STOLEN CHILD

Laura Elliot is the pseudonym of children's writer and journalist June Considine. She is already a bestseller in her native Ireland.

To find out more about Laura Elliot please visit www.juneconsidine.com

By the same author:

The Prodigal Sister

LAURA ELLIOT

Stolen Child

AVON

AVON

A division of HarperCollins*Publishers*
77–85 Fulham Palace Road,
London W6 8JB

www.harpercollins.co.uk

A Paperback Original 2010

1

A catalogue record for this book is
available from the British Library

ISBN-13: 978-1-84756-146-6

Set in Minion by Palimpsest Book Production Limited,
Grangemouth, Stirlingshire

Printed and bound in Great Britain by
Clays Ltd, St Ives plc

Acknowledgements

All stories begin with an idea. Sometimes it arrives fully formed, sometimes it stirs on the breath of a memory. *Stolen Child* belongs to the latter category.

When I was a young girl, I read a newspaper report about a stolen child. She had been snatched when she was a baby and was about to be reunited with her family. Despite my own young years, I appreciated the trauma involved, and the adjustment she would have had to make when she met these strangers, who were her flesh and blood. That memory was the breath that stirred my story into life.

However, *Stolen Child* is fiction. The beautiful and mysterious Burren in County Clare exists, but Maoltrán is my own creation, as is the Valley View Maternity Clinic, St Anna's Clinic and the Chalwerth Industrial Estate. So also, are the cast of characters who journey through these pages.

I'd like to extend special thanks to those who helped me to bring it all together, in particular, Peter Brunton and Mary Coffey for their advice on police procedures and maternity care. Thanks also to Sarah Jane Davis for her valuable input.

I'd like to express my gratitude to Ronan Considine for his wonderful photography, and to Sinead Mullally for the many enquiries she made on my behalf. A special thanks to

Peter Beirne and the staff at Clare County Library for their courtesy and assistance.

As always, my family were supportive and encouraging. Thank you Tony, Ciara and Michelle, my son-in-law Roddy and daughter-in-law, Louise. Thanks to Fran for his technical know-how, and to my extended family and friends for their companionship over the years. Special thanks to the little ones my grandchildren Romy and Ara, for the exuberance and joy they bring to my life.

I appreciate the support I've received from the team at Avon/HarperCollins. Special thanks to Kate Bradley for her insightful and sensitive editing, to Sammia Rafique for being so thoughtful and obliging, and also to Rhian McKay and Jim Blades for their eagle-eyed work on my manuscript. Lastly, a special thanks to my agent, Faith O'Grady.

With love to my husband, Sean Considine.
Thank you for your invaluable support throughout
the writing of *Stolen Child*.

Come away, O human child!
To the waters and the wild
With a faery, hand in hand,
For the world's more full of weeping than you can
    understand.

From 'The Stolen Child'
by William Butler Yeats.

Chapter One

I buried my baby on the shortest night of the year. We were shielded by old walls as I laid her to rest in a shadowy wilderness of lilac and elderberry. She was my almost-child, my shattered dream. Sixteen weeks in my womb before she came away. Born on the longest day of the year, webbed fingers and toes, her veins delicate as skeins of silk. Sweet little monkey face.

The pain took me by surprise. When it came, I was standing by the gate leading into Dowling's Meadow, feeding sugar lumps to Augustus. I heard gunshots in the distance. Mitch Moran, clay pigeon shooting again, and, beyond the lane, the pulse of traffic as cars, driven too fast along the narrow road, signalled an end to another working day. Such a twilight, clouds streaking like lava across the sky, the rooks looping and clamouring above the trees. Then I felt it, the familiar cramping in my stomach, the low drag on my spine.

Sugar crunched like icicles under my feet when I stepped back from the gate. The pain was slight at first and eased quickly, as if teasing me into the belief that I was imagining it. I walked carefully back towards my house, hoping there was still time

3

to save her. But the evening was on fire, a conflagration setting the countryside alight, and the scattering rooks fell through the air like charred scraps of paper. Even the flowers in the hedgerows hurt my eyes, the scarlet pimpernel, the blood-red poppies swaying as I bent over them, cradling my stomach until the pain eased and I could walk again.

I knelt on the bathroom floor and gripped the edge of the bath. The cramps ebbed and surged, each one becoming more insistent, more cruel. Each one signalling the end of another dream. I thought of ringing David but, even before I uttered the words, he would hear my ragged breathing and know. He was too far away to bring me comfort and I could not bear his disappointment, not yet. I thought of ringing my gynaecologist, an austere man with a masterful knowledge of the female anatomy, but he has never been able to answer my most basic question. *Why?* He would shake his head and offer false comfort, assurances and condolences. I thought of ringing my mother-in-law. Miriam is practical and kind. She would come immediately and drive me to the hospital, not saying much, because it had all been said before. But I stayed where I was, knowing that what was about to happen would be swift and soon. No waiting around, no false hope, no time for anything other than the fluid separation between life and loss.

Once again, my body had betrayed me. Once again, it had defied my will and destroyed what David and I, with grim determination, had created.

Body and mind are one, Miriam always argues, the spirit and the flesh, compatible and whole. Wrong . . . *wrong*. The body triumphs every time and I am left holding the husk.

This little one had no fight. She slid cleanly away, so tiny, yet capable of so much brutal force as she left me. I remember wailing. I needed to keen this loss and I was glad to be alone, not subjected to the constraints of a hospital where the feelings of others must be considered. When I could cry no longer, and such a time will always come, I went through the rituals of separation. Familiar rituals by now and usually carried out by efficient midwives, their expressions sympathetic, their eyes gazing beyond me to the other mothers, the ones with reasons to rejoice.

I wrapped my daughter in a soft white towel and rocked her in my arms. I rested my back against the wall. It grew dark outside. I felt hot then cold, my thoughts lucid then drifting. Why fight any longer? Someone would find us eventually.

I ignored the phone when it rang. The caller was insistent. The sound made me quiver but I stayed where I was. The silence, when it stopped, pressed against my ears. I became conscious of other sounds: the creak of old wood, the hiss and gurgle of pipes, the intrusive sighs of a house that has belonged to many generations. The bathroom blind clanged against the window frame and demanded my attention. I wanted to rise and close the window, keep out the scent of the night scented stock I had planted in the spring. It wafted in waves through the stifling atmosphere: sweet and cloying, demanding my attention.

The phone rang again. I became afraid. If it was Miriam, she would drive over to see why I was not answering. Earlier, I had left her working late in her studio. She was probably still there burning the midnight oil, as she usually did when she had an exhibition coming up. If it was David calling from the oil rig, he would ring his mother and the result would be the same. She would drive over immediately to check that all was well. The back door was open. She would enter unannounced and then it would be too late.

I stumbled to my feet and laid my baby, my still and silent

little bundle, on the floor. I opened the door of the living room. My hip knocked against the sideboard. Yellow roses drooped in a vase. Some petals had already fallen and more followed, spilling silently onto the polished wood, as if my laden breath had disturbed their fragile link to the stem. How long had I been drifting? Minutes, hours? Somewhere, in my mind, I was still bending over the blood-red poppies and the rooks were swirling.

My suspicions were correct. Miriam's anxiety was carefully controlled yet it stretched, taut as a membrane, between us. She asked how I was and I told her I was fine . . . fine. My voice was steady. That surprised me. Steady and calm while inside I was howling.

This was the second time she had called, she said, and she waited for an explanation.

I told her I'd been walking – such a fine, balmy evening. She warned me that the lane could be dangerous, easy to trip on a broken branch, to slip on mulching leaves; she knows every step of the lane, as David does, but I am a city woman, transplanted.

'I'll drop in and see you on the way home,' she said. 'I want to show you the new sketches.'

I almost blurted out the truth. But I thought about the last time, and the time before, and before . . . and the well-worn, well-meaning platitudes that stretched thinner and thinner each time she uttered them. Tomorrow, when I was stronger, more able to handle my grief, then I would break the news.

'I'm on my way to bed,' I said. 'I'll look at them tomorrow. Talk to you then.'

I walked to the front door and folded my arms, pressed them against my breast. Light spilled around me but, beyond the porch, an impenetrable darkness stretched across the

Burren. It seemed, as I stood there, that the night was whispering, that even the wind breathed my pain. In the rustle of leaves against the wall I heard the whispers and I heard them rise above a howl that lunged from the darkness. Phyllis Lyons's dog barking at the moon, the sound silenced as suddenly as it started. But still the whispering continued. I felt myself sinking into the powerful refrain, my lips moving, framing the words, making them audible – *No more . . . no more . . . no more . . .*

What does premeditated mean? Is it a conceived plan – or a thought unborn until the moment of delivery? I wrapped my baby in a white blanket and sealed her in a plastic shroud. I carried her gently to the old cottage in the lane. It hulked in the half-light, a crumbling ruin, shouldering briars and ivy, the ground covered in dense banks of nettles. Children once played within these crumbling walls and slept beneath a thatch that hugged them tight. Long gone now, both the children and the thatch. I stumbled through the weeds and the high purple thistles that pushed their heads through the cracks in the stone floor. I laid her down on white bindweed bells and dug her grave outside the walls.

The garden has long lost its form. A low drystone wall marks its boundaries. In the summer the whitethorn and lilac grows wild, and the ripe fruit drops silently from a long-forgotten plum tree during the autumn months. I wanted to name her. Everyone needs a name to stamp their identity on this world, no matter how brief their stay. Joy, I whispered. You would have brought us such joy. My body ached, bled, wept for what I had lost; but when I left that place, my mind was a cold, determined force with no room for grief or doubt.

In the hallway, I paused before a mirror. The weight I had gained during my brief pregnancy seemed to have fallen from my cheeks. My eyes had steel in the blue, a stranger's eyes staring back at me through swollen eyelids, defying me to question or condemn. My hair looked dark, the blonde strands lank with sweat and mud. I was unrecognisable from the woman who had earlier walked the lane; yet, it seemed effortless, this casting aside of an old skin and stepping into the new.

I slept and awakened, slept again. I had no memory of dreams. Dawn was leaching the stars from the sky when I arose and showered dirt from my body, burned my clothes, the towels, the bathroom mat. I washed the floor and walls. I threw out the yellow roses. A bird sang outside the kitchen window, a shrill, repetitive solo, until others took up the song. Their chorus throbbed through the morning.

I rang Miriam and told her I would work from home for a few days. Too many interruptions in the office and I had spreadsheets to prepare, catch-up phone calls to make. Later, David rang from the rig.

'Our baby moved,' I told him. 'Like a butterfly, fluttering wings beneath my heart.'

The words turned to ash in my mouth but they had been spoken and I heard him sigh, as if he had placed his hands upon my belly and felt his child respond. And all around me, in the cracks and crevices of these walls, in the nooks and crannies of this old house, in the chinks of all that had passed since I moved here, the voices whispered – *No more . . . no more . . . no more.*

8

Chapter Two

Susanne
September 1993

Carla Kelly is everywhere. The public face of Anticipation. I see her on billboards and bus shelters, in glossy advertisements. Her white teeth, her full pink lips, her long blonde hair, and that look in her brown eyes, that amber shimmer of contentment; earth mother-to-be, with attitude and glamour.

These days, she's the first celebrity to be interviewed in the media whenever the subject of pregnancy is aired. She writes a column in *Weekend Flair*. 'My Pregnancy Diary' she calls it. How to retain one's sexuality and sense of fashion during those long nine months. Promoting Anticipation all the time. One thing about her, she always was professional.

The Anticipation maternity collection, Dee Ambrose told me when I called into the Stork Club boutique this afternoon, is the most popular label she's ever carried. Lorraine Gardner is an excellent designer and she's touched gold with Anticipation. I was so impressed, I bought a pair of fine wool trousers and a silk twist top.

Perfect for the final trimester, said Dee, and wrapped them in tissue paper before placing them in a carrier bag.

Anticipation was written in gold lettering against a black background. An elegant bag for an elegant collection. On the way out of the boutique, I almost collided with a life-size cutout of Carla Kelly. Dee laughed, noticing how my mouth opened with an apology in the same instant that I realised it was part of the promotion.

Only the big campaigns can afford her now. Her career took off after that lingerie promotion. It gave her an edge, a notoriety, all that sleek flesh and red lace flashing from the billboards. Drivers rang talk radio and complained that her image distracted them during rush-hour. Lorraine Gardner wouldn't have had a chance of running her Anticipation campaign if Carla Kelly hadn't been her sister-in-law.

I carried my carrier bag like a banner to the Nutmeg Café where I'd arranged to meet my mother-in-law. The rain fell steadily as I crossed Market Square and I walked carefully on the slippery cobblestones. A wretched day for the Saturday market, what with the wind billowing the awnings and people scurrying past the stalls towards the nearest shelter.

The Nutmeg was crowded. The smell of damp wool reminded me of crowded buses on muggy school mornings. Women stopped at my table to tell me I was blooming. Even the cashier, a frail, round-shouldered woman, smiled as if she'd known me all her life and said my bump had become enormous since the last time she saw me. I've no memory of us ever meeting but she knew that David had returned to the rig and that I'm planning an end-of-season discount sale at Miriam's Glasshouse. I grew up in the solitude of crowds but here, where the population is sparse, everyone seems to know my business. Miriam arrived at the Nutmeg shortly afterwards and apologised for being late. Something to do with bumping into acquaintances on every corner she turned. She hugged me. Took me quite by surprise. No time to move before I was enveloped in her arms. My mother-in-law has a habit of nudging and hugging and tapping me when I least expect it. I've never grown used to her effusiveness. I expect it's to do with my upbringing – nothing touchy-feely about my parents. I've told her about my childhood. The silence and the separation, two people living on either side of a glass wall of indifference, so steeped in their own unhappiness they were incapable of reaching out to me.

'It explains a lot,' Miriam said, and pitied me for the tenderness I'd never experienced.

I'm willing to endure her pity but not her touch. 'Don't tempt fate,' I warn her when she asks if my baby is moving. Now she no longer seeks permission to rest her hands on my stomach, but today in the Nutmeg she hugged me so tight I thought my heart would flip over.

Phyllis Lyons entered and came straight to our table. No asking, just an assumption that, as Miriam's school friend and my nearest neighbour, she had every right to join us. She picked up my Anticipation carrier bag and placed it on the table.

'Go on, girl,' she said. 'Give us a look.'

I lifted out my new purchases and held them up for inspection. Miriam thought the twist top was a wonderful colour. 'Sapphire blue, a perfect match for your eyes,' she said, and ran her hand over the silky fabric. 'So glamorous,' she added, 'yet it looks so comfortable.'

Phyllis checked the price tag. 'Mother of God,' she said. 'Are you made of money or what? What's the sense of glamour when you look like a whale? If I were you, I'd just keep letting out the waistband.'

What does she know? She's a middle-aged spinster and gone beyond all that now.

Miriam looked apologetically at me and placed my clothes

11

back in the carrier bag. She finds Phyllis as irritating as I do, but neighbours, she warned me when I first came to live in Maoltrán, have long memories. It's wise to keep on their good side.

'I feel sorry for her,' she said, when Phyllis finally left to pick up a prescription for her mother. 'It's no joke looking after a creaking door and that mother of hers has been creaking for as long as I can remember.'

She asked when I was due to see Professor Langley again. 'Next week, I told her. I'll take the afternoon off, if that's okay with you?'

'Of course . . . absolutely.' She nodded vigorously. Her anxiety smothers me. The harder she tries not to show it, the more obvious it appears. She's nervous about the long distances I drive. But I'm her marketing manager. It's my responsibility to meet with customers. She keeps telling me to start my maternity leave and take it easy for the final months.

'But what on earth would I do,' I ask her, 'sitting all by myself in an empty house? I'm fit and healthy. I intend working until the last minute.'

'David warned me to keep a close eye on you and not let you overdo things,' she said. 'It worries me,' she added, 'him being on that oil rig. If anything . . .' She paused, uncomfortable at having to remind me that I've a bad track record when it comes to bringing her grandchildren into the world. I try not to give her cause for concern.

It has not been difficult to maintain the illusion of pregnancy. I've made a harness with bindings that fit snugly below my breasts and under my stomach. I pad it with firm fillings that outline my expanding curve. I'm so conscious of avoiding contact with anyone that my antennae remain on full alert, tremblingly cautious, always watchful. My face

12

looks too gaunt for a woman in her last trimester but people see what they want to see and their eyes are always drawn to my stomach.

Hopefully, Professor Langley has forgotten my existence. His secretary handled my decision to change gynaecologists with chilly politeness and sent me a bill for my last appointment and scans.

At the start of the month, David arrived home on leave, his skin tanned and taut from the harsh North Sea gales. I hid the harness then, and drank so much water every day that my stomach felt as tight and swollen as a drum. My food was fat and starch, it sickened me, but my weight kept increasing. He transformed the spare bedroom into a nursery. He painted the walls a pale apple green and hung one of Miriam's seahorse mobiles above the carry-cot. We travelled to Dublin and stayed for a weekend with my father and Tessa. We bought a pram and the carry-cot, a feeding chair, a changing station. The whispering grew more intense as we made our decisions. Each time I faltered they whispered . . . *Remember us . . . remember us . . . no turning back* . . . Whenever I felt the urge to run free from the shadow of that cottage and bring the dream to an end, they'd whisper *stay . . . stay. Be silent*, they urged, when the truth pressed against my teeth so hard it ached to be heard. *Be brave*, they whispered, when David laid his ear too late to my stomach and said, 'I can't feel anything . . . Well, maybe I do . . . it's *so* hard to tell.'

What he'd felt was my shudder of fear, my womb contracting with dread determination.

That is how our baby grows, carried into being on a whisper.

I met a horse whisperer once. He was small and stout and wore a wide-brimmed hat with a jaunty feather in the side.

To be called a horse whisperer sounded mysterious and powerful, but he said he was simply a man who understood horses. He came to us soon after we purchased Augustus – the horse had too many bad habits for us to handle alone. I'd watched him stand before Augustus, face to face and then cheek to cheek, not threatening, just empathising, reaching deep into the horse's psyche and connecting with the rage that lay at the heart of his flailing behaviour. By the time he'd finished, Augustus was still a spirited horse but he was biddable. He's gone from the meadow now, sold to a horse dealer. I told David he broke loose and almost knocked me to the ground. Seeing him at the gate every time I passed was too much to bear. I want amnesia.

It will happen, my whisperers promise. *Trust us . . . believe in us . . . we are the whispers of what should have been.*

David was reluctant at first to move from my bed, but when I told him I'd suffered some spotting, he understood. Nothing must endanger this new life we've created. I reassured him of my love, explained how hormones go berserk during pregnancy and lovemaking is impossible. 'Afterwards,' I promised him, 'afterwards when our baby is born, everything will be different.'

When I came home from the studio on the night before he left, he asked me to sit down and talk to him. He placed his hands on my arms and sank me into a chair.

'Be still,' he'd said, 'and listen to me. All this rushing around and working such late hours. Apart from our trip to Dublin, I've hardly seen you since I came home.'

He kissed me, his mouth seeking some response. My body clenched in protest, and I accused him of being demanding, selfish, thinking only of his own needs. How was it possible that he could not hear the terrified whine behind my bluster?

'Why,' he'd asked, 'do you spurn me? Do you think I'm a beast, incapable of lying by your side without wanting to invade your body?'

I almost told him. I could feel my knees weakening, the urge to kneel before him and confess. But the whisperers moved from gentle persuasion to implacable authority and straightened my spine. I faced him down, this man whose children I carried so briefly, all five of them, and who now urge me onwards . . . *No more . . . no more . . . no more.*

He drew away from me and wished me goodnight, chastely kissing my forehead. I understand his desire to be part of my experience but this is a journey I must take alone.

The rain had stopped by the time we left the Nutmeg and shoppers were drifting back to the market stalls. A traveller sat on a blanket outside the café. She was young, twenty at most, a baby in her arms, and a dull-eyed small boy hunkered beside her. I searched in my purse for coins but Miriam went back inside to buy coffee and sandwiches for the mother, milk for the boy.

'It's a boy child, missus,' the traveller said. 'A big boy child for his fine strappin' mother.'

Her hard, experienced eyes seemed to sear through my secret. The pavement swayed, or perhaps I stumbled, and the coins fell from my hand, rolling across the uneven surface until they were clenched in the boy's fist.

Phyllis Lyons arrived back from the pharmacy with her mother's medication and asked if she could get a lift home with me. Her car was being serviced and she'd missed the twice-hourly bus that runs past her house. Miriam waved and left us together, glad, I suspect, to escape to her house on the other side of Market Square.

Throughout the journey home, Phyllis talked non-stop

15

about her mother's ailments and her efforts to alleviate them. I stopped outside her gate and waited for her to leave the car.

'Come in and say hello to Mammy,' she said. 'She loves the bit of company.'

I stared at the grey lace curtains on the front window. Her mother would have been watching us, stooped on her Zimmer frame. Inside, the air would be stale and smoky.

'I'm expecting a call from David,' I said, and Phyllis nodded, as if my excuse echoed all the others she'd ever heard.

She stepped from the car and walked around the side of her house, squeezing her stocky figure past the tractor. Farming her few acres and looking after her mother . . . it can't be an easy life but she accepts it without complaint.

I turned down the lane and drove into the grey arms of Rockrose. I locked the front door behind me. Such relief, being alone again, able to breathe, to open my waistband, to allow the silence to settle until only the whisperers were audible.

I speak to women all the time. They look at my bump and confide in me. One woman told me she'd never once, during the nine months of her pregnancy, felt her baby move. He's eighteen years old now, on a track and field scholarship in the United States. Another woman was told by her gynaecologist that he could not detect her baby's heartbeat. That night she felt the first fluttering of life in her womb. Put a group of women together and they'll tell stories that mystify the medical profession.

Carla Kelly writes about them in her pregnancy diary. The happy, clappy stories about babies who kick and jog and elbow their way towards birth. I sent her a letter shortly after

16

that night. I asked her how it was possible to keep hoping when the womb rejects the dream. An anonymous letter, of course. She could not deal with my story. She passed my letter on to Alyssa Faye for her advice column. As a psychologist, Alyssa Faye believes she has a deeper understanding of the human psyche than the average journalist. Human suffering is grist to her mill. For three weeks she analysed my miscarriages, analysed my head, analysed my emotions. I did not write my story to pad her column. I wanted to see if Carla Kelly could understand, empathise. I got my answer.

Last week in Dublin, I saw her in Brown Thomas with her husband. At least I assume that's who it was. He stays out of her limelight but she held his arm in a way that suggested he was her rock. They were looking at baby clothes. I followed them from the department store and up to the top of Grafton Street. The flower sellers were busy. Birds of paradise flamed against white chrysanthemums and tightly coiled rosebuds jutted like spears from overflowing buckets. She bought the roses and continued onwards. I lost sight of them when they entered the Stephen's Green Shopping Centre. I probably could have found her. She's tall and distinctive enough to stand out from the crowd but I was too weak to move any further. I sat down in a coffee bar and asked for a glass of water. The waitress had the experienced eyes of an older woman counting months. She brought the water sharply and asked if I'd like her to call a taxi.

'You think it'll never end,' she said. 'Especially the last months. But it does and then you'll know all about it.'

She spoke with relish, they all do, warning of impending chaos and tiny impetuous demands that will turn my life upside down.

The taxi came shortly afterwards. I caught a last glimpse of Carla Kelly and her husband as I was leaving. They were laughing at something one had said to the other. Her head was thrown back, her hand covering her mouth, as if her laughter was a wild thing she must contain. It's a long time since I laughed that way. Had I ever? I must have, especially in the early days with David. Now I laugh on cue. It sounds natural, spontaneous, even contagious. In public relations, where it's necessary to flatter and admire, I have acquired certain skills. I lean on them now but, from time to time, they slip. Then all I have to do is touch my stomach. Small gestures create an easily translatable language that gives me leave to be tired, anxious, irritable, uncomfortable and, occasionally, irrational.

Was it irrational to follow Carla Kelly that day? Of course it was. I realise that now but she is the face of Anticipation, taunting, flaunting; telling us it's easy, so easy and natural to carry a baby in the womb for nine dangerous months.

I too used to keep a diary. I made the last entry when I was sixteen years old. Hard to believe that's twenty-three years ago. I was pregnant then, eight months gone, on the final stretch, so to speak. And on the verge of becoming a teenage statistic. I lost my boy in March, gone before he had time to draw breath. Lots of blank pages afterwards. The world had become a greyer place, not worth recording. Nothing left for me except my scans and a whisper of what might have been.

'You've had a lucky escape,' my father said when I was discharged from hospital. 'Best thing you can do is get on with your life and forget it ever happened.' He'd taken care of everything and discouraged me from visiting the Angels' plot in Glasnevin Cemetery. It's such a poignant place to visit – that treasured, communal space where the tiny ones rest together.

'It's a new beginning for all of us,' he said. 'No looking back.' My mother was dead by then and he was about to be married again. He'd changed from the grim, dead-eyed man I used to know. His face was plumper and he laughed easily, joyously. I would look at Tessa and wonder how such a small, insignificant woman with rimless glasses and a slight stammer when she was nervous had wrought such a change in him.

I didn't blame him for not wanting to begin his married life with a troubled teenager and her baby. I just wished he hadn't looked so relieved, so determined to obliterate my experience. But it never was obliterated, just lightly buried . . . like my boy. I held on to my diary, kept it safe each time I moved, but I never had any inclination to read it until after that night in the cottage. Funny experience . . . rediscovering the young me. I was on a wild carousal all right, and heading in only one direction.

Now I'm filling those blank pages. Dates don't matter. Time is suspended. Writing about it helps. Otherwise my mind is frantic, thoughts running like ants beneath an upturned stone. How did I work through that wall of pain? There has to be a reason . . . has to be. Three months have passed since then yet the memory clings to my senses. I hear the clunk and clank of a spade, smell the dank, uncovered earth. I see a small bundle resting in that narrow cleft. I feel the clay beneath my nails, the briars tearing my legs, the polka-dot sting of nettles on my skin. And the taste that remains with me is bile, bitter gall.

It's time to close my diary and try to sleep. Close it now and silence the whisperers. Close these musty pages and trap the future as it waits in anticipation.

Chapter Three

Carla
October 1993

Carla Kelly held her hands upwards to receive the wedding dress. Ivory silk overlaid with lace billowed across her shoulders before settling over the defined bump of her stomach. A beautician moved forward to brush blusher across her cheeks and sweep mascara over her eyelashes. One of the dressers briskly corseted Lizzy Carr into the black Goth wedding dress. Her feet were already booted in aggressive spiky heels. A slash of black lipstick emphasised her mask-like white face. In contrast, Carla's make-up was a delicate blending of peach and gold.

She bowed her head as a hairstylist switched off the hairdryer and rippled his hands through her hair, working it with his fingers until it tumbled in dishevelled strands to her shoulders. He clipped an ivory wisp of feathers into place and stood back to check the effect.

Lizzy was handed a bouquet of black roses with one red rose in the centre. Her heavy eye make-up emphasised her emaciated appearance while Carla, carrying a bouquet of orchids sprigged with lily of the valley, looked dewy, fecund, feminine. The backstage photographers clicked around them until Raine signalled at the models to prepare for their entrance.

Lizzy strutted forward into the light and headed towards the foot of the catwalk. She paused, waited for Carla's entrance. The audience gasped, then laughed and applauded as Carla, sexy and pregnant, opened herself to the vibrating music, the piercing strobes, the lens of the cameras stripping her layer by layer as she glided towards the photographers. They called her name. *This way, Carla! That way! The other way!* At the foot of the catwalk, she stood with Lizzy and allowed the audience to absorb the contrast. Then they separated, each move choreographed, each inch of space worked to full advantage. Carla smiled and turned. From behind, she looked like the other models. No weight on her bottom, ankles still slender. The fashion journalists scribbled, the flash of cameras dazzled. This was Raine's most ambitious designer collection to date – and the introduction of the Anticipation wedding dress. Tomorrow the dress would feature on the front pages of the newspapers and Raine, delighted with the publicity, would laugh when the inevitable calls were made to talk radio complaining about pregnant brides glamorising carnal knowledge.

The wedding dress swirled around Carla as the music quickened and the fashion show built to a finale. The other models emerged from behind the screens to sashay down the catwalk and form a guard of honour. They clapped Raine forward to meet her audience. The applause increased as she bowed, grinned self-consciously, longing to be backstage again, organising everything and everyone.

Carla changed into a pair of Anticipation stretch jeans and a midnight-blue top. She had enjoyed her time as the face, or – to be more accurate – the belly of Anticipation, but she was growing tired of the constant publicity.

The baby moved, a gentle jog of heel and elbow that never failed to delight her. She did not know if she carried a boy or a girl, preferring, like Robert, to wait. Life was a series of changes, of adjustments, and the biggest adjustment would take place in three weeks' time. Outside in the auditorium, chair seats snapped back. Voices faded as the audience departed. She emerged from a side door and walked down the empty catwalk. The cleaners had moved in and were removing discarded programmes and press releases. The sound engineer grinned across at her as he packed his equipment and wished her goodnight.

In the ladies' she breathed in the scent of potpourri and tried to imagine a time when she would not feel the constant pressure on her bladder. A woman, heavily pregnant and wearing a distinctive Anticipation top, emerged from one of the cubicles.

'Good show.' She smiled through the mirror at Carla. 'I particularly liked the wedding dress.'

'So did the photographers.' Carla laughed and held her hands under the tap. 'I'm still hallucinating from the flashes.'

The woman ran a comb through her short, spiky hair. Studded earrings glistened on her earlobes. 'It's been a long time, Carla,' she said. 'How are you?'

Startled, Carla paused as she was about to dry her hands. 'Do we know each other?'

'I'm Sue Sheehan,' she replied. 'At least, I was before I married. I used to work for Edward Carter.'

'I'm sorry, I didn't recognise you.' The scent of potpourri breathed sweetly into the space between them. Carla swallowed a hot rush of nausea. Since her pregnancy, her sense of smell always seemed more acute at night.

'Like I said, a long time ago. Ten years at least.' Sue Sheehan tilted her chin, as if checking for any sag underneath. Despite her advanced pregnancy, she had a slim face, her features emphasised by her boyish haircut. Her complexion was smooth, almost waxy, and Carla was suddenly reminded of a doll, an asexual doll with a blue unflinching gaze. Sue blinked and the impression was immediately dispelled. Carla struggled to separate her from the brashly confident team of women who had surrounded Edward Carter in those days. They all had that look, tight haircuts and sharp shoulders, their rippling blouses and pert breasts defining their femininity. She must be in her mid-thirties now, Carla speculated, or even older, if she had been one of the senior executives in Carter and Kay Public Relations.

'Do you still work in public relations?' Carla removed a tube of lipstick from her bag. Her hand remained steady as she applied it to her lips.

'Not since my marriage,' Sue replied. 'I work in the craft industry now. Marketing.'

'That sounds interesting.'

'Yes, indeed it is. Do you ever see Edward these days?'

'No.' Carla snapped her handbag closed and placed it under her arm. 'Apart from on the television, of course. Impossible to miss him.'

'Yes . . . he always had a way with words. When is your baby due?'

'Mid-November, or thereabouts. My gynaey says it's common to go over time on the first though. What about you?'

'Around the same time. Like you say, hard to tell with the first.' Sue glanced at her watch. 'My step-mother's waiting for me in the bar. It's been nice meeting you again.'

'You too, Sue. Good luck with the birth.'

'Yes. I can't wait until all this is over.' She leaned against the counter, as if her weight was suddenly too heavy to carry.

'Are you all right?' Concerned, Carla leaned forward but Sue straightened, moved out of reach.

'I'm just tired. It's been a long day.'

They walked together to the bar where Raine was waiting for Carla.

'Well done,' Raine said as Carla tried to perch on a high stool beside her with as much dignity as possible. 'I've already been interviewed by three journalists and asked if my wedding dress is meant to endorse sex before marriage.'

'Mmmm . . . sounds like you'll have the moral majority on your back tomorrow.'

Raine laughed. 'Bring them on,' she said. 'Are you coming to Sheen's?'

Carla shook her head. 'Do you mind if I take a rain check and head straight home? I'm whacked.'

'Not at all. I'm tired myself but I need to sweet-talk the buyers. Is my bro skulking in dark corners tonight?'

'He should be home by now. How's Gillian?'

Raine's smile faded. 'She's good. Not much energy though. That last chemo session was tough.'

'Tell her I'll drop in tomorrow.'

'Will do.' Raine leaned forward and patted Carla's stomach. 'Night night, little one. Lay off the football for tonight and give your mum a chance to sleep. She's had a busy day.'

Across the lounge, Sue Sheehan had settled awkwardly into a deep armchair beside a slight woman with glasses. Carla felt a fleeting sympathy as she imagined her difficulty when the time came to get up again. All she seemed to notice nowadays were women at the same advanced stage as herself.

Outside the hotel, she hailed a taxi. Lizzy Carr, in jeans and a puffa jacket, all traces of her Goth persona removed, waved as she ran down the hotel steps. She was followed by two other models, who were also heading to Sheen's on the Green. For an instant Carla was tempted to follow but then a taxi driver pulled up and she stepped into the taxi's dark interior.

In the company of models, Carla moved in an assured world where she did not have to apologise for being tall. No more cramped knees from bending to listen to others. No more enduring jokes about giraffe necks or being asked if it was cold up there. Her face, attractive but not beautiful, could be moulded to define a mood, an emotion, an atmosphere. The perfect face, declared the scout who had approached her on Grafton Street when she was sixteen and persuaded her to consider the catwalk for a career. She had acquired the poise and confidence to stand aloof from conversations and discovered that such indifference made people strain upwards so that they could hear what she had to say. But with Robert Gardner, everything was mouth to mouth, eye level to eye level.

He was waiting for her when she arrived home.

'So, how did it go?' he asked and drew her down on his knee. He smelled of soap and shampoo. Nothing about his appearance suggested that he had spent his day working on the grim and secretive side of the city streets.

'The wedding dress was the highlight. I wanted to get married all over again.'

'That could be arranged,' Robert said. 'Only one stipulation. No change of groom.'

'As if I would.' She kissed him but was unable to prevent a yawn escaping.

'So much for my sex appeal.' Robert eased her to the floor. 'Come on. It's way past your bedtime.'

She leaned heavily on his arm as they left the living room. She was glad of his height, his strong arms. During the last week, she had become aware of a slight listing movement when she walked. They would have a tall child. No problem if it was a boy but for a girl, Carla thought, remembering her own lanky teenage years, maybe not so good.

In bed, they spooned against each other and drifted towards sleep. One of them, or perhaps both, stirred with lazy desire and Robert's arms tightened around her. Their lovemaking was passionate but gentle. She moaned softly into the pillow and their baby moved. Robert felt the rippling sensation beneath his fingers and, suddenly nervous, held back until, responding to her touch, he entered her slowly from behind. She clenched him tightly inside her, her energy carrying them swiftly over the edge of desire.

Afterwards, still in the same coiled position, she tried to sleep. Her leg cramped and the baby's elbows seemed wedged under her ribcage. Robert turned, slapped the pillow without waking, and sank his head deeper into it. The room was cold, the central heating off. She pulled on a towelling dressing gown and tied the belt below her stomach. She paused before a full-length mirror and smiled at her bear-like appearance. If the photographers could see her now, there would be a very different photograph on the front of the tabloids tomorrow.

Downstairs, she entered her compact office. Once, rooms such as these had served as dens for husbands who smoked pipes in comfort and isolated themselves from the daily domestic routine. She sifted through the latest batch of letters, answered a few and chose the ones she would use in her column. Shortly before meeting Robert, she had enrolled in a media studies course, fitting her lectures around her modelling assignments. She now had her degree and a regular column in *Weekend Flair*, a Sunday newspaper supplement magazine. Carla was under no illusions that the reason she had been approached by the editor had more to do with her

Anticipation profile than her media degree. But the number of letters kept rising from women seeking advice on morning sickness and weird hunger urges. Some letters amused her, others were so filled with pain and frustration that she shrank from answering them in her column, aware of her own inexperience. In such instances she passed them on to Alyssa Faye.

She was also beginning to receive commissions from other magazines. The feature in *Pizzazz* was excellent. She picked up the celebrity magazine from her desk and flicked through the pages until she came to the 'before and after' feature she had written about the refurbishment of their end-of-terrace Georgian house. When the alterations had first begun, she had taken photographs of the resulting chaos and these photographs had been juxtaposed against a photoshoot of the finished results. So far, she had not shown the magazine to Robert; the memory of the row that followed her decision to write the feature in the first place was still fresh in her mind.

'Absolutely no way,' he had declared when he heard that a photographer intended photographing each room in their house. 'I've no intention of allowing our lives to feature in some cheap, pretentious magazine.'

'Cheap?' Carla, used to having the camera trained on her, had been astonished by his reaction. 'There's nothing *cheap* about *Pizzazz*.'

'The title says it all,' he declared. '"Pizzazz". How could you possibly want us to feature in such a vacuous publication?'

'It's *not* vacuous and everyone wants to feature in it.'

'Everyone?' He scoffed. 'Who the hell is everyone?'

'It's for Raine's sake.' She had changed direction, aware of how shallow she sounded, or rather, she thought, how shallow he had made her sound. 'She's invested everything in her publicity campaign. This is another opportunity to promote Anticipation.'

'Not at my expense,' he had argued. 'I insist you cancel the arrangement.'

'*Insist?*' Carla was outraged by his arrogance.

'You used to protect my anonymity,' he retorted. 'Now you want to splatter my private life everywhere.'

'What's to splatter?' she demanded. 'I don't expect you to appear in the photographs. I'm not *that* stupid.'

'I never said you were stupid. But you need to slow down on the exposure you get. It's different now. You have to think of others besides yourself.'

'Come off it, Robert,' she retorted. 'The average junkie is hardly likely to have *Pizzazz* on his reading list.'

When he paid no attention to her arguments, she cried. Her tears were genuine but under control. She had a modelling assignment the following day and could not afford a ravaged face. Robert had never seen her cry. His anger was immediately replaced by concern and, eventually, by capitulation.

'I want our privacy to be respected, especially when our baby comes along,' he had warned her. 'This is the last time anyone from the media sets foot in our house.'

Looking at the glossy photographs, Carla wondered if he had been right to object. Seen through the lens of the camera, their house looked larger, more luxurious and dramatic than it really was. There was something invasive about the photographs, particularly those taken in the nursery.

Initially, when Colin Moore, the photographer, had entered the nursery, she had moved forward to stop him, then changed her mind. This was a room waiting in anticipation. Somehow, it seemed appropriate to photograph it.

She had painted the nursery herself, a pale yellow shade that gleamed like gold when the sun struck the walls. Before returning to bed, she entered the room and trailed her fingers over the cradle. It had been an extravagant purchase, a replica of a Victorian cradle with a canopy of white gauze. She had bought it at a craft fair, along with the mobile of stained glass seahorses that now hung above it. She sat in a wicker rocking chair and swayed slowly back and forth. Her baby moved, a hard defiant kick that advised her to savour her tranquil moments. They would be gone soon enough. She cradled her stomach as she watched the city drift asleep and tried to imagine herself and Robert as parents.

They had so little in common, or so their friends had claimed when they first met. Bets had been laid on how long their relationship would last. Carla smiled, remembering that first meeting when Raine, in the aftermath of another fashion show, shouted their names across the table in Sheens on the Green to introduce them. Robert had lifted his eyebrows and smiled ruefully at the noise dividing them. Under normal circumstances, he told her later, he would have refused point blank to attend a fashion show. He had never shown any interest in the glitter and glamour associated with his sister's career but this was a charity event to raise funds for breast cancer research. Gillian, his mother, had insisted he support it – not just financially, but physically, by accompanying her.

Gillian, frail but defiant in a red bandana, had the translucent pallor of someone who had stepped close to death. Carla noticed how attentively her son listened when she spoke, as if he appreciated the second chance he had been given to cherish her. She studied their faces, seeking similarities, and found them in their intense blue eyes and the generous width of their mouths. They shared the same bone structure. Cragginess would come to him with age but his features would never sag. The restaurant lights glinted off his black hair. Gillian's lips would have been voluptuous before illness drained their fullness and her son had inherited that same lush curve. A mouth made to be kissed, Carla thought, and Robert, as if attuned to her thoughts, reached out and held her in his gaze. In that single glance, something indefinable passed between them. Carla would later acknowledge it as love and he would agree, his expression still bemused by the suddenness of their attraction. Love at first sight – as romantic as it was ridiculous. If any of her friends had described the sensation, Carla would have laughed and called it a chemical hit. But it had carried them into marriage and would soon carry them into parenthood.

The night-time traffic had slowed. Only an occasional car passed, casting brief, surging shadows across the walls. The mobile tinkled above the cradle and the circle of seahorses, translucent mauves and luminous greens, flashed and danced lightly, as if they sensed her intrusion.

Chapter Four

Susanne

'Why seahorses,' I asked Miriam when I travelled to Maoltrán for the first time to be interviewed for the position of marketing manager.

'Why *not* seahorses?' She had sounded amused. 'The female of the species is intelligent enough to enjoy the delights of courtship and the male gallant enough to carry the consequences.'

She picked a seahorse from a plinth and held it up for me to admire. The shade was a delicate coral that gleamed like mother-of-pearl and deepened to a glistening salmon when the spotlights caught the glass and played with it. She smiled and stroked her index finger over the protruding belly. 'Would that *our* men were so obliging,' she added, and we laughed together, the kind of conspiratorial laughter women share when we discuss our men.

She handed the seahorse to me. I tapped it with my nail. The tinkling sound was as pitched as a tuning fork. I imagined a shoal of pregnant males, their slender exclamation-mark spines camouflaged against wavering sea grasses, their taut, tight bellies pulsing with life.

Her seahorses have names and personalities. Some are

exquisitely etched and encrusted with gems. Others have a more practical design and can be used as bookends, framed on walls or attached to bathroom mirrors. The mobile is one of the most popular items in her collection.

Carla Kelly has one hanging in her nursery. I saw it in *Pizzazz*. That magazine may be devoid of intelligent content but old habits are hard to break and I buy it every month. I used to check it regularly to see which of my clients had been included when I worked for Carter & Kay. Sometimes they didn't make it. Not prestigious or interesting enough. The editor was ruthless when it came to deciding who should feature on her pages. Carla Kelly now obviously fits this profile.

She wrote a 'before and after' feature about the house in Ranelagh where she and her husband live. The before shots look horrendous but the after photography is pure *Pizzazz* and allows her to do what she does best. Her face leaps from the pages and dominates them to such a degree that the furnishings and décor are insignificant props in the background.

That night at the fashion show, she shuddered when I mentioned Edward Carter's name. She covered it up but I watched her composure slip for that instant and I knew she was back there again, with him, intent on destroying what they had so wantonly and carelessly created. I wonder if her husband knows. Probably not. There's something hard and unforgiving about his eyes.

No sign of him in the *Pizzazz* shoot. It's not his kind of magazine. Gloss and dross. Back in those days, apart from the advertisements, Carla Kelly never appeared in her own right. She was just another face, another model climbing on the backs of the older ones, juggling for space in the tabloids. Titbits and gossip, she loved the camera and it loved her. Then she got her lucky break with the lingerie campaign.

She's changed now, of course. Pregnancy has given her credibility. Celebrity and credibility, an unbeatable combination.

She painted the walls yellow for her baby, a neutral colour to suit either gender. A white cradle sat in the centre of the room, muslin curtains trailed the floor. She sat by the window in a white wicker chair, her hands resting below her stomach, her face in profile. Outside the window, a tree was visible, bronze leaves beginning to turn. Her expression was serene, her head bent slightly so that the light streamed through the blonde tendrils. The eternal Eve. I almost expected a serpent to coil from the branches behind her. Signs and omens, they keep appearing.

The whispering voices awaken me at night and insist that I listen to the tinkling call of the seahorses that Miriam fuses in the raging heat of her furnace room; the molten globs are suspended, swelling, mutating. It has to be more than a coincidence.

Chapter Five

Carla
November 1993

Shortly after their marriage, Carla was crossing O'Connell Bridge on her way to a luncheon fashion show when she saw her husband at work. The wind, blowing harshly off the Liffey, tossed her hair across her face, and he had almost passed her by before she became aware of him. A junkie, she thought, summing him up in a glance, his baggy tracksuit bottoms, the grubby trainers minus laces, and the way he hunched into his nondescript anorak, his pale face protected by the hood. More like a dealer, she decided, as his eyes, darting and shifty, sized up everything around him. For an instant, she was swamped in his gaze as his eyes flashed with recognition. Then he was gone, swiftly absorbed in the crowd.

Shocked, she leaned over the balustrade and gazed into the Liffey. The tide was low, the walls of the river dank and brown. She pretended she had not recognised him, knowing he would be furious with himself for dropping his guard, even for an instant. Strange that she, who knew his body intimately, had not noticed his height, nor could she remember anything about his features, other than his eyes, momentarily betraying him. But in that chance encounter,

Carla realised they did share something in common; a chameleon quality that allowed them, when necessary, to dominate or to blend successfully into any landscape of their choosing.

Almost a year had passed since then but she remembered that incident when she watched the evening news. A consignment of drugs had been discovered in the secret compartment of a truck entering Dublin Port. Not discovered, Carla thought, as the news report unfolded. The customs officers knew exactly what they would find when they stopped the truck. The television camera lingered over the plastic bags laid out on a table for maximum exposure. A grave-faced policeman estimated the street value of the seizure. Five hundred thousand punts, a sizeable sum. Uniformed Gardaí moved in the background. Robert was not among them. His role was covert, undercover. He worked the docks area, eliciting information, making contacts, his identity so deeply embedded that twice he had been arrested by uniformed guards unaware of his undercover work. These things he whispered to Carla in the aftermath of lovemaking, coiling her hair around his fingers, his laughter warm in her ear. He skimmed over the dangers, aware that he straddled two worlds but confident of his footing.

'Did you see it?' He rang her shortly after the evening news. The background was loud with voices, laughter, music.

'Yes,' she said. 'Well done, my favourite mole.'

'We've gone back to Sharon's house,' he told her. 'I'm just going to have a few drinks then take a taxi home.'

'A likely story.' She knew he would arrive home in the small hours, smelling of whiskey and, probably, a late-night curry. 'The spare room is ready and waiting,' she warned him. 'In my delicate condition, a drunken detective in my bed is the last thing I need.'

He promised to be quiet, shoes off at the front door. 'You're sure you're okay?' he asked.

'I'm fine.' She wished she felt as serene as she sounded. 'Another fortnight to go. I assume you'll have sobered up by then.'

He was still laughing when she hung up. Their marriage was as separate as a snapped thread from his small, close-knit team. Was she jealous, she wondered as she replaced the receiver. She thought of Sharon Boyle, with her black boyish hair and long, muscular legs, the tough-talking sister in the tight band of brothers. Carla had met her for the first time when she came to their house-warming party with other members of the squad. The group had remained apart from the general gathering. They sat on the stairs, forming a closed-off huddle that showed no inclination to stir outside their pall of cigarette smoke, shop talk and camaraderie. Robert had mingled effortlessly with the other guests but he had joined his colleagues on the stairs by the end of the night.

No, not jealous, exactly, Carla decided. Just envious of the slash of danger that drew people together in a way her safe, glittering world of fashion could never do.

She watched television for a while, searching the channels for light relief, a romantic comedy or an enthralling love triangle she could enjoy without Robert's heavy breathing signalling his boredom. Nothing interested her. Her back ached and the baby appeared to have manoeuvred a vaulting pole under her ribs.

The phone rang when she was climbing the stairs to bed. She reached the bedroom and lay across the bed.

'You sound like you've just run the marathon,' said Raine.

'A marathon would be easier,' she replied and pulled the duvet over her.

'I suppose the bro is on a razz.' Raine had also seen the evening news.

'Celebrations are well underway,' Carla replied. 'I've plumped the pillows in the spare room.'

'Wise move.' Raine laughed. 'Although his powers of recovery are amazing.'

'So I've discovered. How's business?'

'Brilliant, thanks to you. How are you?'

'Solid as the Rock of Gibraltar. That's if I discount kicks, jabs, twinges, aches, and the occasional rugby tackle.'

'Do you want me to come over and keep you company?'

'Not tonight, thanks. I'm already in bed.'

'Sleep tight, kiddo. Enjoy it while you can.'

Carla arched her back to ease a deep cramping pain. Filled with restless energy, she arose and pulled clothes from the wardrobe, folded them into a black plastic sack. Tomorrow she would bring her Anticipation collection to Oxfam and wish good luck to those who wished to wear it.

Midnight came and went without any sign of Robert. She drifted asleep. Her dreams were jagged with pain. Awakening suddenly, she was unable to remember the details, only the discomfort. A moist warm trickle eased between her legs. She hurled the duvet aside, gasped as a spasm rippled across her stomach. Her waters were not supposed to break until later in labour. Her baby was not ready. Another spasm gripped her and she understood that it was she, not her baby, who was unprepared.

Gingerly, she left the bed. Her nightdress clung to her skin. She shivered as she pulled it from her and reached in the wardrobe for a skirt and top. Her bag was packed. All she needed was her husband, drunk or sober, by her side. She was angry with him, then amused, then panicked, her emotions all over the place.

Robert had given her a number to ring in emergencies. Sharon answered, her clipped authoritative voice slurred, too loud. Music blasted in the background. Heavy rock. Sharon shouted at someone to lower the stereo then returned her attention to Carla.

'He's not exactly in the best of health.' She laughed apologetically. 'Actually he's just passed out on the sofa.'

'Then throw a bucket of cold water over him,' Carla shouted. 'And tell him to get his arse over to the Valley View because his child is not waiting around for his health to recover.'

'Message understood.' Sharon snapped to attention. 'I'll call the ambulance. Do you need a Garda escort?'

Carla forced herself to breathe slowly until the cramp subsided. 'That's not a bad idea,' she gasped. 'But you'd better do it fast.'

She debated ringing her parents then decided against it. Her father would cope but she did not want to watch her mother's lips trembling, her hands flailing, her mind ticking off everything that could possibly go wrong.

The ambulance crew arrived. They joked about delivering roadside babies. Carla panted and wondered if they would be laughing on the other side of their faces before the journey was over. The blue lights of a Garda car scattered the darkness as the ambulance driver followed, breaking through traffic lights and heading straight for the Valley View Maternity Clinic.

The pain gained momentum, the spasms coming faster. Robert arrived in a taxi at the same time as the ambulance reached the clinic. He rushed towards her, looking, as she had expected, utterly disreputable, unshaven, his voice excruciatingly precise as he attempted to convince her he was sober. She laughed and allowed him to help her into a wheelchair. Their baby was coming. She sensed its determination, the driving force of its head seeking the light.

'I love you . . . love you . . . love you,' Robert babbled as she was wheeled into the clinic.

She tightened her grip on his hand and breathed into the rhythm of another spasm.

The midwife said, 'This one's not going to hang around. Come with me, Mother. We're heading straight to the labour ward.'

Chapter Six

Carla

GARDNER – Robert and Carla Gardner (née Kelly) are delighted to announce the birth of their daughter Isobel Gillian, born on the 3 November 1993. Sincere thanks to the staff at the Valley View Maternity Clinic for their excellent attention and kindness – and to the ambulance crew, Nikki Nortan and Des Brogan for their swift intervention.

Go raibh mile maith agaibh. *Thank you very much.*

From her bed, Carla watched a fragment of sky fade from indigo to pewter, the light relentlessly moving forward until finally it crashed, harsh and winter-white, against the window. The new day spilled over her and over Isobel, sleeping in a cot at the foot of the bed; two days old now and Carla was finding it increasingly difficult to remember a world where her daughter had not existed.

Until her arrival, Robert had been the most important person in her life. Now, Isobel occupied the same position. But there would be no jostling, no competition, because love was as expansive as the demands placed upon it. A stomach bump, Carla had discovered, no matter how cumbersome, no matter how active, no matter how cherished, had no reality until the moment of birth.

Yesterday, Nurse Clancy – or Amanda, as she preferred to be called – showed Carla how to hold her daughter and bring her gently to her breast.

'Isobel is a natural feeder,' she declared. 'She knows exactly what she wants. I don't see you having any difficulties when you leave us.'

Sudden, fat tears had coursed down Carla's cheeks. Baby blues. Amanda knew what to do. A sensible explanation as to why new mothers often felt weepy and prone to mood swings.

'You've nothing to worry about,' she said as she passed a box of tissues to Carla. 'You're more than capable of managing this lively young lady. Just don't allow her to intimidate you.'

The imminent arrival of photographers had concentrated Carla's mind. She took out her cosmetic case and set to work. By the time they entered the ward she was glowing, ready for action. She had gathered Isobel in her arms and smiled for the cameras. Isobel slept throughout the session, unperturbed by the clicks and flashes, the commands . . . *This way, Carla . . . That way . . . Beautiful . . . Perfect . . . One more . . . Last one . . . Last one . . .*

Amanda had arrived and shown them the door. 'Have you men no consideration for a woman who has been labouring all night to bring her baby into the world?' she demanded. 'Get out of here before I take my broomstick to your hairy backsides.'

The first photographs of the Anticipation Baby had made the evening editions of the *Evening Herald* and the *Evening Press*, and was shown on the early edition of the televised news bulletin. Robert had been tight-lipped when he saw the media coverage. Carla had feared another row and suspected one would have occurred had the ward not been full of people. She had agreed with him that from now on their daughter must be kept out of the public eye. Carla's Anticipation contract was over and Raine had already chosen a successor.

But most of yesterday remained a haze. Her family and friends had called throughout the day, bringing champagne and gifts. Gina Kelly, Carla's sister-in-law, due her first baby in January, had asked for a blow-by-blow account. 'Tell me everything,' she demanded. 'Just leave out the gory details . . . *if* possible.'

'It was as easy as falling off a log.' Carla dismissed six hours of intense labour with an airy shrug. All she wanted to remember was that instant of contact when, trailing blood and mucus, her daughter had been placed across her chest; a withered old woman's face and scrawny fingers (all ten, the midwife assured her, same with the toes) and, in that instant, Carla had fallen feverishly in love. That, she reckoned, would be the abiding memory for the rest of her life.

Robert, pale and sober by then, was equally besotted. 'She's so perfect,' he whispered. 'So beautiful.'

Carla, nodding in agreement, had realised that beauty no longer had any meaning. It simply belonged in the eye of the beholder.

'You have to come and stay with us when you leave the clinic,' her mother said, disregarding the fact that Carla had already discussed this offer with her before Isobel was born and had refused.

'Thanks for the thought, Mother, but Robert's taking some time off work. We'll be fine.'

'Nonsense. You've no idea how difficult it'll be when you go home. I still have nightmares about your first few months. Colic. You never stopped crying. No, no, I insist. Your old

45

bedroom has been redecorated. It's ready and waiting for the three of you.'

'Once we're settled into a routine, we'll come and visit, maybe stay overnight.' Carla's energy had dipped, as it usually did when she was forced to argue with her mother.

'You'll thank me in the end.' Janet's voice climbed a notch. 'It's all very well lying here in a swanky clinic, being waited on hand and foot. But it's a different kettle of fish when you're up all night with a crying baby. And your father is really looking forward to having you stay, aren't you, Gerard?'

'Leave the girl alone.' Gerard Kelly touched his wife's wrist. 'She knows we're here if she needs us.'

Gillian and Raine had arrived with flowers and copies of the evening papers, and the focus of attention was back on Isobel again.

'Welcome, Isobel Gillian.' Gillian leaned over the cot and peeled back the sheet to admire her first grandchild. 'Thank you so much for giving her my name,' she whispered to Carla. 'I'm so honoured.'

The veins on her hands were starkly ridged, her cheekbones accentuated. Despite her insistence that she was responding well to treatment, she was continuing to lose weight. Carla turned away, ready to cry again. She was like a tap, leaking everywhere. Her breasts ached a warning and Amanda, entering and catching her expression, had announced that visiting was over.

'Good morning,' said Amanda, arriving on the morning shift. 'How was the night?'

'Restless,' said Carla, who had left her bed many times to stand beside Isobel's cot, her own breath suspended as she watched her daughter's chest rising and falling. She was unable to resist touching her gently to see her move. Even the flicker of her eyelashes was insufficient to reassure Carla she was safe.

'How's the feeding going?' Amanda asked as Isobel stirred and whimpered.

'I think my milk's come down.' Carla lifted her daughter and lowered the flap of her nursing bra. 'It looks thicker.'

'Excellent.' Amanda nodded, satisfied. 'Usually it takes longer. Like I said, that kid's a natural. Keep it up, Mother.'

'What's the world doing outside?' Carla asked.

'The weather forecast is lousy. Rain and more rain. And this young lady, with her glamorous mother, is on the front page of the *Irish Independent*.'

Carla winced, imagining Robert's annoyance. Nothing she could do about it. She returned her attention to Isobel, whose lips now had a vice-like grip on her nipple.

'You look tired,' Amanda said, as Carla eased Isobel from one breast to the other. 'Why don't you let us take her to the nursery for a few hours so you can catch up on some sleep?'

'No. I'll be fine.' Carla shook her head. 'Leave her with me.'

After Isobel finished feeding, Amanda demonstrated how to bathe her. Carla, seeing the little starfish body with her blobby belly button, lying on a towel, tried to control her tears. Such a bitsy baby to have made such an arduous journey.

'Don't be frightened.' Amanda guided her hand to the bony curve of Isobel's head. 'Babies are tougher than they look but they do need to know you're in control.'

Two more days, then she and Robert would be alone with this terrifyingly tiny individual. No wonder she was panicking. No wonder her pillow was wet with tears.

Robert arrived mid-morning for a quick visit and watched, fascinated, as Isobel's lips searched and latched onto Carla's

47

nipple, her tiny cheeks moving like miniature bellows. When her head lolled to one side and a dribble leaked from the corner of her mouth, he winded her and placed her back in her cot. He settled the bedclothes around Carla, who was almost asleep, and quietly left the ward.

Carla drifted high above the sounds of the afternoon routine and slept.

She continued to weep in her dreams, knowing with the horrendous certainly that comes when the mind is relaxed that Isobel's arrival had triggered off the memory of another journey. So long ago and, until now, safely boxed in the past; a stray wasp that could be swiped aside when it occasionally flew too close. But her barriers were down, her boundaries invaded. Nothing would ever be the same again.

She awoke to the sound of drums tapping out a light, persistent rhythm. The earlier metallic sunshine had been replaced by grey cloud and rain lashing against the window. Carla glanced at the clock on her locker. Three hours since Isobel's last feed. Her breasts felt tender, heavy. Milk had seeped through her nursing bra and the front of her night-dress was wet. When she pulled down the flap and stared at the blue veins, she could see how engorged her breasts had become. Surprising, then, that Isobel had remained silent.

She pulled herself upright. The counterpane on Isobel's cot was bunched awkwardly over the mattress. Impossible to see her from that angle. Carla swung her legs to the floor. Four stitches. She grimaced as they tightened and forced her to walk gingerly towards the cot. She grabbed the counter-pane and stared at the empty space where her daughter, swaddled in a white sheet, had been lying. The undersheet had a slight stain, as if Isobel had marked her territory. A 'wet burp' Amanda had called it when she demonstrated how Carla should wind her after feeding.

She reached for the emergency bell beside her bed and pressed it. Unable to wait for a nurse to arrive, she ran into the corridor. A long empty corridor that silenced her footsteps when she turned to the right, then the left, and tried to locate the nurses' station. She stopped, suddenly dizzy, and leaned against the wall. There had to be a rational explanation. Amanda had taken Isobel to the nursery so that Carla could sleep undisturbed. Her terror gave way to anger. How dare anyone make such a decision without asking her permission?

'My goodness!' Amanda's smile became uncertain as Carla approached the nurses' station. 'What on earth's the matter?'

'You took Isobel to the nursery without asking me?'

'What?' Amanda's head drew back, her eyes widening as she stared back at Carla.

'Didn't you?' Carla shouted. 'You should have told me.'

The nurse's expression changed, her face smoothing out into a professional mask, inscrutable.

'Tell me she's in the nursery.' Air whistled from Carla's throat. 'Tell me.' Her legs buckled. She was vaguely aware that Amanda had rushed from behind the station and was holding her upright, that she was moving, guided by the nurse, back to her ward. As they entered, she experienced an instant of hope. Her imagination had run riot. Crazy baby blues and hallucinations.

The cot was still empty. Carla held the edge of it and screamed Isobel's name until Amanda forced her to sit down into the soft leather armchair.

'Please remain calm, Carla. There's been a misunderstanding!' Her voice penetrated Carla's hysteria. 'If one of the nurses has done what you've suggested, we'll deal with her immediately.'

'What do you mean *if*? Of course they did. Where else can she be?'

'We'll find out, don't worry.' Amanda whipped the bedclothes from the bed. 'But you must remain calm. Sometimes mothers fall asleep when they're feeding . . .'

Now, a new terror had to be considered. The fist clenching Carla's heart squeezed tighter but this thought barely had time to register before the bed was stripped. Nothing there, only the warm imprint of her body. Amanda checked the chart hanging from the bed rail then lifted the phone and asked for the matron. Despite her calm manner, Carla suspected a coded emergency message was being relayed. As the nurse spoke, her experienced glance constantly roved around the room, checking out places where a crazy mother, burdened with baby blues, could have hidden her child. The wardrobe, a drawer in the bedside locker, under the cushions on the armchair.

Carla leapt to her feet and pulled the cushions to the floor, rushed to the wardrobe and opened her suitcase, spilled her clothes across the bed. 'She's not here . . . can't you see . . . she's not here . . .'

Amanda tried to prevent her opening the drawer of her bedside locker but Carla pushed her aside. The matron entered as they struggled. Carla had met her shortly after Isobel was born. Small and sturdy with plump chins and authoritative eyes, she had been smiling then, as everybody had been, and Robert was holding Isobel in his arms, a dazed grin on his face.

'Mrs Gardner, tell me exactly what has happened here.' Her tone was formal, first-name terms abandoned.

'One of your nurses took my child from her cot without asking my permission. How dare she . . .? I have to phone my husband.'

'But first, you need to answer my questions.' The matron's voice was firm. Isobel's disappearance was no longer a misunderstanding. It had, according to Matron, become a serious breach of procedure. 'It's in all our interests to find Baby Isobel as swiftly as possible so please co-operate with us, Mrs Gardner.'

The hospital was sealed off and the entire premises would be thoroughly searched. Amanda draped a bed jacket over Carla's nightdress to cover the milk stains. The police were on their way. Carla had not believed her terror could reach a higher pitch but it clawed more sharply against her chest with every word the matron uttered. Amanda stayed with her until the police arrived. Their bulky shoulders filled the doorway. Uniforms, notebooks, too many people in the ward. They sucked up all the air. She could not breathe if she did not have air but no one was listening. A policewoman sat beside her and probed her with gentle but repetitive questions. How long had she been sleeping? Could she give the exact time she closed her eyes? Did she awaken at any point, disturbed by a sound, alerted by another presence in the room? The most important clues could be hidden in the most basic information. She was an older woman and her motherly tone never wavered when she told Carla to call her by her first name.

'Orla . . .' The name seemed to slide from the side of Carla's mouth. She tried to speak again but everything was shifting, the floor and walls, her words meaningless as she pitched forward into blackness.

She was lying on the bed, Robert's face above her when she recovered. Isobel was somewhere in the hospital, he assured her. She wanted to believe him. He was trained in the art of detection but she saw the truth in his eyes, their bleak fear mirroring her own. The search had now been extended beyond the clinic where all the other babies, tiny labels on their arms, were present and correct.

Carla returned to the armchair by the window and gazed down on the police as they combed the grounds of the clinic. The administration offices, kitchens, bathrooms, each small private ward and the half-finished buildings outside the clinic were being thoroughly checked. The entire staff were being questioned, along with the builders, and all those who visited the clinic during the day.

Her daughter, tiny and helpless, was lost in the rain. Carla moaned and covered her eyes. Amanda and Orla remained with her, each offering reassurances in their own way. There was, Orla insisted, an established pattern to such behaviour. The woman who took Isobel had always longed for children, had, probably, recently lost a child. She would protect Isobel, keep her warm and safe. Orla spoke as if she had a direct line to this unknown woman, whom Carla could only imagine as a monstrous, faceless creature. Amanda displayed the same impassive confidence as she helped Carla pump milk from her aching breasts. It would be kept fresh in the fridge until Isobel was returned to them.

Robert, ashen-faced, rain dripping from his hair and eyelashes, kept entering the ward and holding her, then leaving again, as if he could not cope with her fears. She sensed his desperation to be at the heart of the official search, but he was not allowed to participate. Official procedure, Orla told her. He was emotionally involved.

Raine and Gillian arrived, followed by Carla's parents. Staring at the empty cot, they strove for words of comfort. Janet's hands fluttered. Helpless tears rolled down her cheeks. Happiness, she believed, was contained in nothing more substantial than a fragile bubble, and now her greatest fear had been realised. Unable to endure her distress, Carla begged her father to bring her home. Gillian left with them, her pallor more pronounced than usual.

The day darkened. Spotlights illuminated the courtyard and the raindrops swirled like fireflies before splashing on the cobblestones. Raine sat on the arm of Carla's armchair and held her hand tightly as the new fathers, arriving with flowers and fluffy toys, were directed to another entrance. The car park remained empty. Figures moved over the grounds still. Flashlights lit the shrubbery. Police cars entered and left between the black, wrought-iron gates.

A television van was driven up the avenue. The phone rang shortly afterwards.

'No comment.' Orla replaced the receiver with a clang. 'I'm sorry, Carla. The media have got wind of the story. Don't worry. We'll deal with them.'

'If I talk to them now, it'll be on tonight's news.' For the first time since she awoke and saw the empty cot, Carla's mind focused. She understood optics, publicity, the projection of an image. 'I want to appeal directly to this woman.'

'Leave the media to us,' advised Orla. 'We have procedures in place for dealing with such incidents.'

'Incidents!' Carla bent forward and clutched at her stomach. Her flesh felt flabby, empty. 'How dare you call my baby's kidnapping an incident!'

She brushed aside the policewoman's attempts to apologise but Robert agreed with Orla. It was too early for interviews. The media already had Isobel's photograph. If she was not found soon – he winced and closed his eyes – then a press conference would be organised. Suddenly, the strength left his legs. He collapsed on the bed and lay back, his hands over his eyes. Carla lay beside him. He gathered her close and she, hearing his laboured breathing, his desperate attempts at self-control, became the comforter. She repeated Orla's assurances, soothing him with false words until he felt strong enough to rise again.

It seemed impossible to imagine time moving, yet the hands on the clock turned past midnight and another round of waiting began. Sleep, Amanda assured her, was necessary if she was to cope. When Carla did manage to close her eyes, it was a drug-induced slumber and she sank into a dreamless void until it was time to awaken again into the nightmare.

Chapter Seven

Susanne
Three days later

Go to her, they whispered when I saw her in the papers. Isobel Gardner – a baby with no distinguishing features to set her apart from other newborns who slide into the world a fortnight before their time. I resisted at first. I deadened my ears to the whispering and went to bed instead, pulled the pillows over my face.

The pain awakened me in the small hours. Clockwork precision each month, the bleed so heavy that I'm always nervous going anywhere for the first two days. It was still dark outside. Another hour before dawn lifted over the Burren. The pain was intense, thin and razor-sharp, slicing through my coccyx, through the sacrum, reaching a pitch where I believed I could no longer endure without screaming. Then it eased, ebbed, and I rested in the shallows until it began again.

I knew then that I must leave before the light broke. Before Phyllis Lyons arose to lift her mother upright and plump the pillows behind her head. Before Mitch Moran opened his garage and Stella Nolan switched on her bakery oven. I checked the nursery. All was in order. I prepared your first feed and placed the formula back in the kitchen press. I filled a flask and removed your bottle from the sterilising unit. The pain built again and with it came the bleeding. I had a four-hour journey ahead of me. Eight hours on the road. Heavy rain was expected to fall.

When I reached the Valley View Maternity Clinic, I parked in the most secluded area of the car park. An embankment of pampas grass sheltered me. A wall of cotoneaster caught against my coat as I stepped from my car. I pulled free and the berries fell like drops of blood on the ground.

I gazed through the glass doors into a spacious foyer. The clinic used to be a Georgian family home and the building still smacks of carriages and candelabras. A fire was blazing in the reception area, turf and logs piled in the cavernous fireplace. Armchairs had been placed around it and magazines were stacked neatly on small tables. But no expectant fathers waited in the wings today. The only person I saw was the receptionist, her head bent over her desk. I moved out of sight before she noticed me and walked back down the steps.

At the back of the clinic, signposts directed me to different wards, outpatients' department, the laboratory and the private rooms of gynaecologists. At the outpatients' department, building work was underway. A notice apologised for any inconvenience. The workmen paid no attention to me. I paused outside automatic glass doors. This was the instant when sanity demanded to be heard. Once inside, I was stepping into a zone where rules no longer applied. But it was too late . . . far too late for second thoughts.

The glass doors opened and closed behind me. The noise fell away. Such a calm atmosphere, an empty waiting room, a notice advising me to knock at Reception then take a seat. Through the opaque glass of Reception I saw someone moving across the office. The top half of another person was visible at a desk. I walked past, expecting at any moment to hear the authoritative command that would pull me back from the brink. It never came.

My hands began to sweat. My knees trembled so badly I had to stop and lean against the wall. I forced myself to move on until I reached a long corridor with doors on either side. The smell of food lingered, not heavy and fishy (a smell I have always associated with hospitals) but herby and fragrant. The smell of health and vitality, the aroma of coffee, bread freshly baking, a hint of garlic. I reached a staircase; the banisters formed an elegant swerve. My shoes sank into soft, thick pile. At the top of the stairs, two arrows pointed in opposite directions, leading to rooms 18 to 25 or 26 to 33. On the way to the clinic I'd stopped at a public phone. The receptionist had told me that a bouquet for Mrs Gardner could be sent to Room 27.

I turned left and walked along the corridor until I reached her room. The pain had moved from the base of my spine to my stomach, the cramps doubling me over. I stumbled towards a bathroom. I had tablets for pain control in my handbag. They usually offered some relief but pain was necessary for rebirth. It was important not to interfere with my natural cycle.

Inside a cubicle, I sat on the toilet seat and adjusted my clothes. The harness holding the cushion had loosened. I fumbled, my hands shaking so much they became entangled in the bindings. The door to the ladies' opened and a woman entered the cubicle next door. I remained motionless until she had washed her hands and left. Then I tied the strings securely over my hips and emerged. The white tiled walls cast a hard reflection on my face. My eyes were red-rimmed, shadowed, filled with anticipation.

I splashed water over my face until my skin was raw and flushed. *No more . . . no more . . .* the whisperers drove me forward. I could have stopped at that point. I wanted someone to enter and order me from the premises. A hard-faced matron or an enquiring nurse who would accept my excuse about being lost in this labyrinth of corridors. Then I heard you for the first time. *You*, my daughter, your voice calling out to me. I pushed the door open, hoping I would find Carla Kelly awake, protective and alert. But she was sleeping, one arm resting on the counterpane.

You made no sound when I lifted you. Light as thistle-down, you moulded yourself against my breasts. Swiftly, swiftly, we moved as one, mother, daughter, into the ladies', into the canvas holdall, into the future. Hush little baby, don't say a word . . . walking fast down the stairs with its muffled carpet, past Reception where figures moved behind yellow glass, past the builders who did not stare or wolf-whistle at a pregnant woman, to the car park where I held my bag away from the spiky cotoneaster, safe inside the car, driving away, my stomach cramps beginning to subside, and deep in the depths of the canvas holdall, you moved, jutted an elbow, kicked a foot, struggled to be free from the dark confines. Then you settled back to sleep again.

Rain wrapped the city in a grey shroud as I drove through the traffic and out into the countryside, my foot hard on the accelerator, heading for home.

When you cried I pulled into a lane. The rain dripped like tears from black branches and a cow poked a damp, inquisitive face over a gate. I opened a flask and filled a bottle with your first feed. My hand trembled so much the formula spilled over my trousers. You whimpered, struggled to adjust your mouth around the teat. Your cheeks worked, your lips puckered, your eyes screwed up in outrage. You threw up your feed. The smell was faint but sour. I had to drive on, terrified a farmer would round the bend in a tractor. I wanted to turn back. Leave you where I had found you. But she would be awake by now and already screaming. So I kept driving. Your wailing terrified me – so strident and demanding from such tiny lungs. When I pulled into another lane and fed you again, you sucked reluctantly on the teat and eventually fell asleep.

I drove fast until I came to towns where the rain forced the traffic into a slow, sullen crawl. After Limerick City it wasn't so difficult. I kept expecting to hear the wail of a siren but only the swish of the windscreen wipers disturbed my concentration. When I reached Gort, I noticed the fields were already under water, the same in Kinvara. Water ran from the hills and gathered in the ditches, spilled across the road, splashed dangerously under my wheels. The rocks of the Burren came into view. I drove through Maoltrán and past the craft centre. Lights were on in the windows. Miriam was in London, exhibiting at a craft fair. She'd warned me, before she left, to drive to the hospital if I experienced even the slightest twinge.

The windscreen kept hazing over and the rain was so heavy it flowed under the swishing wipers. I drove past the Lyons' house and, suddenly, I was facing the wet rump of a cow. Cattle fanned across the road and Phyllis, walking behind in a bright yellow sou'wester, looked over her shoulder and moved close to the hedgerow. I skidded, the car waltzing on the scum of dead leaves, but I managed to control the wheel and glide gently into the grassy embankment. The front bumper took the shock, but the holdall slid from the seat. I grabbed it as it was about to topple over and held it steady. Phyllis peered through the window, tapped on the glass. I saw her lips moving and when I lowered the window she stuck her head into the car. Rain dripped from her sou'wester cap, sliding down her nose.

I expected you to cry. Wanted you in a crazy way to do so and end the madness. But you stayed silent, undisturbed by the swerves and jolts.

Phyllis demanded to know if I was okay.

'I'm rushing,' I told her. 'Dying for a pee.'

She kept her hand on the window to prevent me sliding it up again. The road was flooding fast, she said, and she was taking her cattle to the high field. 'Watch how you go,' she shouted when I pressed my foot to the accelerator. 'Take care of the dips. You know how quickly they flood.'

She swiped at the cows with a switch and guided them into a straight line. I squeezed the car past their swaying bellies. The stream running through Dowling's Meadow had burst its banks. Part of the meadow was already flooded, the water rushing through the hedgerows and seeping across the road. I turned into the lane and drove towards Rockrose, grateful for the steep incline that always protected us in times of heavy rain.

The sun peered between two heaving clouds and danced briefly in the sky. The drystone walls glistened as the weight of water swelled the turloughs, those mysterious underground lakes that appear so suddenly and flood the grassy swathes of the Burren. When I lifted you from the car and carried you up the garden path, it seemed as if we'd stepped into a world of glass.

I am a methodical woman and had planned each detail of your arrival. I planned as carefully as a bomber about to take flight, a strategy for survival in hand though he knows he could be blown asunder at any instant. But I cannot claim credit for the weather. I had cloud cover on the night you came to me but the rain that teemed from those clouds led me deeper into my deception.

Three days have passed since then. The flooded fields have swamped the roads and warnings on the radio advise people to stay indoors and only drive if it's absolutely necessary. Two drivers, brave or reckless enough to drive along Maoltrán Road, stalled close to the lane and Phyllis had to pull them free with her tractor. We may be cut off by floods but her role in your birth has already spread the length and breadth of Maoltrán. She is the local heroine. I would have been lost that night without her assistance. I've spoken on the phone to Dr Williamson and to Jean, the district nurse. No need to worry, I told them. I have food in the house and you, my daughter, my miracle child, are in perfect health. When the roads are passable, I'll bring you to St Anne's Clinic for your postnatal checkup. They didn't argue. There's been an outbreak of vomiting and diarrhoea in the area. Not surprising with all that contaminated water.

They told me I was amazingly brave to give birth in such appalling conditions. 'What was brave about it?' I said. Women give birth in war and famine, under trees and in their branches, in igloos, sheds and caves. I brought you into the world under a dry roof and thanked God for a safe deliverance. We lay together between the sheets, nothing stirring except our breath. The whisperers were silent then and have remained so ever since.

'Jesus Christ and his blessed mother,' Phyllis said, when I rang that night and told her I was in trouble. 'How fast are your pains coming?'

'Every few minutes, I told her. It's all happening so quickly. My waters have broken.'

'Must have been the shock from the cows,' she said. 'Maybe it's a false alarm but I'd better ring Dr Williamson.'

'No,' I said. 'Don't bother her. The lane is flooded. Come quickly before it gets any deeper.'

She heard me panting and didn't hesitate. 'I'll take the tractor,' she said. 'Hang in there, girl. I've delivered calves and if you've ever had your arm up a cow's arse, childbirth is nothing.'

She was lying of course and she was very bad at it. 'Hang on,' she warned again, and this time I heard the shake in her voice. 'You can't give birth now. Not with Miriam in London and David still on the rig.'

Phyllis arrived shortly after my phone call, still swaddled in her yellow sou'wester. She had driven down the lane in her tractor and rushed the wet night air in with her. She squished upstairs in her wellingtons, her cheeks flushed from the exhilaration of dangerous deeds.

'Stalled a few times,' she said, 'but here I am, and there you are, and what on earth is that?' She drew back from the bed and covered her eyes.

I understood her fear. She can joke all she likes about calves but childbirth is a mystery to her. All that blood smearing the sheets, my legs, my hands, and you, your hair stiff with it, your tiny, wrinkled face marked with the slime of birth, face down and stretched naked across my stomach. I lifted you and swaddled you in a towel.

'Hold her,' I said. 'Hold her while I take care of myself.'

I forced you into her arms. She held you gingerly, as if she expected you to mew or scratch.

'Sweet Jesus,' she said. 'I've never held a baby that's just been born.'

'Barely born,' I said, and roused myself from the bed. 'Do you mind turning away? I want to . . .' I hesitated and lifted the sheet. I thought she would faint when she saw the blood. 'It's the placenta,' I said. 'It's come away.'

She moved away across the room, still holding you, and

sank onto a stool in front of the dressing table. She looked at me in the mirror as I slopped the liver into a bowl and covered it with a white cloth.

'I never knew what it looked like,' she said when I was lying back again against the pillows. 'Jesus, it's awful.'

'But it's over now,' I said. 'The most frightening part was cutting the cord. If you'd got here on time you could have cut it for me.'

She glanced quickly at the scissors and thread lying beside the bowl then averted her eyes. 'I wouldn't have known what to do,' she said.

'You cut it then clamp it on either end with thread,' I replied. 'That's how you do it in an emergency.'

She came slowly towards me and sank to the edge of the bed. She seemed unable to take her eyes from the bowl. Blood had already seeped into the white covering. She swallowed loudly. I thought she was going to faint or throw up.

'Let me hold my baby now,' I said, and I took you back into my arms.

She stared down at the pair of us and wrinkled her nose. 'Bit of cleaning up needs to done around here,' she said. 'Boiling water.' She laughed suddenly. 'It's what happens in them films. I always wondered what the hell it was for. Now I know.'

She lifted a jug and matching basin from the dressing table, old porcelain, painted with blue roses. Miriam must have used it when David was a baby. His grandmother would have also bathed his father in it. The sense of tradition in Rockrose was never stronger than on that night.

I sponged the blood from the crevices in your skin. I cleansed you from all impurities then wrapped you in a soft white sheet. I wept tears upon your upturned face.

63

'Tea and toast,' said Phyllis. 'My cousin says that's the only thing when the tears start.'

The toast was thick and buttery, the tea stronger than I usually drank it. I'd never tasted anything so fine.

She asked if I'd decided on a name.

'Only one name is possible,' I replied. 'I want to call her Joy.'

We rolled it around our tongues. Phyllis nodded, satisfied, and took you back into her arms. Her smile grew in importance. 'Just as well I was able to manage that tractor,' she said. 'You'd have been truly stranded in your hour of need. I'm just sorry I wasn't here for her birth.'

'But you were,' I said. 'Or as close as makes no difference. I'll never be able to thank you enough.'

She assisted me into the shower. The water coursed over my body, washing away the stain of blood. When I emerged she had a clean nightdress ready to slip over my shoulders. The bed had been made with fresh linen and the old sheets bunched out of sight into the laundry basket. But you had had enough handling by then and David, when Phyllis phoned him, heard you crying . . . such a loud, lusty roar.

'I should have been with you,' he kept saying. His voice broke, as if he too was crying. 'I should never have left you alone . . . is our daughter as beautiful as she sounds?'

'Even more beautiful,' I said. 'She is our miracle baby.'

Gales were blowing across the North Sea. No helicopters had been able to land on the rig for two days. The forecast was for milder conditions and he would be home as soon as humanly possible.

I gave Phyllis instructions on how to prepare your formula and she watched, her eyes moist with longing, as you sucked. But she was growing anxious about her mother who always needed to be taken to the bathroom at midnight.

'Do you want me to dispose . . .?' She hesitated and gestured towards the bowl.

'Leave it be,' I said, when she went to lift it. 'I'll look after it myself.'

She nodded when I told her to leave the sheets in the basket, understanding, as all women do, that dirty linen is best washed in private. I asked her to take our photograph before she left. It's important that David is able to share that priceless moment when I named you into life.

After she left, I rested with you in my arms and imagined the water bubbling behind the drystone walls, forming deceptive puddles and dangerous dips, and raising the river levels that would soon burst their banks. But we were content, you and I; safe and warm in an ocean of calm.

David is in the air, flying towards us. Miriam also, with a full order book, both of them anxious to catch their first glimpse of you. In Rockrose, you sleep by my side, your tiny face puckered with concentration. Your lips move, blowing silent raspberries. I cannot take my eyes off you. Your blonde hair is downy, as fine as my own. Your eyes are still milky, unfocused. Hard to tell the colour; I pray they will be blue.

Carla Kelly will be on the news tonight. Her press conference is due to begin soon. This is her first public appearance, apart from the flurry of publicity that followed the birth of Isobel Gardner. I cannot bear to watch. The deed is done.

Chapter Eight

Carla

Carla braced herself to enter the hotel conference room. Three days had passed since Isobel's disappearance and this was the most important public appearance she would ever make. Bottled water and glasses were laid out on the green baize tablecloth. She sat behind the table and greeted the cameras like old friends sent to comfort her. Each shot mattered. Flashbulbs would illuminate her daughter's whereabouts. Adrenaline pumped through her body as she held up Isobel's photograph. She allowed the intrusive lens to see her devastation, her bewilderment.

Her elder brother Leo, her protector since they were children, had automatically become her adviser and solicitor. Words were important, he stressed before the conference began. He went over the written statements she would read and advised her on how to answer questions. Keep it simple, appeal directly to the woman who had taken Isobel. She would be listening.

The story of her daughter's disappearance had swept like a bushfire through the media. *Anticipation Tot Robbed While Model Mum Slept . . . Mysterious Disappearance of Anticipation Baby . . . Celeb Mum Waits in Anticipation.* The broadsheet headlines were more circumspect than the tabloids. *Two Days Old Baby Stolen from Luxury Clinic ... Shocked Parents Seek Missing Baby.*

The public response was immediate. Sightings were reported and investigated but the Garda had nothing new to report at the end of each day. Borders were checked, ferries searched. Everything that could be done was being done, claimed Detective Superintendent Murphy, who was in charge of the investigation. Initially, Carla believed everything he said. His words were the lifebelt that prevented her sinking.

The Garda Press Office dealt with all the media queries and Detective Superintendent Murphy had insisted she keep a low profile while the Garda continued their investigations. Slowly, she became aware of other ripples in the background.

'For your husband's sake, we need to keep a tight rein on your public appearances and utterances,' the superintendent warned her.

But Robert's career as an undercover detective was over. No more dark deals against the walls of derelict warehouses. A desk job in the future, if there was a future ... and Carla could not imagine their lives moving on if Isobel was not found. On the day following Isobel's disappearance, Matron, stiff-necked with shame, embarrassment and nerves, had discharged her from the clinic. Bookings were being cancelled and investigations of the security procedures in place within her clinic were underway. Journalists hung around the courtyard waiting for staff to emerge and be questioned. They were leeches, the matron declared, feeding off the good reputation of the Valley View Maternity Clinic, which she and her staff had worked so hard to maintain.

Leo stood on the steps of the clinic and issued a statement to the assembled journalists while Carla left by the back entrance. She was driven in an unmarked Garda car to Raine's apartment in Dundrum where Robert had been staying since the story broke. It was safe to weep there. No one to tell her to stay calm and focused. When she had exhausted herself into silence, she tried to eat the meal Raine had prepared.

'I have to face the media sooner or later,' she said. 'I can do the press conference alone. The Garda Press Office should be able to issue a statement as to why you can't appear.'

'I want to be with you,' Robert said. His cheeks were gaunt, his eyes shadowed from lack of sleep.

'What if you're recognised?' she asked. 'I couldn't bear it if anything happened—'

'No one's going to make the connection,' he assured her.

'How can you be so sure?'

'It was my job.' His mouth tightened. 'That's why I was one of the best.'

She noted his use of the past tense. Their lives were out of control and they were powerless to halt the slide. He was in contact with the search team, constantly seeking the latest information. Her antennae had become attuned to every nuance in his voice. She could gauge the information he was prepared to share with her by the shift of his eyes.

'I strongly advise against this press conference,' Detective Superintendent Murphy had said when he heard what Carla was planning to do. 'You could be putting your husband's life in danger.' He was a solid, bald-headed man with a strong neck and intimidating black eyebrows that reminded her of beetles. She found herself staring at them while he spoke, her eyes following their twitching movements in the vain hope that she could read beyond his professional calm. 'You must allow the Garda Press—'

'My wife and I have already made our decision,' Robert had interrupted his superior. 'In this instance, it is my rights as a father that take precedence over any other authority.'

Now, he sat silently between her and Leo, a nondescript figure, his hair slicked sideways, rimless glasses high on his nose. Nothing about his face demanded attention. He was, as the press statement had claimed, an administrative Garda whose job was dealing with driving misdemeanours.

Leo read out a brief statement and reminded the journalists that his clients were undergoing an intensely personal trauma. Their questions should be brief and to the point.

Robert's hands shook as he poured bottled water into a glass and began to speak. He was used to operating in shadows and seemed dazzled by the flashbulbs, appalled by the crouching, crawling movements of the photographers and the blaze of the television cameras. The clicking of cameras became more audible as his voice faltered. He bowed his head, unable to continue. Microphones were shoved forward to capture his harsh weeping. Carla held his hand and spoke for him.

'Isobel is our child,' she said. 'She is only five days old. Please have pity and return her to us. Please . . . please, if you have taken her for some misguided reason, talk to someone you can trust – a friend, a priest, the police. They will treat you with understanding and we are waiting to forgive you. But please . . . please return our darling baby to us.'

Her eyes felt like stones, hard and bright. She longed for tears but they refused to fall and give the photographers the shot they needed. Leo asked if there were any questions from the floor.

'Carla, how did you feel when you woke up and discovered your daughter was missing?' A journalist sitting in the front row raised her pen.

70

'Devastated.' Carla sucked in her breath and wondered why the answer was not blindingly obvious to anyone with feelings.

The journalist, young and eager, waited for a more dramatic response.

'I felt as if a knife had gone through my heart.' Carla winced. Her emotions, veering from manic hope to utter desolation, could not be described in a mawkish soundbite but the journalist seemed satisfied.

'Mr Gardner, as a member of the Garda Síochána, have *you* been personally involved in the search for your daughter?' another journalist shouted from the centre of the room.

'I'll take that question.' Detective Superintendent Murphy held up his hand. 'In any case directly involving a member of the Garda Síochána they are automatically disqualified from participating in the investigation.'

'Are you satisfied with the progress of the investigation so far?' Again the question was thrust at Robert, who nodded.

'I have the utmost faith in my colleagues and appeal to the woman who has our child to trust the Gardaí—'

'How do you know it's a woman?' shouted a journalist. 'Have you inside information that—'

'We don't know who took our child,' Carla swiftly intervened. 'And it doesn't matter. We don't want revenge. We simply want our daughter back in our arms.'

'Carla, has a ransom been demanded?' Josh Baker from *The Week on the Street*, a prime-time television programme, moved forward in tandem with his cameraman.

'We've heard nothing—'

'No ransom demand has been made,' snapped the superintendent. Carla could sense his desire to bring the conference to a conclusion but Josh had now reached the table and the camera was zooming in for a close-up of her expression.

71

'Carla, had you any suspicions that you were being stalked during your pregnancy?'

Carla shivered. She had not believed it would be possible to feel even more terrified. The camera was drawing her terror to the surface, beaming it outwards as she struggled for composure.

'I've no reason to believe I was being stalked.' She forced conviction into her voice and tightened her grip on Robert's hand. He trembled, knowing as she did that she would not necessarily have noticed a stalker. She was used to the gaze of men, indifferent to their eyes studying her as she walked past. No, she would not have noticed a stalker, just as she had not noticed a thief entering the ward where she was supposed to be keeping her daughter safe from harm.

'I agree with Mrs Gardner.' Detective Superintendent Murphy leaned towards the microphone. 'We have absolutely no evidence to back that theory.'

'Is there a link between Isobel's disappearance and the excessive promotion surrounding your pregnancy?' Alyssa Faye asked.

'Excessive . . .?' For an instant Carla's mind went blank. She shuffled the papers in front of her and stared at her statement. 'What do you mean?'

Leo calmly answered the question. 'Carla worked in a professional capacity throughout her pregnancy. There was nothing excessive about her public appearances—'

'The Anticipation advertising campaign exposed you to a wide audience,' said Alyssa. She glanced quickly to either side, aware that she had the media's attention. 'As a celebrity, you were constantly in the public eye. Is it possible that a woman who has recently lost a child could have been influenced by the disproportionate attention you received throughout your pregnancy?'

Once again the superintendent took the microphone. 'Ladies and gentlemen, I agree with Mr Kelly. That theory is groundless. Thank you for your time.' He raised his voice above the protesting babble. 'As you can understand, this is an extremely distressing experience for Mr and Mrs Gardner. This conference is over. No more questions . . . I repeat, no more questions.'

Leo placed his hand under Carla's elbow, raised her to her feet. 'Keep walking,' he whispered. 'Look straight ahead and don't respond to any further questions.'

She followed his instructions, vaguely aware that the journalists were on their feet and shouting her name. It was a familiar scenario. *This way, Carla! That way! The other way!* They stepped backwards, clicking, clicking. She recognised Colin Moore, the photographer from *Pizzazz*. He had phoned her yesterday to offer his support and sympathy. He lowered his camera and smiled encouragingly, jerked his thumb into the air. Instinctively, she found courage in his confident gesture. Her lips moved in response, a grimace, thanking him. Then she was ushered into the anteroom off the conference centre where she collapsed into Robert's arms.

Next morning, her photograph appeared on the front pages of the newspapers. Why was she smiling? She had not smiled from the moment she awoke to find her daughter missing yet there she was, her grimace morphed into her catwalk smile. Years of experience radiating from the pages. Placed beside her smiling image was the photograph of Isobel, her scrunched-up, newborn features partly hidden by a blanket. A photograph of Robert, his face white and haggard, had been placed on the other side; a lost trinity that should have been a family.

Chapter Nine

Susanne
One month later

This morning we christened you Joy Ainé Dowling. In Maoltrán's small Catholic church, where David and I were married six years ago, we renounced Satan, with all his works and pomps. We lit candles to let the light of love shine on you. Fr Davis anointed you with chrism. You did not cry when he poured water over your head. 'Such a sweet placid baby,' he said. 'Such a miracle, born to be loved.'

Phyllis has remained the heroine of the hour. Towards the end of the service Fr Davis mentioned her in his homily: two women sharing the ultimate experience of bringing new life into the world. The art of public relations is about perception. It's not the story that's important but how you tell it.

Carla Kelly had told her story badly. She wore a stretch top, skinny jeans and a fitted jacket, slim as a whippet after giving birth only five days previously. And she smiled for the cameras, such a silly thing to do. She lost the public sympathy with that smile. How could she, a mother so recently bereft, look as if she was enjoying her fifteen minutes of fame?

It gives me courage, that smile. The journalists use it every time they run with the story. The lingerie shots have also been dusted off and the tabloids are having a field day reproducing them. So too is Alyssa Faye. She writes about the woman who stole Isobel Gardner. Clichés and stereotypes, that's all she writes. What does she know about anything? She milked my misery for all it was worth and now she milks Carla Kelly. Each weekend, she picks her bones clean, analyses her need for publicity, and how, by flaunting her pregnancy, she stirred a deep, dark well of longing. As for Josh Baker . . . he was a tabloid hack when I worked for Carter & Kay and now, five nights a week, he brings that same mentality to *The Week on the Street*. He's convinced there's a stalker involvement, which gives him an excuse to use the lingerie shots, and we see her in lacy briefs, her breasts plunging in the cups of a bra, hands upraised to her tousled hair.

Theories and analyses, speculation and investigation. When are they going to stop? Let the story die a natural death. Concentrate on the IRA, Clinton, Princess Di, Yasser Arafat, earthquakes, famines, war; the world still spins yet all they want to do is write about her. But they do not write about me. No one has looked at you and voiced suspicion. And if they did – if, for an instant, a seed of suspicion fluttered to the ground – Phyllis Lyons would crush it under her large, no-nonsense feet. She is determined that *her* story will not die.

I wasn't frightened at first. At least, I don't remember fear. Looking back, I realise I never believed it would happen. Never believed I could pull it off. Was I insane during those months? Living in a fantasy of my own creation?

I constantly surprise myself by remaining calm in the dangerous moments. Like when the district nurse finally drove her car down the lane and met you for the first time. She weighed you, jabbed your heel, dangled you like a monkey, and you clung to her fingers, danced in space, did nothing to betray me. I drove to St Anne's Clinic and sat in the coffee bar with you asleep in the pram beside me. I met Gemma O'Neill who used to go to school with David. She is expecting her second baby and had just emerged from her appointment with Professor Langley. I told her I was there for my postnatal checkup. We talked about Phyllis, how well she'd coped on the night.

'Imagine her having the nerve to cut the cord,' said Gemma. 'Were you terrified to let her do it?'

It seems that Phyllis's version has grown wings. Let it fly. I'm not going to contradict her story.

'I trusted her,' I told Gemma. 'What else could I do?'

'Rather you than me,' she replied, and shuddered at the horror of it all.

'Forget natural birth,' she said. 'I yell for my epidural as soon as the first twinge kicks in.'

David had dinner ready when we arrived home from the clinic. Everything is in order, I assured him. You curled your fingers around his thumb and kicked your tiny feet against his large brown hands.

I write in the small hours when I cannot sleep. I need that space. Afterwards, I feel lighter, as if the weight of words has drained the memory from me. 'No sense in two of us suffering sleepless nights,' I tell David, when he demands the right to lie beside me, the right to rise at night and feed you, the right to be involved.

The dream is reality now. I must live with Carla Kelly on my shoulder. I can banish her during daylight hours but at night she is free to roam through my dreams. I see her bending over your cot or standing at the foot of my bed. Sometimes she cannot get in and then she rages outside my window, her blood-red nails clawing the glass. These are the hours I fear most. What if I call out her name in my sleep, beg her to leave me alone, beg her forgiveness from the mist of my dreams? What if David hears? That is why he must sleep alone.

If you should ever read this diary, I will be dead. All my worldly longings eased. Please do not think of me as an evil woman. Evil is a holocaust of bones, a bullet in the head, a knife in the belly. Fate is evil, smiling from the side of her bitchy mouth as she randomly kicks us about the place. For once in my life, I fought back and took what was lightly left lying around.

The streets of Maoltrán are slung with fairy lights. Carol singers rattle collection boxes and sing about joyful tidings. Miriam buys Christmas presents that ding and ping, and play tinkling lullabies. My father and Tessa arrived yesterday with a teddy bear three times your size, and a caseload of baby clothes. Your eyes widen when I switch on the Christmas tree lights. Your hands move with wondering curiosity to touch the green needles. Christmas suddenly has meaning and magic, says David, and puts his arm around me. We stand together and welcome the season of joy; a family at last.

You stir, wave your fists in the air. You drink us into your gaze then look beyond our shoulders, as if searching for someone we cannot see.

'Angels,' says Miriam. 'Joy is following the flight of angels.'

Chapter Ten

Carla

Christmas was an obscenity wrapped in glitter paper. Carla wanted to go to a hotel and hide in an anonymous room until the festivities died down. The countryside drew her as it never had in the past and she was possessed by a longing to walk along a cliff or gaze at a meadow. But normality had to co-exist with abnormality and the Christmas dinner must be cooked and eaten. Her mother had invited her and Robert to dinner. She wept when Carla hesitated. Now that the sky had fallen, Janet found it an even heavier burden than she had anticipated.

'My grandchild stolen,' she cried. 'I can't endure it. I simply can't endure it. You must spend Christmas with us. Your father will be heartbroken if you don't. We have to support each other through this tragedy.'

On Christmas morning Carla awoke to the sound of bells. Robert was already standing by the window. He leaned his head forward until it touched the glass and Carla knew, before he turned, that he was weeping. They never wept together. An unspoken arrangement kept one of them strong whenever the other fell apart.

Downstairs, they exchanged gifts. She had spent an afternoon with Raine trying to decide what to buy for him.

Everything they looked at was unsuitable, too festive or romantic, too flippant or meaningless. But what did she expect? A gift designed for loss? A cracked heart wrapped in tinsel, crystal teardrops? In the end she bought a cashmere sweater for him. The wool would be soft and kind on his skin, and the sea-blue shade reflected his eyes. He had bought her a painting. Carefully, she unwrapped it from its bubble wrapping and held it before her. She recognised the glacial mountains, the intense blue waters, the white belfry of a lakeside church. They had cruised on Lake Garda during their honeymoon, drifting through a lilac haze of hill and valley, drunk on love and the spreading length of their future together. Then it was her turn to cry. He held her to his chest and allowed her to vent her grief into his new sweater.

At noon they collected Raine and Gillian who had agreed to join Carla's parents for Christmas dinner. Janet, labouring in the kitchen to produce the perfect meal, waved aside all offers of assistance.

'Too many cooks bring on a panic attack,' she warned and poured another glass of sherry. Shortly afterwards, Leo arrived with his wife. Gina's baby was due in early January. She and Carla had talked many times about their pregnancies, comparing symptoms, weight gain and how the two cousins, so close in age, would grow up as friends. From the very early stages, Gina had gained weight and now, with only three weeks to go, her stomach was impossible to ignore. No one made any comment as she settled heavily into an armchair. Music played on the stereo, a little too loud, but it prevented strained silences when conversation died.

Gerard carved the turkey. Janet, unable to break with tradition and serve vegetables everyone could enjoy, passed around the bowl of Brussels sprouts. As usual, everyone took a few to please her. Throughout the meal she drank too much wine. Carla caught Leo's eye. Christmas Day, under normal circumstances, was always difficult when Janet drank too much and they recognised the signs, her flushed face growing more belligerent, her harried movements as she played with her food, her slurred voice insisting on everyone having second helpings. Unable any longer to control her fury, she glared at Robert.

'Who is she?' she demanded. 'Who is the evil bitch who stole my grandchild?'

'Janet . . . please let's finish our dinner in peace.' Gerard's voice was already laden with resignation.

'Peace! How can there be peace in this house?' She pointed her index finger at the remains of the turkey and curled it back. 'God help me, I want to shoot her. I want to shoot her right between her evil eyes.'

Gina, unable to cope with the naked emotion on everyone's face, moved awkwardly around the table and cleared the dishes. Gerard and Leo skilfully guided Janet from the dining room and up the stairs where she took a sleeping tablet and drifted into a peaceful sphere where the sky was secure and eternally blue.

As soon as Leo reappeared, he handed Gina her coat and helped her into it.

'We promised my parents . . .' She glanced apologetically at Carla and hugged her. 'We're already late.'

Gina's parents would plump cushions behind her back, place a footrest under her feet. They would fuss over her and talk about baby names and ask about the last scan and whether she was still suffering from heartburn. Carla sucked in her breath. If she was to continue to stand upright she must acknowledge her sister-in-law's reality. She slipped her hand under Gina's coat and pressed her palm against her taut stomach. The baby kicked. A heart thud, same beat.

'You'll find her, Carla.' Gina struggled not to cry. 'You have to keep believing. Promise me you'll keep believing.'

Gina's baby was born in the second week in January. A baby girl, Jessica, eight pounds, six ounces; one pound four ounces heavier than Isobel. Robert grasped Carla's arm as they walked along the hospital corridor. His grip hurt but she welcomed the discomfort. It kept her walking in a straight line towards the ward where balloons with congratulatory messages bobbed above the beds and bouquets of flowers scented the air. Gina's family were already in the ward. They fell silent when Carla and Robert entered. The weight of all the unspoken thoughts gathered together in the small ward was almost too much to bear. Carla was acutely aware of the discomfort of Gina's family, the sympathy they longed to express if they could only find the right words. Tragedy had turned her and Robert into pariahs, doom-laden victims of an unsolved mystery. The visitors began to talk again but their voices were hushed, as if an inadvertent word would break the brittle calm. Carla bent and stroked her niece's cheek. Jessica rested in her mother's arms, cocooned in a pink sheet, a tiny, red-faced chrysalis with a shock of black hair.

'We're meeting friends so we can't stay,' Robert said and Gina nodded, accepted the excuse along with the baby present in bright wrapping paper. She did not order Carla to have hope. The time for platitudes had passed. Words were no longer an adequate response for people consigned to limbo.

By the end of January, the decision was made to wind down the Garda search. Isobel's file would remain open but the team was being disbanded and assigned to other, more pressing cases. Another unsolved mystery. There were so many of them. The great void where the 'missing' existed.

Isobel would become past history, someone who would feature sporadically in the media when she was tagged to a similar tragedy. Not that Carla could imagine anything remotely similar but children disappeared all the time. She had read about such disappearances, tug-of-love children, kidnapped children, slave children, and, sometimes, disappearing mothers who abandoned or killed their babies. She no longer wanted to hear such stories, nor read comparisons. Any extra strain would send her over the edge. She felt herself stepping nearer to it every day; the smooth perimeter of a deep black hole.

Detective Superintendent Murphy broke the news as gently as possible. He had been in regular contact with them throughout the search, his reassurances ringing with less conviction each time. On this occasion, Carla watched his eyebrows moving as he detailed all the avenues that had been explored, the leads followed and abandoned. How strange his face would look if they were shaved off. Like a moon without a shadow.

That night Robert sat in the kitchen with a bottle of whiskey at his elbow. It was after two o'clock in the small hours when he entered the bedroom.

'Carla . . .' His voice shook as he leaned against the doorway. 'Carla . . .' His voice thickened when he repeated her name. He slumped to the floor, his back arched as he encircled his knees. 'I know you're blaming me. But I couldn't prevent the decision . . . I couldn't even do that much for her . . .' He began to cry, an ugly sound, brutal, bare.

'I don't blame you.' Carla helped him to their bed. 'But it's up to us now. We must do everything possible to keep her name in front of the public.'

Once he fell asleep, she entered the nursery. Isobel's photograph was pinned above the cradle. It was *so* out of date.

83

She was almost three months old now, the colour of her eyes clearly defined. Carla hoped they were brown but they could just as surely be the same intense blue as her father's searching eyes. She was smiling and gaining weight, standing sturdily on the lap of some strange woman. Two little ramrod legs determined to stay upright.

The light struck the seahorses. She had forgotten how delicately they moved. The slightest sway of air set them in motion. She remembered the day she and Gillian had bought them. The glass artist had admired the cradle and held the seahorses over it, rainbow colours glancing off the white gauze.

'It's for my first grandchild,' Gillian had confided to the artist, who smiled as she bubble-wrapped the seahorses and told them she would soon also become a grandmother. She was probably enjoying her grandchild now, whereas Gillian could only live with the longing.

Chapter Eleven

Susanne
Four months later

Miriam called this afternoon. No warning. She just walked into my kitchen as if this was still her house. Country people do not understand the nature of privacy, the value of distance. They were used to dropping into Rockrose when she lived here and don't see why things should be any different now.

Phyllis Lyons does the same. She opens the back door and shouts, *Yoo hoo, anybody home?* Do I need anything in the village? Would I like to sample her homemade jam? Would I like to put my feet up while she takes you to her house to see her mother? She wants to hold you, kiss you, cuddle you. As if she has earned the right to possess you.

Like Phyllis, Miriam is also oblivious of boundaries. 'Come into my arms, my little cabbage,' she says, and takes you from your pram or cot without asking my permission. 'We're a small community here,' she reminds me when I suggest a phone call in advance would be appreciated. 'We don't stand on ceremony, especially in a village where everyone knows everyone else. Just be glad to have such good neighbours. Remember Phyllis. Where would you have been without her?'

'Let's have lunch,' she said when she came today. 'It's ages since you and I have had a chance to talk. I've brought food.'

She unpacked a flask of homemade soup and sandwiches. You were sleeping upstairs, quiet for once, and we had the kitchen to ourselves.

When did I intend returning to work? Miriam's tone was polite but she was looking for an answer. 'It's four months,' she added when I make no reply. 'I'm coping without you but only just. Have you considered the crèche at the craft centre? It's the perfect solution.'

'Not yet,' I said. 'I need more time with Joy. In fact, I think I should stay at home for the foreseeable future. I'm sorry, Miriam. I'd no idea she would take over my life but I honestly believe I'm making the right decision.'

She accepted my decision to resign from her company. If she was disappointed, she showed no signs. I used to believe she liked me. Now I'm not so sure. It's something about her eyes that makes me nervous. Does she suspect? I rationalise my feelings. I see that same speculation in everyone's eyes, even in the eyes of strangers, which means my imagination is playing up again. That's what I tell myself, repeating it, every time I take you into Maoltrán and people stop to admire you, to talk about Phyllis Lyons, and how amazing it was that she managed to bring that tractor through the flood, and ask if I'd like to join the mother and toddler club. The sweat starts at the back of my neck and I want to run . . . just run, you in my arms, *run . . . running* . . . back to my house, locking the door and keeping the world away from us.

When Miriam left I took you in my arms and told you about the day I first came to Maoltrán and how the seahorses brought David and me together. You stared at me with those round eyes, as if you could understand every word I said, and I was back there again, eight years ago, driving through the summer heat, heading towards my future.

Maoltrán, in English, means a bare hillock. As I drove through this small country village with its wide main street and the usual assortment of shops, I could see how it had acquired its name. The surrounding countryside is hilly and pastoral, but the grey rocky outline of the Burren is its most distinctive landmark. I'd passed a one-storey school with stencilling on the windows, and high stone steps leading to a Catholic church. I'd sped past lichen-covered tombstones and a small Protestant church, its ancient heritage diminished by the steel frame of an ugly creamery erected next to it. On reaching the new craft centre I searched for a sign that would lead me to Miriam's Glasshouse. The small compact buildings exuded fresh cement and paint, the sheen of creativity and hope. Miriam had recently moved from a small studio in the back garden of Rockrose to larger custom-built premises and she planned to expand her business. We'd spoken on the phone and I was confident I'd be her marketing manager by the end of the interview.

My job in public relations was a mystery to her. She read a press release I'd written about an age-resistant moisturiser and asked how I could write with such conviction when I knew there was no truth to the claim. She touched her face, the laughter lines deep around her eyes, the pull of middle age against her mouth.

She was right. What I'd written had no substance but I worked in the business of persuasion. I used words to capture the imagination, to trail it towards desire and the ultimate dream of eternal youth.

'Why would you change your career,' she asked. 'You're at

the heart of everything in Dublin. Why bury yourself in a small country village?'

Silence is golden. I'd learned that lesson early, knowing that an inadvertent word from me could spark against the tinderbox of my parents' marriage.

Her fingers were adorned with rings. Celtic swirls and knots, but no wedding band. Not even a Claddagh. My fingers were bare. The indentation where my engagement ring had rested was a stark reminder that I was planning a new future. I couldn't stop touching it. Like a tongue to a broken tooth, I would find my thumb rubbing against the white circle, as if, somehow, I could hasten its slow fading.

I held up my ring finger. 'A man,' I said. 'I need a fresh start.'

She noticed the white circle left by my engagement ring and nodded. Richard, the villain. No further explanation was necessary.

Richard was my rebound man. Not a good basis to start a relationship but I needed calm in my life after Edward Carter. I was twenty-eight when we met at a party and we became engaged two years later. Richard was upwardly mobile and ambitious, his career in the financial sector giving him the authority to wear pinstripe suits without looking ridiculous. What can I say about our relationship? It was safe and steady and Richard was an eager lover, who only became impatient when I mentioned babies.

'Plenty of time when we're married,' he'd say, whenever I brought up the subject. But I was anxious for a baby, aware of time marching smartly by. The brief mad spell after my mother's death, when I'd tumbled so heedlessly and head-long into sex, now seemed like someone else's shambolic nightmare; but the memory of what followed was indelible.

Without telling Richard, I stopped taking the pill. A year passed, hope fading each month. My gynaecologist advised me to bring him along for tests. Deceit had me by the ankles and, just when I'd plucked up the courage to confess the truth, he arrived home one night with champagne and roses. He'd been offered promotion, along with a three-year transfer to his company's headquarters in New York. We would move the date for our wedding forward and honeymoon in the Big Apple.

'No babies,' he wagged his finger at me and said, 'New York is no place for children. We'll start a family after we return to Dublin.'

As we drew up wedding lists, booked our hotel and church, I felt myself closing down. How could I describe it? A tight coiling inwards, mentally moving away from his words, physically from his touch, from everything he planned for our future, until, when it was finally time to walk away, I did so without tears or regret. I moved from his apartment, surprised at how little I had to carry with me.

I did not blame him for hating me. Our wedding plans had been cancelled for no reason that he could understand, apart from the reason I gave him. Incompatibility. As an excuse, incompatibility was vague enough to cover a multitude of reasons, yet serious enough to break the foundations of any relationship.

Miriam offered me the job and, when the interview had ended, she invited me to her house for a meal before I began my journey back to Dublin. I followed her car from the craft centre for about a mile. Ancient walls, ridged as the selvaged edges of a rough-knit jumper, ran over the hills. The Burren lay around me, flat pavement rocks marked by dolmen tombs and fortresses. She slowed after we passed the grey house, where Phyllis Lyons lives with her mother, and took a sharp right-hand turn into a narrow lane. Grass grew along the centre but tyre marks had grooved the edges. A tumbledown cottage was almost hidden by hedgerows and the grassy embankments were aflame with red-hot pokers, poppies, foxgloves and dense pockets of maiden pink. The lane rose sharply until I reached the line of cedar trees sheltering her house. The grey limestone walls blended into the rocky landscape and the name Rockrose had been carved into a gate pillar.

I fell in love with Rockrose as soon as I saw it or perhaps it was David who moved my heart so violently that, for an instant, I needed to possess everything within my gaze. He was dressed in shorts and a singlet, well-worn trainers, a sweatband tied around his forehead. He was playing with a small boy, chasing him around the garden, pretending, with exaggerated gestures, to be unable to catch him.

I parked outside the low drystone perimeter wall binding the front garden and stepped from my car. I watched as he hoisted the boy to his shoulders. David looked so young that day, like a teenager, far too youthful to be a father. I assumed the boy belonged to someone else until Miriam introduced him as her grandson.

Susanne . . . David lowered the boy and spoke my name slowly, as if anxious to memorise it. His face glistened with perspiration. The faint musky smell of youth oozed from his skin as he took my elbow and directed me into the kitchen.

The long wooden table looked as if it had served generations, as did the six sturdy chairs and the high upright dresser. A sofa was pushed against one wall and the cushions, deep and sagging, provided a trampoline for the boy to bounce upon. The open window looked out into the front garden and a jug of meadow flowers sat on the ledge.

Miriam served beef bourguignon from a large earthenware tureen. David ate heartily, sopping up the sauce with chunks of crusty bread, breaking off pieces and feeding them to his son. By then I had established their relationship. Joey was three years old and David would never be able to deny him: the same dark brown eyes and brown curly hair, the high, broad forehead, the easy grin.

Outside we heard the sharp blast of a horn, repeated three times. It broke like glass into our conversation. Joey jerked his head and looked up at his father. A blue car was parked outside the gate. The driver was female, with long black hair, impatient hands that once again sent out a demanding summons.

'Time to go, big boy,' said David. He lifted his son in his arms and ruffled his hair. He carried Joey down the path and handed him over to his mother. The exchange was brief. He returned to the house and went upstairs, muttering an excuse about phone calls he had to make.

'Young people,' Miriam had sighed then, 'so reckless with their happiness.' For a while after Joey's birth, Corrie O'Sullivan and David had tried to make their relationship work, she explained, but their son was all they had left in common. Corrine had recently become engaged to a local carpenter and they planned to settle in Canada. Miriam hinted at custodial battles, lost before they would even reach the courts; a single father in his early twenties, no chance.

David's expression when he had returned from handing Joey over to Corrine had been hard and angry. I recognised what lay behind it. Loss. I understood, as only I could, how he felt as he watched his son being lifted away from him. But at least he and Corrine O'Sullivan could lay claim to their son's identity.

I'd no idea who had fathered my baby during that crazy year after my mother died. Cervical cancer, the symptoms diagnosed too late. For months afterwards, my father had wandered around in a daze, twitching at sudden noises, as if he expected her to emerge from dark corners or behind closed doors and shriek at him.

I escaped into the arms of Shane Dillon, then Liam Maguire, then Jason Jackson. Dark lanes, the back seats of cars, my bedroom when my father was out. I didn't enjoy these furtive encounters, the impatient fumbling and tumbling, the brief satisfaction gained by them, not me. Yet my need seemed insatiable. I understand it now. The need to be loved unthinkingly, unconditionally. Such a demanding, primal need. Why else do we perpetuate our race? Why else would we subject our bodies to such grotesque man-oeuvrings, the animal grunts and heaves, the savage satisfaction that is instantly forgettable and, in my own case, always dispensable?

'Slut,' my father said, when Tessa brought the strain of my stomach against my school shirt to his attention. Five months gone by then, too late for an abortion, which was his first intention. 'Off to London on the next flight,' he said. 'Quick fix.'

But Tessa was determined that he was not going to export my problem. 'Too late,' she insisted, 'and even if your daughter wasn't five months gone, it's against the laws of the state and the law of God.' The country was not yet riven by abortion referenda and opposing views, but Tessa knew which side she was on. Actively pro-life, she'd decided that adoption would be the perfect solution and that's what probably would have happened in the end.

I'd argued loudly against either option. How I hated them, him and her, smug with happiness, and my mother hardly cold in her grave. None of us realised that it was my boy who would decide whether or not he would make that hazardous journey towards the light.

I didn't see David again until it was time for the official opening of Miriam's new studio. A lively occasion compared to the usual formal launches I'd once organised. No muted and strained conversations as strangers sipped tepid wine and struggled to find common ground. The people who crowded her new studio were loud and boisterous. They had gathered to celebrate her seahorses, those gentle males with their protruding bellies who mate for life and sing their love songs under the silver rays of the full moon. David had just qualified as a geologist. No surprises there. He'd grown up with sand and fire, flint and oxides, and was familiar with the melting and moulding of brittle substances. Petroleum exploration and oilfield development were his fields of expertise. Soon afterwards he left on contract for the oil-fields of Saudi Arabia.

I settled into Miriam's Glasshouse and was soon travelling across Ireland, meeting customers and building up her market base. I rented one of the new townhouses being built in Market Square and she invited me regularly to Rockrose. In David's room I browsed through his music collection. The Chieftains and Horse Lips sat uneasily beside Alice Cooper, Judas Priest and Black Sabbath. I was familiar with the Chieftains but heavy metal was not a taste I'd acquired. I was repelled yet fascinated by the lyrics: death, pain, anger, loss. I absorbed his presence and thought about his absent father.

By then I knew Miriam's story. I asked her if she felt any animosity towards her ex-husband, who had walked out on his family when David was six years old.

She shrugged and admitted her only emotion was indifference. 'And David,' I asked, imagining him as a young boy, alone in his room, playing his harsh angry music, giving the finger to the man who had deserted him. 'At first they used to meet,' she said. 'But not any more, not since he was thirteen and stopped mentioning his father's name.'

David arrived home from Saudi Arabia six months later. In Molloy's, the local pub where set dancing was a tradition, he stood out from the crowd, a tanned, mature man with a new firmness about his mouth that suggested authority. He was immediately whisked to the floor by an impetuous young woman.

'Imelda Morris,' Miriam nudged me. 'She's been friends with David since their pram days.'

More than friends, I thought, watching her heels flashing.

Miriam nudged me again when another young woman danced past. 'Corrine O'Sullivan,' she whispered.

Up close, Corrine was pretty in a blowsy way that would, I suspected, soon turn to flesh. Her boyfriend was sturdy and straight-backed, a squared-off chin that would brook no arguments. I watched David dancing with Imelda and Corrine dancing with her husband-to-be. They seemed oblivious of each other, yet I sensed the tensions that could be released by an inadvertent glance. I thought of Nina, my mother, cold and silent in her grave, and wondered where all that angry energy went when it could no longer be contained within the body. But the night passed off without incident. David asked me to dance. I suspect a hint from Miriam sent him in my direction. I shook my head, having no wish to compete against the fleet-footed Imelda, who claimed him once again.

When he came home on leave again I'd learned to set dance. In Molloy's, I wore a sundress with a discreetly plunging neckline and my toenails were painted red as sin. What was ten years between a man and woman, I asked myself. Nothing . . . if it was the man who carried the years. But for a woman, trapped by time, by a biological clock, it was different. I had squandered my time with too many men and had no more to waste.

Imelda had youth to flaunt but I was skilled in the art of pleasure. I knew how to give, if not to receive. How to stroke and caress a man's flesh, to apply firm or gentle pressure, to moan deeply, to breathe urgently, to gasp, as if pain and pleasure had clashed then melded. I often wondered if the sour coupling that led to my conception was responsible for my inability to experience pleasure; but David, on our first night together, had no reason to doubt my satisfaction. No condoms. I reassured him. Everything was under control.

We were together every night until it was time to start his next contract. I didn't write and tell him I was pregnant. Time enough when I was sure. Two months later, I was in Dublin, attending a meeting with a department store buyer, when a cramping pain forced the breath from my lips.

'It happens,' said the doctor in the family planning clinic. 'First babies, it's tricky. No reason why it should ever happen again.'

Miriam, busily crafting glass, did not notice my shadowed eyes when I returned to the studio, and David never knew.

Six months later, when he came home again, I'd chilled white wine in the fridge and red wine was breathing on the hearth. I served beef roulades with blue cheese and walnuts, a blackberry crumble for dessert. He carried me to the bedroom. Afterwards, I brushed his hair from his eyes and whispered endearments. Sweat beaded his chest. I leaned my palm against the beat of his heart and, for once, I wished I could experience that hot, racing sensation where nothing else exists outside the boundaries of our desire.

We slept and awakened, made love again. Three times he came inside me and when he finally left my side, his eyes dark with spent passion, I lay still and sensed his strong determined sperm shouldering each other in the rush to create something wonderful between us.

Three months passed before I wrote and told him I was pregnant. I assured him he'd no reason to worry. Nothing would be demanded from him, no commitment, no support, no strings. I imagined him reading my letter, surrounded by the scorching sands. He would be alarmed at first, then reassured, then wincing, thinking, no doubt, about his son, who now lived with his mother and stepfather in Canada.

He rang and proposed. We would be married when he came home on leave. He spoke with certainty. This child would carry his name.

I asked him if he loved me. We'd had so little time to know each other.

'Yes,' he said, and I believe he spoke sincerely. 'I love you, Susanne. That's all we need to begin our lives together.'

A week later the pain began. Miriam drove me to the hospital.

'First babies, it's common enough,' she said, and cried with me, held me gently, as if she was afraid I'd shatter at her touch. She faded quietly into the background when David returned from the oilfields to comfort me.

'We will still be married,' he said, 'and we will have many children.'

We married that summer in Maoltrán. I'd achieved what I desired yet I was haunted by ghosts; the ache was unbearable. Miriam moved into my house and I moved to Rockrose.

'Less clutter, more space,' she insisted. 'Two women together in the family home, not a good idea.'

The Burren billowed into the distance, a grey patchwork quilt stitched in green. I imagined the earth seething beneath the limestone ridges and dolmen tombs; and on the surface, the gentle orchids and gentians, the woodruff, harebells, eyebrights and rockrose spurting from the cracks. This grimly beautiful landscape would absorb my grief. We would have more babies. They would grow up wild and free and happy.

I was in the business of persuasion but fate mocked my hopes one by one. And then they began to whisper to me, my lost children: *no more . . . no more . . . no more.*

They don't whisper any more. Not since you came to me. The only sound that breaks the night silence are your fretful cries, as if you are trying to break through the walls with your voice.

Today, sitting at my kitchen table that had once been hers, Miriam asked how I was feeling. Her expression was guarded, as if she was picking her way through thistles. She wanted to know if I'd seen Dr Williamson.

I shook my head and told her everything was under control. I'd seen a doctor when I was in Dublin visiting my father. He prescribed antidepressants to get me through the next few months.

She frowned, as if I'd suggested lacing my tea with arsenic. 'They will only mask your symptoms,' she said, a hint of ice in her tone. 'We're not exactly a backwater here,' she added. 'Dr Williamson is highly qualified and a trained counsellor to boot.'

'I'm suffering from exhaustion,' I replied. 'I've a child who doesn't sleep at night.'

She bit her bottom lip and looked away. 'I'm not for a

moment suggesting you need counselling,' she said. 'But I suspect you're suffering from a touch of postnatal depression.'

You, as if hearing her words, awakened and cried. Miriam waved me back into my chair and went upstairs to pick you up. Moments passed. I heard her footsteps crossing the landing. The creak of old wood tells its own story. I walked silently up the stairs, skipped the fifth step, which always squeaks, and paused at the top. She was holding you in her arms. Her chin rested on your head and her hand patted your back, *pat-pat-pat*. You gurgled against her, content in her embrace as she stared into David's bedroom.

A sweater lay over a chair, a book and his Walkman were on the dressing table. I had not touched his room since he left last week and it was obvious we no longer shared a bed. That's the worst of knowing the geography of a house. It's possible to figure out what should be other people's private business. I turned before she noticed me and waited for her in the kitchen.

'What you and David need is a break,' she said when she returned. 'I can take a few days off work and move into Rockrose to look after my little cabbage.'

I took you from her and sat you on my knee. You began to cry, to wriggle in my arms, your legs kicking against me.

'Colicky,' said Miriam. 'David was exactly the same for the first few months.'

She loves making comparisons and is delighted that your eyes turned out to be brown. 'Bog pools,' she calls them. 'Exactly like her father.'

'Later, in the summer,' I promised her. 'Maybe then we'll go away.'

She refused to be fobbed off, believing, no doubt, that our friendship allowed her an inappropriate level of inter-ference. 'Living down the lane, so far removed from others, it's isolating you from normal life,' she said. 'Too much solitude is for men with beards who like to perch on rocks.'

She waited for me to share her laughter and looked at her hands when I remained silent.

I saw her to the front door. She kissed your cheeks.

'I'm sorry you're not coming back to the studio,' she said. 'But you now have everything you need to make this a happy home. Look after my son. He lost one child. Let him enjoy his daughter. It's a shame he has to spend so much time away from home.'

'It's his own choice,' I replied.

'Is it?' Her question was rhetorical. She had already decided on the answer.

I locked the door behind her. I allowed the silence to settle. You stirred, restless, your eyes searching, always searching. Miriam was right to call them pools. I want them to pool with love for me but more often they pool with tears and you awaken in the night with a shriek that jerks me upright in the bed. I rock you . . . rock you . . . walking the floor until you exhaust yourself back to sleep.

Chapter Twelve

Carla

The letters had started to arrive shortly after Isobel's disappearance. Mostly they were messages of support, offering prayers and hope. Medals, mass bouquets and holy pictures fell from the envelopes. Good luck tokens also came, small packages with crystals and dried bunches of four-leaf clover, amulets and phials of sand or strange-coloured liquids. The latter ones were usually accompanied by long, rambling descriptions of guiding spirits and psychic predictions. But other letters – Carla was unable to tell if the senders were unbalanced or unbelievably cruel – claimed she was being punished by God for her past wanton behaviour. These letters were mostly linked to the lingerie advertising campaign that the press had unearthed. Photographs had been cut from newspapers. Much folded and with suspicious stains, they were enclosed with the anonymous letters. She saw herself in lingerie and transparent tops, boldly posing. How thoughtlessly she had worn such clothes, proud of her body, enjoying the caress of the camera, blissfully unaware that such images would haunt her future.

   Whore of Babylon . . . Scarlet Bitch . . . Shameless Hussy . . . God Has Seen Fit To Punish Thy Wickedness.

Since the Garda search had been scaled down, the number of letters had decreased. Carla flung the morning's post on the table and made a cafetière of coffee. She read every letter she received, searched them for clues, hoping that somewhere in the crazed ramblings she would find the key to Isobel's disappearance. So far, nothing had been deduced from the well-meaning messages of sympathy – or from the dark sponges that soaked up her misery and squeezed it out again in vile capitals.

A psychic called Miranda May had sent a prediction in this morning's mail. For once, the letter claiming psychic intuition was short and to the point.

Dear Carla,
I have received strong psychic signals from your
daughter. Look for her in a place of stone. She is safe and
well-nourished. Do not be downhearted. Keep the candle
of hope burning. Your patience will be rewarded.
Miranda May.

Carla grimaced and folded it back into the envelope. The next letter belonged to the ugly category. Even before she opened it she knew, could almost smell the stale air of venom and religious wrath that possessed the senders. She stared at the scrawling handwriting. *You deserved God's retribution . . . Your child has been spared a life of shame and debauchery . . . Harlot.* The words no longer shocked or alarmed her and nothing she read brought Isobel's recovery any closer.

She was cupping a cold mug of coffee and staring into space when she heard the doorbell. Two hours had passed since she had picked up the mail. She had no idea where the time had gone or what she had thought about while she was

102

in that vacuum. It happened regularly, snatches of time disappearing, as if her mind closed down in an effort to bring her through the day. Earlier, the sun had been shining but the sky had greyed now and the rain had started falling.

'I was just about to give up,' said Raine, shaking out her umbrella. 'I've been standing outside for ages.'

'Sorry. I didn't hear you.' Carla walked back towards the kitchen, conscious, suddenly, of the groceries she had purchased yesterday and dumped on the floor, intending to unpack them later. The frozen food would have to be binned. The smell of last night's cooking still lingered in the kitchen but she had no memory of the meal she had prepared. She lifted a bundle of laundry from a chair and gestured at Raine to sit down.

'Coffee?' she asked. 'It's just made.' She lifted the cafetière, touched the cold glass and placed it back down on the table, switched on the kettle.

Usually at some stage during the day, Raine called to see how she was faring. The Anticipation collection was no longer being produced. Mothers-to-be refused to wear a label with such tragic connotations and Raine, who had invested all her finance in the promotional campaign, had been forced to place her small design company in receivership. Ripples upon ripples, thought Carla. Robert in a desk job and she, sitting here day after day, waiting for . . . what? Her heart to leap whenever the phone or the doorbell rang? To find a clue among the mail she had scattered across her table? To read the papers to see if her daughter had been mentioned? To wait for Robert to come home?

The editor of Weekend Flair had been apologetic but firm when she had phoned Carla to tell her that her contract would not be renewed. Readers of Weekend Flair wanted to be entertained on Sundays, not reminded of the frightening things that could happen if they lowered their guard for an instant. Returning to the catwalk, even if she wanted to do so, was impossible. Her life, she knew, had changed irrevocably. She had no idea what shape her future would take. The future was the next hour. Thinking beyond that was impossible.

She made fresh coffee and carried the cafetière to the table.

'What's all this?' Her sister-in-law pointed to the morning post.

'They come all the time,' said Carla. 'The good, the mad and the ugly.'

Raine, reading one of the letters, shuddered and dropped it back on the table. 'Sick bastard,' she muttered. 'He needs help, preferably from a straitjacket.'

'Could be a woman.' Carla shrugged. 'As usual, it's anonymous.'

'Why don't you destroy this obscene rubbish as soon as you read the opening line?' Raine demanded.

'Because . . . I don't know . . . I keep hoping there'll be a clue.'

'A clue?' Raine impatiently interrupted her. 'We're talking about the ravings of sick, crazy people. How could you possibly give credence to any of this crap?'

Carla hesitated, swallowed. 'Maybe this is a punishment . . .'

'For what?' Raine demanded.

'For the things I did in my past.'

'Ah! The past.' Raine tapped the sheaf of envelopes on the kitchen table until they were aligned together. The sound, growing more insistent, echoed her agitation. 'We've all done things in our past that make us wince. Show me someone who hasn't and I'll stick pins in them to see if they bleed. No one has the right to sit in judgement—'

'God has—'

'God? When did you start believing in God?'

'It's easy to mock, Raine.'

'I'm not mocking you,' Raine replied. 'But I want to hear about this God who freeze-framed your past and is now demanding retribution. Is he the same God who said, "Suffer the little children to come unto me"?'

'It's the emptiness,' Carla said. 'Nothing can fill it. There has to be a reason—'

'Yes,' said Raine. 'A terrible crime was committed. What happened to you and Robert is a tragedy, not a punishment. Have you any more of those letters?'

Carla opened a drawer and emptied the contents over the table.

'Jesus!' Raine caught some of the mail in her hands as the letters began to slide over the edge of the table. She placed the letters out of Carla's reach and pointed towards the kitchen door.

'Go upstairs, Carla, and change out of that hideous dressing gown. You look like a grizzly bear. You need to get out of here and fast. I've some good news for a change. I've been offered a job. I'll tell you about it over lunch.'

When Carla returned downstairs, Raine had sorted the mail into two piles.

'This stuff has to go.' She pointed towards the smaller bundle. A much smaller bundle, Carla realised, yet those were the letters that filled her mind. Raine opened the back door. The rain had stopped. A ray of sunshine flared through the clouds. She pulled a barbecue set into the centre of the terrace and flung the letters into the tray.

'The people who wrote this filth have nothing to do with you . . . or your past.' She handed a box of matches to Carla. 'Torch them,' she ordered.

The first match blew out but Carla managed to light

the second one. She flamed one page then another. They watched the letters curl and brown, the obscene words startlingly visible for an instant before they were consumed.

Over lunch in Sheens, Raine told her that Fuchsia, the British chain store group, had plans to open six fashion outlets in Ireland. They had commissioned Raine to design their rainwear collection.

'Raine-Wear,' she said and clinked Carla's wine glass. 'What else can it be called?'

'Here's to Raine-Wear.' Carla glanced out the window to see that the rain had once again started falling. 'Looks like you could be onto a winner with this one.'

'It's going to involve a lot of travel.' Raine frowned, her earlier excitement replaced by anxiety. 'Mum seems well at the moment, but I suspect she's doing what she always does, keeping us in the dark about the real situation.'

'I'll take care of her.' Carla reassured her. 'I need to keep myself busy. This could shorten her life . . .'

'That's not true.' Raine shook her head. 'If anything it's made her stronger. She has no intention of dying until Isobel is back with us again.'

Carla spun the stem of her glass until the wine slopped over the edge. 'Four months,' she said. 'I never thought I'd survive three hours.'

'You're strong,' said Raine. 'Stronger, I suspect, than my brother.'

'That's ridiculous.'

'Is it? Has he been drinking much?'

'Not much.'

'What does that mean?'

'He hates working at a desk.'

'Would he prefer a bullet in his head?' Raine snapped.

'He may look like Mr Average Nice Guy but his face is recognisable now.'

'He's well aware of the risk. Everything's changed, Raine. *Everything.* I wake up in the morning and wonder if my legs will take me from the bed. Will they take me to the shower, to the kitchen? Will they take me from this restaurant? The phone rings and I think maybe this is it . . . maybe today . . . and it never is . . . *oh Jesus.* I'm going to cry and make a show of myself.'

'No, you won't.' Raine grasped her hand and held it tight. 'Small steps, Carla. That's how you keep moving.'

That night, waiting for Robert to come home, she saw Edward Carter on *The Week on the Street.* Usually when she saw him on television or heard him on the radio, she immediately switched him off but she stayed sitting, the remote control untouched. He was being interviewed about a tribunal, something to do with a conflict of interest and corruption in high places. The weight he had gained since entering politics added to his authority, she thought, and his dark hair, now veined with silver, was long enough to suggest a streak of rebellion.

Carter & Kay Public Relations had become Kay Communications when he had ended the partnership and entered politics. What better occupation? He could juggle words like a set of clubs, knowing exactly where they would land after he had flung them into the air.

Josh Baker was the journalist who first referred to him as 'The Spur'. The name stuck. Carla suspected he encouraged its use, enjoying the inference that he was a spur in the belly of the government, a needling, digging-in, jolting-them-into-action spur.

The following morning she rang his constituency office. His secretary was apologetic. He was in the Dáil and not available to speak to her. If she wanted to leave her name, the secretary could pass it on to him.

'Tell him Carla Kelly would like to speak to him.'

The pause at the end of the line was laden with sympathy. 'Of course I will, Ms Kelly.'

An hour later he rang her back. They arranged to meet the following day.

The scent of tiger lilies filled the kitchen. Some of the blooms were open, the speckled petals curling away from the aggressive stamens. Carla had read somewhere – she could not remember where, and she must have been pregnant with Isobel at the time – that a tincture made from the tiger lily was good for nausea and vomiting in pregnancy. But she had not needed a tincture. Not once during those nine months did Isobel make any demands on her body, apart from pattering it with her hands and feet.

She accepted the flowers from Edward Carter and arranged them in a vase. He nodded when she offered him coffee.

'The Garda have stopped searching for her,' she said. 'I need you to convince them it's too soon to give up.'

'What makes you think I'd have any success?' Edward Carter stretched his legs under the table and drank his coffee.

It unnerved her to see how easy he was in her surroundings.

'You're a politician—'

'On the Opposition benches,' he reminded her.

'If anyone can do it, you can.' She sat opposite him, forced herself to stay still. 'I have to find her,' she said. 'Otherwise I don't know how I'm going to go on.'

'I'll do my utmost to help you, Carla.' He spoke confidently, as suave and as persuasive as she remembered. 'A baby simply cannot disappear without trace. There must be something the guards have missed. No one could carry this off on their own. Someone must have information that can help. I'll bring it up in Question Time in the Dáil. I'll also check out my contacts in the media. Once the story dies away, you're forgotten. If I've anything to do with it, you'll share the future with your daughter.'

She wondered whose conscience he was trying to appease, hers or his own.

'How do you spend your day?' he asked.

'Waiting for the phone to ring,' she replied.

'That will destroy you.'

'What else can I do?'

He shook his head and stood up. For an instant she thought he was going to touch her. She drew back, an involuntary gesture that he immediately noticed.

'I treated you badly . . .' He fell silent when she raised her hand, holding it like a barrier across her face.

'I need to concentrate on the future, Edward. Not the past. Can you help us?'

He nodded, acknowledging the futility of his apology.

'How are your family?' Carla asked before he left.

'All grown now,' he replied. 'Gone their own way. I'll soon be a grandfather.'

'And your wife?'

He held her gaze for an instant then looked away. 'Wren is as busy as ever with her charity work.'

After he left, Carla opened the back door and flung the lilies into the bin. Their odour was too strong to endure in the small space she now occupied.

Edward Carter called his wife after a bird. A pet name. Once, in the early days of their relationship, Carla had imagined her as a chirrupy woman with a beaky face, tilting her head this way and that. But the woman who had sat in the front row at the gala fashion show she had organised for charity had been slight and petite, brown hair winging her cheeks in a soft bob, her thin hands folded demurely on her lap. Carla's stride had not faltered as she advanced towards her along the catwalk, nor had Renata Carter's gaze. She had observed Carla and then dismissed her as another one of her husband's brief dalliances.

She was right, of course, and now, if Carla could speak to her, she would ask how long it took to reach that level of acceptance, indifference, whatever was necessary to make the unbearable bearable.

Chapter Thirteen

Susanne
Seven months later

Midsummer. Her anniversary. The longest day of the year. I understand why she, more than the others, has stayed with me. Other hands took my babies away but she was in my arms until I was forced to let her go. In the spring I covered her grave in crocuses and snowdrops and, later, primroses, cowslips, bluebells, violets, forget-me-nots; small, delicate flowers that will come and go as the seasons dictate.

I feel peaceful there. When the plums fall in the autumn they will sweeten the earth. It's a green and fertile grave, unlike the Burren tombs with their box-like caverns and slanting slabs of stone. Bodies have been excavated from these tombs, along with stones, beads, pendants, crystals, all suggesting rituals and grieving. Did they worship the sun, I wonder, these megalithic people who walked across those pavement rocks? Kneel and bow before the solstice?

In Newgrange, that time. The winter solstice. I've never forgotten it but the memory was particularly vivid today. I remembered the silence, not a word from anyone as we pushed our way along the narrow passage and crowded into the burial chamber. I had stood there with Edward Carter, my hand hidden in his. We watched that slant of sunrise steal through the narrow shaft of that ancient tomb, faintly at first, then glowing stronger until it had illuminated the chamber where old bones and ash once rested. Such exquisite precision, such exact timing. In that instant I believed in miracles. I believed he would leave his wife. I believed we would have children. I believed we would play happy families and grow old together. Truly, I was bewitched by an ancient spell. I wanted to bow my head in honour of those who had walked there before us, five thousand years, and more.

Later we went to a hotel and lay beside each other until it was time for him to return to his real life.

I loved him for eight years. We came together in discreet hotel rooms. And there were many such occasions: overnight trips, weekend business seminars, client conferences, promotional campaigns that took us to strange locations where we walked among strangers and were freed from the shadow of his wife.

She's neurotic, he would say on the brief occasions when he mentioned her name. Wren does not understand me.

I believed him. I, who worked in a world of persuasion, allowed myself to be conned by the greatest persuader of them all. How sad is that? To fall for a cliché . . . but love ruled my heart over my head and I was young enough to believe time was on my side.

Did Wren suspect? Maybe . . . maybe not. He was always plausible with excuses. I believed them myself when he began to cancel weekends, offer reasons why I couldn't accompany him to conventions. When I accidentally (and it was an accident) clicked into his private line and heard him speaking to Carla Kelly, I was not, at first, suspicious. I recognised her voice: that low, fruity growl was quite distinctive. We used her regularly for photoshoots and there were many reasons why they should be having a conversation over the phone. But I'd grown up with the growl and snarl of unhappiness and I recognised the vibrations of an argument. I stayed perfectly still, afraid they would hear me breathing.

The clinic was one of the best in London, he assured her. And yes, he sighed heavily, he would accompany her. I visualised him jerking the white cuffs of his immaculate shirt and checking his watch as he searched for an excuse to bring their argument to an end.

She was crying when she hung up. I leaned forward and silently clicked out of the call. I wondered how he had made such a mistake. Was it blind passion or something sordid like a faulty condom? She was eighteen, not much older than I was when . . . I veered away from the memory, unable, as ever, to go there . . . and waited until he left his office. The address and phone number of the clinic were scrawled on a piece of paper in the top drawer of his desk.

When he returned from London I informed him I was leaving the company.

'Leaving?' He rested his hand fleetingly on mine. 'Surely not? Whatever will we do without you?'

I wanted to tell him what I thought of him. To splatter the words across his handsome face. But I said nothing. I did not want to endure his lies, his excuses. Remonstrations belong to wives. So do the spoils of marriage. Vengeance belongs to the mistress.

Midsummer is almost over. Earlier, when darkness fell, I stood in the cottage garden and tried to remember what it was like that night but I can't. I have to read this journal to feel it again, the pain and the loss and that dread determination that drove me into a new reality. I was passive for so long. Richard with his ambitions, my father and Tessa demanding that I give my child away, those boys with their animal grunts and heaves . . . and Edward Carter.

I try not to dwell on the past but he makes it impossible for me to move forward.

He took on the Garda, stood tall and straight in the Dáil and demanded that more resources be provided to protect the most vulnerable in our midst. Such passion in his voice. Every time I switched on the radio I heard him, the same message. Find Isobel Gardner or no child in the nation will be safe. Only in the silence that followed did I hear the truth. A guilty conscience, an unpaid debt, and Carla Kelly was demanding payment in full.

It worked for a while. The Gardaí renewed their search for a few more weeks but, eventually, they were forced to wind it down again. I hoped that would be the end of it but it continues . . . on and on . . . Isobel Gardner's name is never out of the headlines. Carla Kelly is never out of the news. No more lingerie shots or that awful inappropriate smile. Instead, her interviews are carefully chosen. To the unobservant eye, this may not be obvious but I know what's what. Edward Carter's hands are all over it.

Last month they held a press conference to launch the 'Find Isobel' campaign. Oh, it was well orchestrated, no doubt about that. He offered an initial reward and the public have started contributing to a fund for a private detective. Even Alyssa Faye with her tired questions about the psychology of celebrity could not crack Carla Kelly's composure. Her hair is slick now, tied in a knot. No more shaggy mane falling over her eyes. No more inappropriate smiles or skinny tops. She dresses in black, a ballerina in mourning, that's her image now that Edward Carter has become guardian of the truth.

Her updates to the media on her campaign always get front-page coverage, even though she has nothing new to say.

I was wrong. It's a week since Midsummer; a week when her name was not mentioned once by the media . . . until this evening, that is.

Yes . . . this evening there was nothing controlled about her. She looked as if she'd been crying all day and her hair was loose, streaming like her tears. I was in the kitchen preparing your bottle when David shouted from the living room that there'd been a breakthrough in the search for Isobel Gardner. The spoon slipped from my hand and the powder spilled across the counter. I leaned against the wall until the dizziness passed. I wanted to run upstairs to my bedroom where you were sleeping and barricade the door behind me.

Carla Kelly was being interviewed on *The Week on the Street*; a scoop for Josh Baker. He could hardly contain his excitement as he quizzed her on the progress of the search. The interview took place in the nursery. She sat on that same chair in that same position by the window. I could see the cradle . . . empty . . . and the seahorses.

'Look at Miriam's seahorses,' said David, and turned the volume higher. 'Imagine,' he said, 'when we were celebrating Joy, she was weeping. No one should have to endure what she's going through. Maybe soon the agony will all be over for her and her husband.'

A woman had phoned Garda Headquarters last night and confessed that she'd stolen the Anticipation Baby and had now abandoned the child in an empty factory in a disused industrial estate on the north side of Dublin. The search had been carried out in secret until the media got wind of it. Carla Kelly turned directly to the camera and made her appeal.

She knelt beside the cradle and placed her hand protectively over it. Those wretched eyes and that catch in her voice when she mentioned her child's name . . . Isobel . . . Isobel . . . not Joy . . . and I wanted to wrench my face from the television and curl myself into a tight umbilical coil.

I went upstairs. You were still sleeping. You lifted your arm and flung it over your shoulder. Your chest rose and you gave that shuddery sigh that used to terrify me in the early days.

Later, when the evening news came on, I saw high walls and yellow tape surrounding them. Guards stood on duty outside the gates and inside, where the cameras were not allowed, spotlights were visible. I reached for the remote control and switched off the television, silenced David's protests with my lips. I sat beside him on the deep sofa where we used to make love in the early months of our marriage, lazy drifting times when we were too comfortable or too lazy to head for our bedroom.

I kissed him, gently at first, as he likes to be kissed, then more urgently. I understand desire. David is easily distracted and tonight he was eager for me. His tongue parted my lips and we sank into the cushions, into familiar positions, almost forgotten. He joked that we were out of practice, as indeed we were. 'Nothing strange about that,' I said. 'New babies equal havoc.'

But there was something wrong. He moaned when he came into me, as if it was pain, not pleasure, he was experiencing in my arms, in the curve of my legs, in the clench of my vagina as I sought to bring him to the peak. He wanted to slow down, to wait until I too experienced the same hot thrill. It was selfish, in a way. Why could he not take what I willingly offered? Why insist on prolonging it when all he really wanted to satisfy was his own male ego? He pulled

116

away from me and laid me on my back. He caressed my breasts, kissed each nipple with such slow deliberation I wanted to scream. He drew his tongue over my ribcage, over the mound of my stomach and beyond, his breath warm between my thighs. I shuddered, a sign he mistook for pleasure, and after that it was quickly over.

You began to cry, your sobs shrill on the baby monitor.

'I'll go to her,' David said, and I thought there was relief in his voice as he adjusted his clothes and left the room. He has been patient about the bedroom situation, too patient for a young man whose body responds instantly to pleasure. I wonder, sometimes, about Imelda Morris. She travels from Dublin occasionally to visit her parents but those trips always seem to coincide with David's leave.

He is back in my bed now. You awoke when we entered the room, not with your usual fretful cries, but with gurgles of delight as you stared through the bars of your cot at him. Now you are both asleep and I am sleepless, drenched in fear.

Chapter Fourteen

Carla

Abandoned . . . abandoned . . . the word kept beating against Carla's head as she drove over O'Connell Bridge. The moon, a scimitar blade, was pale and waning. She passed the Rotonda Hospital where Gina had given birth to Jessica, and where Robert had wanted her to have Isobel until she insisted on the luxury of Valley View. The windows of the hospital were dark, mothers and babies safely sleeping. Onwards she drove, around Parnell Square and past the Black Church with its high spires and the legend that claimed the devil would appear if anyone had the courage to run three times around it at midnight.

The engines in the Broadstone bus depot were silent, as were the sleeping streets of Phibsboro. Glasnevin Cemetery, shadowed with yew trees and grey hulking tombstones, was visible behind railings as she swept towards the valley of Finglas. This was urban Dublin – flyovers and vast sprawling housing estates – but the imprint of a one-time country village was still evident in its winding main street. She drove past modern factories and offices until she reached a country road where an industrial estate sat like a desolate and deserted fortress. Fields spanned out on either side of the perimeter walls. White plastic bags fluttered like abandoned kites from the trees. This was her first time to see the industrial estate in reality. Its façade was even grimmer than the television images had led her to believe.

'*Abandoned!*' she had cried when Robert told her about the woman's call to Garda Headquarters. 'What exactly did she say?'

'You mustn't get your hopes up,' Robert had pleaded with her. 'We get calls like this all the time but they have to be investigated. She's probably a crazy—'

'But the woman who took Isobel *is* crazy,' Carla interrupted him. 'Please don't tell me the guards aren't taking her seriously?'

'We always take such calls seriously. A specially trained search team with dogs is combing the area right now.'

'Where is this place?' she had demanded, imagining herself already speeding towards this unknown destination.

'It used to be called the Chalwerth Industrial Estate,' Robert replied. 'It's between Finglas and Cabra, and is a wasteland of old buildings that have been closed down for years.'

A place of stone: grim factories and warehouses, high walls and narrow abandoned roads.

'She's there, Robert,' Carla had cried. 'I know she is.' She rummaged in the drawer and pulled out the letters, desperately seeking the one she had received from the psychic. 'I have to go there and search for her.'

'Carla, please calm down.' She heard iron in his voice. 'That's absolutely out of the question. Let the guards do their work. If there's any possibility Isobel is there, they'll find her quickly. I'm sorry you have to go through this . . . but please *don't* talk to the press?'

The search would be carried out in a planned and structured way.

120

'They're an expertly trained team and they'll cover every square inch of the area with the dogs,' Robert assured her. 'But every instinct tells me that this is a hoax call.'

The search had continued throughout the night. Raine had arrived with hot food. They tried to eat and make conversation but the strain of small talk had become impossible. Robert had left early in morning and promised to stay constantly in touch with her.

'Remember what I said,' he warned her before leaving. 'Hang up if anyone from the media calls. They're sure to have heard rumours by now. The Press Office will handle all enquiries. I've contacted Leo. He should be with you shortly. Let him deal with any phone calls.'

A short while later, her phone rang. Josh Baker wanted to know where the search was being carried out.

'Come on, Carla,' he had said when she denied any knowledge of the location. 'Of course you know. We can help each other. Give me the information and I'll give you prime exposure this evening. This woman will be glued to the television. The rest of the media will feed off *The Week*, as they always do. Use your head, Carla. You can't let this opportunity pass.'

'Leave me alone, Josh. I've told you, I can't help you.'

'Can't or won't?'

When she stayed silent he had said, 'You owe me one for all the exposure I've given you.' His anger was contained but he was known for his ruthlessness when he wanted information and for his ability to hold a grudge if it was denied him.

'Exposure!' she snapped. 'You've used me at every opportunity. I don't owe you anything.'

'But you owe it to your daughter,' he retorted. 'If she were my child, I wouldn't hesitate to use every opportunity at my disposal to find her.'

'I have to go, Josh.' She could no longer bear to listen to him. '*Don't* contact me again.'

'If this turns out to be a hoax, don't come looking in my direction for any further—'

She hung up on him and ran to the nursery, fell to her knees. It had been seven months since Isobel's disappearance, and she no longer wept for hours on end, or collapsed into people's arms, or sat motionless staring into space. Her knees had strengthened, so had her spine. But, suddenly, she was back again to that moment of discovery, gripped with the same rudderless terror. She had stopped believing in God when she was fourteen. The breaking away had been sudden. No more rituals, no more confession, childhood prayers forgotten. Now, kneeling beside the cradle, the prayers that had comforted her when she was a child spilled easily from her lips. She had bargained, demanded . . . *Please God . . . please . . . please please . . . make it happen . . . I beseech you . . . implore you . . . I lay myself open to your mercy . . .*

Leo had arrived shortly afterwards. The phone continued to ring throughout the afternoon. When she looked out her front window she saw journalists in her garden and drew back before they noticed her.

As the hours passed without word, she wondered how she would stay sane. Her head had filled with images: a baby, surrounded by rusting machinery, lying unnoticed on a factory floor, cobwebs drooping from the walls, rats scurrying. A dark narrow road filled with weeds, the stink of mould and desolation. How could her daughter survive in such conditions? She had to appeal to this woman. Beg her to reveal where, in this place of stone, her daughter lay waiting to be found. Overriding Leo's objections she had phoned Josh Baker.

He had conducted the interview in the nursery. 'Let's go

for maximum impact,' he said. 'The nursery is the perfect backdrop for your appeal.' It made no difference in the end. The search was called off after twenty-four hours when the search team and the sniffer dogs failed to find anyone. Robert was pale and tight-lipped when he had finally arrived home.

'I hope you're satisfied,' he said. 'The whole operation was turned into a media circus. For once, couldn't you have kept your head down and stayed out of our way?'

'I wanted to appeal to her. She would have been listening . . . watching . . .'

'It was a hoax, Carla, a *fucking* hoax. I warned you not to get involved.'

'How can you be sure?' she screamed. Her eyes glittered, tearless but feverish. 'You weren't there. It's too soon to call it off.'

'They combed every square inch of space. Do you understand what I'm saying . . . every square *inch*. If a needle had been missing, they would have found it.'

He held her arms, shook her into silence. 'You've no idea what I'm going through. To stand by and watch . . . not to be able to search for my own child. I hoped as much as you did. But she was *never* there.'

She refused to heed his desperation. 'You're wrong. She's there . . . *here's* the proof.' She showed him the psychic's letter. 'Don't you see? A place of stone. Robert, she could be dead by now and we're sitting here doing nothing. They *have* to keep searching.'

Robert crumpled the letter and flung it into the wastepaper basket. 'Jesus Christ, Carla, how many times must I tell you? She wasn't there. They would have heard her . . . seen her. It's over. Accept it.' She removed the letter and clutched it against her chest. Unable to watch her desperation, he walked to the sideboard and poured a large whiskey. His drinking had increased. Some nights he drank to the point of incomprehension, blurting out his anger, his frustration, his hatred of his desk job. She had had to listen to him rambling, watch his eyes redden, his face tautening with grief. Tonight, unable to watch, she left the room.

In the small hours when he came to bed, she pretended to be asleep. His arm reached across her hip, cradled her flat stomach. Soon his breathing had deepened and he turned over on his back. He began to snore. He never used to snore, or if he did she had slept too deeply to hear him. He had forgotten to switch off his bedside light. Anxious not to awaken him, she had left the bed and walked around to his side. She stared down on his face, chalky white, his expression slack, shadows like bruises under his eyes.

To be a detective and be unable to search for your own child. How long were they supposed to endure the waiting?

She had pulled a pair of trousers from the wardrobe. The waistband was loose and she notched the belt tighter. She dragged a jumper over her head, slipped on socks and boots, zipped a parka to her neck. Robert turned, heavy as a log, and uttered a low moan. She switched off the bedroom light but did not bother closing the door softly, knowing he would not awaken until morning.

She parked now beside the perimeter wall of the industrial estate. Yellow tape fluttering across the entrance gates was the only visible sign that the Gardaí had spent the day scouring the grounds. The gates were padlocked and too high to climb over. She walked along the side of the wall and stopped when she reached a narrow opening. A pitted bollard, bent sideways, was cemented into the centre, obviously placed there to obstruct cars. It would once have been used by workers as a short cut to the factories and warehouses. Few people went there now, and those who did came in secret; she shone her torch over syringes, condoms, empty beer bottles and cans.

Narrow roads stretched before her. Clumps of weeds moved, as if night creatures scurried within the foliage. The urge to run shivered through her. She walked past an open shed, once used for bicycles. The pungent smell of urine caught against her breath. Black circles marked the spots where dead fires had blazed, charred wood crunched under her feet. She imagined homeless men and women seeking warmth around the flames. The Garda search must have scared them away. In the waning moonlight she sank on her haunches and buried her face in her knees. Her daughter was not here, never was. Robert had been right all along. No wonder he had heaped scorn on the psychic's letter. Mad psychic. Mad God, claiming omnipotence yet unable to grant her, the smallest sparrow, a simple request.

She rose and crashed her foot down on a piece of charred wood, stamped the fragments until they turned to ash. She walked away from the grey walls. Nothing there but ghosts.

A shuffling sound caused her to pause; slowly, frightened for the first time, she looked over her shoulder. The isolation of this abandoned place bore down on her. Her shadow moved . . . no, not her shadow, another person, a woman. She was falling. Straight and rigid as a plank, the woman fell forward and hit the pavement with such force that Carla expected it to vibrate. Nothing moved, except the woman's long blonde hair as it flopped forward and covered her face. She was unconscious, her body frighteningly still.

Carla ran towards her and knelt, lifted the woman's wrist and felt her pulse. The woman moaned softly but otherwise showed no other sign of life. Using all her strength to push her over, Carla placed her hands underneath her chest and managed to turn her sideways. The body was heavy, a dead weight, but the face, now in profile, was male. In the light from her torch, Carla noticed stubble on his chin. He was dressed in an anorak and jeans, trainers that had once been white. His forehead was bleeding. Blood matted the front of his hair. He collapsed over on his back and opened his eyes. The pupils were dilated, his eyes rolling in their sockets until only the whites were visible. He was young, early twenties, his face hard and angular.

'Don't . . .' He shielded his gaze from the torch. 'Don't shine your fucking light . . .' His voice was hoarse, as if he had not used it for a long time.

'You need help.' She fought back the urge to walk away. 'I'm going to find a phone and call an ambulance.'

He touched his forehead then stared at the blood on his hand. When he tried to stand, she reached out to support him but he brought them both to the ground. He was unconscious again as she pushed him off her and scrambled to her feet. Madness, this was utter madness. She ran towards the bollards and squeezed through, reached her car and drove to Finglas village.

She found a phone kiosk and dialled 999. Briefly, she gave a description of the location. This was the time to leave, to return to her bed before Robert awoke and discovered she was missing. She drove to the end of the main street then turned back, driven by an impulse to see him safe. He was still lying in the same position. The ambulance team arrived shortly afterwards. She hurried to the main entrance and directed the paramedics to him. The driver of the ambulance was a woman. She seemed far too young and small to be in charge of such a large ambulance but there was no doubting her authority as she took details from Carla.

'Your name?' she asked once the man was strapped into the ambulance. Her tone was informal, her gaze inquisitive.

'Does my name matter?' asked Carla.

The young woman nodded. 'I need to fill in the details.' She glanced closer at Carla then looked beyond her to the perimeter wall.

'I recognise you.' Her expression carried a wealth of understanding. 'You should not be here.'

'You drove me to the Valley View clinic . . .'

'Yes, I did.' The driver closed the doors. 'Will you go home now, Carla?'

'Yes.' Carla walked towards her car. She waited until the blue light flickered and disappeared.

Dawn was edging the horizon when she returned home. Robert was still sleeping. In the bathroom she opened the medicine cabinet and took out the bottle of sleeping pills. She held a pill in her hand, placed it on her tongue, filled a glass with water. A stranger was reflected back at her from the mirror. Once before, the same reflection had stared back at her, younger then by ten years, glassy-eyed, hollowed out. Ten years . . . She tried hard not to think about it but the memory was alive and tearing her apart; an eye for an eye, a child for a child.

Chapter Fifteen

Susanne
One year later

You are one year old today. 'Where does time go?' said Miriam. 'My little cabbage is growing up.'

I worked so hard to make your first birthday a success. I'd bought you the prettiest pink dress and a matching hair band with a little butterfly attached. You immediately pulled it off, and did so each time I replaced it. Such will power, your face red, your bottom lip the size of a plum. David insisted that the hair band was hurting you. He lifted you from your high chair and tossed you in the air. You shrieked when he caught you and he tossed you again. It's your favourite game. I warned him you'd throw up, which of course you did, all over the lace and appliqué. He carried you upstairs under his arm and changed you into a pair of dungarees and a T-shirt. You ended up looking like a boy, bold and triumphant.

I didn't know most of the people who came. David's friends, most of them, with their children.

'Now is your chance to meet new people,' he'd said when we were drawing up the guest list. 'Maoltrán may seem like a one-horse town to you but there's lots of clubs to join. It will help you to cope with your postnatal depression.'

I hated the way he said that . . . postnatal depression . . . as if the very idea made him irritable.

Some of the others I know. Phyllis and Lily, her mother Kathleen O'Sullivan, Corrine's mother, and, needless to say, Imelda Morris was invited and came back from Dublin for the occasion. Joey sent you a birthday card. Corrine has evidently softened her attitude from a distance. She sends us regular photographs and video tapes of their son. Joey now wears a baseball cap and swings an ice hockey stick. He signed your birthday card with his name and a line of kisses.

Everyone made a fuss of you. Lily Lyons hobbled across the floor and said, 'Joy's got the look of the Dowlings, right enough.'

'Same eyes as Joey,' said Kathleen O'Sullivan.

But you look nothing like Joey O'Sullivan. You look like me. Except, of course, for your eyes. They're too dark for your pale complexion and flaxen hair.

Phyllis bought you an enormous doll's house. Far too extravagant, I wanted to tell her, but I hid my annoyance. She boasted again about your birth. I could see that the women were tiring of her story. Fifteen minutes of fame, said Andy Warhol. Phyllis will feed off it for ever.

Miriam looked around the house and said, as she always does, that she hardly recognised it. I reminded her that nothing had changed since her last visit, nothing major, and tried not to sound defensive.

I carried in your birthday cake. We sang 'Happy Birthday' and everything was going well until someone turned on the television. The evening news came on. The first anniversary of Isobel Gardner's disappearance. Everyone in the room turned to watch, even David.

Carla Kelly sat beside her husband. I couldn't believe I was watching the same woman. Almost impossible to believe

130

she ever strolled down a catwalk. Gaunt and grim, nothing to her face except bone. And her husband looked just as haunted. A wall exists between them now, invisible to most but obvious to anyone like myself who understands body language. They never touched or exchanged a glance until she broke down at the end of her statement. Glassy tears rolled down her cheeks. He gripped her hand then, a white-knuckle grasp against the green baize tablecloth.

Their solicitor held up an artist's impression of what Isobel Gardner should look like at one year of age. The camera zoomed in for a close-up. 'One year and two days,' he stressed. 'Two days was all they shared with their child before she was taken from them.'

No one looked in your direction as you dipped your finger into the icing on your cake, sucked it, grinned with pleasure at the taste. I held you close to my chest. You must have felt the palpitations, thumping like a bird's wings against glass. And the pain in my chest, across my shoulders, the dizzy, swooning sensation, as if everything was slipping beyond my grasp.

I understand the symptoms now. It's anxiety, not a heart attack. I'm glad I discussed it with Dr Williamson. My symptoms had become too serious to ignore. When I visited her surgery last week, she'd checked my heart and my blood pressure.

'It's nothing to do with your heart,' she'd said. 'What you've just described are the classic symptoms of a panic attack.'

She shook her head when I asked if I'd imagined my symptoms. 'Panic attacks can occur out of the blue for no discernible reason,' she said. 'But they can also have a deep underlying cause.' She asked if I was anxious, distressed. I assured her that everything was fine but she wrote a name and phone number on a prescription pad and tore off the page.

'This woman is an excellent counsellor,' she said, and handed the page to me. 'Give her a call if you think there is an underlying cause for your anxiety.'

Anxiety. It was so obvious. I tracked back to the moment the first attack occurred. I had been driving home from Dublin and you were strapped in the car seat. We'd spent the weekend with my father and Tessa, and I was anxious to get away from the city before the peak-hour evening traffic. I was driving along the quays when the pain had clamped my chest. I braked at the red lights. I'd wanted to run from the suffocating atmosphere in the car but your face was framed in the rearview mirror. I couldn't run away. But that was what I wanted to do, abandon you in the traffic and run into a mist too dense to ever find me. The traffic lights changed and I'd moved forward. I struggled to control my terror. And I did. I managed to get you home safely. But the attacks continued and, when Dr Williamson gave her diagnosis, I understood.

The Liffey had been flowing on a high tide that day and cranes were visible beyond a high hoarding. Posters fluttered on the hoarding; rock bands and theatre advertisements. But one poster stood out from the others. A poster of a baby, one day old. A stolen child – an image almost bleached from existence.

Anxiety. I've got the pills. But they just deaden me. I still know what I have done.

Chapter Sixteen

Carla

Once again, the journalists were ranged before them. And the photographers . . . *click . . . click . . . click.*

Initially, the questions were predictable.

'How do you feel on the anniversary of your daughter's disappearance?'

'Do you think Isobel is still in Ireland?'

'What do you want to say to the person or persons who took her?'

'Are you going to model again?'

Josh Baker stood up and fixed Robert with his hard, speculative stare. 'Is it true that the Gardaí suspect a criminal involvement in your daughter's disappearance?'

'What exactly are you implying?' Robert asked. Carla sensed his tension, his withdrawal. His elbow remained rigid on the table.

'Was your daughter's disappearance linked to the drug seizure at Dublin Port that took place the day she was born?' Josh asked. 'Is it possible that through your undercover work with the Drugs Unit, her disappearance is an act of revenge?'

Criminals . . . drug traffickers . . . revenge . . . For an instant Carla was unable to catch her breath.

'There is absolutely no evidence that there was any criminal involvement in my daughter's disappearance.' Robert sounded stern and certain. He refused to answer any further questions and Leo, shepherding them from the table, almost lifted Carla from her seat. In the anteroom Robert collapsed into a chair. She sat opposite him and gripped his hand. His skin was cold and clammy, his eyes bloodshot from the shock. To be considered responsible for Isobel's disappearance. She understood the emotions whirling inside him. She experienced the same rush of guilt every time a journalist asked her about the Anticipation promotion.

Over the following week, the tabloids and broadsheets ran with variations of the story. Journalists listed the gangland figures who, allegedly, could have ordered the revenge kidnapping or worse. One tabloid ran a headline – '*Dad-to-be Drinks in Anticipation*' – and published a photograph of Robert, his arm around Sharon Boyle, celebrating the drug seizure on the night of Isobel's birth. They held their glasses towards the camera, smiling broadly, two half-smoked cigarettes resting on an overflowing ashtray in front of them.

The photograph had been cropped, Robert insisted. He pointed to his other arm, truncated from the crop, and insisted it was around Gavin's shoulder or Victor's or Jimmy's; he was at a party with friends, and had only the vaguest memory of who was sitting beside him.

'Who gives a fuck . . .' He sounded too weary to care. 'They're my mates. We were celebrating.'

'Some mates!' The image of Robert and Sharon Boyle laughing and drinking together while she was suffering labour pains ran like a wire through Carla's brain. She picked up the newspaper and tore it into shreds. 'Find out which of your *mates* gave that photograph to the papers. But

I doubt if you'll succeed. They can't even find your own daughter.'

He watched her fling the pieces to the floor. 'Don't ever speak to me like that again.' His anger, tightly suppressed, was visible only in his eyes. 'I've enough on my mind without having to endure your petty jealousy.'

'I'm not jealous. Not of her—'

'Then what?' he snapped. 'Is it because I'm the centre of media attention for a change?'

Something inside her shrivelled. It could have been her heart or something less tangible, the knowledge that they were stepping into new, dangerous territory where forgiveness could soon become impossible.

'What exactly do you mean?' Her voice was shrill, accusing. 'Do you believe I enjoy the notoriety . . . that I seek it out for my own satisfaction rather than from a desperate need to find Isobel? If that's what you mean, then say it. Say it straight to my face, Robert.'

'I'm sorry . . . sorry. I didn't mean it.' He rubbed his hands over his cheeks and swayed forward. 'Forget what I said . . . *please* forget it. How can anyone enjoy what we're going through? But you're able to handle it . . . you're used to it.'

Her voice, when she was able to speak, was hoarse. 'I hate them . . . the whole fucking circus feeding off us. But if it means keeping Isobel's name out there, I'll endure it. And you're right. I am jealous. Jealous to my bones of the woman who stole our child. She's out there somewhere and she's getting further and further away from us with all this nonsense about gangsters. We need to step up the campaign—'

'What campaign?' He shook his hands in frustration. 'It's over, Carla. We have to move on with our lives. You talk about jealousy. Have you any idea how I feel about Edward

135

Carter? "*The Spur.*"' She flinched back from his mocking tone. 'What is it with you and him? I hear the remarks, the speculation—'

'What speculation?'

'That you're having an affair with him.'

'So? What do you think, Robert?'

'I know it isn't true. I just don't understand why he took such an interest in our case.'

'Because I asked him. I told you we used to know each other.'

'How well did you know him?'

'For Christ's sake, Robert—'

'I need to know.'

'But that doesn't give you the right to ask such questions. I've never questioned you about your past.'

'This is different. Everything humanly possible was done by the police to find Isobel yet the two of you are constantly criticising my superiors. It's implicit in everything you say, especially when you launched that campaign.'

'So this cross-examination is about your superiors and what they think of you . . . and, by extension, me?'

'No, Carla. I'm asking you as your husband. What is Edward Carter to you?'

'A friend,' she replied. 'Someone who is willing to help us.'

She bent down to pick up the newspaper pieces. He hunkered beside her and helped. If he touched her now they would tumble to the floor and make love, swift love, hurting and intense. Perhaps, afterwards, they would be able to reach each other's thoughts, share the pain, her secret. His face was turned from her. Perhaps he was waiting for her to reach out to him. Robert, as if suspecting her turmoil, allowed the scraps of paper to fall from his hands. He made a sound; animals must moan in the same bewildered way when they were caught in traps, she thought. He straightened and walked away from her, away from the room, from their house, from the hope that if he had stayed an instant longer, they could have broken the back of their grief together.

Chapter Seventeen

Carla

The letters had continued to ebb and flow, depending on the publicity she received. Since the anniversary of her disappearance, it was becoming more difficult to keep Isobel's name in the public eye. The day marked a watershed for the public who had been following each twist and turn of the search. They were moving on. This morning only one letter lay in the hall when Carla came downstairs. She left it unopened on the kitchen table. She was running late this morning and Gillian would be waiting for her.

Gillian's strength was waning, although she still insisted on getting up each day, even for a short while. When the day was fine, they usually walked along Sandymount Strand, which was only a short distance from Gillian's house. She had refused any further chemotherapy, settling instead for pain management and home assistance. Her determination to live until Isobel was found was a fragile hope but she never wavered in her belief that her grandchild was alive and would eventually be reunited with her parents.

She was downstairs in her kitchen when Carla arrived at her house.

'I suppose you haven't eaten,' she said as she removed eggs and smoked salmon from the fridge.

'I'm not hungry.' Carla flung her coat over a chair and sat down. 'You don't have to make anything for me.'

'Who says I'm cooking for you?' Gillian busied herself at the cooker. 'I happen to be hungry and I don't like to eat alone.'

'Then let me do it.' Carla stood behind her and placed her hands on her hips, shocked by the thinness Gillian disguised under her chunky cardigan and loose trousers.

'I need to do it,' Gillian replied. 'Please, let me cook for you, Carla.'

The scrambled eggs, flavoured with pink slivers of salmon, were fluffy and light. Carla forced herself to eat and knew that Gillian was making the same effort. Food, the great comforter. She had become Gillian's chief carer. An end was in sight and, although Carla dreaded its inevitability, her days now had a structure and a purpose. When Gillian's phone rang, she knew it was Raine calling from Hong Kong or Japan or wherever her job dictated. She knew it was Robert ringing from his desk, grabbing a few moments to enquire about his mother. A ring on the doorbell meant a nurse or a doctor. They arrived with relief-inducing morphine for Gillian and advice for Carla. Gillian's friends also came with homemade soup or casseroles and offered to sit with her while Carla did the shopping or met Steve Robson, the private detective Edward had hired for the 'Find Isobel' campaign.

She forgot about the letter until she returned to the house that evening. She glanced at the postmark. Co. Clare. When she was a child, she went there once with her parents for a holiday. A cottage overlooking the sea in Lahinch. She rode a donkey on the beach and Leo buried her in sand, only her head protruding, like a character from *Endgame*.

She remembered the Burren, the strange rock formations, the exhilaration of jumping over them with her brother, then lying down, pretending to be dead, under the dolmen slabs.

Rockrose
Maoltrán
Co. Clare

22 November 1994

Dear Carla,

I'd like to offer you and your husband my deepest sympathy. Your struggle has moved me deeply. I hope constantly that there will be a breakthrough in the search for your daughter and, like the rest of the country, I hoped that the search of the industrial estate would be the end of your suffering. Sadly, that was not to be. How anyone could be so cruel is beyond belief – so I have to assume that the person who made that phone call was deeply disturbed. I wanted to write to you then and tell you how much I admire your courage and endurance. But I did not want to intrude on your privacy.

However, after last week's appalling press conference and the media's behaviour since then, I simply had to make contact to express my disgust at the coverage you have received from certain newspapers.

Do not allow them to deflect you from your search or diminish your courage. If faith can move mountains, then you have the power to create an earthquake. What lies beneath the surface is fragile and constantly shifting. Sooner or later, and I hope with all my heart it will be sooner, the cracks will appear and you will be reunited with Isobel.

*Please do not think I'm comparing my loss to yours –
but I do understand the pain of being parted from a
child. My son lives in Canada but I'm fortunate to be in
contact with him and able to foster a close relationship. I
hope that soon you can put this dreadful time behind you
and look towards the future with your precious daughter
by your side.*

Yours sincerely,
David Dowling.

Robert rang to say he would be late. Sharon Boyle was
leaving the force, moving to Australia. Tonight was her send-
off party. Carla wondered what it would be like to fly away
to the other side of the world. Abandon everything and
start over. Sometimes, when she was exhausted, when her
strength was at its lowest ebb, she wondered what life would
be like if Isobel had been stillborn. Dead and buried and
mourned. If she had never felt the warm touch of her baby's
skin, the pull of her baby's lips against her nipples, would
her agony be more endurable? If she had never smelled the
newborn baby smells, sweet and sour, heard those kitten
whimpers or the arrogant wail that demanded space for
Isobel Gardner in the bright, big world she had entered,
could she and Robert have moved painfully forward into
a different reality? If Isobel's brief presence on earth was
marked by a small white cross then they might have had a
second chance at happiness instead of being caught in a static
web of waiting.

She unpacked bags of groceries and tidied the kitchen.
Midnight came and went without any sign of Robert. She
answered David Dowling's letter. Her hand shook and she
misspelled Maoltrán. Too tired to write another envelope,
she crossed out the word and rewrote it.

The front door slammed. Robert stood in the kitchen doorway.

'How long have you been drinking?' she demanded, knowing from his expression of concentration that he was very drunk.

'Not long.' He carefully enunciated his words.

'Sleep in the spare room tonight.'

'I told you I'd be late.' He sighed heavily and swayed forward, gripped the frame of the door.

'But not drunk.'

'It was Sharon's send-off party. Don't make a drama, Carla.'

'You're drunk, Robert. I don't want you in my bed.'

'Drunk or sober . . . it doesn't seem to make any difference.'

'It might, if you occasionally came home to me.' He is my husband, she thought. I love him . . . love him . . . love him . . . The words were meaningless.

She guided him up the stairs. When his hands fumbled she helped him undress. Help was all they had to give each other. They lay together. His body was flaccid, hers unyielding, but, gradually, they grew warm and moved closer. They took comfort from this heat. Nothing else was possible.

3 Longley Crescent,
Ranelagh,
Dublin 6

25 November 1994

Dear David,

Thank you for your letter. I appreciate the time and trouble you took to contact Robert and me. We are heartbroken over Isobel's disappearance but the letters of support we receive help us to cope with each day. You called me courageous. I've never seen what I do as courageous. There is simply no other way to behave. If I don't hold on to the hope that Isobel will be found, it will be impossible to continue. She was in my life for such a short sweet time, yet now she dominates my every waking moment. She enters my dreams where I hold her close to me. You may think I would find it difficult to awaken and discover I was only dreaming, but when the dreams are kind, they nurture me through another day.

You wrote about your son and your separation from him. How very sad. But continents cannot separate you and you must use every opportunity to see him. I wish you every happiness in your life and thank you again for your kindness.

With my best wishes,
Carla Kelly-Gardner.

Chapter Eighteen

Susanne
Eighteen months later

Last month we were seven years married. Seven years since we exchanged rings and vowed to love each other for eternity. Miriam insisted on babysitting.

'Go . . . go . . . go!' She waved us away from Rockrose, ordered us to be happy. Like my mother used to do. I swore I would never sit opposite my husband in silence and I never do. It's easier since you came. Eighteen months of age and running like a sprinter, you bind us together. Or so I believed.

We dined by candlelight in Giuseppe's Bistro on Howe Street. Throughout the meal, we talked about you, laughed over your antics and wondered if there was another child in Maoltrán with your intellect and cuteness.

Imelda Morris entered with her brother Angus and a man with a sinister black goatee, whose name is Marcus. His pale grey eyes bulged slightly when she introduced David.

'I've heard a lot about *you*.' He stared pointedly at David and, behind the goatee, his smile hid secrets. He's gay, I saw that at a glance. Her gay best friend, her confidant. What had she told him about my husband?

'You *must* come to Molloy's later,' she said. 'No . . . *no*,' she insisted before I could even open my mouth. She wagged her finger warningly at me. 'I don't want to hear excuses about your babysitter. Life's too short. We must grab the moment and enjoy.'

Molloy's is not enjoyment. It's cigarette smoke and loud music and the impetuous Imelda with her clattering shoes and flouncing hair.

'I hope you don't mind me borrowing your husband,' she said, coy and determined as she pulled David to his feet. 'We were dancing together when we weren't making mischief in our prams.'

For some reason she seemed to find this hilarious and so did Marcus.

I watched them twirl and come together, separate and form fantastic manoeuvres. The crowd stood back and gave them the floor, whistling and stamping them on. I saw her red lips aching for the touch of him. And he held her firmly to him, his strong supple body bending her every which way.

Marcus stood too close to Angus, their fingers just touching, their minds dancing fast and furiously to the same tune. But this is a country village where discretion is a necessary tool for survival.

'Watch your back,' Marcus whispered into my ear. 'Imelda's claws are long and sharp as hooks.'

Seven years married. Seven-year itch. Something was definitely going on.

What else was I to think when he left for Dublin the following day? Men cheat. It's a fact of life. My father cheated on my mother. Tessa did not enter his life suddenly. She let the cat out of the bag once when she'd had a glass of wine too many. So did David's father. Edward Carter cheated, double-cheated, treble, probably.

David claimed he was meeting someone called Paul.

Someone he'd never mentioned before. He wanted to talk to him about a consultancy he plans to set up in Miriam's converted studio. That's where I searched first. Nothing. No indiscreet Visa payments or crumpled hotel receipts. But I found a letter in a drawer in his desk, postmarked Dublin, the writing carelessly formed and slanting. Impetuous.

Carla Kelly.

Her signature seemed to leap from the bottom of the page. Five months hidden in his desk. How come the wood was not scorched or burned to ash? How dare she . . . how dare *he* . . .? I replaced it where I'd found it and ran outside.

I entered that green hollow space where it all began. Nettles stung my knees when I knelt and cursed her. Was there no end to her intrusion? She had entered my space. I had to vanquish her.

You had awoken from your afternoon nap. I heard you crying when I entered the house, your outraged howls at being ignored. I carried you downstairs. I kissed your wet, angry face and held you tightly in my arms. When you were calm again, I strapped you in the car seat and drove to Doolin, drawn there by the violence of my mood. The waves were high, roaring and raging against the rocks, flinging question marks into the air. I left you in the car and walked to the edge of the rocks. A dangerous place to stand on a wild day when the wind is high and the spume salts my face. But I stood there and tempted fate. One wave was all it would take. But you drew me back. A cloud, black and flat as a tabletop mountain, crossed the sun and the world darkened. That is how it will be in death but I could not go there, not when you still needed me.

I've done a terrible thing but there's no going back. One deed borrows another and when, on the way home, I stopped off at Miriam's Glasshouse, I knew what I had to do. Miriam was delighted to see us and agreed immediately to mind you for a long weekend. Things between myself and David have not been easy, I admitted. Hormonal. I sighed and she nodded in agreement.

Those cursed hormones, she joked – cursed with them, cursed without. She's in the throes of the menopause, hot flushes, mood swings. She wrapped her arms around you. Even the most adorable babies can play havoc with a marriage, she said. Paris is a wonderful place, perfect for a short break. She went there once with her husband. A wonderful city, she said, especially for lovers. Her mind drifted back to younger days, then she shrugged, unwilling to allow her faithless husband space in her busy thoughts.

We've been here for three days now. Tomorrow we'll fly home. Miriam was right. Paris is wonderful. We swooped in a taxi along the Champs Élysées. The city lights twined around us like a necklace as we circled the Arc de Triomphe. We relaxed in cafés along the banks of the Seine and talked about you. We shopped for baby clothes and wooden toys that spin in dizzying loops or chime gently. When we rang home, Miriam assured us you were both getting on like a house on fire.

David stopped at an open grill and bought two cones of roasted chestnuts. Above us, the Eiffel Tower glittered like an arrow winging towards heaven. We showed your photograph to a pavement artist and watched you come to life on parchment.

We lay together on a vast bed and made love. Afterwards, he was silent as we rested. The emptiness between us was so vast I was afraid to move in case he heard the sound of our breaking apart.

My memory is a storehouse of useless information, lying dormant until the moment it becomes useful. Then it opens like a flower and the scent is sweet and powerful. The post boxes in Paris are yellow. We sent you a postcard, a picture of a kitten chasing butterflies, knowing we'll be home before it arrives. I slipped it through the slit of the post box. The letter to Josh Baker followed. Anonymous. He can do with it as he wishes. A mother will always protect her young. It is written in our genes.

Chapter Nineteen

Carla

Carla placed the tray on Gillian's bed and settled the pillows behind her. She drew back the bedroom curtains and looked down over Sandymount Strand. The tide was a shimmer on the horizon, the beach busy with joggers and dog walkers. Her mother-in-law was feeling energetic this morning and hoped to manage a short walk after breakfast.

They walked slowly across the hard-packed sand. Occasionally, Gillian's lips compressed but she was determined to stay on her feet as long as possible.

'A day at a time.' Gillian stopped and gazed out towards the frill of the retreating tide. 'I wish I'd had the good sense to live my life like this, cherishing the little things, the moments like this. But the years went so fast. They ran away on me, Carla.'

The sun continued to shine and the wind stayed soft. Josh Baker was upon them before Carla became aware of him.

He had rung her earlier before she left her own house and asked if he could interview her.

'I already told you I'm not prepared to do any further interviews unless they have been arranged through Kay Communications,' Carla had replied.

'You mean *Carter* & Kay.' His tone, filled with the same brash confidence he had shown at the last press conference, unnerved her.

'Carter & Kay no longer exist,' she snapped back. 'If you ring Norma Kay, I'm sure she'll give you any information you need. Goodbye.'

She had debated ringing Edward; then, anxious to reach Gillian, she had left her house, half-expecting Josh to be waiting outside.

But he had waited until now. He walked alongside her and Gillian, the cameraman moving backwards as he filmed them. She tried to compose her features, to protect Gillian, who had stumbled when the journalist appeared.

'Why did Edward Carter take such an interest in your daughter's disappearance?' He held the microphone towards her.

'He wanted to help us find Isobel.'

'Did he offer his help or did you approach him?'

'I approached him. What is this about?'

'What is your relationship with him?'

'He's a public representative. Why are you asking me these questions?' Aware that the camera was still rolling, she resisted the desire to cover her face. 'People have been amazingly kind. In particular, we appreciate the massive effort the police have invested in their search for our daughter.'

'But they would not have extended the search if Edward Carter had not used his political influence.'

'Isobel's file was still open.'

'A file will always remain open until a case is solved,' Josh replied. 'That's police procedure. But demanding that tax-payers' money be used to further the search when there were no further leads to follow suggests an abuse of political power. Was there a personal reason why he took your case and not any of the *other* unsolved cases, whose files still remain open?'

'My husband and I are grateful for any help we receive . . .' She put her arm around Gillian whose breathing had become shallow. 'Please, Josh, turn off the camera. My mother-in-law does not need to be involved in this. You can see—'

'You used to work for him.'

'Not directly. I modelled briefly for some of his clients.'

'How long ago is it since you worked for him?' Josh held the microphone closer to her mouth.

'I already told you . . . I didn't work for him—'

'Was it eleven years ago?'

'I can't remember . . . what has that to do with this inter-view?'

His mouth frightened her. It was tight and hard, like a trap that would snap the spine of small animals.

'Would you call yourself his friend?'

'No.'

'Or his mistress?'

She heard Gillian gasp and step forward. Before she could stop her, Gillian had swiped the camera with her arm. Her face, gaunt and pale, was set with determination.

'Leave us alone,' she shouted. 'Haven't you inflicted enough hurt on us as it is? What more do you want?'

The cameraman, taken by surprise, jerked the camera upwards and almost fell. He regained his balance and focused the camera back on Carla, who was too stricken to move.

'What kind of question is that?' Her voice rasped.

'A straightforward one,' Josh replied. 'You can answer yes or no.'

'I certainly am not his mistress. How dare you suggest otherwise.'

'You've denied an accusation I never made. I simply asked

a question. As a journalist, it's my responsibility to establish whether or not there is an intimate link between you and Edward Carter. My source alleges that the link dates back over eleven years when you worked for Carter & Kay. My source also suggests he travelled to a clinic in London with you when you terminated a pregnancy.'

The cameraman moved nearer. She was aware that her face was being captured, every nuance, blink, twitch, wince, her soul stripped bare and exposed. Saliva flooded her mouth. She wanted to throw up. She tightened her lips, forced herself to swallow, aware that Gillian was holding her upright and that she was clinging desperately to a dying woman, drawing on Gillian's strength, her unflinching bravery.

'I am not, and never was, Edward Carter's mistress.' She spoke slowly. 'If you dare suggest otherwise, I will sue you for slander. My husband and I are fortunate that he took an interest in our case. He gave us fresh hope that our daughter will be found.'

Chapter Twenty

Susanne

Anticipation Mum Denies Affair.

Publicity feeds publicity. She knew better than most how it worked. Like a snowball on a downward slope, it grows in proportion to the distance it travels. *Spurious Claim, Insists Politician.* For the tabloids it was a soap opera made in heaven. As the storm gathered force around her, she refused to make any comment. Her poise on the beach was remarkable. Years of catwalk experience stood her in good stead but she faltered in the end. The truth was written across her face. And she was dealing with the wrong journalist. Josh Baker is a snake who can ease his way through the densest lie. He had followed the trail to the clinic and infiltrated the records. The director of the clinic protested loudly at the unethical nature of the leak, ordered a major investigation of his staff, then quietly faded from the story. Unknown sources came out of the woodwork and declared that the affair between Edward Carter and Carla Kelly had been an open secret. They lied. Edward Carter understood how to use publicity and how to hide from its glare. No hiding now. He fronted the headlines, posed the question. Should a politician use Dáil privilege to forward his own personal agenda? The press were determined to have an answer.

For three weeks they waited outside her house but a story can only run for so long, especially when the fuel runs out, which it did when he resigned from politics. *Spur Removed from Body Politic.*

His bird-wife stood beside him and said he had always been a good husband, a family man, a servant of the state. A politician's wife to the core of her faithful heart.

But Carla Kelly continues to jerk at the even rhythm of our lives. I opened the *Irish Times* this morning.

Gillian Gardner. Beloved mother. Died peacefully and courageously at her home after a long illness.

Chapter Twenty-One

Carla

A breath and then silence, absolute and forever. Carla tried to absorb the enormity of the break. No jagged edges, just a clean snapped thread between the space Gillian had occupied and the next stage . . . life . . . existence . . . wherever her spirit had gone.

'I want to pass my belief on to you,' she had whispered before drifting into unconsciousness. She clung to Carla's hand, her grip weak but insistent. 'Isobel is alive. No matter what you are told, believe what I tell you now. My husband is waiting for me to join him. But I've no sense of Isobel's stillness in this place where I'm going.'

Carla, looking at Gillian's face as it settled into the rigid posture of death, tried to believe that her mother-in-law's belief had, by some form of osmosis, entered into her. But the only emotion she felt was grief and a shaming sense of relief that she would no longer have to witness Gillian's optimism being quenched as the months passed and hope faded.

Robert held her hand as they walked away from the graveside. She was aware of stares, eyes flicking sideways then away again. The notorious Carla Kelly. *God has seen fit to punish thy wickedness.*

'When I asked you for the truth, you looked into my eyes and lied,' Robert had said when she told him about her confrontation with Josh Baker. 'How could you say you loved me, knowing, all the time, you were deceiving me?'

'I was afraid you wouldn't understand—'

'Understand what? Have you any idea of the risk you were taking? Ireland is a village. Everyone knows everyone. It was bound to come out.'

'No one knew,' she said. 'I never told anyone, nor did Edward. Afterwards, I never met him again until now. *Never*.' She had hugged her arms, numbed by the exposure that was opening up before her. 'I didn't mean to hurt you, Robert. All I thought about was our daughter.'

'Yes,' he said. '*Our* daughter. But she never was mine, was she?'

'What do you mean?'

'She was your trophy, Carla. And then she was your tragedy. All the publicity . . . you were addicted to it.'

'Stop it, Robert. You know that's not true. Are you trying to destroy our marriage?'

'I don't have to lift a finger. You're managing it all by yourself.'

She had shook her head, unable to believe the power they had to hurt each other. 'I take responsibility for what has happened now . . . but my past is my own business.'

'Your past belongs to everyone, Carla. Every two-bit hack and gossip columnist. And you've no one to blame but yourself.'

'If it helped to find her, I'd do it all again,' she told him.

'I love you, Robert. But I can't live with an unforgiving man.'

'And I can't live with a woman who shares everything with me except the truth. Because, Carla, when that *everything* is weighed against trust, it doesn't amount to a hill of beans.' His mouth clenched. He buried his face in his hands. She thought he was crying but he was as tearless as she was.

On the night the programme was aired, Carla had walked from the house, her footsteps drawing her in the direction of the Grand Canal. Head down, her eyes following the line of the water's edge, she had walked past lock gates and bridges, past the barges and the swans that emerged from the reeds to trail ripples in their wakes. Ripples upon ripples spreading outwards as television sets flickered and her secret was exposed, fodder for an evening's viewing; her life destroyed, and Edward's too, ripples rippling . . . She collapsed onto a bench and wept violently, her hair shielding her face, giving her a privacy that had come too late. She was still weeping when Robert had found her and brought her home.

The phone was ringing when they entered their house.

'Gillian wants to see us,' he had said. 'We'd better go immediately.'

They had driven without speaking to Sandymount. Gillian was in bed. She looked drained, her eyes bruised with pain.

'Make your marriage work,' she had said and her grip on both their hands was a tight command. 'Ignore the publicity. It will pass and be forgotten. All that matters is that you are together when Isobel is returned to you.'

Later, alone in bed and unable to sleep, she had waited for his footsteps on the stairs. He would have started drinking as soon as she left the living room, she believed, and he would sleep in the spare room, probably forever. Eventually he crossed the landing and paused before entering their bedroom. He sat on the edge of the bed, his shoulders slumped, his hands dangling between his knees.

'I love you,' he said. 'But I don't know if it conquers all. I don't know anything any more.'

She drew him down beside her and removed his clothes, slowly unbuttoning, unloosening; each piece of clothing sliding to the floor. When he was naked, she straddled his back and worked her hands into his neck, releasing the hard knots of tension, fanning her palms over his shoulders, working her way down his vertebrae and back to his neck until she felt the stress ease from him. They did not speak. Words were redundant as they sought each other and grappled with the truth that their future together depended on whether it was more painful to be together than to be apart.

Isobel would never be found. Carla forced herself to confront this bleak truth. The campaign had been wound down, and her Garda file, open still, was quietly gathering dust. Steve Robson had admitted defeat. His disappointment was personal as well as professional. He was an experienced detective, stoical and tough, but, like the police investigations, all his leads had petered out. So also would the donations from the public, now that *The Week on the Street* had aired her past. Too many famines, earthquakes and other worthy causes where results could be achieved.

Nothing left now except to file away Steve's final report with all the other material she had accumulated since

Isobel's disappearance, including the letters of support. Her daughter would not be returned to her by detection. The trail was cold, had ever been thus.

'So, what now?' said Leo when she called into his office a week after Gillian's death. He signed off on the audited accounts from the 'Find Isobel' fund and wrote the last cheques for services rendered. 'What will you do with your time?'

'I don't know.' Time without purpose was her enemy. But she was unable to think beyond the immediate.

Leo opened the top drawer on his desk and drew out a manuscript. 'Take a look at this for me,' he said. 'I wouldn't mind a second opinion.'

'What is it?'

'A memoir of sorts. There's a whiff of sulphur from it, not to mention gelignite. I've to vet it for any possible legal issues that could arise after it's published.'

Leo specialised in the laws of libel and worked with a number of publishers offering pre-publication advice. Carla skimmed through the foreword, which had been written by a well-known peace activist. From what she could gather, two men from Northern Ireland, former terrorists from different religious backgrounds, and now middle-aged, had become involved with a cross-community project after they were released from jail. As part of that project, they had written their life stories. They wanted to publish them within the one book cover, under the one title. As a symbolic gesture to the tortuous peace process, it had merit, but Carla placed the manuscript back on Leo's desk.

'Sounds like a project that could give either of them a bullet in the head,' she said.

'A bullet in the head is their concern,' said Leo, pushing the manuscript back towards her. 'A libel case is the publisher's concern and that's where you come in. You've a sharp mind. Read it and see what you think.'

'Come off it, Leo.' She laughed and placed the manuscript out of his reach. 'I used to write a beauty column. That hardly gives me the expertise to vet the lives of two murderers.'

Northern Ireland did not interest her; she despised the Unionist politicians with their clenched mouths and closed minds, and felt the same contempt when she listened to the rhetoric of Sinn Féin.

'Times are changing, Carla,' said Leo. 'Peace may be dropping slow and tortuous but it's coming to Northern Ireland. This is a timely book but it needs careful scrutiny. Take it with you. Read a few chapters before you make up your mind. If you're still definite, I've other manuscripts that might be more suitable.'

'Are you offering me a job, Leo?'

'Could be,' he said and groaned. 'My brain has gone into serious decline since the twins arrived. Twenty-five-hour shifts, that's what life is like in the Kelly household. Let's see how you get on with this. Then we'll talk again.'

A fortnight later, he asked her to attend a meeting in his office with the publisher, Frank Staunton. The publisher's eyebrows lifted when she placed her notes in front of him.

'Impressive,' he said when he finished reading them. 'I hope to have the pleasure of working with you again.'

To her surprise, she had been drawn into the two stories from the moment she began reading them. Two separate encounters, two separate environments that were remarkably similar if one looked behind the slogans and dominating murals. She had been impressed by the writers' honesty, repelled yet fascinated by the journeys they had taken: death, pain, anger, despair, and, finally, a tortuous redemption. She recognised within herself the steely hatred that had driven them forward before they realised that blood, when it flowed from a dying man, made no distinction between creeds and classess.

Chapter Twenty-Two

Susanne
Three years later

You have no concept of time. 'Next month,' you shout when David goes away again. 'When is next month? Is it now? I want Daddy now!'

You sit defiantly on his office steps, knowing the office is empty but your face is mutinous when I try and persuade you to come back inside. Such tantrums, screaming and flailing, leaving me with no option but to carry you to your bedroom and leave you there until you quieten down. Then you cuddle against me and ask why Daddy keeps going away. I explain that he needs to find oil so that Mitch Moran, the man in the garage, who always gives you a lollipop, will have petrol to put in our car, and all the other cars in Maoltrán. For a while, at least, you seem to understand. You help me bake an apple tart and cut gingermen shapes from the leftover dough. I read stories to you at night and we laugh at *The Cat in the Hat* and *The Gruffalo*. We feed the swans and ducks on the river and build sandcastles on the beach. The days are long and calm. We are happy.

David brings noise into the house, the whiff of oil and

rock and hard earth. How loud his footsteps, how soft his laughter when he holds you. I ask him to put you down, afraid you will fall when he throws you in the air. You are not used to such boisterous behaviour but he catches you securely in his tawny arms and you shriek *Again, Daddy . . . again.* He marvels at how big you've grown in his absence and you dance together around the kitchen, your small feet planted securely upon his mountain boots. He carries you on his broad shoulders through the Burren, takes you to the ocean, and you return with bunches of wilting wildflowers tied to the handlebars. You look apologetic when you offer them to me, as if you are making amends for preferring his company to mine.

'She needs company,' he said tonight. 'A sister or a brother. Whatever was wrong has righted itself. Why don't we make an appointment and talk to Professor Langley?'

I'd demanded to know why you were not enough for us. How could he be so selfish and demanding? Had he forgotten the heartache we endured before you came into our lives? My voice was sharper than I'd intended and he stepped back as if my words stung his face.

Demanding? He sat on the sofa in the kitchen and drew me down beside him. 'I'm trying to talk about our future,' he said. 'Even if we don't have another baby, we can't continue living like this. I don't know what you want from me, Susanne. If you tell me, I'll try and change whatever it is that makes you so unhappy.'

Tears glistened in his eyes but – perhaps – that was my imagination.

'I'm not unhappy,' I rushed to reassure him. 'I have everything I need.'

'And what about me,' he asked. 'What am I to you? Was I just a stud, convenient until you achieved what you desired?

Your bed was always a cold place, Susanne. But at least there was space in it for me.'

He is not good with words. They come out the wrong way and are difficult to forgive.

'You still share my bed,' I said. 'And I never refuse you.'

'Like a teacher,' he said. 'Offering me a star for being a good boy.'

It was a bitter argument. We'd kept our voices low. Afterwards, David moved back to his old bedroom. I'd made a comment but he claimed it was an accusation. Such a shame that you had to be the cause of a row between us, and over something so trivial. Usually, I have to coax you awake in the morning. You are a grouch until you finish your breakfast. Not when David comes home. Then you run to our room and leap into our bed, sprawl across his naked chest, cuddling under the duvet, clinging tightly to his lanky body. He sleeps only in a pair of boxers and for a little girl so finely tuned and imaginative as you, I believe it's unseemly to lie so intimately with him. It makes me uncomfortable.

The colour drained from his face when I tried to explain how I felt. He accused me of trying to destroy the loving relationship he shares with you. His voice shook when he called me 'a jealous, paranoid bitch'.

The accusation reverberates through my brain. How can he speak to me in that way? I did not suggest his behaviour is inappropriate. We both understand the coded nuances associated with that word. I'm positive I said 'unseemly'. In the heat of the argument, he must have misunderstood. He immediately pulled his clothes from the wardrobe, turning his back on me when I tried to apologise, explain my point of view. Every word only added to the tension. I waited until he was in bed before entering his room. I sat on the edge of his bed and placed my hand on his cheek. He turned away, as if my touch repelled him.

'What do you want from me,' he asked. His voice was low and hoarse.

'I want us to be happy,' I replied.

'You and I will never be happy together,' he said. 'Joy was meant to hold us together . . . but the love we feel for her is the wedge that drives us apart. Why is that?'

Some questions can't be answered, and I made no effort to do so.

'You have destroyed the spontaneity I shared with my daughter,' he continued. 'When I'm away from home, earning the money you insist is necessary to refurbish this house, I think only of her, how she will run to greet me. I think about her laughter, her joy. You named her well but I will never be able to embrace her again without wondering what vile thoughts are going through your mind. I can never forgive you for tarnishing the love I feel for her.'

How many times is it possible to ask for forgiveness? I looked into his eyes and knew that our marriage was over. But we have time on our side . . . and we have you. You are our purpose in life. We will stay together for your sake.

We are home again. Canada was good. I felt free for the first time in years. The month flew. David visits Vancouver every year to see Joey but this was your first opportunity to meet your half-brother. The apartment we rented was within walking distance from Joey and Corrine allowed him to spend as much time as he wanted with us. At first, not being used to other children, you were cautious around him and his two sisters. But, gradually, you relaxed. You fought with Leanne and Lisa. 'He's my brother too,' you shouted and demanded to know why Joey couldn't live with us in Rockrose.

He taught you to write your name. 'Just an E between us,' he said, as you struggled to form the letters.

Visiting Whistler was the best part of the trip. While Joey and David skiied, you and I build snow boys and snow girls. 'Joy and Joey,' you chanted, and wrote your names on the snow . . . 'just an E between us.'

But the journey home was a nightmare. The air hostess tried soft drinks and lollipops. Nothing stopped you crying. In desperation, David searched our bags in the luggage rack and found the furry polar bear Joey bought for you at the airport. You clasped it in your arms and sobbed yourself to sleep. Why is it that you only cry for those you cannot have? I am here for you, my darling child. See *me*.

I don't know why or how . . . but the news broke tonight. The remains of Isobel Gardner have been found.

Chapter Twenty-Three

Carla

For three years Carla had steeled herself to hear such news. Now the waiting was finally over, the last flicker of hope blown out, the file closed.

The industrial estate where a crazed woman claimed to have abandoned Isobel three years previously was being razed to the ground. A complex of apartments and small townhouses would soon rise in its place. Tree-lined avenues and street lighting would replace the rubble-strewn paths and, according to the developers, there would be a water feature to admire and a small playground for children. But all that was in the future. Asbestos had been discovered in the roofing of some of the factories and the ground around a chemical plant had proved to be contaminated. Development work had been stopped until a thorough investigation of the site was carried out. In the process of this investigation, a tiny, fragile skeleton, badly degraded, had been discovered in the soft earth on the perimeter of the chemical plant.

'The state pathologist is at the scene,' Robert said. 'We'll know the results as soon as possible . . . but they've so little to go on . . .' He placed his head in her lap and began to weep. She noticed how grey his hair had become. Funny not to have noticed sooner.

'The preliminary tests show she died within the first few days of life.' Robert slowly gathered himself together and stood upright. 'DNA tests are being done on the remains. We'll have this information immediately the results come through.'

She wanted to cry with him but that would offer her some relief. Her body seemed incapable of seeking such comfort until the tiny bones were officially identified.

The media arrived shortly afterwards. Carla had no comment to make. She did not leave her house. All her phone calls were monitored by Leo before she accepted them. Her DNA was taken, such a simple procedure to establish such a momentous truth.

The baby was naked, not even a fragment of fabric had been found on her, but when the results were finally released, they were inconclusive.

Once again, they sat in front of Detective Superintendent Murphy.

'I thought DNA was an exact science,' said Carla. 'Why can't the tests reveal whether or not you've found our daughter?'

'It *is* an exact science,' the superintendent replied. 'But this is a most unusual situation. You do realise that the area where the bones were discovered was contaminated by a number of dangerous chemicals?'

'Yes. Robert explained everything to me,' said Carla.

She tried to follow the lengthy explanation that followed. When a leakage of chemical fluids had occurred at the chemical plant, the seepage had gone unnoticed or unreported by the owners. An investigation to establish the facts was already underway. There would be repercussions; the superintendent's eyebrows beetled as he contemplated the punishment that would be meted out to the owners. But, sadly, the contamination had created problems and the forensic team who had examined the bones could not reach a definitive conclusion.

Carla was aware of phones constantly ringing in the background of the Garda station, and of Robert's hand clenching hers, willing her to absorb the information.

'Sadly, the bones were too badly degraded by their exposure to the chemicals to give us an exact result,' said the superintendent. 'We believe that the woman who made that call is the same person who buried the remains.' He shook his head, still capable of being amazed by the random cruelty of people. 'She is obviously deranged. I'm so sorry, Carla. So sorry.'

That night, Carla awoke in the small hours, her body jerking with shock. Rocks, slabs of rock, a dolmen tomb. She tried to hold the nightmare before it slipped away. She had been crouched underneath the leaning stone, unable to move as it began to collapse on top of her. Already the dream was breaking into watery particles, floating away from her. Something . . . a child crying . . . that was why she was underneath the stone . . . reaching towards that cry.

She sat up in bed and switched on the light. Robert, blinking, rubbed his eyes and squinted up at her.

'What is it?' he asked. 'What's wrong?'

'I had a dream . . .' Unable to continue, she buried her face in her hands.

He pulled himself upright and embraced her. 'It's okay . . . okay . . . you're all right now. It was just a dream.'

'No.' Her voice steadied. 'It was more than that.' She drew back from his embrace and stroked his face. 'That was not Isobel.'

'What do you mean?' His stubble grazed her skin as he moved his head sharply to one side. 'Everything tallies.'

'Everything *seems* to tally.' Her hand sank limply into the folds of the duvet. She stared down at her fingers. She had been crawling, not crouching, under the slanting stone, her fingers clawing the earth, freeing her child's cry. 'But we don't know for definite. Even the superintendent said—'

'Carla, stop this right now.' Robert sounded too weary to argue any further. 'If you go into denial—'

'Are you suggesting I'm delusional?'

'I didn't say that. Denial is an inability to accept facts. Delusional is a flight of fancy. Our daughter is dead. We have to bury her and grieve over her and then, Carla, we *have* to move on.'

'No . . .'

'*Yes*. I want to live with the hope that some day . . . but it's not going to happen. I'm a policeman. I work with facts. And these facts are indisputable.'

'How can you say that? Forensically, the results are inconclusive. That's the only fact I'm prepared to accept.' She lay back down beside him. 'Why do you want this little scrap of bones to be our daughter?'

'I don't want it to be her. I just want an end to this interminable wait. Otherwise, I'm going to go crazy.'

She believed him. He was gaunt and depressed, utterly defeated, unable any longer to disguise his feelings over the direction their lives had taken.

'A new beginning,' Robert said after an inquest was held to determine the cause of death. The coroner had returned an inconclusive verdict and, as DNA tests could not definitively prove that the remains were those of Isobel Gardner, he was unable to give a ruling on her identity.

They accepted the remains as their own, and buried her. Carla refused to allow Isobel's name to be mentioned throughout the bleak short service. They called her Angel and laid her to rest in the Angels' plot in Glasnevin Cemetery.

The media hung around the perimeter. They had invested their emotions in the story of the Anticipation Baby and it was only fitting that they should witness its conclusion, said Josh Baker when Carla asked them to leave.

Grieving Mother Weeps as Anticipation Baby Buried. Her tears dominated the pages the following day. She refused to look at *The Week on the Street* or the newspapers. But the headlines lied. She had been weeping for an unknown mother who had buried her child in that bleak industrial estate. She had wept also for Robert, who believed their search was at an end. He grasped this belief, unaware that it was their marriage, not her hope, that was ending. Only then did she realise the weight of the gift Gillian had passed on to her.

'We go together to Australia or I go alone,' he said when the inquest was over. An ultimatum. No going back. Strange that they had weathered the publicity following the revelation of her affair with Edward Carter but this find, this miniature tragedy with its own history, had snapped something inside Robert. It could prove the breaking of them. But that was too simplistic. Her marriage was over, and she had known it instinctively when Josh Baker walked across Sandymount Strand and held a microphone to her mouth. Since then they had been marking time, drifting towards this inevitable conclusion.

The desire they had known in the early years claimed them again, sweetened by the realisation that they could soon part. Neither admitted that their decisions were made, each hoping the other would be the one to capitulate and stay, capitulate and go.

*   *   *

175

In the end they compromised on a trial separation. He would go ahead and she would follow within a year. Then they would make a final decision on their future. They sold their house without difficulty. Before they moved out, Carla entered the nursery for the last time. A fine layer of dust lay over the cradle and the seahorses still danced, luminously restless on the slightest drift of air. Slowly, carefully, she unhooked the mobile and dismantled it. She wrapped each seahorse in layers of tissue paper and laid them in a box. She took them with her to her new apartment. She donated the cradle to Oxfam.

Her only feeling as Robert's plane took off was one of relief. Her world seemed lighter, as if gradually the weight of other people's sorrow was being lifted from her. It was similar to the emotion she had experienced when Gillian released her last battling breath and, as then, she knew her relief would be equally fleeting.

He joined the Victoria Police Department. He phoned her every morning, her day beginning, his ending. It seemed an appropriate portrayal of their lives.

Chapter Twenty-Four

Susanne

Dublin has become an alien landscape. I see cranes every-where. They dominate the skyline. Glass towers mushroom along the docks. I remember when there was nothing there but derelict warehouses and grey gloom. All the talk is about the Celtic Tiger and economic growth, opportunity and capital investment. I once drove through the city centre with one hand on the wheel, the other beating time to music. Now I clutch the wheel and am terrified by the pulsing lines of traffic and one-way street systems.

I stayed for a week with my father and Tessa, and was relegated to the background as they swooped you up into a whirl of activities.

'Meet your friends,' he said. 'Catch up on old times. You look like you need a good break.'

I met Amanda and Julie in the Gresham Hotel. Amanda is a senior executive with Kay Communications and Julie runs her own PR company. 'The corporate sector,' she said. 'Big business. Big bucks. What have you been doing with yourself?'

'Full-time mothering,' I replied. 'It's demanding but very rewarding.'

She played around with a salad leaf and flicked a glance at Amanda. Childcare never rated highly on their list of career choices.

'Rewarding, my arse,' said Amanda. 'I tried it for six months then clawed my way from the grave and back to life again.'

She has three kids now and a full-time nanny. Julie hasn't bothered. Her career is more important than nappies and feed-formula. I envied them their freedom. I want to be part of this great Celtic Tiger but you, my precious child, you have become my gaoler. Every time I think of escaping, you draw me back into the shadows. Four years of age and tyrannical with your power.

You returned that evening with bags from Brown Thomas, dresses and dungarees and trainers with flashing heels that you insisted on wearing to bed.

You wore them to St Stephen's Green when I took you to feed the ducks. I sat on a bench and watched you run to the edge of the pond with your bag of bread. Your trainers winked red and bright each time you moved. I could see your ankles below your dungarees. You are stretching like a beanpole before my eyes.

Then you tripped on an undone lace and howled, as only you can howl when you hurt yourself. Someone else reached you before I did. Edward Carter. He set you back on your feet and hunkered down to your level. A duck nosedived at the edge of the pond, its tail feathers fluttering as wildly as my heart.

'Hello, Edward,' I said. 'I see you've met my daughter, Joy.'

He rose to his feet. I'm not sure which of us was more flustered. Strange that, seeing him flushed and at a loss for words. But not for long.

'Well, I'll be damned,' he said. 'Sue Sheehan . . . this is a pleasant surprise.'

'Equally so, Edward,' I replied.

'So, you have a child,' he said. 'A beautiful daughter. Joy. What an appropriate name.'

You stared up at him, the tears still on your cheeks, but you sobbed quietly, as if the words he'd spoken had soothed you.

'Sit with me for a while, Sue,' he said. 'It's so long since we've talked. Tell me what you're doing with yourself? What's new in the world of spin?' He took my arm and guided me back to the bench.

'I really couldn't say, Edward,' I replied. 'I'm not involved any more. Like you, I've moved on.'

He watched you bend to examine a duck as it waddled towards the bread you held in your hand. The sun gleamed on your hair, honey-spun tendrils hiding your face.

I wanted to run from him, wild and terrified, clutching you to my chest, but I stayed by his side. What else could I do?

He talked about the scandal.

'You must have hated me when you discovered I'd been involved with her,' he said.

'For a while, yes,' I replied. 'You squandered eight years of my life with false promises. But not any more. I'm too busy to waste time over past mistakes.'

Perspiration trickled down the back of my neck, a single trail like a tear. His shoes were scuffed, the upper coming away from the toe. His tie had a stain on the front. An egg stain. I wanted to lean over and scrape it off.

'I'm glad you've moved on,' he said. 'Everyone is moving on, except me . . . and her, of course. She'll never move on.'

'You have an egg stain on your tie,' I told him.

He glanced down and lifted his tie, scraped ineffectively at the silken fabric.

'How is your wife,' I asked. 'Still as neurotic as ever?'

He shook his head. 'Wren has left me,' he said. 'Gone to live in Italy. But she stood by me when it mattered. I suppose I couldn't ask for more than that. Funny thing, I never really saw her when she was with me. Now that our marriage is over, I see her everywhere.'

I imagined a small, strong bird flying higher and higher until her song was inaudible and there was nothing left, not even a black speck against the sun.

'The political establishment fucked me over well and truly,' he said. 'But I've enough information in my diaries to fuck every one of them to hell and back again.'

I heard his anger then, vicious and bitter.

'I'm going to publish and be damned,' he said.

'Dishing the dirt,' I said.

'If you want to call it that, feel free. I prefer to call it telling the truth,' he replied.

'You've never told the truth in your life, Edward,' I said. 'How do you expect to start now?'

He threw back his head, laughed loudly.

'You always had a wasp on your tongue, Sue, and motherhood hasn't swatted it away. She is a darling child. So tall for her age. Who does she resemble? Those eyes . . . magnificent. Her father's, I presume?'

I walked to the edge of the lake and took your hand.

'Goodbye, Edward,' I said.

We walked slowly from the park. Your heels winked and mine clicked as Edward Carter shuffled forever from our lives.

Chapter Twenty-Five

Carla
Four years later

She sat alone in the most secluded area of the café. Even there she felt exposed. The coffee looked disgusting, tar-black and tepid. She sipped and shuddered, pushed the cup to one side. She should go back to the counter and order a fresh one but she lacked the energy to rise. Two old men in peaked caps sat at the table next to her. They talked loudly to each other and would have looked more at home in the corner of their local pub than this city-centre café with its stainless steel coffee grinders and glass tabletops.

The midday rush was over. A group of young people entered and settled around a circular table. Trinity students, Carla guessed, as they dropped backpacks and canvas satchels to the floor. They were followed by two middle-aged women with Brown Thomas carrier bags. They looked alike, probably sisters, tanned and bleached and wearing too much gold. Everyone seemed relaxed, interested only in coffee and chat, but Carla saw normality as a veneer that could crack at any moment. The man sitting by the window listening to his Walkman could suddenly materialise into a journalist and shove a microphone under her mouth. A photographer could be lurking behind the tall dracaena, shielded by the shiny green leaves as he waited for her to relax her guard.

'Paranoia is alive and living in your head,' Robert would say if he was with her. But he was in Australia and no one could tell her to get a grip, get a life, get real.

Frank Staunton had contacted her shortly after Robert's departure and asked if she would be interested in ghost-writing a book for Vision Publications. He booked a table in an Italian restaurant. The waiters obviously knew him and they had fussed over Carla, asking her to sample the wine and pasta dishes.

'I know from the work you do with Leo that you've an eye for detail,' Frank said. 'The libel snags and snares. But you can also write. I need a ghostwriter. I'd like you to take a look at a manuscript that's been submitted to me. It's a tough story and doesn't make comfortable reading. There'll be publicity when it's published, controversy and denials. But it's a true account of one man's life story. His literacy skills aren't great and the book needs rewriting. Will you meet him and hear him out, then ghostwrite his story without losing his voice in the transition?'

'What makes you think I'm the right person to do it?'

'It's about a stolen childhood.'

'Stolen?'

'By the state. There'll be a lot more stories like this one. Read it and let me know what you think.'

He was right. Brendan's manuscript, littered with bad grammar and misspellings, horrified her. After his mother's death when he was five years old, his father had placed him in care. Sixty years later, he was dying from emphysema and his only wish was to launch his book before he died. Carla worked closely with him, teasing from him the story of physical and sexual abuse that had marked his eleven years in the St Almus Home for Boys. When *Screaming in Silence* was published she was acknowledged as his co-writer under the pseudonym Clare Frazier.

Today, she was meeting Frank in the Gresham Hotel to discuss another commission. She was early for her appointment and would have been equally content to sit all day in the café, watching the sun streaming through the stained-glass window and listening to old men scolding.

'Wouldn't fill a sparrow's belly,' said the man nearest her as he inspected his sandwich. His friend agreed and scornfully dismissed the salad on the side as 'leftover swill for rabbits'.

At the next table, the students talked urgently, argumentatively. Their voices forced the old men into silence. They settled their caps more firmly on their heads and left. A young man, older than the students, entered and carried a mug of coffee to the vacated table. His blond hair, cropped tight against his skull, emphasised his angular features. An old-wise face, she thought, comparing him to the students, who – despite their dishevelled hair, ripped jeans and sludge-coloured tops – moved and spoke with the sleek assurance of wealth.

The man opened a book and began to read. After a few minutes he glanced up and caught her eye. Apart from his gaze, which openly appraised her, he looked neat and unremarkable in black jeans and a T-shirt worn under an open denim shirt. He closed his book and walked towards her table.

'Do you mind if I sit down?' He rested his hand on the back of a chair.

'Yes,' Carla replied. 'I do mind.'

Once she had believed that journalists were her friends,

her co-conspirators. Once she had deliberately attracted their attention to gain a brief flurry of exposure and believed, in those silly carefree days as she tossed her flyaway hair and cast alluring glances at the camera, that they were feeding off each other's needs. She had not known then, as she knew now, that they were waiting to plunder her soul.

He nodded and removed his hand from the chair. 'You don't remember me.' He did not seem offended when she shook her head. 'I didn't expect you would. I'm Dylan Rae. We met one night but—'

'I'm sorry, I don't give interviews.' She attempted to rise but something about his steady gaze held her still.

'In the industrial estate,' he said. 'You called an ambulance.'

Suddenly she was transported back to the circles of burned wood, the shadow that moved within the greater shadows and became human. She had never been able to envisage his face, only the trail of long blond hair and the shock of his body falling.

'I hope I haven't startled you.' He sounded nervous. The premature lines around his eyes carried a hard history, yet there was something unspoiled about his mouth. A choirboy's mouth, she thought, which was an ironic comparison considering the substances he must have smoked or swallowed. He was off drugs now. She could tell by his eyes, dark grey and alert, waiting for her reply.

She gestured towards his hair. 'You look different.'

'I *am* different.' He laughed and, without asking again, pulled out a seat and sat down. 'Can I get you another coffee?'

'No, thank you. I'm just about to leave.'

'I want to thank you—' He studied his hands for an instant. His fingers were long, the nails clipped short. She noticed scars that would probably never fade. 'I've no idea what I took that night,' he said. 'In fact, I know nothing about that night except what Nikki told me.'

'Nikki?'

'The ambulance driver.'

'Ah, yes. She drove us both . . .' She swallowed, unable to continue.

'Yeah. She told me. She came to see me in the hospital, said she'd scraped me off the ground. Turned out she'd lost a brother from an overdose and decided I was worth saving.'

'She obviously succeeded.'

'She had her work cut out, so she had. Rehab was fucking grim, I can tell you that for nothing. Don't know how I stopped myself running from the place. Would have too, I reckon, except for you.'

'Me?' Astonished, Carla stared at him.

'Yeah.' He nodded, vigorously. 'You stepped out of your own agony long enough to help me. Every time I wanted to run, I'd think of you wandering like a ghost through those empty buildings. At least you knew who you were searching for, whereas I hadn't a clue what I'd lost.'

'Have you found it?' She struggled to control the rush of tears.

'I've been clean as a whistle since I came out,' he said. 'Nikki kicked me into shape and persuaded me to go back to college. I'm going to counsel young people. I know all about the shit that goes on in their heads when they've lost their way.'

'I'm glad things are working out for you,' she said.

'I'm sorry they haven't worked out for you. To lose a child . . . I can't imagine how awful that must be.'

His directness appealed to her. She was used to people shifting their gaze, speaking too fast, avoiding any subject to do with babies.

'Some days are more difficult than others,' she said. 'On

days like today, meeting you, well . . . it's good . . . really good.'

'I'm glad we met. Just in time, too. Me and Nikki are moving to the sticks next week.'

'For good?'

'I want to leave the past behind, make a fresh start. We've a kid to think about now.'

'A kid?'

'A little lad. Billy.'

'Sounds like you have everything you need.'

'I walked a hard road to get it.'

'Sometimes that's necessary.'

They walked together down Grafton Street and parted when they reached the turn-off into Nassau Street. She shook his hand. His grip was firm and warm. She wanted to stand with him for an instant longer. He too seemed reluctant to leave her.

'I'd better go.' She half-turned from him. 'I have an appointment.'

He bent forward and kissed her cheek. 'My life began that night,' he said. 'I've you to thank for everything.'

'I did nothing—'

'You picked me up when you'd every reason to walk away.'

He crossed the road and rounded the railings of Trinity College. She watched him striding confidently towards his future. When he disappeared from sight, she hurried across O'Connell Bridge, already late for her appointment. Strange twists of fate. Her child had been taken from her and, as a result of that taking, Dylan Rae had found his life again.

Chapter Twenty-Six

Susanne
Six years later

I almost lost you. It could have happened so easily. All my fault. I dropped my guard for an instant and believed I could be free. I will never return to Dublin . . . never. I need a fortress to keep you safe. Miriam can think what she likes. They all can. This is where we will remain. But the walls are too thick, the windows too small. I want a conservatory filled with light that will look out over the countryside and alert me to danger.

Last week Miriam phoned and asked us to call into her studio. For inspiration, she has moved from the sea to the land. 'The Blind Stallion of Leamanagh Castle' is the centre-piece of her new collection.

There's a story in these regions about a fierce, red-haired woman, known as Maura Rua, and her blind stallion. In the 1600s she lived in Leamanagh Castle and battled as hard as any warrior to retain her lands and property. Her blind stallion was equally spirited, and lashed out so wildly with his hooves when he was released from the stables that she had special niches built into the gateposts where the grooms could leap to safety. This fierceness is what Miriam has captured and turned into glass.

When we arrived at her studio, the stallion was revolving slowly in a display cabinet. She took it out and handed it to me. The glass hooves were raised in a flailing movement. Each fierce muscle was delicately etched, and the smooth barrel-belly was tense with energy. The stallion's eyes bulged with awareness, yet were lost in an opaque sightlessness that sensed but could not see the enemy ahead.

I held the stallion carefully, knowing how hard she had worked on its design, the numerous sketches that littered her studio floor, the many failed attempts before she was satisfied with the finished model.

You clamoured to hold the horse. To my horror, Miriam took it from me and placed it in your hands.

'Don't worry,' she said calmly. 'Joy knows it's precious. She won't let it fall.'

To have such faith in a four-year-old child is ridiculous but you, as if respecting Miriam's belief in you, solemnly inspected the figurine. You stared into the eyes and said, *Cross horse.* You looked at the frenzied body, the anger that seemed to exude from the thin nostrils and drawn-back mouth, and you repeated, *Cross horse . . . The horse is cross like Mammy.*

Miriam hunkered beside you and said, 'He's a very cross horse indeed but your mammy is not cross. She loves you very much and only gets cross when you've been a naughty girl.'

You begin to chant. *Mammy is naughty. Naughty Mammy . . . cross, naughty Mammy.* Your eyes raked me from under your long eyelashes, those dark eyelashes, curving over your judgemental eyes. Miriam removed the horse from your grip and placed it out of reach. She pointed through the glass doors of the showroom. 'Why don't you go out and say hello to Rita,' she said.

She asked me if I would assist her on the stand during the Finest Crafts Fair.

'It's only three days,' she said. 'David will be on leave then and if the two of you could help out, it would make a huge difference. I'm sure Phyllis would be delighted to mind Joy. She's always looking for an excuse to do so. Think about coming back to the studio,' she added. 'Joy will be going to school soon and you'll have time on your hands. You could consider working on a part-time basis. I'm going to need someone with experience to market this new collection.'

I held the horse again. This job was created for me. I could imagine the stallion on display, the interest it would create at trade fairs, the gallery exhibitions, the publicity. Suddenly, the walls of Rockrose expanded outwards. The future ran beyond the lane, ran past Dowling's Meadow and out into the world again.

At the Finest Crafts Fair, Miriam's seahorses tinkled, clinked, jangled, and the customers came in their droves to see the blind stallion. The exhibition stand became crowded. Everyone seemed to be demanding my attention at once. I could see David on the opposite side of the stand, hear his laughter as he lifted one of the stallions and displayed it to a customer. The translucent hooves flashed and dashed against the lights as he twisted his wrist this way and that. Something about his laughter alerted me. A frisson of excitement, perhaps, or nervousness, but I was unable to see who was causing that reaction. A customer shook Miriam's hand and left the stand, leaving me with a clearer view. Carla Kelly swept her long blonde hair over her shoulders and she was smiling at David, her long fingers brushing his as she took the stallion from him. His posture reminded me of the way he had leaned forward on the night she appeared on

The Week on the Street, watching her intently as she knelt beside the empty cradle. He had watched her again with that same intensity when her secret was exposed, and, after the programme ended, he had called Josh Baker an exploitative gutter rat.

My heart began to palpitate, just a flutter at first but building steadily. I slipped into the galley where we kept the chilled wine and coffee machine, and gripped the counter for support. The pain spread across my shoulders. The moment I had always dreaded was about to happen. I would collapse, lose control, open my mouth and scream my secret. Above the boom of my heart, I heard the low rumble of water preparing to burst its banks and I was swept back again to that night, the fields turning to glass as I carried you safely into my world.

When it seemed as if the noise could grow no louder, the level increased. From my vantage point, I watched a government minister, surrounded by officials and photographers, walk onto the stand. Miriam emerged from the crowd to speak to him. They posed together for the photographers, holding the stallion between them.

She entered the galley, beckoned to me. 'Susanne, come and have your photograph taken with the minister,' she said.

The floor shifted. I sat down on a high stool and pressed my head between my knees.

'What's the matter with you?' Miriam's gaze was speculative, flickering with hope. 'Is everything okay .... anything I should know?'

I straightened and whispered an excuse about a stomach bug, hardly aware of what I was saying. She shrugged and returned to the minister. One of the photographers aimed his camera towards David and Carla Kelly. She turned away and stepped off the stand before her face was framed in the lens.

Later, Miriam said, 'Did you notice who else was on the stand? That poor woman whose child was stolen. She bought one of the stallions. God love her, can't be easy, never knowing.'

Today, I called into the studio and told Miriam I would be home-schooling you.

'Thanks for the offer,' I said, 'but I can't possibly take on a job outside the home.'

'Home-schooling?' She made no attempt to hide her annoyance. 'Why on earth would you prevent Joy making friends her own age? No wonder she's highly strung. She's forever stuck down that lane with only you for company and now you want to educate her yourself. Really, Susanne, I've never heard such nonsense in my life. What does David think about this ridiculous notion?'

It's unusual for Miriam to be so forthright. I tried to make her understand that you are too sensitive and highly strung for the rough and tumble of a country schoolyard. She bristled, as she always does, if she suspects I'm criticising anything to do with Maoltrán. But I'm staying with my decision. I'll research the subject thoroughly and devise a curriculum that will keep you abreast of the national one, if not surpass it. It will be a perfect balance of study and outdoor activity, free from the constraints of the classroom.

'I'm committed to home-schooling Joy,' I repeated. 'I can't accept your offer.'

The floor was steady yet I walked carefully from her showroom. It was filled with delicate, brittle creations that would shatter if I made a wrong move.

Chapter Twenty-Seven

Carla
Five Years Later

After three long and tedious flights, Carla finally landed in Melbourne airport. She moved in a daze through the passport channel, knowing that within the next few minutes she would exit into the arrivals hall and see her husband for the first time in a year. She was relieved that the glass stallion had survived the flight in one piece.

At the Finest Crafts Exhibition she had recognised the seahorses immediately. Initially she had turned away, unable to watch them swaying in a kaleidoscope of coloured glass, then stopped, undecided. She was joining her husband in Australia and that meant letting go of the past. The stallion had attracted her attention. Such energy etched into every line of its design, its blindness only adding to its determination to clear the way forward. The man who sold it to her had lines around his eyes. White lines against a ruddy skin, as if he spent his life outdoors, squinting into the sun.

A woman in the passport cubicle examined her passport then handed it back without a flicker of emotion. No one cast a sideways glance in her direction as she walked towards the luggage reclaim area. She was alone in a crowded space, flowing through the indifference of others. No wonder Robert did not want to leave. Her hands shook as she waited for her luggage. She steadied them on the handle of the trolley. Like the prisoner who learns to love his cell, she was falling into freedom, terrified by the open vista before her.

Robert looked slim, tanned and fit. The bagginess around his eyes had disappeared. His complexion was clear. He had slotted effortlessly into this continent of tall, outdoor people. Their eyes locked when she emerged into the arrivals hall, the same direct, searching glance that once sealed their future. By the time she reached him, his face was flushed and raw with longing. They clung together, mumbling unintelligible endearments into each other's ears.

He drove confidently from the airport, obviously familiar with the route. She smelled his aftershave, a hint of something citrus, and longed to touch his face again. He was nervous; there were little signs she had forgotten, the way he rapped his fingers on the steering wheel when he stopped at traffic lights, the anxious way he cleared his throat when they fell silent, his sideways glance, speaking of pleasure to come. She asked about his work. As always, he remained vaguely informative. She wondered how he enjoyed being back again on the dark side of the city streets.

'I saw you once on O'Connell Bridge.' She was surprised to hear herself blurting it out after so many years. 'I thought you were a junkie at first.'

'I wondered.' He braked at traffic lights. 'Why did you never mention it?'

'I thought you'd be annoyed with yourself.'

'I'd have had little to worry about.' He caught her hand and pressed it against his cheek. 'Jesus Christ, Carla, I missed you so bad it never stopped hurting.'

His skin was as smooth as she remembered. She wondered

how long it would take to reach his apartment. Her body ached for him. She was alive in a way that had not seemed possible an hour ago. He brought her hand down to his crotch. She felt his hardness and laughed as he quickly accelerated when the light turned green.

'What if the law finds out you're breaking driving regulations?' she said as she was jerked back against the seat.

'Fuck the law,' he replied and grinned.

'I will,' she promised. 'Just drive a little faster.'

It was good to laugh and tease each other. To run from the car, abandoning her luggage, and slam the door closed on the world outside. She had a brief impression of a tidy living room then she was pulled behind him down a narrow corridor and into a bedroom with a king-sized bed.

He lifted her in his arms and carried her to the bed, laid her down on the duvet, a masculine duvet with a red and black zigzag pattern. They did not remove their clothes. No foreplay or lingering kisses. Their mouths were hard and searching, his hands seeking her panties, pulling them to one side and her body, wet and eager, arched towards him. It was so familiar yet so strange to be in his arms again, as if something broken was being repaired, only the edges were too jagged ever to match perfectly again. It did not matter. He groaned loudly as he plunged inside her, and the cry she uttered tore against her throat. She wondered if it was agony or ecstasy that caused her to writhe and shudder and bite down on his lip. It seemed, in that instant of capitulation, as if only the taste of his blood would ease her longing.

When it was over, they lay, limbs coiled, too exhausted to move. Eventually the phone roused them from their stupor. She rolled away from him as he sat up on the bed and cleared his throat before speaking.

'Yes, she's here.' He moved his shoulder, only a fraction but she noticed, and that gesture, even if she had not heard the voice at the other end of the line, would have been sufficient for her to know the identity of the caller.

'We'd like that . . . but not tonight. Carla's absolutely jetlagged.' He smiled down at her and winked. 'Yes, it was a long flight. But you're very kind. I'll tell her.'

'Sharon?' she asked when the call ended.

He lay back down and drew a sheet over them. 'The one and only.'

'How is she?' Carla kept her voice neutral.

'In love,' he replied and laughed. 'She moved in with her boyfriend a few months ago.'

She tried to decipher the sound – relief, envy, or simply pleasure that his friend was happy?

When he had first arrived in Melbourne, Sharon had introduced him to her circle of friends. They had accepted his past without being shackled by the publicity that had haunted him in Ireland.

'I've found myself again,' he said. 'Today is what matters to these people, not what went before.'

Tomorrow Carla would meet some of his friends and she too would understand what it was like to walk free from the lens of a camera. Then they would leave Melbourne and fly to Brisbane. He had worked out the itinerary for their holiday: a tour of the Gold Coast then a flight to Cairns where they would explore the Great Barrier Reef.

Robert turned into an estate of detached houses, each one individually designed and surrounded by large gardens. For an instant Carla did not recognise the attractive woman who answered the door. Sharon had grown her hair long and dyed it blonde. She had gained weight, not a lot, but enough to round her figure and make her look a little less like one of the lads.

'Welcome . . . welcome.' She led them outside to the terrace where a group of people were already assembled. Lights hung from trees, candles flickered on the table. Carla was introduced to the other guests. Some were Irish, the rest Australian. She could tell by the height and sturdiness of the men that they were probably in the police force. She was not so sure about the women. Sharon, accompanied by her boyfriend, Harry, a tall, thin Englishman with sloping shoulders, emerged from the kitchen with wine and beer.

'Food will be ready shortly,' she announced and handed Robert a bottle of Victorian Bitter without asking what he wanted.

'Wine or beer?' she asked Carla, who accepted a glass of white wine. She sipped the wine and answered the obligatory questions about her flight, the connections, the delays she experienced, the food and films. Apart from Sharon, only one of the women in the group belonged to the force, a slightly built woman, whose parents, she told Carla, were originally from Thailand. She quickly lost interest in Carla when the men began to talk about work. The other women, who had formed a book club the previous year, began to discuss their latest read, *The Conversations at Curlew Creek*.

Sara, an Irishwoman sitting next to Carla, asked if she was familiar with David Malouf's work. Carla shook her head and sank back into the shadows. The night was balmy. She was content to simply observe.

'You should read him,' advised Sara. 'There's quite a strong Irish element to *Conversations*. The lawmaker and the lawless. Both sides of the same coin.' She laughed and flicked her hand towards the men. 'Thankfully, we sleep with the law.'

'I'm from convict stock and proud of it,' said Kerry, an Australian woman sitting opposite Carla. 'Both sides. I traced my ancestral line all the way back to West Kerry and Mayo. I'm writing my thesis on it.'

'What did they do?' Carla asked.

'She stole a sovereign from her employer,' replied Kerry. 'And he was a sheep smuggler who didn't run fast enough. She was transported first and he followed two years later. They married in New South Wales and had twelve kids. I have copies of the marriage and birth certificates. Amazing, every one of their kids survived.'

'Have you ever been to Ireland?' Carla asked.

'Next year, I hope. I'd like to find their homesteads.'

'You'll probably find them buried under Bungalow Blitz,' warned Sara.

Sharon bustled between them with a bowl of salad and slices of home-baked soda bread.

'Angels on horseback for starters,' she announced as Harry leaned forward and placed a large platter on the table. 'Hold onto your cutlery for the main eats.'

She was flushed and a little breathless as she stood back from the table and clapped her hands. 'Eat and enjoy,' she ordered and gave Robert's arm a brief squeeze.

Was their relationship as platonic as he claimed, Carla wondered. Was it possible to be so close to someone and not have occasional desires, especially when they shared so much in common? With three glasses of wine inside her, and a companionable buzz of conversation around her, it was not a question to be tackled at the moment. She was enjoying the evening. Kerry's convict relations had lost their Irish families yet had managed to build a new future. That was the answer: moving forward. In this new world there was nothing to slap her in the face and demand sorrow. They could have more

198

children. She allowed herself to feel Robert's conviction. Across the fluttering candle flame, she caught his gaze. He smiled, as if linked to her thoughts, and lifted a bottle of white wine, poured it into the glasses as he moved around the table. Sharon had prepared lamb. The smell of garlic and rosemary wafted across the terrace as she emerged with it from the kitchen. Harry followed with bowls of baked potatoes.

He sat beside Carla and talked about the reef where he regularly snorkelled among the shoals of multi-coloured fish and the wavering banks of coral. He planned to honeymoon there later in the year.

'How long have you been in Australia?' Carla asked him.

'Eleven years. Where does time go?' He leaned closer and lowered his voice. 'We're all hoping you'll settle here.'

'I haven't made up my mind yet.' Carla also instinctively spoke more softly. She was aware of Sharon standing in the doorway, a bottle of wine in one hand, her arm raised against the door frame. She was silhouetted in the light from the kitchen, the outline of her legs visible through the transparent material of her skirt.

Harry whistled and shouted, 'Go, girl, go!' as Sharon jutted her hip provocatively before disappearing back into the kitchen.

'It's a good life here,' he said. 'We all settle in the end.'

'I have family in Ireland—'

'We all have family back home. But a man needs a woman out here. Robert's waited a long time for you to join him.'

It was a warning, discreetly given, and Carla gave a slight nod in acknowledgement.

Robert trailed his fingers along the back of her neck. His fingers were icy from the bottle.

'We'll eat and run,' he whispered. Her skin tingled. She raised her shoulder in acknowledgement.

Three weeks of swimming and lovemaking lay ahead. Long, relaxing lunches, romantic dinners, their hired car eating up the miles, music playing too loud, drowning out the need to ask the inevitable question. They would not mention Isobel's name. They would not think about tomorrow. They would gave themselves over to pleasure and clasp it savagely, selfishly from each other. They would explore the Great Barrier Reef, holding hands under water, weightless and adrift in that silent world of perpetual movement.

They were relaxing on the deck of a cruiser, returning from a snorkelling trip to the Barrier Reef, their legs dangling over the edge of the bow, when the sky darkened. Clouds bunching on the horizon broke apart and hurtled towards them. The boat rocked and the easy-going motion of a few minutes earlier was replaced by more turbulent waves. As sheets of rain slanted across the sea, passengers hurried under the canopy for shelter.

'Get under cover.' Robert got to his feet and stretched his hand down to her. 'This will be a beast when it hits.'

She ignored his outstretched hand and gripped the railing. 'You go,' she shouted back. 'I need to be by myself for a little while.'

'I'll stay with you,' he shouted. The rain flattened his hair and ran in rivulets down his cheeks.

'No!' The wildness of the storm had entered her. 'You heard me, Robert. I want to be alone for a while.'

He hesitated; then, reading her expression, turned and hurried under shelter with the other passengers.

The rain gathered force against the speed of the cruiser and needled her face, forced her eyes closed, whipped her hair into drenched tendrils. She must look crazy, she thought, the only person on deck, a demented figurehead at the bow of the cruiser as it ploughed onwards through the squall. She gripped the rail tighter as the anger she had controlled for so long lurched through her. She screamed into the wind, screamed at Robert for turning his back on their daughter, preferring to believe that she was dead rather than live with the pain of not knowing. Her throat hurt but still she continued to scream. The wind carried her voice over the bow and dashed it against the waves. The rain stopped as suddenly as it started. Raindrops glistened on the rails, water ran from the deck. Her anger passed with the same speed. Robert ran towards her with a towel.

'My crazy mad fool,' he said, knowing that her decision had been wrestled from the turbulence of the storm.

'Do you despise me for running away?' he asked when they were in bed that night.

She shook her head. To stand in judgement and apportion blame was to hang one more weight around her neck.

'I could never despise you, Robert,' she replied. 'I fully understand why you left.'

'Do you understand enough to stay here with me?'

'Isobel's alive,' said Carla. 'I can't stop trying to find her.'

'She's gone from us.' He spoke so quietly she had to lean forward to hear him. 'Dead or alive, it no longer matters.'

'Yes, it matters, Robert. It matters more than anything else.'

'More than our happiness?' he demanded.

'Come back to Ireland with me,' she pleaded. 'We can start again, have another child.'

'Another child would live in her shadow,' he said. 'It could never be otherwise with you.'

'You think I'm obsessed?'

'I think you're in love with a memory. There's nothing for either of us in Ireland.'

'Except hope,' she replied.

'Platitudes, Carla. I can't live with them any more. I've found my own reality here. I'll never stop loving you. But I'm prepared to settle for less.'

They made love gently then, afraid any sudden movement would break the fragile peace they had reached with each other. She had no memory of sleeping but she must have drifted in and out of oblivion, waking to touch him, or he, equally restless, reaching towards her. Three days later she returned home.

Chapter Twenty-Eight

Susanne

You've been so excited since Joey arrived. He swaggered through the airport, his rucksack sitting lightly on his shoulders, and danced on the spot in mock-alarm when he heard your shrieks. Corrine and Jack followed with their daughters. Joey is staying at Rockrose for the duration of their holiday.

It's strange, having a boy in the house. He's boisterous, abrasive almost, with his clattering boots and awkward hands that seem incapable of touching anything without knocking it over. He's tall for a fourteen-year-old, moody at times, and his hair, like David's, needs sheep-shears to keep it under control. Perhaps he doesn't shout, yet his voice reverberates through my head. He is constantly on the move and gets restless if we're not going somewhere, doing something.

Miriam has taught him to blow glass, shapeless pieces, of course, but she believes he has a natural talent. He wants to visit Leamanagh Castle where the blind stallion once lashed his hooves so violently that the grooms had to barricade themselves from him. You want to see the castle too. You are his echo, his shadow, his adoring younger sister, fiercely jealous of Leanne and Lisa. We'll go there on Sunday and drive on to Lake Inchiquin for a picnic.

Yesterday, we brought him to Lahinch for the surfing. He rode his surfboard over the rollers, cocky and assured as he crested ashore. He showed you how to belly-ride your own small surfboard. I could hear your triumphant yells above the crash of waves.

You both turned to watch a windsurfer in a black wetsuit skim across our line of vision. He tilted the rig and worked the board so that he became part of the great curving wave carrying him onwards. When he collapsed his rig on the sand, Joey sauntered towards him. I wanted to dry you off but you followed like a puppy at his heels. Joey and the wind-surfer ignored you. He has David's habit of gesticulating when he speaks and it was obvious they were talking about the waves. You drew a circle around them in the sand and wrote your names. Joy/Joey.

A small boy toddled towards you. You shovelled sand for him, built a sandcastle, both of you collecting shells to decorate the turrets. You ran back to me and rummaged in my beach bag for your polar bear and showed it to the boy, placed it on the top of the castle. The man finished talking to Joey and scooped the child in his arms. A woman, who was lying on a rock, an open book across her face, sat up and held out her arms for the boy.

'My friend Dylan is going to lend me his board and rig,' Joey said. 'He's cool.'

'No, he's not,' you chanted. 'You're cool, Joey. You're very *very* cool.'

Chapter Twenty-Nine

Carla

Gina, aware that her children's birthday parties were difficult occasions for Carla, always sounded slightly apologetic when she rang her sister-in-law to invite her. Not to do so would have marked her out as a social pariah and Carla, aware of Gina's conflicting emotions, always made a brief appearance to mark each event. Balloons were bobbing merrily from the front gate when she arrived for the twins' party and a banner slung across the door announced that Shane and Stephen Kelly were three years old today. Much to Gina's relief, the weather was fine and children were noisily tumbling on the bouncy castle she had hired for the occasion.

Leo, in a butcher's apron, was busily barbecuing and swigging from a bottle of beer. A group of fathers stood around him while their wives, relaxing in deckchairs, kept an eye on their bouncing children. With her antennae honed to the reaction of others, Carla noticed the almost imperceptible silence that fell as the guests became aware of her arrival. Carla Kelly, the unyielding face of every parent's nightmare. People began talking again. Their lips moved but she knew that, instinctively, each parent had cast a protective glance towards their shrieking children.

'I'm over here, darling.' Janet, sitting in a secluded area of the terrace, beckoned her across. The gesture was imperious and could not be ignored. Her mother gave the empty chair beside her an authoritative pat. 'How are you, darling?' She tilted her cheek for a kiss. 'I rang you three times yesterday. Didn't you get my messages?'

Carla sank into the chair and accepted a glass of wine from Gina.

'I've been so busy,' Carla lied effortlessly. 'How you've been?'

'In good health, thank you.' A touch of asperity entered Janet's voice. 'Were you too busy to ring your parents?'

'I'm sorry. I'd other things on my mind.'

'Like breaking up your marriage, you mean?'

'I'm not . . . Look, Mother, this *really* is none of your business.'

'Don't be ridiculous, Carla. Of course it's my business. You're offering your husband like a sacrificial lamb to that woman . . . what's her name . . . Karen . . .'

'Sharon. And she's Robert's friend, nothing else.'

'Carla, my dear child, I've been too long on this earth to believe there is such a thing as platonic friendship between a man and a woman. You might as well ask a tom cat to stay home at night.'

'Sharon is getting married in a few months' time to a wonderful man.'

'If I was a betting woman, I wouldn't be putting odds on that. Honestly, Carla, you're being very foolish. Robert is offering you a second chance. He stood by you when other men would have walked away. That dreadful programme . . .' She shuddered and dabbed her forehead with her handkerchief. 'He wants to make a fresh start and the least you can do is meet him halfway. If you don't, it will break your father's heart—'

'I don't want to break anyone's heart,' Carla replied. 'But I've made my decision and Robert has accepted it.'

'But it's hopeless . . . how long are we expected . . .?' Unable to contain her distress, Janet slammed her fists against the arms of the chair. 'If Isobel had died at birth you'd have moved on by now . . . had another child.'

'It's not the same. Can't you try to understand? It's the not knowing that makes it impossible to accept.'

'Even though Robert and the rest of us believe she's dead?'

'That's what you've chosen to believe.'

'But even if we're wrong . . . even if, by some miracle, you did succeed in ever finding her, she's someone else's five-year-old girl. How can you possibly expect to form a relationship with her? I'm sorry if I sound harsh, Carla, but people deal with tragedy all the time. They don't allow it to define them for the rest of their lives.' Janet's lipstick, too red for her thinning lips, had blurred into the lines above her mouth. 'It's destroying us all. Gina worries—'

'Worries about what?' snapped Carla. 'Is she afraid I'll spoil the party atmosphere?'

'Stop being so dramatic, Carla. That's not what I meant.'

'Then why don't you say it straight out, instead of using Dad and Gina as a shield? You'd prefer I wasn't here to remind everyone that awful things happen. But, unfortunately, they do and I can't magic them right again by disappearing from sight. So stop telling me my child is dead. I'm the one who'll make that decision and I'll only make it when I believe it to be true.'

Janet, flushed and agitated, fanned her face with her hand. 'You are always *such* a drama queen, Carla. I never wished . . .' She turned her head and looked over at her husband who was talking to Gina's father. As if attuned to Janet's distress, he stood up and walked towards them. Carla had always been fascinated by the invisible signals her parents relayed to each other. Perhaps that was the enduring legacy of their long marriage, the ability to communicate without words.

'I'd like to go home now, Gerard,' said Janet. 'The sun is giving me a headache.'

Gerard glanced from his wife to his daughter then bent to pick up Janet's cardigan from the back of her chair.

'She worries so much about you,' he said when Janet was saying goodbye to Leo and Gina.

'You all do. I'm sorry . . . I wish . . .' Unable to continue, she hugged her father.

'You've done what you believe is right, Carla,' he said. 'That's all any of us can ever do.' He patted her awkwardly on her back, a diffident man who never had a way with words. He was the listener in the family, preferring to absorb their problems rather than advise.

In a sudden gesture of sympathy, she hugged her mother. 'I'm sorry for being so snappy,' she said. 'I didn't let Robert go lightly. I still love him but I need to be here. He needs to be there. There's no middle ground.'

'I want you to be happy again.' Janet's taut expression softened. 'That's all I want. And it won't happen as long as you continue chasing a dead dream.'

Leo lifted burgers and sausages from the grill and called to the children. They all looked identical to Carla as they jumped from the castle and ran towards the table. One of the children fell and his mother darted towards him. Like penguins in a snowstorm, each to its own.

She wandered away from the party and strolled along the garden path. This was an old garden, long and winding, and the trees still carried the luminous green of early summer.

'Aunty Carla!' The voice came from within the branches

of a shrub. Bending down, Carla saw her niece's face peering between the leaves.

'Come into my den,' said Jessica. 'It's my secret place.'

The branches arched above them, creating a dome-like space carpeted with dusty soil and pine needles. Carla crouched beside her niece. The smell of earth and dead leaves reminded her of her childhood, of the seclusion children seek in hidden dens from an adult world.

'This is a wonderful hidey-hole,' she said. 'Is it your special secret?'

'Yes.' Jessica's black curls bobbed vigorously. 'Only Isobel knows. She comes here with me.'

For an instant Carla thought she had misheard.

'Isobel?'

'My cousin,' said Jessica. 'But she's my best friend too.'

Carla wrapped her arms around her knees and swayed forward. 'Is she here now with you?'

'Yes.' Jessica patted the earth beside her. 'She has her party dress on. It's beautiful.'

'Is she with you all the time?'

'When we're here, she is. But she never talks to anyone. Only me.'

'Have you told Mammy and Daddy about Isobel?'

Jessica shook her head.

'Then how do you know her?'

'A girl in my school told me.'

'What did she tell you?'

'That she was stolen by a witch.' Jessica's eyes were anxious, cornflower blue question marks. 'Isn't that right, Aunty Carla?'

'Not a witch, Jessica. We don't know who stole her.' Carla leaned forward and lifted leaves from her niece's hair, kissed the black corkscrew curls. The delicate scent of lilac drifted from a nearby tree. 'Will you tell her that I love her very much and that I'm going to bring her home some day?'

Jessica held her hand to the side of her mouth and whispered into the leaves. They rustled and sighed, and, somewhere above the green foliage, a bee droned.

'She loves you too, Aunty Carla. Next to me, you're her best friend. Do you want to bounce on the castle with us?'

'Yes. I'd like that very much, Jessica.'

Carla held hands with her niece. As the noise thundered around them, they sprang together on the bouncy castle, their laughter lost among the clamour of childish voices. Between them, they held hands with an imaginary child who leaped higher and laughed louder than any of them.

Chapter Thirty

Susanne

Why does reality never measure up to imagination? We should have had a wonderful day by the lake but it turned into a disaster, almost a tragedy. It started going wrong at the castle. I don't know what you expected. Buckingham Palace, if the tantrum you threw was anything to go by.

Leamanagh Castle is on a crossroads. It's a ruin, four storeys of a ruin with rows of windows staring blindly across the surrounding fields. The tower attached to the main building is the only aspect of the castle that matched your imagination but it too has that same bleak façade. It's not a place to linger but you wanted to climb over the gate and look inside.

You shrieked when I tried to lift you down, flailed in my arms until David, joking that you were worse than any blind stallion, carried you to the car. You created such an atmosphere. How you sulked. Your arms folded and your heels kicking the back of my chair, just the occasional kick to remind me that you were behind me and still brooding.

When we reached Lake Inchiquin, I laid out the picnic. Marinated chicken breasts, cheeses, crispy bread rolls, homemade scones, relishes and salads. I wanted this to be a special day that you would carry from your childhood. Joey wolfed the chicken, tore open a packet of crisps. You peered at him through your fingers then stretched out your hand for a crisp. He laughed and pulled the packet out of reach, teasing you out of your mood.

Three swans swam across the lake and in the distance we could see the ruins of another castle. Miriam told you a story about a mysterious swan maiden who arose from the lake and went to live in the castle with the chieftain, Connor O'Quin. Your eyes filled with tears when you heard she returned to the water three years later and disappeared forever. David lifted you onto his shoulders and walked with Joey to the shore. The three of you were silhouetted against the sun. Miriam took a photograph with the castle in the background then lay back down on the rug.

'Give Joy a break,' she advised me. 'She's just pushing the boundaries a bit. Why do you persist in keeping her so isolated? This home-schooling may work for other children but Joy needs company. Why are you so afraid for her?' Her glance was sharp, as if she was on the edge of some discovery.

David lowered you to the ground and you ran along the cement wharf, Joey in pursuit. Watching him following you with exaggerated slowness, I remembered the first time I came to Rockrose. A day like today, powder-blue sky and the future shimmering.

'Academically, Joy will be on a par, if not ahead of children in the same age group,' I told Miriam.

'It's nothing to do with academic results,' she said. 'It's to do with company, interaction with children her own age. The local school was good enough for David. Why is it not good enough for his daughter? Look at her now. I've never seen her so happy.'

Joey stretched out his arm and pushed you. You staggered

forward, your hands reaching out in a vain effort to stop your fall. I heard the crack of your skull on the cement as you crashed to the ground. You lay perfectly still and silent. I was on my feet instantly and running but David reached you first. He lifted you in his arms. I knew from the way he held you that something dreadful had happened. Your blood ran freely from the deep gash in your forehead. He tried to stem it with his handkerchief but he was unable to stop the flow.

I didn't mean to hit Joey so hard, or to shake him. He staggered back and almost fell when I hit him again. I don't know what I would have done to him if Miriam had not held me. I saw what happened, no matter how shrilly he claimed you tripped on a crack in the wharf.

In the car I held you in my arms. David turned his shirt into a makeshift bandage but your blood still seeped through. I believed you were going to die. In the rearview mirror I saw Joey in the back seat. He rested quietly against Miriam, his face as pale as yours. The mark of my hand was a red imprint on his cheek.

The doctor on duty in St Anne's Clinic was worried about concussion. You had X-rays and scans, blood tests done. He assured me you'd make a full recovery. There might be a scar on your forehead but, in time, it will be hardly noticeable. I stayed overnight with you and slept in a chair beside your bed. David arrived with your polar bear. Only then did you fall asleep.

Next morning you boasted about your good blood.

'*Really* good blood,' you said. 'Nurse Carson said I have to give lots of it away when I'm a big girl.' You gazed at me with your demanding eyes and said, 'Have you got good blood too, Mammy?'

'Yes,' I told you. 'We all have good blood.'

You nodded, satisfied, unaware that your words had turned my own blood to ice. This is lineage, a haemoglobin echo, corpuscles so minute yet so overwhelmingly powerful they can destroy me. You are rhesus negative. David and I are rhesus positive.

You and I do not need ancestral echoes to bind us. We belong to the moment, to that instant when a decision is made and life, as we know it, tilts in a new direction. You were the answer to my dreams yet the happiness I expected has always escaped me. There have been flashes, yes. Instances of such profound pride and joy that they've branded themselves into my brain and bring me comfort during the dark times. But there have been too many dark times, haunting and terrifying. They come out of the blue when I least expect them, hit me when my defences are down.

I can never be ill. *Never*.

Joey was staying at his grandparents' when I brought you home from hospital. Corrine insists he'll never again set foot in Rockrose. If David wishes to see his son, he can make alternative arrangements. From David's expression when he told me, I at first assumed he had been arguing with Corrine, but it soon became obvious his anger was directed towards me. He insisted, as Joey had, that you'd tripped. Nothing to do with his son. An overreaction on my part. He accused me of seeing what I wanted to see, of trying to destroy his relationship with his son. Just as I constantly try to destroy your feelings for him. Such an unjust accusation, so hurtful.

You cried silently in your bedroom. I looked at your face, the bruising and swelling, the mummy-style bandage on your forehead. I wanted to comfort you but you pulled the duvet over your face and said you hated me for sending Joey away.

The swelling had gone down, the bruising fading to a

214

muddy yellow by the time he returned to Canada. You insisted on accompanying David to Shannon airport to say goodbye. He ignored my protests and lifted you from your bed. You were still weak, staggering on your feet, but determined, so determined to defy me.

It's over a fortnight since it happened but word spreads quickly in a small village. They don't say it to my face, of course. They're grimly polite and greet me with closed expressions when I enter their shops or fill my car with petrol at Mitch Moran's garage. Joey O'Sullivan is one of them. I've lived in their midst for twelve years but I'm the outsider, always will be. I can ignore the gossip but I can't ignore you. You are in my face, sullen, resentful, accusing, siding with them, as David has, and Miriam too, everyone united against me.

Today, Corrine's mother Kathleen crossed to the other side of Howe Street to avoid me. As far as she's concerned, I struck her grandchild, shook him until his teeth clashed. As president of the local Irish Countrywomen's Association, her word carries weight and she's responsible for the gossip and innuendo. You ran after her, darting out in front of the traffic. I screamed but my voice was drowned by the blare of a car horn. I ran after you and grabbed your arm before you reached her. You faced me, dared me to lose my temper.

Kathleen stared coldly beyond me and bent to whisper loudly in your ear, 'I'll tell Joey you sent him kisses.' Still ignoring me, she kissed your cheek then swept on her way.

This ostentatious show of affection was for my benefit. I hated you for exposing me to it. The shock of this hatred ran like a current through my body. How was it possible to swing from loving you to hatred? It won't last, of course. Your anger, my hatred, fleeting emotions, but they change the balance between us. I can no longer pierce your thoughts.

Chapter Thirty-One

Joy

Clang, clatter, roar, growl, smash. Joy draws the yellow duvet over her head and tries to block the sounds of anger.

She reaches for Polar's paw.

Polar says, 'Silly buggers,' and makes her laugh because Joy is not allowed to say that word. He says, 'Silly buggering buggers,' and Joy laughs louder.

'Why are you laughing?' Her mother enters the room and pulls down the duvet. Her eyes are red and her mouth is a straight line that means no nonsense. She does not hear Polar. No one ever hears him except Joy.

'Go to sleep, Joy,' she says. 'Eleven o'clock is far too late for you to be awake.'

'Why are you and Daddy fighting?' Joy asks.

'Fighting?' Her mother laughs with her straight mouth. 'We're not fighting, darling. We're just playing a game. Did we wake you?' She kisses Joy. 'A grown-up game, Joy. That's all it is.'

Polar winks and smiles, a real smile. 'Liar,' he mouths. 'Bet they're still fighting over Joey. She's an *effing* liar.'

Another forbidden word. Joy loves Polar. Her mother says she's far too old to sleep with a bear but Joy doesn't agree.

He's her only link with Joey now that he will never be allowed to stay in Rockrose again.

He phoned tonight. He told her a knock-knock joke and said Leanne and Lisa are doing his head in. He wishes he had only one sister and her name was Joy. She made up the last bit but she knows it's what Joey really thinks, and Polar agrees.

Her father comes in to kiss her goodnight. His face is long and sad the way it always is when he and her mother fight. He does not pretend it was a grown-up game. Instead, he hugs her so tight she can't breathe and tells her she is an ace.

'My ace kid,' he says. 'What story do you want me to read tonight?'

'The swan maiden,' she says.

It reminds her of Joey, although it hurts her head, thinking about the picnic. Her mother cried because Joy went to the airport to say goodbye to him. She wrote all about it in the Judgement Book. Joy saw her when she woke up and went down to the kitchen for a glass of milk. She was sitting at the table and writing so fast that she didn't look up for ages. She saw Joy standing there, staring, and slapped the book closed. When Joy asked her what she was doing she said, 'I'm entering Joey's name in the Judgement Book.'

That's bad. Only bold behaviour goes into the Judgement Book. Her mother keeps saying Joey shoved her. Joy doesn't remember anything about the fall. Only her toes catching in the ridge of concrete and lunging forward. She doesn't even remember hitting her head. She touches her scar. It's still bumpy and sore if she presses it.

The Judgement Book used to be in a box with a padlock in the back of her mother's wardrobe. Joy found it once when she was searching for Polar. He was in the washing machine, but her mother never said, and Joy had been frightened that he was lost forever. She'd searched everywhere before she found the box. It wasn't locked and there were three Judgement Books inside. One smelled musty but the other two were new and the one on top had lots of blank pages. Her mother came into the kitchen and made a noise like a kitten when she saw Joy drawing on them.

'You are a bold *bold* girl,' she said, and smacked her legs for being naughty again. Joy had cried softly after her mother left the room but she must have heard because she came back and rocked her . . . rocked her . . . sobbing big whooshing sobs, *Hug me . . . kiss me . . . love me.*

Joy lies back in bed and listens to her father's story about the swan maiden. She imagines the beautiful maiden rising from the lake and taking the chieftain's hand. They walk together into his wonderful castle and sit on thrones and everybody bows down in front of them. Then the picture changes and it's her and Joey on the thrones. Their golden crowns are as bright as the sun.

Tomorrow her father is going away again to make money so that they can have the nicest house in Maoltrán. She clings to his neck when he kisses her goodnight. It's no use asking him to stay. He never does. The row tonight was not about Joy. It was about school. Joy is afraid of school. The children who go there pull hair and pinch and kick and bite. She could kick back, if she went, and bite their arms. But her mother says home-school is the best.

Home-school is boring. She hates sitting at the kitchen table and writing words that no one but her mother can see.

After her father finishes the story she kisses Polar and lies in the darkness. The swan maiden went back to the lake after living for three years in the castle. Her grandfather went away after living for six years with her father. That's why her father

219

will never leave her. And Joy will never leave Joey when she grows up. She will live in Canada and lock Leanne and Lisa in a dungeon. But, until then, she will be extra good so that her mother doesn't put her name in the Judgement Book ever again.

'Or mine either,' says Polar. 'Blasted buggering bloody book.'

Chapter Thirty-Two

Carla
Six Years Later

November came and went. Six years since Isobel's disappearance. Robert rang on the date of her birthday, as he always did, but their conversation was brief, his uneasiness evident in the stilted words they exchanged. When he rang again a week later the reason was clear. His voice broke when he spoke Carla's name. In the breathy silence that followed, she braced herself for bad news. *But what is bad news*, she wondered. The bad news he was about to deliver was his way forward and up. She fingered her bracelet. The tiny shells felt sharp under her fingers. Robert had bought it for her in a souvenir shop on the Barrier Reef and she had worn it ever since.

'What do you want to tell me, Robert?'

Unable to bear his silence she repeated the question and heard him sigh.

'It's about Sharon,' he said. His voice strengthened. 'She's not getting married to Harry. She and I . . . we're together now.'

'I see.'

'Do you, Carla? I don't. It happened and I can't leave her. She needs me.'

'Is there anything else you should tell me?'

'I'll always love you . . . no matter what—'

'Robert, what do you want? Is it a divorce?'

'In time . . . perhaps. I don't want to talk about that now. But she's going to have a baby in April and . . .' He stopped again, as if this truth clogged his throat.

She sank to the floor, her back hunched against the wall. Everything was motion, momentum. Even grief had an antidote. He had told her he was willing to settle for less but, now, when he mentioned Sharon's name, he no longer sounded as if he was speaking about a mate, a colleague, one of the lads.

'Your baby, Robert?'

'Yes.' He was sorry, deeply sorry . . . he had not intended it to happen but Sharon had been good to him . . . supportive when Carla returned to Ireland . . . and she and Harry were never suited.

Carla cut off his ragged apologies and quietly replaced the receiver. In the living room she poured a shot of tequila, then a second one. She had expected to feel jealousy, anger, grief. Familiar emotions that pulverised her but could always be tamed. But not this, she thought, how can he do this to me? How can he hold his voice steady and break the news that he will soon become a father?

She arose, stiff, her legs cramping, and entered the kitchen, heated a saucepan of milk. Her father had always insisted on giving it to her when she was a child and unable to sleep. She poured the bubbling milk into a mug, added another generous measure of tequila, and stood on the balcony, allowing the mixture to cool before taking an occasional sip.

She lived in a sealed-in chamber, the walls soundproofed. Impossible to hear the sounds from other apartments. Often she wondered if she was the only person living in the complex. Initially, she had sunk gratefully into the protective anonymity but tonight she wanted human company. She wanted to cry on someone's shoulder. Raine was in Dusseldorf. Janet would look bewildered and probably say, 'I told you friendship isn't possible between a man and a woman. Something always gets in the way and it's called *sex*.'

On the Grand Canal, a black satin ribbon splintered by street lights, the swans were sleeping. The only sign of movement was a lone prostitute walking slowly back and forth along the bank. Carla had seen her on other sleepless nights and recognised her peculiar walk, her limp exaggerated by the high heels she wore. Heavy make-up and tight clothes made it difficult to guess her age but Carla reckoned she was young, probably still in her teens. Usually, she was with other women but tonight she was working alone. A car passed and slowed. The prostitute stood beneath the street light and tilted her hip. Sharon came to mind, the same provocative tilt when she stood in the doorway of her house. Robert had not turned to look, not then. He had kept his eyes on Carla, believing they could still begin again.

The prostitute entered the car. It moved forward, indicated, and turned into a side street, sandwiched between tall glass buildings. The banks of the canal were now deserted, the silence absolute. Unable to bear her thoughts any longer, Carla pulled on a coat and left her apartment. She often walked at night when she was unable to sleep. Usually it was quiet where she walked, apart from the prostitutes who ignored her as long as she did not loiter near their space. Cars slowed but seldom stopped, the drivers moving on when she increased her stride and refused to look in their direction. She only returned to her apartment when she was exhausted but tonight she had energy to burn.

She stepped from the path and approached the wooden lock gate spanning the water. In the glow of street lights she saw the night's litter trapped between the slats: Styrofoam cups, hamburger boxes, condoms, beer cans. The tall reeds rustled and swayed. A lone bird began to sing and a duck, as if alerted by this false early morning alarm, emerged from the reeds and swam in a circle before disappearing back between the stalks.

The words of a song her father always sang at parties came to mind. *Why stand I here like a ghost in the shadows. It's time I was going. It's time I passed on.* A hot surge of tears pricked her eyelids. She leaned forward and looked down into the chasm below her. The water frothed and poured down into the next level. She was a step away from oblivion. *Was it so easy*, she wondered, *so sudden, this desire to let go?* She had always imagined suicide as a long, drawn out, mentally torturous process but now, poised, she realised that an unconscious momentum had driven her towards this moment.

She released one hand from the gate rail. Her heart pounded. Urine trickled between her legs, the sudden, warm gush reminding her of the last time she experienced this loss of control. Her midnight dash to the hospital and Robert, running towards her, wild-eyed and drunk with exuberance. She leaned further out, felt the strain on her other arm as her body slowly tilted sideways. *Let go . . . let go . . . let go.* Her body released tears and snot and sweat and urine but refused to release her hand.

The prostitute with the limp watched from the bank. She was a flicker on the edge of Carla's gaze before she moved into full view and stopped under the street lamp. Her gaze was hard, unflinching. She will not stop me, Carla thought. She will watch me fall then walk towards her next trick.

'I'm goin' for a fag and coffee to Naffy's,' she shouted across at Carla. 'D'ya wanna come?'

Slowly, Carla swung her arm back and grasped the rail. Her teeth chattered, an uncontrollable tremble that travelled through her body and weakened her knees, forced her to cling tightly to the rail as she stepped carefully to the bank and moved towards the path. She rubbed her face with the sleeve of her coat. The prostitute limped awkwardly yet she moved fast, her thin frame visible for an instant when she paused beneath a street light and glanced back. Carla stopped and stepped out of her panties, stuffed them deep into an overflowing litter bin. She was stripped of dignity, a madwoman who had decided not to belong to the night's debris. The prostitute waited for Carla to catch up, her cardigan hastily buttoned, the buttons out of alignment. Such a trivial thing to notice at such a time and Carla noticed also how the fabric shimmered, a gaudy metallic shade that belonged to the night. It was at least three sizes too big for the young woman and she, as if realising she was being scrutinised, clasped her arms across her chest.

She pushed the door open. Naffy's was a late-night greasy spoon, grimy lace curtains, paint peeling. The air inside was steamy. A few taxi men sat together with mugs of tea on the table. They nodded at the woman and settled their jaded gazes on Carla. Perhaps they thought she was a ghost. She felt like one, featureless, without lustre.

'Sit there.' The prostitute pointed to a corner table. Her skirt was short and narrow yet it sagged against her thin hips. Her feet slipped in and out of her high heels and the clacking of her footsteps was an uneven beat as she limped towards the counter.

Carla obediently slid into the seat and rested her elbows

225

on the oil cloth. The woman, noticing her cardigan, opened the buttons and fastened them correctly.

'Wha' was all tha' about?' she asked when she returned to the table with two mugs of tea. 'Were ya tryin' to bleedin' top yerself?'

Her harsh inner-city accent grated against Carla's ears. The fluorescent light shone through her heavy make-up and revealed a waif. No more than fifteen years old, Carla reckoned.

'I was thinking about it,' she replied. She sipped the tea, which had been sugared and milked. Her stomach kicked against the sweet, strong taste but she continued to drink it. As it warmed her insides, the taste no longer mattered. 'Would you have stopped me?'

The girl – Carla could no longer think of her as a woman – shrugged. 'Why the fuck should I have?'

'No reason. How old are you?'

'None a yer bleedin' business.'

'I see you sometimes. Are you not afraid being out there on your own?'

The girl glanced towards the door. 'It's the same as anyplace else.'

'No, it's not,' said Carla. 'It's extremely dangerous.'

'Ah, Jasus . . . don't lay the bleedin' good Samaritan shit on me.' She fidgeted with her mobile phone, turned it over in her hand. When it rang, she hunched her shoulder away from Carla. 'Yeah, Naffy's. Yeah . . . yeah . . . see ya.'

She turned her attention back to Carla, her gaze weary-wise. 'Hangin' off a fuckin' bridge, that's what's dangerous. What's yer name?'

'Carla. What's yours?'

'Anita.'

'Thanks for the tea, Anita.'

'Yeah . . . well, see ya 'round.' The door of the café opened and a man stood waiting for her. Carla remembered Robert on O'Connell Bridge, the same shifting gaze that seized everything in a glance. Anita immediately arose and left with him. Carla watched them through the lace curtains until they were out of sight.

Chapter Thirty-Three

Joy

Polar is missing. This time he's not spinning around in the washing machine. Her mother says, 'He was in rag order, Joy. I'll buy you a new teddy for Christmas. Stop making such a fuss.'

Joy finds him in the bin. Tea bags and baked beans have soaked into his fur. One eye is missing and his mouth is stuffed with something horrible that smelled like the cabbage she refused to eat for dinner yesterday. She holds him under the shower but the stains won't come out and the stuffing keeps falling into the bath.

'Effing cow,' says Polar. 'She's trying to kill me. I *hate* her guts.'

She wants to ring her father and tell him but he's in the middle of an ocean earning money to do lots of things to the house because her mother says it's a mausoleum.

'What's a mausoleum?' Joy had asked Granny when she came to dinner last Sunday.

When Granny said it was a grave, Joy became frightened there were ghosts in the house.

'No ghosts,' said Granny. 'Just a difference of opinion on what makes a house into a home.'

She left soon afterwards and didn't hug Mammy. She never does any more, not since Joey.

Joy shakes Polar and feels her anger rising. It's a hot, fuzzy feeling. She can't think straight with it.

'You threw Polar into the bin,' she shouts.

Her mother looks up from the nature table. Yesterday, they went on a winter walk and gathered cones and branches of holly and ivy. Today, for home-school, they are going to make a Christmas scene, but Joy flings the cones on the floor. They bounce like balls. When one of them rolls against her foot, she crunches it to bits.

Her mother grabs her arms and forces her to stop. 'Polar was filthy,' she said. 'Full of filthy germs. You're forever sucking his ears or putting his hands into your mouth. It's disgusting. You'd swear he was the only toy you have.'

'He's my favourite,' she sobs. 'Fix him. Make him better again.'

'I can't do that, Joy. You've had him since you were a baby. You're a big girl now. Six years of age and you want to play with a baby toy. What about all the beautiful soft toys we've bought for you? They're sitting in rows on the bottom of your bed. That's not where they should be. Polar has served his time. We can bury him if you like. Have a special funeral in the garden.'

Joy looks at Polar. She wants him to say something really rude and disgusting. He might even say, 'Fuck off.' She shudders and waits for him to speak. But he's like a rag, all limp and dripping and his head is hanging like a dead flower.

'Fuck off,' she says to Mammy. 'Fuck . . . fuck . . . *fuck* . . . off.'

Her mother slaps her face. Just like she slapped Joey. That's what Joey felt, stinging and scorching, and dots dancing.

'I can't take this any more. You're more trouble than you're worth.' Her mother puts her hand to her mouth. Joy thinks she's going to be sick but she turns her back and walks from the kitchen. She slams the back door behind her and runs down the garden path. Joy watches her from the window.

One side of Joy's face feels really big. She touches it and grimaces. Is that what Joey did when her mother hit him? She grimaces again. Her mother doesn't come back. Joy waits and waits. It's so long now, nearly an hour. Maybe she's run away. Polar lies on the nature table and stares at her from one eye.

'Where do you think she is?' she asks but still he can't speak.

She runs from the house and out the front gate. It will be dark soon. Everything is brown and dead, the bracken and the grass and the bare branches. With all the leaves gone, she can see the cottage now. Daddy's ancestors used to live there. Some day he's going to leave the rigs and build a hostel there for the people who want to visit the Burren to see the butterflies and flowers.

Joy runs past the cottage then stops. Something moves behind the branches. She returns and pushes through the hedge. Her mother is kneeling on the grass. Her hands are joined like the statue of Holy Mary in the church.

'Mammy . . .' she whispers.

Her mother looks up and there are tears all over her face and dripping off her chin. Joy forgets the pain in her face, and Polar too, and can think of nothing except how much she loves her mother.

'I'm sorry, Joy. I'm so *so* sorry.' Her mother holds out her arms and Joy runs into them. She almost knocks her mother to the ground because she's still kneeling, her blue dress wet from the grass and the dead flowers.

'Don't put my name in the Judgement Book,' Joy cries. 'I don't want Holy God to know I said "fuck".'

'I won't tell him.' Mammy is still sobbing and, in between, whispering, 'You must never come here again . . . it's dangerous . . . Hug me . . . kiss me . . . love me.'

They bury Polar in the flower bed under the kitchen window. Her mother sings 'Nearer My God To Thee' and says, 'He was a good and faithful bear. May be rest forever in peace.'

In the summer she will plant a rose bush over his grave and Joy will remember him every time a rose blooms.

Joy has no time to be really sad because Mitch Moran drives down the lane the next day with something very special in his car for her.

'He's weaned from his mother,' he says. 'And he's yours if you want him. Miriam tells me you've had a sad funeral for Polar.'

The pup lies in a basket in the back seat. When he sees Joy he jumps against the window and scrabbles his paws on the glass. He's black and tiny, like a little splotch. And that's what Joy will call him.

'Can I have him, Mammy? Can I?' she shouts.

She nods and opens the back door. Joy is surprised at how really pretty her mother looks when she smiles.

Chapter Thirty-Four

Carla

The new Millennium came and went. Despite the dire predictions, no planes fell from the sky. Toasters did not burst into flames. Nor did computers crash and bring about a global economic collapse. A pool of calm had settled around Carla and she clung to its order, rising at the same time every morning and working in her apartment until lunchtime. In the afternoon, she spent an hour catching up on emails, checking details with the person whose memoir she was ghost-writing, and speaking on the phone to Frank. She worked on her laptop for a further two hours then went to the gym where she exercised and swam with the same discipline.

Her apartment was surrounded by office blocks. Glass bee-hives of activity. From her balcony she watched men and women at their desks. She envied their camaraderie yet knew she would hate the enforced closeness, the closed gossip of the water cooler, the tedium of waiting for five o'clock. But was she any better in her self-imposed isolation, ghost-writing the lives of other people?

Frank's ambition was to publish the uncomfortable books, the memoirs that no one else wanted to handle. At the start of each new commission, as Carla became familiar with the author and the manuscript, she was gripped by fear. The stories she encountered were so ragged, so personal, how could she possibly do justice to them? Then gradually, so gradually she was aware of it happening, she slipped inside the other person's skin. It was a comfortable place to be. For months she soaked up their emotions, their thoughts, saw the world through their eyes. With each book she felt a little more of herself slipping away. She had become a true ghost-writer, ephemeral, insubstantial. When once the books were written, proofread, and sent to the printers, when it was too late to change a word or a comma, she emerged slowly and reluctantly into her own reality.

She awoke one morning after she had spent the night with Lizzy Carr and tried to grasp back that reality. But with the phone ringing and reverberating through her head, it was already too late.

'Carla, can I ask you a personal question?' Janet demanded.

'If I can find my head, I'll be able to answer you.' Carla groaned but Janet was in no mood for jokes, nor was she offering sympathy.

'What exactly are you doing with your life?' she asked.

'Minding my own business.'

'Not when your face is plastered all over the papers. Your father is horrified by that photo. And not, I might add, for the first time either.'

'What are you talking about?'

'Have you seen the papers this morning?'

'Hardly. I was fast asleep until you rang.'

'I'm amazed you got to bed at all. Why do you insist on attracting the most unsavoury publicity every time you appear in public?'

'I wouldn't worry too much about it, Mother. I discovered

long ago that today's news makes an excellent bin liner for tomorrow.'

'You won't be pleased when you see this one,' Janet warned. 'And I sincerely hope Frank Staunton is not lying beside you listening to our conversation.'

'What?'

'You heard.'

'I haven't a clue what you're talking about.'

'Then I suggest you get to the nearest newsagent and clue yourself in.'

Anticipation model Carla Kelly and radical publisher Frank Staunton enjoy an intimate moment in Kim's Cave.

Back in her apartment, dark glasses discarded, Carla moaned and dragged herself back to bed. She stared at the ceiling and tried to project last night onto the white surface. She had no memory of being photographed. But that was not her main concern. Frank Staunton, she shuddered, and pulled the duvet over her head. He was the last person she would have expected to see in a nightclub. Now that she remembered, he had seemed equally surprised to see her. He was accompanied by an author. Carla tried to recall her name, something American, Samantha . . . no . . . Savannah, that was it, an American author named Savannah, who was promoting her book in Ireland. She talked a lot about post-modernism and Carla had been just as eloquent, considering she had had absolutely no idea what they were discussing. Wine and tequila had turned her into a literary bore, moaned Lizzy Carr, and she had dragged Frank up to dance.

He had danced stiffly, only his shoulders moving, and Carla could remember quite clearly how his expression moved from mild embarrassment to alarm as Lizzy's dancing became more exuberant. Savannah continued to talk about objectivity, nihilism and deconstruction. She agreed with Carla that Robert Gardner was the ultimate post-modern shit to give birth to a son – well, he didn't give birth, that would be *too* post-modern, said Carla. It was that bitch Sharon who had had his baby and was, right at that moment, drinking champagne, well, probably not at that *precise* moment because they were on the other side of the world, but that didn't change the fact that all men were shits, untrustworthy post-modern bastards, except Frank, who was a darling and good in bed, said Carla, just to see Savannah's face, and when he came back to the table, Savannah said, 'I believe you're a stud in bed, Frank, five stars from Carla here,' and Frank bent down to say in his precise, polite voice, 'I think I'd better take you home, Carla.'

Carla remembered the taxi ride and dropping Savannah off at the Westbury Hotel and walking with Frank, well, maybe not walking, she remembered Frank supporting her into the elevator, and the elevator doors sliding closed, just like her mind slid closed on the same instant. This morning she was looking down into a black pit of amnesia. How many brain cells had she killed last night? Billions, probably.

She emerged from under the duvet when the phone rang again.

Lizzy assured her she had done nothing wrong like dancing on tables or flinging her shoes at the DJ.

'But what about Frank?' wailed Carla. 'What did I do to him?'

'Frank the stud, you mean. The five-star guy?'

'*Tell* me.'

'Well, after he dropped Cassandra—'

'Savannah.'

'Whatever. After he dropped her off at the Westbury

and me at my apartment, you said, "Home, James, and don't spare the horses. I fancy a good ride tonight."'

'You bitch! I didn't.'

'Would I lie to you?'

'Oh, God. Lizzy, I'm going to be sick. I'll talk to you later.'

After Carla emerged from the bathroom, she prowled around her apartment, terrified she would find a tie or an odd sock or two wine glasses sitting intimately on the draining board. She checked the bed, relieved when the second pillow looked smooth enough to suggest it had not supported her boss's head throughout the night.

Her five-star boss. She slumped to the edge of the bed and buried her face in her hands.

Frank Staunton, who had treated her with kid gloves. Never by word or deed had he implied that he thought of her as anything other than an efficient and reliable ghost-writer. And she had kept him at the same distance, until now . . . Could she really have called him a stud? Yes, she had. She remembered every word of that free-whirling conversation, as if her mind was flying loose, scattering words at random. But her conversation with Robert was just a jagged memory, retaining only one fact. A son.

He was weeping when he told her, and she had wept too, her voice too choked to do more than wish him well. Lizzy had phoned shortly afterwards and had insisted a night on the town was in order. Lizzy was funny. She made Carla laugh. And that felt good. Almost as good as not caring. And better, infinitely much better, than living in limbo.

'Just remember,' said Lizzy when Carla rang her back. 'A hangover is occasionally necessary to make us appreciate sobriety. I wouldn't worry about your boss. From the look on his face last night, I've a strong suspicion he'd be more than happy to prove you were right when you called him a five-star stud.'

That evening, driving back from dinner with Gina and Leo she recognised Anita's distinctive walk. The young girl turned when Carla drew up beside her and peered suspiciously into the car.

'Ah, jeez,' she said. 'I thought ya were me first punter for the night. Bugger off, Carla. You're ruinin' me chances.'

'Why don't you take a break?' Carla leaned over and opened the passenger door. 'Fancy a bite in Naffy's?'

'Might as well.' Anita shrugged. 'Business is shite anyway.'

'How's life treating you?' Carla asked after Naffy had brought the coffee, and placed a plate of chips for Anita on the table.

'I need me own gaff.' Anita stirred four spoons of sugar into her coffee but made no attempt to drink it. 'The Celtic Tiger is givin' them punters notions. They want clean sheets an' all, now.' She tossed her head back and laughed so loudly that heads turned in their direction.

Since their first meeting, the young girl had flitted in and out of Carla's life. Some nights she worked the canal, sometimes the docks, or, if she had enough money, she took the night off and spent it with friends. Usually, when she came back to the canal and Carla coaxed her to Naffy's for a meal, she was bruised and wasted, withdrawing into herself if Carla asked too many questions.

'I saw ya in the paper.' Anita tilted her head to one side and stared at Carla. 'Me friend says you'd a child stole on you.'

'I did. A little girl called Isobel.'

'Jeez . . . that's rough. Them cops are fuckin' useless.'

'They did their best. I'll find her some day.'

'Wha' age is she now?'

'She's six and a half years old.'

'Me sister is tha' age.'

'Have you many sisters and brothers?'

'Five, last time I counted. Could be more now. Me Ma pops 'em like peas.'

'How long since you've seen her?'

'Mind yer own effin' bisness.'

Carla shrugged. Every time they met she was treated to the same sudden mood swings and had discovered the only way to pacify Anita was to change the subject.

'Anita, I made an absolute arse of myself last night.'

'Wouldn't be the first time. Hangin' off tha' fuckin' bridge—'

'That was then. This is now. I called my boss a stud to his face.'

'An' is he?'

'I haven't a clue. That's the problem.'

'Is tha' the geezer with the beard in the pitcher?'

'That's him.'

'He'll be warmin' yer feet soon.'

'Oh, really?'

'Yeah, really. Ya can always tell by their bleedin' eyes. Everytin' else they can hide but not the eyes.'

Anita was growing restless. Her hand shook when she lifted the mug of coffee. The effort seemed too much and she placed it back untouched on the table. Robert would have mingled with young people like her, gained their confidence, elicited information on the network of suppliers ringing their lives. Carla's only aim was to rehabilitate her. Unwittingly, she had helped Dylan Rae at a crossroads in his life but Anita scoffed at the idea of a rehabilitation centre and grew angry every time Carla mentioned the social services. She had been through them all and had no interest in going back.

'You didn't make that meeting I set up with the counsellor?' Carla kept her tone neutral but Anita instantly picked up on the rebuke.

'Fuck off.' She pulled her mobile phone from her pocket and spoke to someone, her back turned to Carla.

'See ya then,' she said and clicked out of the call.

'It's me mate.' She looked at Carla, her gaze unflinching. 'He wants ta meet me now.'

'Are you all right?'

'Bleedin' great.'

'Don't go, Anita.' Carla leaned across the table and gripped her hand, held tight when Anita tried to wriggle free. 'I can help if you'll let me. You don't have to live like this—'

'Yeah . . . yeah . . . that's what they all say. Tanks for the coffee.' She walked towards the door then turned and came back to the table. 'Must be shite to have a child stole. I'm real sorry for ya.'

Chapter Thirty-Five

An early-morning haze hung over the canal and a barge, making slow progress through the water, flitted in and out of view in the gauzy air. Carla poured coffee from the cafetière and carried the mug to the balcony. A siren sounded, then another. Looking down to the street, she became aware that other Garda cars were parked nearby. The peak-hour traffic, always heavy, was being diverted and further along the bank of the canal yellow tape fluttered.

By the time she reached the cordoned-off area, a group of people had already gathered. She recognised Bev, an older prostitute, who always kept an eye out for Anita. Four days previously she had stopped Carla when she was leaving her apartment and asked if Anita had been in touch with her.

'I saw you and her in Naffy's the other night,' said Bev. 'I've checked all her usual haunts but no one's seen sight nor sign of her since.'

Carla had gone with Bev to the local Garda station to report Anita's disappearance. The guard who took the details believed it was too soon to start a full-scale search, considering Anita's usual pattern of behaviour.

Now, as Carla hurried towards the canal, she recognised Bev's distinctive red hair among the crowd.

'Is it Anita?' she asked, knowing it was a rhetorical question.

One look at Bev's raddled face had given her the answer. The crowd were already being dispersed by the guards. As they were herded back from the scene, Carla noticed a television van parked nearby.

'Let's go to Naffy's,' she said.

Bev nodded and they pushed free from the onlookers. As they walked swiftly along the canal bank, they passed the statue of Patrick Kavanagh. The poet's arms were crossed in his reflective pose, his wish granted. No tomb . . . just a seat where he could stare forever into still waters, mouthing splendid words into the green morning. Carla thought back to the night she had first met Anita and how the young prostitute had crossed her arms in the same way. She had clasped her thoughts deep into her skinny body, a pied piper, leading Carla towards Naffy's and sanity.

'It wasn't the cops that found her,' said Bev. 'It was a woman out with her dog. The dog found the shoe, you know the red pair she loved, and brought it back to the woman. Then she found Anita . . . half in and half out of the water, she was. Been there since Sunday night, I reckon. A knife he used, the bastard, and all because she owed him money.' Tears puddled Bev's eyes, streaked her cheeks with mascara. 'They'll probably want to talk to you, the cops, I mean. Looks like you were the last one to see her alive.'

Bev was right. The guard who had originally taken the details interviewed Carla that afternoon. She was unable to add anything further to her original statement. The only time she had seen anyone else with Anita was the first night they met.

'He was outside the café,' she told the guard. 'I wouldn't be able to identity him. But a man rang her on her mobile on Sunday night. I don't know if he was the same person.'

'Was she a close friend of yours?' The guard made no attempt to hide his curiosity.

'She was a friend when I needed one. I wanted to help her too. But I couldn't. I let her walk to her death and did nothing to stop her.'

'From what I can gather, she was too far gone for help.'

'No, she wasn't,' Carla replied. 'She was lost. But as long as she was alive, there was hope.'

She had examined the identity files without success and left the Garda station. A group of photographers and journalists were waiting outside. She recoiled from the flash of cameras, the shouted questions.

'Carla, how did you know Anita Wilson?'

'Did you realise she was a prostitute?'

'Did you know she was a drug addict?'

'Why were you with her on Sunday night?'

'Do you know many prostitutes?'

'Do you know her supplier?'

'What information did you give to the police?'

'Do you still believe your child is alive?'

The questions hit her like bullets and her anger had a velocity that forced her through the milling journalists towards her car. When a photographer ran alongside her, she screamed and lashed out at him.

'You fucking vultures, why can't you leave me alone? Leave me alone . . . leave me alone. . . .' She ran to her car and tried to zap it open. The zapper fell from her hands and was kicked aside by someone's foot.

'I have to open my car.' Anger gave way to fear. There was nothing between her and them now except the lens, a scalpel, cutting deep into the brittle veneer she had built around herself. Tonight on *The Week on the Street* and tomorrow in the newspapers, she would be laid bare; cleanly sliced for consumption.

Colin Moore bent down and picked up the zapper. He zapped her car and opened the door, assisted her inside.

'I'm sorry, Carla,' he said. 'It's a lousy job but someone has to do it.'

Only one thing to do, thought Carla. She must become invisible to remain visible.

Chapter Thirty-Six

The hairdressing salon Carla entered was suburban and unassuming. A notice in the window offered ten per cent discount to senior citizens on Thursdays. The atmosphere suggested efficiency rather than the hyped glamour of the salons she had once frequented.

The Polish hairstylist who flicked her fingers through Carla's hair was called Florentyna. 'You need just a little trim to mend broken ends, yes?' she stated in her precise Eastern European accent.

Carla stared back at her in the mirror. 'Cut it all off,' she ordered.

Florentyna looked as if she had been asked to perform an amputation.

'Cut it *all* off?' she exclaimed. 'Please, Madam, do I understand you to tell me that your beautiful hair is to fall on the floor?'

'That's precisely what I'm telling you,' replied Carla. 'I want you to cut it as close to my scalp as possible without making me bald.'

'But blondes . . . they have the fun.' Florentyna looked shocked. 'You have most beautiful hair. Irish women, they are blondes, many of them . . . so many. But not natural like you. Why you want it so short?'

'It's a long story, Florentyna. I also want you to dye my hair black.'

'Black!'

'Jet black.'

'But you have one Sinéad O'Connor. You cannot have two.'

'Please, Florentyna, I've had a very difficult day. Do as I say.'

'Black is dull and not interesting, yes?' said Florentyna when the transformation was complete. 'You change your mind, please, you come back to me and be a fun blonde again.'

'I won't change my mind.' Carla stared at her hair, tight as a skullcap, and felt the satisfaction of a snake shedding the last of an old skin.

When Janet called in to her apartment the following afternoon, she greeted her daughter's new appearance with a mix of horror and disbelief.

'How could you do something so drastic?' she demanded. 'I'd pass you on the street without a second glance.'

'That's the idea, Mother . . . and this is only the first step. I already use a pseudonym. I'm going to talk to Leo and change my name to Clare Frazier by deed poll.'

'A name change?' Janet sank into the sofa. 'Did I hear you correctly?'

'Yes.' Carla sat opposite her and tried to calm her down. 'As long as I'm Carla Kelly, I'll never be left alone.' Frazier was Gillian's maiden name and Clare is my second name, so it's a family name.

'You may think so.' Janet's voice rose. 'But I hope you don't expect me to call you anything except the name I gave you at birth.'

246

'No one outside my family is to know otherwise. Do you understand, Mother? This is very important.'

Janet leaned closer to Carla. 'What in the name of God have you done to your eyes?'

'Contact lenses. Purely cosmetic.'

'But they're *green*.'

'An appropriate choice, don't you think?'

Janet's lips tightened. Her red lipstick had blurred into the lines above her mouth and Carla had a sudden impression of how her mother would look when she was an old woman. Time was laying stealthy hands on all of them. Six years . . . and Carla was still upright, still fighting.

'I did warn you about Robert,' said Janet. 'Now you're facing into a divorce, and he's facing into a new life with that one . . . that *strap* of a one who threw herself at him as soon as your back was turned.'

'What do you want, Mother? Marks out of ten for being right?'

'I take no pleasure in being right. I'd give anything . . .' Janet's eyes watered as she stared at Carla. 'You were so beautiful. And now . . . your father will be heartbroken. He loved your lovely hair.'

'Dad will understand. He always does.' Carla handed her a box of tissues. 'I need to protect myself—'

'But you ask for trouble. Honestly, Carla, what do you expect when you hang around with prostitutes?'

'Anita was a child, Mother. And I didn't *hang around* with her. She was my friend.'

'Your friend?' Janet was becoming increasingly agitated. 'You can see why the media would want to know *those* details.'

'There were no details. But that's never stopped them writing about me. I'm selling my apartment and buying one

247

on the other side of the canal. I'm moving on, Mother. Isn't that what you keep asking me to do?'

'Yes. But not by changing into a green-eyed *man*. Honestly, Carla, this is the most ridiculous thing you've ever done. I wish I hadn't been right about Robert. But he made a decision to get over things and now he has a son. What do you have? Tell me, what do you have?'

'A daughter who is waiting for me to find her.'

Frank's reaction was equally disbelieving when he called to Carla's apartment the following evening. Her initial embarrassment over her behaviour in Kim's Cave had been swept aside by Anita's death and all that had followed. When he had phoned in the morning to discuss a new commission she had invited him to dinner on an impulse.

'Even your own mother wouldn't recognise you,' he said when he had followed her into the kitchen.

'I should be so lucky,' Carla replied.

He placed a bottle of white wine in the fridge, uncorked a bottle of red. 'You've had a terrible week.' He pulled a high stool over to the counter and handed her a glass. 'You really socked it to those guys.'

'I lost control, Frank. I'm not proud of how I behaved. As for last weekend . . .' She blinked her eyes against the pungent smell of garlic rising from the wok. 'This is my apology.' She gestured towards the dining area where she had laid the table for two. 'I dread asking this question, but what happened when you brought me back to the apartment?'

'I carried you to your bed, resisted, with great self-control, your request that I join you, and left you snoring into your pillow.'

'This is *so* embarrassing.' Carla added chicken to the wok

and stirred it vigorously into the sautéed vegetables. 'I'm really sorry.'

'Don't be. I enjoyed every moment of it. But as you have absolutely no recollection of the night, I think it's best we both put it behind us. Just one question.'

'Yes.'

'Who's Sharon?'

'My husband's partner. The mother of his son.'

'I see.' Frank nodded thoughtfully. 'That would explain your desire to hack her body into very small pieces and feed them to crocodiles.'

'Is that all I wanted to do?' Carla laughed and lifted her glass in a half-salute. 'Just shows how much self-restraint I have, even when I'm drunk.'

Later, when they had eaten, she carried two glasses of brandy to the living room. He slid his arm along the back of the sofa and rubbed the stubble at the nape of her neck. 'Was Anita's death the reason you did this?'

'Yes. That media scrum triggered everything off again. I'm not able to cope with it any more. Drastic situations call for drastic remedies.'

'I wouldn't call it drastic. Striking and quite beautiful, actually.'

'Thank you, Frank.' His beard brushed against her lips when she leaned across and kissed his cheek.

'Frank Staunton is a single-minded warrior,' Leo warned Carla when he heard she would be writing for him. 'He'll stand shoulder to shoulder with his authors when they have stories to tell. But when it comes to emotional involvements he'll always put himself first. Don't get involved.'

But Carla did not want commitment. Nor did she want love. She simply wanted to forget and Frank's touch, easy and undemanding, was a spark she could ignite and change everything. As he waited for her to make the next move, she drew back and held his gaze. She had never noticed his eyes before, would previously have been unable to tell their colour. Dark hazel and questioning, they demanded a response. Desire, when it came, was swift and sudden.

They undressed each other, flinging clothes to the floor, kicking off shoes, stopping to kiss deeply then to separate and free another piece of clothing. She stretched beneath him and he, holding himself back, stared down at her and said, 'I've wanted to do this from the moment I first set eyes on you.'

Her lips silenced him and he moaned as her body yielded beneath him. Head to toe, mouth to mouth, she moved into a sphere that was sweetly familiar yet startlingly different. He stopped and reached into his jacket for a condom. She closed her eyes, willed herself to stay with him, to forget everything in the melding of passion. But she could feel it draining away, and he, sensing the change in her, collapsed at her side and cradled her against him.

She traced her lips over the bony arch of his shoulder and kissed his throat. He had pale skin, almost like porcelain, and the hair matting his chest was a deep auburn.

'I'm sorry, Frank,' she said.

'So am I, Carla.' He lifted his shirt and spread it over them. 'What do we do now?'

'We don't do anything,' she said. 'That would be nice for a change. Just to do nothing.'

'My mind agrees,' he said. 'But my body tells me that that would be quite impossible.'

'I'm the last person you need in your life, Frank.'

'Let me be the one to make that decision. All you have to do is decide whether or not *you* want to be in my life. But this is obviously the wrong time. When you come into my bed, I don't want anyone else sharing it.'

He dressed quickly, without self-consciousness, and left. She smiled wryly as she switched off the bedroom light and pulled the duvet over her. She should have asked him to stay, scratched and clawed her way to oblivion. He would not have known what hit him and she would probably have ruined her career as a ghost.

Chapter Thirty-Seven

Joy

Splotch is the bane of her mother's life. Joy stares at the pool in the middle of the conservatory. He does wee-wees on the floor and big jobs too. She tries to clean it up so that her mother doesn't shout about the bane of her life and how Splotch is a slow learner when it comes to house-training. If he doesn't improve, he will have to live outside in a kennel.

The conservatory is her mother's private space. She doesn't like anyone else going into it, especially since Splotch chewed one of the cushions from the cane armchair and left teethmarks on the legs of the settee. Her father says the conservatory looks like a boil on the side of the house but her mother loves to sit there writing . . . writing. She will write Splotch's name in the Judgement Book if she sees the mess he made.

Her mother is upstairs hoovering. Joy grabs the pup in her arms and runs to the kitchen for newspaper. The pages soak up Splotch's wee-wee and turn yellow. Splotch scampers over the paper and leaves wet pawmarks on the floor.

'Get out, Splotch,' she whispers and chases him out the door. She adds another sheet of newspaper. This one is not so wet and that's when she sees the photograph. It's the hair she notices first. It's blonde like her own and hanging over the woman's face. She's wearing a jacket with shiny buttons and skinny black trousers, and she's leaning back against the car. Her mouth is open, like she's screaming, and one hand is pushing against someone. Joy can see just the edge of the other person and she doesn't know if it's a man or a woman. She reads the headline. *Model Linked to Pro . . .* it's a long word and she tries to break it into pieces, the way her mother showed her with the word, *To-Get-Her*. Joy knows what a model is. They're super and skinny and wear beautiful clothes. But the other word, *Pros-Tit-Ute*, she's never heard it before. She speaks it aloud. '*Pros-Tit-Ute*.'

'What did you just say?'

Joy glances sideways. Her mother's ankles come into view.

Caught in the act. She presses the paper into the floor and watches Splotch's pee soak into it. Her pup must have a lake inside him.

'Pros-Tit-Ute,' she repeats the word. 'It's in the paper.'

Her mother kneels down and leans so far over the newspaper that Joy thinks she will fall. But she pulls back in time and crumples the paper in a ball. She has that look again, like she doesn't know Joy's name, and she makes a sound like a frog when she clears her throat.

'Your dog is chewing the arm off your Barbie,' she says. 'Keep him under control or he's going outside for good. Do you understand?'

She's right about Barbie. One of her arms is pulp. But Joy doesn't care. She has six Barbie dolls. Granny Tessa brings one every time she comes to stay. Joy never plays with them. They can't talk, not like Polar could. No one is like Polar, even Splotch.

They have to leave him whimpering in the kitchen, the floor covered in newspapers, when her mother brings her to

Maoltrán the next day. Since they started getting the groceries delivered, it's ages since they've been to the village. She drives past the school. Joy lowers the car window and hears the children shouting in the yard.

'You're letting the heat out,' says her mother. 'Put that window up immediately.'

The hairstylist's name in *Cutting it Fine* is Mary. She tucks a black plastic cape around Joy's shoulders and fastens it at the back. Joy stares at her reflection as Mary lifts her hair and lets it fall again.

'Nits,' says her mother to Mary. 'Don't ask me how she got them but we've had two infestations. Cut it as short as possible.'

'Most of the kids tie their hair back in a ponytail and that takes care of the problem,' says Mary. 'It's a bit drastic, don't you think, to get rid of it all?'

'She chews the ends,' says her mother. 'It's unhygienic. Please do as I say.'

Joy wants to tell Mary that she doesn't chew the ends of her hair. She did, for a while after Polar's funeral, but not for ages. Mary brushes the fringe back from her face and drags the brush to the ends of her hair. The strands spark, like they're wired, and Mary smiles in the mirror at her. Joy smiles back even though she wants to cry, and she bends her head so that she doesn't have to look when Mary starts to cut. *Snip . . . snip . . . snip.*

She feels the air on the back of her neck and shivers. Her head is so light she thinks it might take off like a balloon.

'Shorter,' says her mother.

Joy touches stubble on the back of her neck. She's afraid to look into the mirror. A stranger stares back at her. She has such a tiny face. Even Splotch won't know her.

When they come home her mother has to clean the kitchen

floor. She goes down on her knees with a bucket and scrubbing brush. The smell of Dettol is all over the house. But still she keeps scrubbing, even though there's nothing left to scrub except spotless floorboards.

Her father is home again. Joy thinks his eyes will pop from his head when he sees her.

'Don't you like it, Daddy?' she asks. 'Don't you?'

He doesn't speak for a long time. His Adam's apple goes up and down. 'Let me have another look,' he says, when he sees her tears. 'Some things take a bit of getting used to.'

He turns her around and examines her from all angles. 'Do you know who you remind me of?' he asks.

'Who, Daddy? Who?'

'A beautiful pixie,' he says. 'The most beautiful pixie ever.'

He stares over her head at Mammy and doesn't speak again. Joy feels the shiver on her arms. She calls Splotch and runs upstairs to her room. She knows the signs. The silence is filled with thunder.

Her father says that the Burren is a unique place. It was formed from the compressed shells of sea creatures that lived at the bottom of the ocean over three hundred million years ago. Then, fifteen thousand years ago – which seems like yesterday in comparison to the sea creatures – the ice age came and glaciers scraped the Burren clear of topsoil. When the glaciers melted, fifty square miles of pavement rock was left exposed. By rights, nothing should grow here but it is full of rare and wonderful plants nestling in the warm limestone cracks.

He teaches her the names, in English and in Latin: the mountain avens, *dryas octopetala*, spring gentians, *gentiana verna*, early purple orchid, *orchis mascula* and the flower with the same name as their house, hoary rockrose, *helianthemum canum*.

He takes her hand and they walk across the flat rocks. 'Grikes are the crisscrossing cracks in the limestone,' he says. 'And the clints are the isolated sections of rock.'

Her parents' marriage is full of grikes, large cracks that they pretend not to notice. Joy often wonders what warm space they found in the grikes to create her.

'Were they happy before I was born?' she asked Miriam once when they were in the stockroom sticking barcodes on the seahorse boxes.

'Yes, they were happy but things happened and it was tough on both of them,' her grandmother replied.

'What things?' Joy finds it impossible to imagine life before she arrived and became a bone for her parents to argue over.

'Babies that were not meant to be born,' said Miriam. 'Not like you, my little cabbage. You are their miracle.'

Phyllis says much the same thing, and puffs out her chest every time Joy asks her to tell the story. 'Lucky for some I was around. You were one fortunate baby to survive.'

Her mother never wants to talk about that night. 'You came quick,' is all she says. 'Fast as lightning.'

Joy imagines the snow and the panic and Phyllis's rough, red hands carefully drawing her out into the light, and her father, far away on the rig, listening on the phone to hear her first cry.

Chapter Thirty-Eight

Susanne

Last week she was photographed in Kim's Cave. I remember it well. The nightclub for celebrities and wannabes. Her eyes are as smudged as night and behind the drunken sparkle I saw the bleakness ... oh ... the bleakness ... And now this. *Model Linked to Murdered Prostitute.* Publicity follows her like a bad smell. I saw the resemblance immediately. I never noticed it before but you are growing into her.

'Why ... why ... why,' said David. 'Joy's hair was beautiful. Her crowning glory. Now she looks like an urchin. Are you jealous of her beauty? Is it possible that you resent your own child, the attention she receives from others?'

When I mentioned nits he called me a liar.

Our gloves are off, our marriage reduced to bare knuckles. It's a charade and you are beginning to see through it. I wonder about other women. They must exist. He is young and virile but he has never come to me since that night when I said it was inappropriate (yes, I did use that word) to hold a small child against his naked chest.

He was in Dublin yesterday talking to my father ...

about me. Neither will admit it but that has to be the reason my father came today.

You heard his van entering the lane and were gone before I could catch you, running up the lane, your hands waving. He stopped and flung open the driver's door. You disappeared inside and when he braked outside the house you were sitting on his lap, your hands on the steering wheel, the two of you laughing uproariously.

'It was just for a few yards,' he said, when I warned him about the risk. 'Isn't she the great little rally driver? In control the whole time.'

I asked why he hadn't phoned in advance. I didn't intend it to sound like an accusation but I'm losing my ability to speak normally to people. He claimed he had to visit a client in Limerick, some new hotel signage, and, as he was so near, he decided to touch base with his only daughter. This *was* an accusation and was not meant to sound otherwise. 'Just be glad to see me,' he replied. 'A cup of tea in my hand is all I want. That and a chance to hug my favourite grandchild.'

'Silly Granddad,' you shouted, giddy from the drive. 'I'm your *only* grandchild.'

I made him tea and he nibbled around the edges of a biscuit. 'So,' he asked, when you'd gone into the living room to watch your video, 'how's life treating you, Susanne? It must be lonely all on your own down here, especially when David is away so often. I hear he's interested in finding a job closer to home.'

I shrugged, refused to be drawn.

He picked up a pine cone from the nature table and examined it intently. The questions began. Why were you not attending the local school? Why does David believe I was bullied throughout my school days when nothing of

260

the sort happened? Why have I turned my back on an interesting career in Miriam's studio? Why did I strike another
woman's child and accuse him of attacking Joy when
everyone present agrees it was an accident? He flung the
pine cone back on the table. It rolled to the floor and
reminded me of your fury that afternoon, the hatred in your
gaze when you cursed me.

No sense fooling myself any longer. He's right. You hate
home-school. You lie listlessly across the kitchen table and
suck your thumb. You tickle Splotch under his chin and allow
him to walk across the table on your school books. You find
it impossible to memorise the simplest sums yet count the
days until David's return.

'Home-schooling,' my father said, 'is for cranks and
Creationists. Why are you involved in this ridiculous charade
when Joy is crying out for the company of other children?
Why are people talking about you? Are you aware that they
call you a recluse? They claim you're neurotic, an unbalanced
mother.'

How easy it is to fling accusations of neurosis into the
air. I thought briefly of Edward Carter and his bird-wife but
my father was in full spate, incapable of stopping.

'I believe you're suffering from agoraphobia,' he said. 'Fear
of open spaces,' he added, as if I was unfamiliar with the
term.

He suggested I see someone, a counsellor, someone who
can understand my fear of human contact; someone in whom
I can confide the reasons why I have such a compulsion to
hide myself away.

He felt responsible . . . at this point he stopped and seemed
to lose his way.

'You were not brought up in a happy environment,' he
said. 'It has obviously affected you.'

I saw my parents' faces then, cameo-sharp in my memory: Nina and Jim, the ticking of their unhappiness loud in the silence surrounding them. I'd longed for a brother or a sister, or both, but there was no space for them to survive the briar of my parents' anger.

Is that what you see when you look at us, I wonder. *My brittle smile ordering you to be happy? David's brooding resentment leaching the energy from the air around us?*

This afternoon, my father was determined to tackle old ghosts. 'That first unfortunate experience . . .' his voice trailed away.

'You would have had my baby adopted,' I said. 'You would have given him away, no matter what I wanted. You'd no interest of starting your married life with me and a baby hanging on.'

'That's not how I remember it,' he said. 'You were young. How could you cope with the responsibility of a child when you could not even name its father?'

Until this afternoon, that instant, I was unaware of how much I hated him.

We heard you singing, the light beat of your feet on the wooden floor as you danced with the orphans. *Annie the Musical* . . . again. Miriam bought it for your birthday. You play it every day, singing about ashtrays and art and lost parents. Singing with such pathos, such longing.

You sang about a hard-knock life this afternoon, held a hairbrush like a microphone to your mouth.

'She's made for the stage,' my father said. 'But she'll never get beyond these four walls if you have your way.'

I imagined you exposed in spotlights. The hairs lifted on my neck. It can never be. And yet it must.

I watched him leave. *Sheehan Signs* is written large on the side of his van. As a sign maker, he works with neon and

262

metal, oak and vinyl. I always recognise his signs wherever they are erected. The graphics, the colours and imagery do not intrude on the landscape. Their function is to attract attention without jarring the eye, to guide the customer without effort in the right direction, to seem invisible while being actively visible. I am the sign that jars the eye. The one that points the way to strange behaviour, leads towards speculation and innuendo. Invisibility has made me conspicuous in a community that would notice a blade of grass growing in the wrong direction. I'd forgotten about perception. It's not the story that counts but how it's told.

You and I must face them, become one of them. We must become visible to remain invisible.

Chapter Thirty-Nine

Carla

Robert's son was eight months old when Raine married Jeff Boyne, the European manager of the Fuchsia chain. Under different circumstances, Carla would have been her chief bridesmaid. Raine understood her reasons for refusing. Too much exposure could destroy her hard-won freedom. As Carla waited with Frank and the other guests for the bride to arrive, he nudged her with his knee and whispered, 'Is that Sharon in the front row?'

'Yes.' Carla folded her hands calmly on her lap and watched as Sharon lifted her son to her knee and silenced his cries with a kiss. 'How did you know?'

'She's your clone.'

'Not any more, she isn't.'

'True,' he replied. 'But you know what I mean.'

A wide-brimmed hat added to Carla's anonymity. Her arrival at the church had not caused an intake of breath, or a head to turn, yet when the organist played 'Here Comes the Bride' and Raine walked up the aisle on Robert's arm, he recognised her instantly. His eyes widened and his mouth opened, as if he was going to speak her name. Then he recovered. His expression smoothed out. He too was used to invisibility.

When they reached the hotel where the reception was being held, Carla went directly to the ladies'. She ran cold water over her wrists until her hands felt numb and her cheeks grew pale again.

'Carla . . .' He was waiting for her outside.

'Clare,' she said, softly.

'Raine told me.' He nodded in acknowledgement and gestured with his hand, taking in her slimline shirt and short jacket. 'You look stunning.'

'Thank you.' She removed her hat and ran her hand through her hair, ruffling it back into shape. 'I still get a shock when I look in the mirror.'

'You've moved apartments, I believe.'

'Yes. I'm settled in now. And you . . . a family man. Are you happy, Robert?'

'Sometimes I believe I am,' he replied. 'In my own way. And you?'

'I'm content. It suffices.'

'I think about her every day.' He spoke so quietly she had to lean forward to hear him. 'I visited the Angels' plot yesterday. She would be seven years old now.'

'She *is* seven years old.'

'You look different,' he said. 'But you haven't changed at all.'

Sharon, pushing the baby in a buggy, stopped beside them. 'I was wondering where you were.' She glanced at Carla without a flicker of recognition. 'Hi,' she said. 'I'm Sharon Dowling.' She waved towards the baby. 'And this is our son, Damian.'

'Congratulations, Sharon.'

'Carla . . .' Sharon's gasp was audible. For an instant no one moved. Even the baby seemed gripped by the currents playing across their faces. 'I saw you in the church but I'd

266

no idea . . .' Her voice trailed away and the little boy, as if unable to bear the tension, began to wail.

'He's hungry.' Sharon bent and laid her hand like a protective wing over Damian's head. Her bleached hair showed dark at the roots. She was obviously letting it grow out. Perhaps she was tired of being the alter ego of a past memory. 'I'm going to take him to our room and feed him.'

'I'll join you in a moment,' said Robert.

She nodded and glanced from him to Carla. 'It's good to see you again.'

'You too, Sharon.' How civilized we are, Carla thought. How immune to pain we have become. Who would have believed it would be possible to stand in the same space without drawing knives?

'Can I call and see you?' he asked when Sharon walked away.

'No.'

'Just to talk?'

'*No.*'

'I wouldn't—'

'Yes you would.'

He nodded. 'You're right. I would. But would you?'

'I'm not going to risk finding out.'

'That man you're with? Who is he?'

'Frank Staunton. He's a friend.'

'Ah, the publisher. Raine says he wants to be more than that.'

'He does.'

'Will you let him?'

'I believe I will.'

He reached out and grasped her hand. 'Jesus Christ, Carla . . . how did we lose each other?'

'I don't know, Robert. But we did. And now there's absolutely nothing we can do about it.'

267

Frank had organised a table and ordered drinks. 'I was going to send a posse out to look for you,' he said when she sank into a chair opposite him.

'I was talking to Robert.'

'I thought you might be. If you want to break for the border, we don't have to stay for the reception.'

'The border sounds good. Raine and Jeff will understand.'

'Where would you like to go?' he asked.

'How does my apartment sound?' she replied.

'It was a dangerous place the last time I visited it.'

'No, Frank. It was an uncertain place.'

'And now?' His expression was quizzical.

'It's filled with certainty.'

She was surprised at how easy it was to love Frank. He delighted in controversy, the edginess of living close to the wire, and it was this recklessness that continued to attract her to him. If she had been asked to define her feelings she would have admitted that it was a convenient love, one that made few demands on her. No questions asked. No turbulence, no rows. She experienced none of the fire that had drawn her to Robert or any of the giddy, foolhardy excitement that had attracted her to Edward Carter. Frank's true passion was paper and print and he, while appreciating her past, was not burdened by it. At forty-two, he was, he admitted, a confirmed bachelor with a set lifestyle he had no intention of changing. They suited each other's needs and the move from being friends to becoming lovers was effortless.

Chapter Forty

Susanne
Twelve Years Later

Tonight you were a star. I sat with David in the front row of the assembly hall of Maoltrán National School and watched you strut into the spotlights; that radiant smile, that cocky walk that could, in a heartbeat, slow to a languid glide. Your mop of red curls was a thin disguise but no one sat alertly in their seat and added two and two together and, even if they could, they were too absorbed in their own children's performances to notice the resemblance that beamed at me from the stage.

From the time the auditioning for Annie began, I knew you'd be chosen. Your music teacher loves your voice.

'How proud you must be of your daughter,' she said, when we went backstage. 'Where does she get her talent from?'

After the show, I wanted to sweep you into my arms and tell you how wonderfully you had performed. My voice sounded strained, the words empty. I saw your face fall, your expression harden. You tossed your head defiantly and turned your dazzling smile upon those who came to congratulate you. You believed I'd dismissed you and I was in too much pain to care. Fear and pain, I wasn't sure where one ended and the other began. My stomach cramped and I was afraid blood would flow . . . it gets worse each month and I'm frightened . . . oh Jesus . . . I'm frightened.

Discipline, that's what matters. Yoga and religion. I've discovered the power of prayer . . . and property. It was Miriam's suggestion that I call in to Breen's Auctioneers and talk to Victor Breen about a job. 'If only you'd come to me sooner,' she said, sighing and pretending to be disappointed when I'd asked if I could work again in her studio. Our relationship changed after the Joey incident and has never been the same since. For your sake, we occasionally have Sunday dinner together, but in the years that have passed we've grown more distant. Busy people, both of us. Pillars of the community, each in our own way. Occasionally, I think back to the early days but thinking back is to stand still and I don't have time to pause. Not with Victor breathing down my neck and prices spiralling.

I never thought I'd be good at selling property but it's a piece of cake. Victor believes we're cut from the same cloth. I guess he's right. Commitment. That's his mantra. One hundred and ten per cent commitment. 'The property market is going through the roof,' he shouts. 'We have the Celtic Tiger by the balls and by Christ we'll make him roar. Apartments and town houses, manors and mobiles, castles and chateaus, duplexes, semis, terraces, bungalows, barns and shoe boxes. This is our time, Susanne. Big is beautiful. Property is king. Sell, sell, sell.' Maoltrán seethes with life. It's not unusual to hear Polish voices in the shops or the deep roll of an African accent. Stately black women in peacock colours address me by name, as do the slim Latvians and brown-eyed Romanians. Sell . . . sell . . . sell . . .

Tonight, you sold yourself to a packed audience. You got a standing ovation. Cameras flashed. *This way, Annie . . . That*

way . . . The other way. Sing 'Tomorrow' . . . 'Maybe' . . .
'Hard-Knock Life'. Encore . . . encore. Miriam led the standing
ovation.

'Aren't you glad you changed your mind about home-
schooling,' she said.

She finds it hard to resist these small verbal nudges but
she's right. I *am* glad I set you free. I never realised how
claustrophobic our relationship had become until you walked
away from me that first morning when I brought you to
school. You held my hand tightly, your eyes round with fear
when I knocked on the classroom door. We both cried in
the beginning, morning after morning, and then, slowly, I
felt my grip loosening on you.

Initially, Lilian Marr, the school principal, was cool with
me. Home-schooling was a challenge to her authority but
she mellowed when I offered to join the school management
committee. After that it was the Chamber of Commerce and
the Tidy Towns committee. In the end, it was easy enough
to assimilate. People in country villages understand depression. The grey sky. The grey rocks. The isolation. It can
happen to anyone.

Months passed without writing in my journal and, even
when I remembered its existence, I had no desire to pour
my dread into it. Carla Kelly had disappeared. Nothing to
suggest she had ever existed. The relief was slow to come. I
kept expecting her to stare at me from screen and paper.
Then, finally, I was able to breathe deeply into my lungs and
walk freely into the world.

You asked where the Judgement Book had gone. I hadn't
realised what terror it held for you. It was mixed up in your
head with the Day of Judgement when all our sins shall be
revealed. I never intended it to become a weapon of fear but
you had found its hiding place. If I hadn't discovered you

drawing those pictures you would have shown them to David. You always showed him everything you did, hanging on to his words of praise. I lashed out . . . forgive me. In that instant I saw a terrifying future . . . everything we had achieved . . . our lives wrenched apart. I'd forgotten to lock the box. How could I have made such an incredible mistake?

But now I write again, write late into the night. The whisperers came back to me after David's father died. Six months now since he was laid to rest in the graveyard. Last week Miriam erected a headstone. I never knew the man. When I saw him for the first time he was laid out in his coffin. Miriam had received the call from the Mater Hospital in the middle of the night. Since he left her, there had been many women in Kevin Dowling's life but none were by his side when he died. Miriam and David went to Dublin and brought his body back to Maoltrán. He's at peace now, if peace is what awaits us on the other side. But on this side I'm in torment. In his will he left the cottage and the land surrounding it to David. Now my husband has ambitions. There's a sparkle in his eyes and you've been fired by his enthusiasm. He's had plans drawn up by an architect. The two of you pore over them, discuss how the lane will be widened and the cottage demolished so that a hostel can rise in its place. Dowling's Meadow will become a wildlife sanctuary. They'll come to Maoltrán, the botanists and lepidopterists, the hill walkers and those who seek mystical significance in the ancient tombs. I imagine the claws of diggers reaching deep into her tomb. My almost child. My secret exposed.

I tried to find her, tried to remember the exact spot. You came upon me as I was digging. I though you were in Lucinda's house but you came home early. Some row over a boy. You dropped your bike in the lane and ran into that wild place, stared at the mound of earth. I told you I was uprooting wild primroses to replant in my garden.

They will be destroyed when the cottage is demolished, I said, and you were too absorbed in your argument with Lucinda to wonder.

Your eyes sparked with indignation. 'Lucinda's *such* a cow,' you said, and spent the next ten minutes explaining why. An hour later you were on the phone to her, giggling and whispering secrets.

David came home the next day. It's too dangerous to search for the past. He will not believe vague excuses about uprooted plants. Victor Breen is my only hope. He dislikes competition and he has plans to build a new hotel on the outskirts of the village. There's four of them involved in the conglomerate, all members of the Chamber of Commerce, all friendly with Mattie, the local county councillor. It's how things work here, a nod, a wink and a brown envelope slipped sleight of hand.

The entrance to your lane is narrow, a traffic hazard, says Victor when I tell him what David plans to do. Can he honestly expect to get planning permission under such circumstances? Tell him it's a pipe dream. Don't let him waste his money.

Tonight, at the musical, he slapped David's shoulder and wished him luck with his planning permission.

'Sly bastard,' said David. 'He'll do everything he can to scupper my plans.'

He dislikes the fact that I work for Victor. They went to school together. They know each other's warts. He advises you to avoid Danny Breen. 'Like father like son,' he says. 'I don't want him supping at my table.'

But Danny Breen's house is the honey pot. It's where you

all gather around the swimming pool, the pool table, the home cinema. Soon you will be a teenager. Already you show the signs. A touch of acne on your forehead sends you spiraling into anxiety. Your mood swings cast you high and low, fill you with sunshine or dark, brooding clouds. You argue for the sake of it, challenge my authority, disagree with me over every change I make to the house. You obsess over your weight, your looks, your clothes, your friends. You are typical of your age group yet to me you will always be unique.

The pain has eased since I started writing. The house is silent, except for the whisperers. So low they whisper . . . *Beware . . . beware . . . tread carefully . . .*

The blind stallion glints on its pedestal. I will finish now. I found a hiding place that will never again be breached unless I decide otherwise. If there comes a time . . . it will not happen . . . but if it should . . . then you will know the truth.

Until then, only the eyes of the blind see what I write.

Chapter Forty-One

Joy

Joy cycles down the lane. In the distance she can see the Burren rising and falling like the back of a great grey beast. She shouts over the hedgerow at her father who is walking through the meadow. He lifts his arms above his head and waves them back and forth, as if he's sending a distress signal. Maybe he is. She resists the urge to stop and go to him. Lucinda was expecting her an hour ago and it'll take at least twenty minutes to cycle to her house. Living in the back end of nowhere is a pain. She has to either cadge a lift from her parents or cycle.

'See you later,' she shouts at her father.

'Be careful,' he shouts back. 'Make sure Splotch doesn't follow you.'

Splotch pants behind her. He'll stop when she reaches the top of the lane and be back there again waiting for her return. An amazing dog who knows what she's going to do before she does. Her father walks slowly now, his head bent, his hands clasped behind his back. She cycles faster. It upsets her to see him so depressed but that's the way he's been since his plans were turned down.

The cottage is almost invisible under the summer leaves.

What use is it to anyone? It's so long since her ancestors lived there that it's crumbling back into the earth. She slows to allow Splotch to catch up and he passes her, scampering after a rabbit that has darted from the hedgerow. The rabbit streaks along the green grass in the centre of the lane. Silly rabbit. It should run into the bushes and hide. She shouts at Splotch to stop. His tail is up, his ears back as he races towards the T-junction at the top of the lane. The rabbit keeps going, a grey flash across the main road where drivers drive too fast and her parents always warn her to stop, look and listen. Splotch follows the rabbit and disappears from view. She screams but her voice is drowned by the squeal of brakes. She knows what is going to happen the instant before she hears the thud, a high anguished yelp, then silence.

She drops her bicycle and runs forward onto the main road. The car has been driven into the grass verge and the driver's door is open. A man bends over Splotch, his back curved as if he is praying. Joy huddles against his car, her hands over her face. Her father runs from the meadow and snatches her into his arms, almost lifts her off the road and presses her against his chest. His heart beats hard and fast like a drum.

'I thought . . .' he swallows loudly and holds her tighter still, holds her upright or maybe she's the one holding him because he's trembling so much his legs will surely sink him to the ground. 'I thought it was you—'

'It's Splotch,' she sobs loudly. 'He's dead. I know he's dead.'

The man looks over his shoulder and gestures at them to come forward. 'Is he your dog?' He speaks so softly she can barely hear him.

Still sobbing, she nods and leans down. The dog's body quivers as if he is wired to electricity. His eyes remind her of the blind stallion, that same milky glaze. The man strokes

276

Splotch's throat, a slow stroking movement that keeps the dog still while his other hand probes for injuries. He finds one when he touches the left hind leg. An anguished yelp and Splotch's head shoots up, his body convulsing for an instant before succumbing once again to the gentle strokes and the low, soothing voice.

'He only glanced off the side of my car.' The man moves aside and allows her space to kneel beside him. 'He's injured but not seriously.'

'We'll take him to the vet.' Her father rings the vet on his mobile phone and turns back towards the lane. It will take him ten minutes to walk back for his jeep and Joy is relieved to hear the man offer to drive them to the clinic.

She sits in the back seat with Splotch and keeps him calm. He's stretched on the flattened cardboard box the two men used as a stretcher to lift him into the car. Her father sits beside her. Occasionally he reaches over Splotch and pats her cheek, pats her hand. The lines around his eyes are deep. She never noticed them before. In the rearview mirror she sees the man's reflection. He catches her gaze and smiles.

'Not much longer to go,' he says. 'Your dog will be as right as rain as soon as that leg heals. A bolt from the blue, he was. Just as well I'd slowed coming to the junction or the little mutt wouldn't have had a chance, so he wouldn't.'

The man's hair is blond and spiky. He's from Dublin. She recognises his accent.

'What's your name?' he asks.

'Joy Dowling.'

His eyes narrow, then he switches his attention back to the road. 'Have we met before?' he asks.

Now that the shock has subsided, she can think clearly again. He looks familiar, deeply tanned like her father, as if he spends most of his time outdoors. She remembers then, the waves and the surfboards, and Joey talking to the man with the rig. She drew a circle around them but they were too busy discussing jibs and sails and wind speeds to notice her.

'In Lahinch. I was with my brother Joey.'

'The Canadian lad with the surfboard?'

'He's my son,' her father says. 'He's actually Joy's half-brother.'

'Ah, I wondered. The name's Dylan Rae.'

'I'm David.' Her father lifts his hand in a half wave and Dylan does the same. 'Do you live around here?'

'A few miles outside Ballyvaughan.'

'You from Dublin originally?'

'Born and bred.'

'So is Susanne, my wife. How've you settled down?'

'We're well settled now. I'm a counsellor and my wife drives the ambulance for St Anna's Clinic. The kids are native, through and through. If we dared move back to the smoke, they'd disown us.'

Sandra, the vet, is waiting for them. 'He's going to be fine.' She echoes Dylan's words and hugs Joy. 'He'll stay here overnight and you can collect him tomorrow afternoon. That's a dangerous junction. You'll have to keep him on a lead in future.' She speaks fast as she administers a sedative and Splotch's eyelids drift closed.

Dylan drives them back to Rockrose and comes into the house when her father insists. Her mother is sitting in the conservatory. She makes tea and serves scones with cream and jam.

'What part of Dublin?' Dylan asks her.

'Clontarf,' she says.

Dylan grew up in Howth. Joy knows Howth. She can see Howth Head from her grandparents' house. At night it glistens with lights. She goes walking along the cliff with her grand-father and Tessa. Dylan knows people in Clontarf. He keeps mentioning names he hopes her mother will recognise but she doesn't know them.

Her mother rattles her cup in her saucer and checks her watch. She has a meeting about the organ fund with Fr Davis in the church hall.

Dylan takes the hint and says he must be on his way.

He stops to admire the blind stallion.

'What a magnificent piece,' he says.

'My mother designed it.' Her father sounds so proud. 'She has her own studio. Miriam's Glasshouse.'

'I know it. Nikki buys stuff there every Christmas. But I've never seen this beauty before.' He bends forward to lift the stallion but it's attached to the table.

'It's a precious piece.' Her mother rests her hand on the stallion's head. 'Joy is always galumphing around the place so I had to take precautions.'

Galumphing! Why does her mother always make her feel so hefty? And in front of strangers too. Joy hates the way she does it, the slight smile that suggests it's just a joke but they both know she means it. Every word. Her mother is petite. She has small hands and takes size three in dainty shoes and moves as if the wind is behind her back, blowing her forward too fast.

Dylan touches one of the stallion's hooves, traces his finger over the blind eyes.

'"The Blind Stallion of Leamanagh Castle".' He reads the words engraved into the base of the stallion. 'Leamanagh Castle,' he says. 'A grim edifice.'

Joy shows him the scar on her forehead. Her mother walks from the conservatory. She hates it when Joy mentions that time.

279

Dylan nods when he sees her scar. It's hardly noticeable any more but he says, 'It's hard to get through life without a few scars.'

He runs a counselling clinic. Mostly it's a hang-out place for young people to spill out their troubles. At least that's the way he makes it sound. He looks back at the stallion.

'I was blind too,' he says. 'Blind to everything but my own needs.'

Chapter Forty-Two

Susanne

Victor Breen's house is an impressive edifice. It sits on the summit of a hill, a proud tribute to our Celtic Tiger. David may pour scorn on its brash brickwork and the statues of soaring eagles above the doorway, which are, I agree, over the top, but Victor has made his money through hard neck and hard sell. He deserves to flaunt it as he chooses. Annette, his wife, is of the same opinion and Victor's fiftieth birthday gave her the perfect opportunity to entertain.

The butler took our coats and escorted us into a reception room where we enjoyed a pre-dinner drink and made small talk with the other guests. Apart from Dr Una Williamson, my bridge partner, and her husband, Andrew, I knew most of them from the Chamber of Commerce and the Lions Club. I was surprised to see that Dylan Rae and his wife, Nikki, had been invited. They were underdressed for such a formal occasion. He was in casual trousers and an open-necked shirt. She wore a dress of crushed velvet that looked as if it had been pulled from the back rail of a charity shop. As it turned out, I was wrong. It had belonged to her great-grandmother and is a genuine antique.

She's a friendly, talkative woman but I never feel comfortable in his presence. It's his eyes that unnerve me; too direct and challenging for small talk. Last year he helped Lisa, Victor's daughter, who'd stopped talking to her family for a year and had demanded all her meals in her room. She joined the party for a short while and kissed her father's cheek, so, it's possible Victor has reason to be grateful to Dylan.

Initially, they looked out of their depth until David insisted we join them. He's become quite friendly with Dylan since Splotch's accident and they've gone surfing together on a few occasions. Una and Andrew joined our circle. As an ambulance driver, Nikki knows her quite well and we made polite conversation until we were led into the dining room.

Victor drank too much and became quite belligerent towards the end of the meal. I don't know who was responsible for bringing up the subject of drugs. Victor, I suspect. He believes his daughter's odd behaviour was directly related to substance abuse and is of the opinion that the state should bring back hanging for drug pushers. Black and white, that's Victor's view of life. It's easier not to argue with him when he's drinking but Dylan wasn't prepared to pander to his views. He insisted that the lack of government funding for rehabilitation facilities was disgraceful and that there was a serious lack of Garda initiative in the fight against drugs.

Victor demanded to know where personal responsibility came into the equation. He became so flushed I thought he was going to have a stroke. Annette Breen looked furious with the pair of them. This was her big occasion and the lively chatter around the table a few minutes earlier had died down under the force of their argument. Nikki shot her husband a warning glance which Dylan caught full on. He apologised to Annette and admitted the reason he became so emotional when the subject of drugs came up for discussion was because he had been an addict in his younger days.

'Only for Nikki's intervention and perseverance, I would have died,' he said.

'Nonsense,' said Nikki in her brisk, matter-of-fact voice. 'It was Carla Kelly who forced you to take stock of your life.'

She spoke so casually I thought I'd misheard . . . or that my inner demon had uttered her name aloud. I almost expected everyone's eyes to turn in my direction, demanding answers. But they were looking from Nikki to Dylan with undisguised curiosity. Even Victor had calmed down sufficiently to ask if Nikki was talking about the Carla Kelly whose baby was stolen?

'The very person,' said Nikki, and told us a story about a crazed woman wandering aimlessly through a desolate wasteland searching for her child. I began to bleed. I knew the instant it started. I left the table and asked one of the maids to direct me to a bathroom. I was bleeding heavily. Fortunately, I had protection and was able to manage the situation but I knew I would have to leave soon. I opened my evening bag and used blusher on my cheeks. I brushed my teeth and reddened my lips. I still look youthful in a good light. My main asset is my eyes. They are serene. They do not mirror my soul. For that I am fortunate.

I returned to the dining-room where the conversation had flowed from dangerous memories to the ever present reality of spiralling property prices. And everyone looked perfectly at ease discussing how their houses had increased in value and wasn't it amazing how the money markets had lost all sense of reason.

That was a week ago. I've stopped bleeding now . . . but only just. Each month it comes, and sometimes twice, heavy, prolonged. But it passes, everything passes. I want my body bleached, scoured, freed from the unending demands of hormones and cyclical calendars. I want my womb ripped out but then . . . what? Would the truth be revealed, laid bare beneath the magnifying lens of experts, sleuths, busybodies? Can it reveal the fact that it has never pulsed and released you into life? The thought terrifies me yet I must seek help. It's too dangerous to wait any longer.

Dr Williamson is my bridge partner on Tuesday evenings. Over the years we have attuned our bidding so well that we know what cards the other holds. But in her surgery, where we were separated by a desk, not a card table, I was lost.

It was difficult to subject myself to her probing. She asked too many questions. Was I feeling fatigued? My blood pressure was up, she said. Only slightly, which would suggest white-coat syndrome but, on the other hand, it would be worth further investigation.

'There's nothing wrong with me other than the onset of the menopause,' I said. She checked my file. 'You're healthy,' she said. 'The last time you attended my clinic you were showing classic signs of anxiety. That's quite a long time ago. You're probably in need of a good overhaul.'

'You make me sound like a clapped-out car,' I said, but she was not amused.

'The body is a delicate engine,' she replied. 'It's tougher to repair when we drive it into the ground. Victor Breen is a hard taskmaster. Have you been overdoing it? You're involved in so many committees. How long since you've had a smear test? Blood tests?'

'Six months ago,' I replied. 'My gynaecologist carried it out. The results were clear.'

She tapped her pen on the desk, narrowed her eyes. 'You must go for blood tests,' she said. 'We need to check you out for iron deficiency. Ask your gynaecologist to forward the results of your smear test to me. Or, better still, I'll contact Professor Langley myself.'

'I don't attend Professor Langley,' I replied. 'I have a gynaecologist in Dublin.'

'Tell me his name and I'll write to him,' she said. 'I don't want to alarm you but the kind of excessive bleeding you've described means we could be talking about a hysterectomy.'

What does she mean by *we*? I swung my legs down from the examination table and told her I'd organise everything myself. If *we* were talking about a surgical procedure, I'd prefer to deal directly with my own specialist. I tried to soften my voice but I could see her puzzlement. She drew back, as if I'd offended her and pulled off her rubber gloves, throwing them away.

Everything is disposable except the past.

David is her patient. Last year he had blood tests done to check for a bug he'd picked up in Mexico. Your blood results when you were hospitalised would have been sent to her from St Anna's. What else could I do but walk away?

At night, the blind stallion leaps through my dream and fastens his teeth into my stomach. I scream but no sound emerges. My mouth fills with sawdust. I fight him off but my limbs are flaccid. His teeth sink deeper. Blood begins to flow ... flow ... flow like a river in spate and I awaken, cursed, yes, they named it right, cursed with a womb that hates me.

The whisperers grow more insistent ... *take her away ... take her away* ... Tomorrow we fly to Spain. I wonder will they come with me, those soft, insistent voices.

We'll stay in Victor's villa. We've gone there every summer since I started working with him but this will be a working holiday to gauge the potential in the Spanish market. I'm the perfect person to run an overseas office. I've studied Spanish property law and have a working knowledge of the language.

I must do as Dr Williamson suggests. A smear test. In Spain I can seek medical assistance, start with a clean slate. They'll miss me in Maoltrán but life moves on. David needs a holiday. He's upset about his hostel but he'll get over it in time. Spain will be good for him, take his mind off things. Our marriage may be in name only but I've tried to be an understanding wife.

Sometimes, I look at him and see him with a stranger's eyes. I imagine him in bed with other women, his supple body rising and falling, his tousled hair falling over his forehead, his head arched back in deliverance. I long for him then, but it's too late . . . far too late for regrets. You and I will face a new future . . . with or without him.

I love Spain. The dusty hills stencilled against the blue sky. The lazy afternoons when the sun glistens on the red rooftops and nothing stirs except the palms swaying lazily, and the terracotta clay crumbling under the claws of a ginger cat. No cheesies and English breakfasts here, no Irish pubs with their shillelaghs and shamrocks, no karaoke bars or stumbling drunks in this quiet resort where the only language spoken is Spanish and the only tourists are the Spaniards escaping their big cities.

We are strangers among strangers and the beast at my shoulder is quiescent.

Chapter Forty-Three

Joy

'Isn't this wonderful?' Joy's mother says as they walk along the esplanade at night, the two of them in sundresses and sandals, showing off their tanned shoulders. She looks younger, prettier, and she smiles as if she really means it. 'I love the sun, don't you, Joy? Such a change from grey. I love blue. Don't you love blue too?'

Joy nods and agrees. It's easier to agree than to remind her that the sky is also blue in Ireland. Only her mother never notices when the sun shines and the turloughs sparkle like emeralds before disappearing back into their underground caves, and the Atlantic Ocean, the same ocean she sees from her Spanish bedroom window, is speckled with gold. The villa belongs to Mr Breen, Danny's father. It has white walls and a terrace with tiles and sun chairs arranged in a circle around a glass table. There is a swimming pool and steps leading up to a solarium. Today the weather is stormy, torrential rains and an overcast sky, which should prove to her mother that blue is not a given fact anywhere.

Just thinking about moving from Rockrose makes her nervous. The row downstairs is a marathon one. Her father seems to be winning, which as far as Joy is concerned means nothing. Her mother will keep on and on, the way she always encourages him to go work abroad, and in the end she will get her way. She always does. He will fly to Texas or Mexico or Japan or wherever there is oil to be found, and Joy will live with her mother in Spain.

'Susanne could sell sand to the Arabs,' Mr Breen said when he came to dinner one night. 'And snow to the Eskimos.'

And now she wants to sell Spanish apartments to Irish people who long to escape the rain.

Joy opens her laptop and emails Joey. Joey/Joy. Only an E separating them.

> *Hi Bro,*
>
> *Shit going on downstairs. What's new? How's things your end? How are Leanne and Lisa? Is Leanne still stealing your Pixies CDs? Cut her hands off . . .*

She stops writing and clamps her hands over her ears. This time her father is *really* digging in his heels. She some-times wonders what her life would be like if her parents were divorced like Lucinda Brennan's parents. Lucinda spends every second weekend in Ennis with her father and his new girlfriend. They eat takeaways and watch horror DVDs.

'It's fun,' Lucinda says. 'Better than Irish stew and *effing* homework.'

Her parents will never divorce. She asked her father once and he told her about the anger he felt when his own father left home. He does not want her to experience those bad emotions. When he was eighteen, his father tried to come back into his life again but by then they had nothing to say to each other. The next time he saw his father he was in a coffin. Definitely too late then.

288

'Some families have quantity time together and they squander it,' her father often says. 'We have quality time and that makes us appreciate that our time together is precious.'

Her mother slams the living-room door and runs up the stairs. Her bedroom door closes and the lock clicks. Just as well it's a three-bedroom villa. Unsettling to think that her parents ever had sex but even more unsettling to think of them sealed away from each other in their own private, lonely worlds.

Her mother has been locking her door since last month when Joy walked into her bedroom without knocking. Just thinking about the blood makes her sick and scared at the same time . . . Her mother gathered up the sheets from the bed, unable to hide the stains that had seeped through the white cotton onto the mattress.

'Get out of my room immediately.' Her voice was different, shrill and shaky, not calm at all, and her face was waxy white, as if all the blood that should have been in her body had drained into the bed. A new mattress was delivered that evening and the old one taken away in a skip, the rust-coloured stain jagged as a map. Six months ago Joy's first period came. She is used to it by now, the cramps and the moody feelings for a few days beforehand. It's no big deal – not like what she saw in her mother's room, as if someone had been stabbed and then stabbed again.

Later, when her mother hummed a tuneless tune and laid the table for dinner, Joy asked about the blood.

'It's the menopause,' her mother said. 'Nothing at all to worry about. It's perfectly normal for women to occasion-ally have a heavy bleed. Say nothing to your father. Do you hear me now?'

'But if you're sick—'

'What did I just tell you, Joy? I'm not *sick*. Your father

hates hearing about women's problems. All men do. I'm perfectly okay now.' She sounded fine and strong and she was as busy as ever. Only for the click of the lock Joy could have imagined the entire scene.

The rain stops. Just like that, as if someone switched off a tap and opened curtains on the sun. Joy walks out onto the balcony and watches her father diving into the pool. She should join him but she doesn't want to feel his anger bouncing off her. He swims a few lengths and emerges, grabs a towel and rubs his head vigorously. Working off his frustration. He will run now, all along the dusty roads and down to the hard-packed sand, and return covered in perspiration, his brown skin gleaming, his curly hair falling across his forehead. Her mother will draw back, as if she cannot bear the smell of male sweat, and he will pretend not to notice, except for the way the vein in his forehead moves.

If Joy is forced to live in Spain she will run away. And if she is brought back, she will run away again. What can her mother do? Lock her up like Rapunzel in a Spanish tower?
    Probably.

Chapter Forty-Four

Carla

St Vincent's Hospital

3 July 2007

Dear Carla,

I'm aware that you probably have no wish to hear from me but, nonetheless, I feel compelled to write to you. A dying man can ignore certain niceties and, as I'm now facing the great void, I claim that privilege. Knowing the date of one's imminent departure leaves one with a harrowing sense of responsibility . . . how to make amends . . . where to begin . . . and with the grim reaper scything time, a certain panic sets in. You, my dear Carla, my lovely, brief love, are to the forefront of my thoughts at this moment.

I do not expect you to visit me in hospital but if you are passing this way and feel a surge of pity, then I will be happy to see you.

Yours with deep regret,
Edward Carter.

What is it about men in pyjamas, Carla wondered, as she walked towards the ward. They looked so lost, so forlorn as they shuffled past in plaid slippers and sparked off the nurses to try and cover their dread. Edward Carter was no exception. She was shocked by his weight loss, his pale bony ankles, the vulnerability of his bald skull. Chemo was a vicious beast and Edward had suffered from its ravages. He sat on a chair beside his bed reading the *Irish Times*, his glasses low on his nose.

He had sent his letter to Leo's office for her attention. Reading it, Carla had the urge to throw it away, but Edward Carter was dying and, somehow, the brief past they had shared seemed of little consequence when weighed against this new reality he faced.

'Jesus H. Christ!' he said when he recognised her. 'It's bad enough one of us going bald.' He ran his hand over his pallid head. 'When did this happen?'

'Some years ago. I got tired of the media throwing fruit into my cage. You can call me Clare.'

'I absolutely refuse to do any such thing.'

'Have it your own way, Edward. What's all this nonsense about you dying?'

'Don't patronise me, Carla.' He removed his glasses and placed them in his dressing gown pocket. 'If you can't handle it, leave now.'

She pulled up another chair and sat beside him. 'I can handle it, Edward. What's the prognosis?'

'Two months, if I'm lucky. Prostate. They got it too late. My own fault. I ignored the danger signals. Too busy fucking up my life as usual.'

'I'm sure that's not true.'

'You know bloody well it is.' He smiled and cupped her chin. 'God, but you're still a beauty. You always filled my eyes.'

'Your eyes were *always* easily filled, Edward.'

His neck rose long and thin from the collar of his dressing gown. She had never seen him in a dressing gown, or slippers, or, come to think of it, in pyjamas. He was either impeccably dressed or naked, his body sleek and muscular, primed for pleasure.

'Wren has returned from Italy,' he said. 'She's promised to be with me at the end.'

'I'm glad, Edward.' She was surprised by his composure. She would have expected him to rage at death, defy it with fists flying until he exhaled his last breath.

'It's a funny thing, Carla. You think you want it all . . . the power and the pleasure, and when it's there to be taken you don't hesitate.' He spoke so quietly she had to lean closer to hear him. 'I took my share of it and never weighed it against the pain I caused. Then this happens and suddenly I'm staring into an abyss that's so deep I can't imagine ever reaching the bottom of it. That's the most terrifying thought, free-falling forever through my past. So I started making reparations. Nothing dramatic, just an apology here and there, and suddenly the abyss is not so deep any more, nor so dark.'

He stroked her cheek with the side of his finger. Then, almost primly, he folded his hands on his lap. 'I didn't bring much luck into your life.'

'It wasn't your fault—'

'I wanted to contact you after the story broke. But I figured it was best for both of us if I stayed away. Not that it saved either of our marriages. The past . . . Jesus . . . it's a snake in the grass. You never know when it's going to strike. Impossible to be in politics and avoid making enemies.'

'You got your own back with your diaries.'

'And lost my friends. No one likes a tattler, unless he's a journalist. Josh Baker certainly worked you over. I don't blame you going undercover.' He paused, deep in thought before speaking again. 'I keep thinking about the past, that time in London. Remember the traffic jam?'

'Yes.'

'At the last moment you begged me to take you home. I refused. In my arrogance I believed I knew what was best for you. Can you forgive me for being such an condescending shit?'

'There's nothing to forgive. I was always free to walk away and change my mind. I chose not to.'

'You've walked a long road since then.'

'Uphill, most of it.'

'But look at you. Standing straighter than ever. Do you still believe you'll find her?'

'I'm not sure any more. All I know is that she's alive.'

'Despite everything?'

'Despite everything,' she repeated. She glanced at her watch. 'I have to go, Edward.'

'So soon.'

She leaned over and kissed his cheek. He moved his head until their lips met and his thin arms held her captive. She resisted the urge to pull away from his withered mouth and the submissive smell of impending death.

Renata Carter entered the ward and stopped at his bed. She tilted her head to one side and lifted her finely arched eyebrows.

'Another reparation?' she said.

'This is Clare,' Edward said and Renata nodded, as if an understanding existed between them that had moved beyond jealousy or hate. She still wore the same bobbed hairstyle and her face, unlined and almost girlish in its softness, wore an expression of polite puzzlement. Without speaking to Carla, she opened a holdall and removed pyjamas that had been ironed and meticulously folded. She bent down to

294

place them in Edward's locker, her movements swift and decisive.

Carla left the ward and had reached the elevator before Renata came towards her. She walked with light, short steps, as if she was picking her way through stubbled grass.

'Have coffee with me,' she said. 'I think it's time we spoke.'

'I've an appointment—'

'Five minutes is all I want. Is that too much to ask . . . considering?'

'Tea or coffee?' Renata enquired when they were seated in the coffee bar.

'Neither, thank you.'

Renata pulled her chair closer to the table. 'My husband has a guilty conscience,' she said. 'I'm glad you came and eased it for him. But I was surprised when I saw you. I thought I knew them all. Then I recognised you. Carla Kelly in the flesh.'

'I'm sorry, Renata. You've no idea how much I regret—'

'Please don't insult me with an apology.' Renata flicked her fingers dismissively. 'I made a decision to forgive my husband but my forgiveness does not extend to his mistresses.'

'Then what do you want from me?'

'There were others, many others. He treated you all the same way. I endured his infidelities for my children's sake until it was no longer possible to endure any longer. You were the one who broke me. You and the cheap publicity you trailed in your wake wherever you went.'

Carla stood up and pushed back her chair. 'Go back to your husband, Renata. I've been punished enough for my stupidity without having to listen to your—'

'I never believed I'd feel sorry for you but I do.' Renata

295

continued as if there had been no interruption. 'You've paid for your so-called *stupidity* and even I will admit that your punishment far outweighed your crime. Edward believes he was a victim of politics. He's wrong, of course. There's no fury like a woman scorned and it was probably Sue Sheehan or one of the others who brought him down. Did you even know she existed? Her or any of the others? Or were you so caught up in your ego that you believed you were the only one?'

'Goodbye, Renata. I hope you feel better now. Although, somehow, I doubt it.'

Edward Carter was wrong about snakes in the grass, Carla thought, as she hurried from the hospital. The past was a bird-wife with fury in her eyes. And when she struck with her killer beak, the venom sank deep.

Chapter Forty-Five

Susanne

I don't think it's very professional to have a discussion about blood tests in the middle of the bakery section but Una Williamson stopped me in Costcutters today. She'd received my letter explaining why I could no longer be her bridge partner but she was not content to leave it at that. She asked why the results from my gynaecologist had not been forwarded to her.

I said I'd contact him and see why there was such a delay. 'Thankfully, all the tests were clear,' I told her. 'The treatment he recommended has been successful and the matter we discussed is now regulated.'

She has steely eyes. Does she suspect? How can she?

'You've lost weight,' she said. 'Have you been dieting?'

'I'm so busy,' I said. 'Skipping lunch. Things will quieten down as soon as I settle in Spain. You must come and stay with us. A break in the sun is just what should be ordered for the doctor.'

She smiled politely at my attempt at humour and muttered something non-committal, moved her trolley aside to let me pass. I could feel her eyes still watching me when I turned the corner. You were sulking in the make-up section, sampling the lipsticks, your hand covered in slashes of peach and pink. You've been moping since David accepted the Arizona contract. It's probably the reason you turned on me. I saw hatred in your eyes; it scared me, then drove me to anger. What is so bad about moving to Spain? You'll make new friends. It will be a mind-broadening experience. Danny Breen will be flying over regularly with his father, and you can invite Lucinda for holidays.

The row started as soon as we got into the car. What a cruel tongue you have when you don't get your own way. I know what's best for you but you rail against me . . . as he does . . . and Miriam too. She had the audacity to suggest you stay here with her while I set up the Spanish office. You're my daughter. How dare she? I can't wait to leave this place. Just knowing I can escape has made it even more unendurable. Two weeks and we'll be there.

It's late now. Even the whisperers are silent. I looked through the album tonight. It is my record of your existence. The record of my reality as I have shaped it. I added the last photos we took in Spain. How content we all look. Our lips flinging smiles at the camera.

Then I turned to the beginning . . . to when it all began. The years called out to me. The heartache and disappointment . . . the whisper of what might have been. In the end I closed the album and turned to my Judgement Book, where one day we will all be judged according to our works.

Chapter Forty-Six

Carla

She finished reading the manuscript and stacked the pages together. At least this memoir had a happy ending. She had become fond of endings with redemption. The clock chimed seven. Frank would be arriving in an hour. Time to switch on the oven. Before leaving her office, she opened the www.FindIsobelGardner.com website. All the features and news items, all the audio and visual material relating to Isobel's disappearance were linked to the archival pages. She found it impossible to read through the contents, clicking instead on the contact page at the end of each day. Occasionally, she found emails from students requesting interviews they hoped to include in their theses. Journalists and documentary makers also emailed her but she remained steadfast in her refusal to give personal interviews or quotes. The internet was the shield that protected her and she had no intention of allowing it to be breached.

Only one email this evening. Miranda May again. Carla sighed and debated sending it directly to her spam folder, but, as usual, curiosity got the better of her. Over the years she had received letters and, latterly, emails from Miranda. They were usually variations of the same message: look for your daughter in a place of stone.

Once, after seeing Miranda's advertisement for psychic readings in the classified section of a newspaper, Carla had visited her. She entered a small roadside cottage that smelled overpoweringly of turf smoke and incense. Miranda's ears and throat had glittered with cheap jewellery. Bangles jangled on each arm, and her rings flashed each time she moved her hands. Her hair, which looked as if it had not been touched since it was combed into a fifties beehive, was studded with diamanté combs.

'It's tat,' she confided to Carla. 'But I like to shine and when you get to my great age your options are limited.' She lifted Carla's hands and glanced at her palms. 'You, on the other hand, with all your options, are a shadow. A ghost.'

As assessments went, Carla was impressed. Miranda released her hands and swayed forward, as if buried under the weight of prediction. 'You love a man who keeps your bed warm,' she said. 'You love him with your mind and your body. But not here.' She straightened and pressed her hand to her chest. 'You do not love him with your heart and you never will.'

Tonight, Miranda's email was more cryptic than usual and had a strong biblical overtone.

Dear Carla,
    Your faith will be rewarded. Your daughter resides in a place of stone but she is still out of reach. Be brave. The largest boulder is being rolled aside. Deliverance will soon be at hand.
    Your faithful friend,
    Miranda May.

Definitely, Carla decided, as she switched off the computer, Miranda deserved to be classified as spam but somehow she always remained in the inbox.

Chapter Forty-Seven

Joy
Fourteen Years Later

Rockrose is silent as the sun rises above the Burren and the hoary rockrose mats the limestone with yellow petals. The aspen leaves shiver and the skeletal cottage, twisted in bindweed, peers through the pearly light. All is silent yet Joy's body quivers. She has awoken for a reason. A sound crashed through her dreams. She leaves her bed and opens her door, hesitates, then, gripped by fear, runs to her mother's bedroom and bangs on the door. She calls her name repeatedly until she hears a whimper. The frail sound terrifies her because she knows her mother is calling for help and beyond the locked door there is blood everywhere.

'Turn left at Dowling's Meadow and drive to the end of the lane,' she shouts into the phone, unable to understand how she can speak so clearly when all around her the world is screaming. The ambulance is already on its way. She runs towards the door and kicks at it the way they do on television, all those cops splintering wood, but the door does not budge. Splotch, barking uncontrollably, runs back and forth across the landing.

Yesterday they had a row over Spain and Joy's refusal to move there. She crashes her shoulder against the door and remembers each careless word she flung at her mother.

Anger races like fever through her when she rings her father and gets his answering machine. She hates him for being on the other side of the world when she needs him here, now, this instant, forcing her mother's bedroom door open with his big strong shoulders. She phones Miriam and huddles on the landing until she hears the ambulance. Miriam comes running behind the paramedics, taking the stairs two at a time, dragging Joy into her arms. Her grandmother's eyes are still crusted with sleep but she tries to smile, tries to pretend that everything will be all right.

Nikki is the ambulance driver. She looks different in her luminous jacket and boots, not like on the beach in her wetsuit, surfing beside Dylan. She blocks Joy from entering the room but Joy sees everything before she closes the door. It is as she feared. She waits outside with her grandmother until the door opens and her mother is carried out on a stretcher.

'I'm sorry . . . sorry . . . sorry . . . it's my fault. I didn't mean what I said.' Joy walks beside the stretcher, not feeling any pain as her mother's grip on her hand tightens and she can't stop saying *sorry . . . sorry . . . sorry . . .* until Nikki tells her she needs to be calm and give her mother strength.

In the ambulance her mother's eyes glisten, bright as sapphires. She grasps Joy's hand, holding on to something familiar, drawing her nearer, whispering all the time, the words garbled . . .

Anticipating . . . see my dead babies and the blind stallion trampling my dreams . . . and the truth written in blood . . . in the book . . . in the blood . . . the book . . . the blood . . .

'It will all work out . . . it will . . . it *will*,' says Nikki. She presses her foot on the accelerator and sounds the siren. Time is precious, passing through a sieve, each grain matters.

Chapter Forty-Eight

Susanne

Life is a fleeting glance . . . moments flickering on the reel of memories . . . press forward and another comes . . . sepia tinges lightening . . . and the paramedic says, 'On a scale of one to ten, how would you rate your pain?'

I tell you about the blind stallion but you don't hear and the paramedic asks again, his voice cutting through my terror, forcing me to concentrate. On a scale of one to ten – 'Ten . . . ten . . .' I hit the word off my teeth and the driver, breaking through traffic lights, says, 'Not to worry, we're nearly there . . . nearly there.'

Dylan's wife . . . I can't think of her name . . . it doesn't matter . . . names mean nothing . . . except that name . . . I must say it . . . must . . . it terrifies me, this weakness that came on me when I awoke and tried to reach you . . . clutching the edge of the dressing table . . . further than I realised and I pitched forward . . . forcing my voice through the silence to summon you, as once you summoned me to your side . . . my footsteps soft as we fled together into our future . . . the rain falling silent . . . seeping . . . seeping . . . slipping through the mist that comes and goes before my eyes . . . control . . . control . . . I must keep control . . . you are weeping, apologising,

begging forgiveness for words neither of us can remember ...
the Judgement Book ... you must find it ... you shake your
head and apologise again ... unaware that it was my wailing
wall, my deep depthless well where secrets moulder ... the siren
is a requiem ... I left it too late ... Dr Williamson warned me
... hospital lights ... I grip your hand and pull you nearer ...
the cottage ... dead babies ... the blind stallion ... you say,
don't talk, your voice a scared whisper as hands lift me ...
hurry me ... the ceiling swaying ... voices shouting ... your
arms outstretched, and Miriam too ... masking her fear but
it burns her eyes ... faces behind masks ... real masks ... a
needle pinching my hand and the light above me is butter ...
a blob of melting butter ... and I melt with it ... into a dark
space where they remove my womb ... such a small cocoon to
have caused so much heartache ... and now ... this final act
of betrayal ... but what does it matter ... I sink deep, deeper
until the light shines again and voices call my name ...

Susanne ... Susanne ... Mammy ... Mammy ... how
long have I been sleeping ... why are you crying ... your head
bent ... and Miriam's arms tight around you ... David
running ... why is he here ... his face above mine ... his
breath fast as the wind when it rushes through the sycamores
... stay, stay, he cries, his hand hard as a rope pulling me back
but he has long since lost the power to woo me ... life is a
fleeting glance ... I see your long legs dangling over the sofa
... giggling phone conversations with friends ... David leaving
... returning ... Dowling's Meadow at sunrise ... a gaunt
castle ... a child falling ... the whispering ivy tangling my hair
as I bend over an open wound ... a bed of bluebells and forget-
me-nots ... and the blind stallion waits ... impatient ...

Voices talk about transfusions ... I do not want a stranger's
blood in my veins ... even your blood, which you have given
generously ... knowing it takes priority over all blood groups ...

*and the truth will be revealed . . . it is written in our blood . . .
in the book . . . and the reel of memories flicker . . . sepia tinges
. . . my limbs entwined . . . David . . . Richard . . . Edward . . .
faceless boys . . . my nails red as sin . . . you beg me to stay . . .
beg my forgiveness . . . why do you beg when it is I who must
beg and be absolved . . . the stallion paws the earth . . . ready
to carry me on his broad fierce back . . . carry me towards the
silver lining of the sky . . . while you . . . with your bog-brown
eyes that belong to her . . . you draw me back towards pain . . .
pain of the soul . . . and the past is so close I can touch the
flickering moments . . . the blind stallion tosses his mane . . .
your voice is thick and scared because you know I am letting
you go . . . setting you free at last . . . my mother beckons . . .
serene Nina . . . no bitter lines . . . no bitter gall to drink . . .
her mouth generous with smiles . . . and hiding behind her long
yellow skirt I see them . . . my slender whispering children . . .
my hair, my eyes . . . they call me through a path of moonlight
. . . high above the grey pull of the Burren . . . but there is one
last face that binds me still . . . her eyes, deep as the bogs that
preserve their secrets . . . pleading . . . always pleading . . .
where is my child . . . give me back my daughter . . . but she is
trailing behind me now . . . fainter . . . fainter . . . and I am
beyond that flash, that instant when all of life is revealed and
abandoned . . . a shell . . . an empty womb . . . what is done is
done . . .*

Chapter Forty-Nine

Joy

For three days her mother struggles to live and, when she dies, the nurses transform the small ward into a mortuary. They lay her out in her nicest dress and light candles. Impossible to believe she's dead. When Joy blinks and looks again, she believes she can see her mother's chest rising and falling. Her face has collapsed into softness, the way it had in Spain, as if her skin has been released from invisible clasps. She should have looked like that all the time. Such rows over the Spanish office and her father being so stubborn, refusing to listen. He must feel the same way because when he weeps the sound crashes against the silence surrounding her mother and Joy expects her to open her eyes and say, 'Get a grip, David.' But she is beyond them by then, separated by a breath.

Joy wants to hit her father. He should have made her mother happy. He should not have left her all alone so that when she fell Joy was unable to save her. Her anger is too deep to be contained. She shoves him away when he tries to hold her and runs from the ward, her footsteps clattering along the corridor, her heartbeat pounding in her ears.

'Joy!' She stops and looks up at the man standing in front of her. 'I'm so sorry, Joy. I came as soon as Nikki phoned.'

Dylan always sounds calm, even now, and she wants him to stroke away her terror, the way he soothed Splotch on the road that time.

'I need to let Splotch out,' she sobs against him. 'I have to go home to Splotch.'

Why does she keep thinking about her dog when her mother is dead and it's all her fault? Dylan leads her to a chair, he must be used to people crying all the time in his clinic, pouring out all their sorrows, knowing he will understand what it's like to be lost in the middle of nowhere.

When they return to Rockrose from the hospital, the neighbours have gathered in the kitchen. The women have made sandwiches, plates and plates of sandwiches and cake and scones, and her father pours whiskey and Guinness for everyone. All the talk is about her mother ... what a loss she will be to Maoltrán, and Fr Davis – who drove to Rockrose once a week to share a bottle of wine and a beef stroganoff with her mother and her various committees – says, 'We must pray together so that our dearly departed sister will rest peacefully in the arms of our Lord Jesus.'

Joy wants to laugh out loud at the idea of her mother resting anywhere. Laughter seems better than crying, or throwing up, but Fr Davis won't understand that if she cries she will never be able to stop. She keeps her hands in front of her face when he decides to say a glorious decade of the rosary. Why not sorrowful, she wants to shout. Nothing glorious about death. She laughs silently when everyone stops eating and drinking and bows their heads to pray. Her shoulders twitch and the tears run so fast into her mouth she tastes salt.

She sleeps that night with Miriam, awakens and sleeps again. Each time her grandmother is watching over her. 'Hush hush, my little cabbage. Rest now. You're safe in my arms.'

She says, 'Don't be troubling your head with such foolish thoughts,' when Joy tells her about all the times she stormed off to bed in a huff over things so stupid she can't even remember what they were . . . And it doesn't matter any more . . . they will never be important again.

Chapter Fifty

Carla

Robert had proposed to her in the curve of a Tuscany valley. They sat outside a small Italian restaurant, sharing a bottle of Chianti. The purple evening settled around them and the cicadas, tired from their serenading, gradually fell silent. Into this silence he asked Carla to marry him and she accepted on the same exchange of breath.

When Frank proposed, they were in the middle of an argument as to whether or not he should publish a celebrity kiss-and-tell memoir. Carla had glanced through the opening chapters and let the pages slide to the floor. The story, written by a rock singer who hoped to save his waning career with his lurid revelations, was testosterone-laden and turgid. But Frank, aware that he would sell more copies of this particular memoir than all his hard-hitting exposés put together, was anxious to agree a publishing deal.

'It's absolute junk,' said Carla. 'I'm not going to work on it, so you can find yourself another ghostwriter. In fact, you can find yourself another full-time ghost because I'm sick of writing other people's stories. But at least they were worth writing. Not like this piece of self-regarding *rubbish*.'

'Since when did you become so self-righteous?' Frank

demanded. 'You were part and parcel of the celebrity culture once.'

'Yes . . . and it broke me.'

'No, it didn't. You were never broken, Carla.'

'You're wrong. I broke when Anita died. That's why I live like this.' She ran her hands distractedly through her short hair and spiked it upwards. 'Do you know what I've been doing lately? Putting myself in the way of people I used to know. It's like a sick game I play. I don't want to be recognised yet, at some crazy level, I'm hoping they will see through this face and call me Carla.'

'If they did, how would you feel?' He picked up the scattered manuscript and slipped it into his briefcase.

'Alive again, I expect.'

'*Alive?*' He stared down at her. 'So am I to understand I'm in love with a corpse?'

'Don't be ridiculous. You know that's not what I mean.'

'Then what do you mean? Are you going through the motions of being *alive* when I make love to you? Are you *alive* and listening when I tell you I love you? We've been together seven years now so I should have noticed I was living within the pall of the grave. I don't give my heart away lightly, Carla. When I do, it would be reassuring to know it's in safe hands, not in a dead-claw grasp.'

His complexion had deepened as he spoke, flushing high spots of colour into his cheeks. She was used to his outbursts and allowed his anger to run through her. That was the advantage of being a ghost.

'Trust you to play semantics with a word, Frank.' Her voice was mild when he paused for breath. 'Would you feel better if I used the word "affirmed"? It's difficult living in another skin. I know . . . I know . . .' She shook her head, warding off his retort. 'It's my choice and I must accept the consequences. It's just . . . occasionally . . .'

'You'd like to be a celebrity again?'

'No, Frank. Occasionally, I'd like to feel I was living a normal existence. Like Robert with his two sons.'

'Then move on with me.' His indignation forgotten, he stood up and drew her to her feet. 'Marry me, Carla. We could have a baby, maybe two . . . or none, if that's what you'd prefer. What do you say?'

'Why on earth do you want to change anything between us?' She was unable to hide her astonishment. 'You've told me often enough you've no interest in marriage.'

'I haven't been *that* definite.'

'You certainly have. You said you were genetically programmed to remain single and change the world by the might of the pen.'

'I talk a lot of horseshit, Carla, as you well know. I'm in love with you. I'd like to marry you, if you'll consider my proposal. I should have gone for violins and roses, not shooting from the hip like this . . . but it comes down to the same answer in the end. Yes or no?'

She imagined waking up every morning beside him, turning to kiss him last thing at night. Perhaps he was right and they could have a child. At thirty-nine, there was still time but the thought brought her no joy. They would grow old together, send invisible signals to each other, as her parents did, learn tolerance, patience, understanding. Just thinking about it made her exhausted.

'We've everything we need in our relationship as it is,' she said. 'And we have our independence. You'd hate sharing a home with me. You're always on at me for living in a pigsty—'

'Steady on, Carla. I occasionally comment on your untidiness. But that's part of your charm.'

'Charm quickly fades when you live cheek by jowl with its flaws,' she said. 'Forget marriage, Frank. We don't need it.'

'What if I do?'

His face set stubbornly as she continued to argue. Leo had been right when he warned her that Frank Staunton would always put his own needs first. Now that he had decided he wanted marriage, he would give her no quarter until she made a decision.

'I can't deal with this at the moment,' she protested. 'It's too sudden.'

'You don't *deal* with a proposal of marriage, Carla,' he replied. 'You either accept or reject it.'

'Or you take time to consider it,' she retorted. 'If you want a genuine answer from me, you must give me that space.'

He nodded, his features relaxing. 'You're right. I'm too impatient when I make up my mind about momentous decisions. Come to me when you're ready and let me know your answer. But if you say yes, I need to know if it's Clare Frazier or Carla Kelly who's accepting me.'

'Which one would you like to marry?' she asked.

He answered without hesitation. 'The one who will love me most.'

Chapter Fifty-One

Joy

On the Colorado River, Joy's father steers the speedboat between the canyon walls. Pillars, minarets and colossal cliffs soar above them. Joy feels terrifyingly insignificant as their small craft shudders in the backwash from other boats.

'Vishnu schist is one of the oldest layers of exposed rock known to man,' he says. He does not look in the least bit fazed by his towering surroundings. 'No one knows its origins but geologists reckon it's over one thousand, seven hundred million years old.'

The rock, gleaming like a wall of dark chocolate, looks far too cracked and raddled to be the basement structure for the Grand Canyon. As her father steers around the pinhead bends, Joy grips her seat, terrified they will be washed overboard and disappear forever. Sometimes he slows to gaze upon the eroding rock face and describe the strata of the earth's skin, but she is unable to relax until they are back again on the open plain of the Colorado River. Then he releases the throttle and laughs. He throws back his head. The wind whips her hair and flings it like a banner behind her. She has been growing it for nine months. Soon it will reach her shoulders.

In Arizona, everywhere she looks, there are rocks. Not like the rocks of the Burren but enormous, aloof boulders bulging from the landscape. They appear to be balanced on their toes, tilting so precariously she can imagine them tumbling over when the breeze stirs across the desert earth. Not that the breeze stirs very often. She has never known such heat, but at night, when the hot desert air finally cools, they sit on the veranda, or sometimes soak in the hot tub, and gaze up at the stars. She listens to him making plans and waits for him to mention her mother's name but he never does; nor does she. She'd like to ask him how he really feels. Is he relieved that her mother is no longer going on about Spain and the oil fields and locking her door so that no one would know she was dying? If Joy asks, he will tell her the truth, as he always does. But she's not yet ready to ask such questions. Not until she understands how she feels about this hole that has opened up in her life.

'Change direction,' are words he regularly uses. He cheered and shot his fist in the air when Miriam rang to tell him planning permission to build the hostel had been granted. He has done enough travelling. This is his last contract. Joy is glad she decided to come with him instead of staying with her grandmother, who has moved back into Rockrose to be with them when they return home

Not that she can forget what happened, but in such a strange empty landscape it is possible to escape. The desert seems too barren to hold seeds, yet it sprouts with blood-red claret cup and scarlet gillia, carpets of verbena and poppies, prickly posies; everything is prickly here and, when the sun sets, the land turns to blood, a sudden haemorrhage that paints the truncated limbs of the tall saguaros and the brittlebush. Then it is gone. A heartbeat is all it takes for darkness to fall and quench the flame.

She has made friends with three girls in high school. They have the whitest, most perfect teeth she has ever seen. She hangs out with them by their swimming pools and in the shopping mall where they have their nails painted and sip cappuccinos. They talk about their families, the complicated labyrinth of half-sisters and half-brothers. She has told them about Joey and Miriam. She never mentions her mother since the night Hannah cut her off in mid-sentence and said, 'Let's change the subject. Life's too short to dwell on tragedy.'

Hannah's mother has a house like a ranch and runs a vegetarian restaurant. She feeds Joy tofu scramble and black bean *chilaquiles*, and makes batwing eyes at her father when he collects Joy in his four-wheel drive. He looks younger these days. She suspects he would like to sit longer over the *papadzules* that Hannah's mother serves him, but he always thanks her and leaves as soon as he finishes eating.

She drinks tequila one night when Hannah's mother is out. Egged on by the girls, she rings Joey and puts the call on conference. He hears them giggling because he hangs up while she is in the middle of speaking to him. He doesn't email her for a while afterwards. When he does, it's a real big brother lecture about underage drinking. It makes her so angry she vows she will never contact him again but he keeps popping into her mind at the most unexpected moments, especially when he finishes art college and goes to Ireland to work in Miriam's studio. He's staying in Rockrose for six months then moving to Italy to continue his training with a famous glass designer. He surfs with Dylan in Lahinch and Doolin, and emails the photos to her. Hannah and the others pretend to swoon when they see them. He was a boy when Joy saw him last, all elbows and big feet and a wide, cocky grin. He's different now, more serious and sleek, like a panther. Joy has to agree with her friends. Her half-brother is the most handsome man she has ever seen. But that doesn't mean he has the right to treat her like a kid.

'There's an email from Joey on the laptop if you want to read it,' her father says when they return from the boat trip. 'He'll still be in Ireland when we return home. We should have a party before he leaves for Italy. What do you think?'

She shrugs. 'As long as he stays out of my hair.'

'Don't tell me you're going to get a lip about Joey. What did he do to annoy you?'

'He thinks he can boss me around.'

'The nerve of him.' Her father laughs and opens his laptop, clicks into the email. 'I think it's about time we had some dancing in Rockrose, don't you?'

Chapter Fifty-Two

Joy

Miriam and Joey are waiting to welcome them home. The house looks different, not so tidy any more. It even smells different, a warm smell, which is ridiculous because *warm* doesn't have a smell, yet that's the only way Joy can describe it.

Soon she doesn't notice it any more. She's settled back into the house and pulled it around her again. She's forgiven Joey for being such a pain over her drinking but the pleasure she feels in his company is mingled with guilt, knowing her mother would never allow him to stretch out on the armchairs or sleep in the spare bedroom or to stand at the Aga and toss pancakes in the air. He flicks batter at her and she does the same to him until they are splattered and there is no one to yell, 'Stop . . . *stop* . . .'

Everything they do together would be impossible if her mother was alive. Perhaps that is why his simplest gestures, like holding her hand as he helps her down from the rocks, or ruffling her hair, or accidentally touching her hand when he steadies her surfboard, seem wedged in her mind.

They confide in each other. She lies on the sofa and dangles her bare legs over the arm while he sprawls with his back against the side. If she moves her toe, she can touch his hair. It's springy on the crown, standing like a question mark. When she dips her toe, she does it so fast he never notices. The sensation of his hair against her skin is like a feather flicking the pit of her stomach. He talks about his stepfather, who kept going on and on at him about finding a proper job when he graduated from art college instead of 'gadding around Europe like a ponce' and got jealous every time Joey's mother tried to defend him. And all the time, Joy's toe is as light as air, stroking, stroking.

She tells him about the noises she keeps hearing in her head. The smash of bottles and jars falling to the floor. The strange whimpering cry that sent her crashing against her mother's door.

'You can't blame yourself,' Joey says. 'It wasn't your fault. I doubt if even I could have broken that lock.'

Looking at his shoulders, she knows he could have smashed it open with one heave.

Rockrose is full of people, Dowling's Meadow full of cars. Miriam and Phyllis have baked and roasted, prepared salads, sliced hams and turkeys, dressed a wild salmon, all to celebrate their arrival home and Joey's departure.

'Just like old times,' Miriam says. 'Whiskey and Guinness, music, dance and song.'

As if to make up for the long absence, people dance harder, laugh louder, sing sweeter, and the musicians, sweat pouring down their faces, play with a wilder than usual abandonment. Joy is unable to imagine her mother anywhere, not in the kitchen, which is laden with food and bottles and a Guinness keg, not in the living room. Not even in the conservatory where she used to sit in the evening to watch the sun setting. No one mentions her name. She might never have existed.

Nikki and Dylan arrive with their children. 'Well, would

ya take a look at yer one,' says Dylan, exaggerating his Dublin accent and holding her at arm's length. 'Isn't she the bee's knees with her fancy new hairstyle and them high heels? Ya'd never take her for a boy now, so ya wouldn't.'

'I never mistook her for a boy at any time, you blind old bat,' says Nikki, nudging him out of the way and hugging Joy. 'You beautiful girl,' she whispers. 'Welcome home.'

Joy *feels* beautiful. She swishes her long hair. It settles like silk on her bare shoulders. It was a relief to let it grow and not to have to meet the searching gaze that had followed her all her life, the disappointment flickering deep in her mother's pale blue eyes. An eternal quest that nothing Joy did was capable of satisfying. She had never been so aware of her mother's disappointment until it was no longer visible.

Joey grabs her hands. 'Come on, sis. It's time to dance.'

He is as agile on the floor as he is on a surfboard. She spins in his arms, faster, faster, until she is dizzy and collapses against him, hot and breathless, laughing, and he spins her again and again, not allowing her to relax until the dance is over and Imelda Morris claims him.

When Dylan dances with her he stamps all over her feet. 'Born with two left ones,' he says. 'A terrible curse altogether. Don't know how Nikki puts up with me. When are you and Joey going to call over and see us?'

'Soon.' She waves as Nikki dances past, her cheeks red, her head jerking as Mitch Moran swings her into a star pattern.

The floor vibrates, crash, stamp, thump. Old women with stiffly waved hair and floral dresses waltz around with the same ease as the strutting young men who stamp the floor and swirl their partners through each intricate movement. She walks outside with Joey. The stars punch the sky, so bright they dazzle her when she looks upwards. Joey leans against the wall and rolls a cigarette.

'You must miss her a lot.' He dips right into her thoughts and the guilt comes back because this is a wonderful party, one they would never have had if her mother was alive and Joy is glad . . . glad . . . glad that Joey is here, standing with his shoulder touching her shoulder, the roll-up between his teeth, the tip sparking the darkness.

Without replying, she leaves him and runs upstairs. In her mother's bedroom, she searches through the dressing table for perfume. She wants to sprinkle it on the walls and floor, on the new bed and the bedclothes that have replaced the sheets and counterpane. She wonders if Miriam burned the ones that wrapped her mother when the haemorrhage began. She does not want to remember that morning but, no matter how hard she tries, she can't stop thinking . . . thinking.

The drawers are empty. She lies on the bed and buries her face in the pillow, seeking her mother's scent, but she smells only newness – a change of direction, closure. She begins to weep. Tears will destroy her face but the relief they bring swells inside her. She does not hear the door open or Joey's footsteps on the floorboards.

'I figured you'd be here,' he says.

'I've haven't cried since the night she died.' The pillows muffle her voice and the mattress moves when he sits down on the edge of the bed. He puts his hand on the back of her head and strokes her hair. She sobs louder. Why is she crying so violently? Is it because she misses her mother or because she is freed from her unending expectation of love? *Hug me . . . kiss me . . . love me . . .*

Joey emerges from the *en suite* with a handful of tissue. 'Come here,' he says. 'Let me wipe away those tears.'

She sits up and hugs her knees. 'I must look a sight.'

'You'll be fine.' He dabs her cheeks, wipes her eyes. When

he is unable to remove the mascara smudges he wets the tissue with his saliva and rubs again. He pushes aside her fringe and touches the scar on her forehead. She jerks her head back, her skin flaring at his touch. The tassel on the window blind raps against the glass and his fingers shiver suddenly. She wants him to move closer. To kiss her on her lips and open her mouth with his tongue. She is shocked by the longing that opens like a warm wound inside her, pain and pleasure oozing from a dangerous core. What would her mother think if she knew? Joy imagines her shame, her disgust, but still she cannot stop . . . if he kisses her she will kiss him back, the way she kissed Hannah's brother one night, kissed him until her lips were sore, and she is seized again by that same clamping excitement. She giggles, hating the sound but unable to stop until the words in her head become audible.

'I don't miss her eyes,' she says. 'They never left me alone. Even now, I feel her watching me, judging me.'

'Why should she judge you?' He sounds puzzled.

'I never knew. That's the problem. She died without telling me.'

They can no longer ignore the noise from downstairs. This is supposed to be a party and she is monopolising him with her moods when they should be downstairs mingling with the others.

'That phone call . . .' She covers her face, cringing. 'It was *so* stupid. I was drunk and lonesome and all over the place . . . oh my *God* . . . what a hangover. Those Arizonian girls sure know how to drink their liquor.' She mimics Hannah's accent and he tells her to cut it out, shakes her shoulder, amused or angry, she doesn't know. He moves away from her and stands beside the window.

'Like I said, kiddo, you shouldn't be drinking at your age.'

'Who are you to tell me what to do?'

325

'I'm your brother.'

'Half-brother.'

'Same difference. I think you should talk to Dylan.'

'*Dylan?*'

'Yeah. He understands things.'

'Like what things?'

'Like your mother being dead and how you feel about her.'

'I don't need a counsellor.'

'He's a friend.'

'He's a fucking counsellor and you're telling me I'm a basket case just 'cause I said some shit when I was off my head. Go to hell, Joey, and mind your own business.'

He grabs her arm to prevent her walking from the room. She turns into him until suddenly there is nothing between them except the hard pressure of his body. But she must have imagined the sensation because he shoves her back and says, 'Okay . . . okay . . . let's forget this conversation ever took place. I was just trying to help. I'm worried about you.'

'No one's asking you to worry.'

'I don't need to be asked, Joy. I care about you. Is that so difficult to understand?'

He is in her dreams that night, tall and suntanned, astride a surfboard, crashing ashore. She is on the sand waiting, knowing she will be knocked asunder by the advancing wave. Joey/Joy. Separated only by an E.

Chapter Fifty-Three

Joy

Dylan looks different. Not like a parent or a windsurfer, which is the way Joy always perceives him. She tries to imagine him as a drug addict, sleeping rough. Impossible. A certificate hangs on the wall before her and others are displayed around his office. Is this an office or a clinic or a nuthouse? From the outside it looks like an ordinary stone cottage with apple trees in the garden and herbs in window boxes. This is their third session. He is dealing with what he calls her 'reckless behaviour' which means her drinking, and her 'unresolved grief' – namely sleeplessness and a tendency to weep for no apparent reason.

Her father was furious when he discovered she had been drinking in Molloy's. No one asked for ID and it was cool being part of the gang and laughing until her sides ached. Danny Breen dropped her off at the top of the lane. She insisted she was okay, no need to drive her down, and Danny took her at her word. His father had bought him a Boxster for his eighteenth birthday and he was frightened the police would pick him up for drink-driving or speeding, or both. She never made it to Rockrose. Her father found her outside the cottage but she has no memory of collapsing. She is barred from going near Molloy's until she is over eighteen and her father has threatened to report Jimmy Molloy if he ever again serves underage drinkers.

Afterwards, she was so sick it seemed impossible to imagine ever doing anything so foolish. But she did, and only a week later, six of them hanging out in the long grass in Dowling's Meadow. Danny bought the cider in Molloy's off-licence and they would have been safe from discovery if he hadn't wanted to show off the stereo sound on his new Boxster. When he turned up the volume, the Children of Bodom blasted her ears and it felt good, the grating hate songs. Pity it didn't dawn on any of them that the sound could probably be heard in the next county. It was certainly heard in Rockrose and her father looked as if he wanted to take a lump hammer to Danny's new car. She didn't make it to the bathroom on time and threw up on the landing. Then she sent the email to Joey. Just thinking about it still brings her out in goosebumps.

'How was your week?' Dylan interrupts her thoughts.

'Boring.'

'Tell me about it.'

'What's to tell about boring? I got up, did stuff, went to bed.'

'Stuff?'

She shrinks deeper into the chair and uncrosses her feet. 'School, homework . . . emails. Like I said, boring.'

'You sent boring emails?'

'I suppose . . . can you think of a better way to pass the time in this one-horse town?'

'You tell me.'

'Apart from drinking, I mean.'

'How's that going?'

328

'Well, it's not, obviously. Isn't that why I'm here?'

'That's the reason you gave me. But is it why you are here?'

'You tell me.'

She hates it when he allows the minutes to elapse without either of them speaking. It never seems to bother him but the silence itches against her mind and she finds herself saying stupid things just to break it.

Pens and an envelope opener sit in a jade-coloured holder on the desk. She studies the blade of the envelope opener. Letters are definitely safer. They need to be folded and placed in envelopes, addressed and stamped. Even if she changes her mind after the letter is posted, Mildred in the post office will allow her to remove it before it is taken on the next stage of its journey. But not with email. That is an instant communication.

She had written the email on the night her father marched her home from Dowling's Meadow. Alone in her room, his voice still ringing through her head, she wrote to Joey. The following morning she had no memory of what she wrote and almost threw up again when she discovered it in the sent mail folder.

Darling Joey . . . do you know that only one letter separates us? Joey/Joy. E is for eager and I am eager to see you again. E is for escape and I want to escape into your arms . . . I miss you so much since you left . . . I hate Italy for taking you away from me. I miss you . . . miss you . . .

She had immediately sent Joey another one and excused the first on the grounds that she had been delirious with drink. His reply was cold and distant.

Joy, I'm worried about your drinking. You're only fifteen and have no idea of the damage it's doing to your organs.

*I understand why you want to escape from the shock of
your mother's death but drinking and hanging out with
that Breen creep is not going to help. I've deleted your last
email on the grounds that you were, as you wrote,
'delirious with drink'.*

*I'm extremely busy at present and will email again
when I've time. Please remember what I said. Dylan has
been through his own horrors and will understand.*

Joey.

She had called Dylan that afternoon to arrange her first
appointment.

He sits so still she wonders if he's still breathing. She studies
the photograph on his desk of Nikki and his two children.

'I don't know why everyone is so worried about my
drinking,' she says. 'It only happened a few times but
everyone's going on as if I'm on the fast track to skid row.'

'Who's everyone?'

'What?'

'You said everyone's worried. Who exactly do you mean?'

'Well, my dad and grandmother . . . Joey as well.'

'How is Joey?'

She shrugs. 'How should I know?'

'You don't keep in touch?'

'Hardly ever.'

'Yet you believe he's worried about your drinking?'

'That's 'cause I do stupid things . . .' She stops and sucks
in her breath. 'My mother never liked him.'

'Have you any idea why?'

'She blamed him for this.' She pulls back her fringe, runs
her finger over the fine white ridge. At night when she is
unable to sleep, she touches it. An almost invisible scar, yet it

is as familiar to her as the rest of her body. 'She wanted me to blame Joey but I refused. I disappointed her . . . as usual.'

'As usual?'

'It's difficult to continually disappoint someone but I managed it.'

'How, in particular, did you disappoint her?'

She wonders how much longer she will have to sit here making idle conversation. 'By being me, I suppose. She wanted a blue-eyed baby for starters.'

She is surprised by the tightly coiled memory that springs from nowhere. Years since she thought about it . . . lying in bed with her mother, eye to eye, arms around each other, and her mother had sighed, 'If only you had blue eyes. Then you would be perfect.'

What age was she – two, three years old? And was it said once or many times? Why is the memory so sharp, as crystal clear as the feeling it evoked? The longing when she looked in the mirror that her eyes would change, lighten, be as beautiful as her mother wished them to be. But they always stayed the same muddy colour and her mother would look away, press her lips tightly together in disappointment.

It's easier to talk about her mother than to discuss Joey. The words come easy. She remembers the quiet years, the silence and the solitude that settled over Rockrose when her father left. The silence she had needed to break by screaming and flailing against her mother, and how, when she was left alone in her room, she would cry herself back to silence.

Home-schooling, the only way to go. 'I know what's best for you,' her mother had said. 'A mother always knows what's best.'

'But I want to go to real school. I don't want to be here all the time with you.' She did not mean to say the words aloud and her mother smacked her legs for being bold again. Joy had cried softly after her mother left the room but she must have heard because she came back and rocked her . . . rocked her . . . *Hug me . . . kiss me . . . love me . . .*

Dylan's face is impassive. He looks almost nondescript in his grey jumper and trousers, but perhaps that is a deliberate attempt to make himself invisible so that people's emotions can flow like a rip tide over him.

'She used to write things down in a book when I was a child. She called it her Judgement Book. Every time I did something wrong she'd record it so that God could see it and use the information on Judgement Day. It frightened me so much . . . every time I saw her writing, knowing I'd disappointed her again. How could she . . .' She breaks off, sobbing now, and Dylan waits for her to continue. She believes he will wait all day if necessary.

'She greeted death with anticipation.' She ground out the words. 'She preferred to die than to continue living with me . . . living with her disappointment.'

Dylan looks up from his hands. 'Have you ever considered the fact that her disappointment was with herself, not you? Perhaps that's the reason you cannot understand it?'

'Why? I was supposed to be her miracle baby.'

'It's hard to live up to the expectations of a miracle. Why did she look upon you in that way?'

'She had a number of miscarriages before I was born.'

'I never realised.'

'Why should you? She never spoke about them. My grand-mother told me, otherwise I wouldn't have known. She wanted to be with her babies. That's what she said before she died. She anticipated a better life with them than the one she had with me.'

Dylan hands her tissues. She wonders how many boxes he uses in a week. Dozens, if everyone who sits in this chair is like her.

'What exactly did your mother say to you?' he asks when she can speak again.

'I told you—'

He leans forward. 'Tell me her exact words.'

The morning comes back to her in fragments. Nikki in her luminous jacket and boots and how, as she broke through the traffic lights, she kept telling them everything was going to be okay.

'Joy . . . Joy . . .' Her mother seemed too thin, her body hardly defined under the cover, yet her grip was claw-like, drawing her nearer, whispering all the time, the words garbled . . . such a fierce glittering gaze, looking beyond her daughter towards her lost babies.

'Her anticipation babies.' She is unaware that she has spoken aloud until Dylan stands up and walks to the window. Usually he never moves until it is time for her to leave.

'Anticipation baby?' he says.

'Babies,' she corrects him. 'I told you, she had those miscarriages.'

Joy also stands and crumples the tissue in her hand. Time has passed so quickly. Dylan's expression is intent, troubled. Something has changed between them. Something so subtle and inexplicable that she has already forgotten it by the time she leaves.

Chapter Fifty-Four

Carla

She passed the day reading a manuscript written by a woman who spent three years crossing continents in search of her tug-of-love son. The woman's story was amazing, yet she had managed to make her fight for custody read like a social worker's report. Carla's job was to breathe life into it but it was too raw, too close. She would reject the commission. Her skin had been absorbing the molecules of other people's experiences for too long.

She sent an email to Frank to that effect, then clicked into www.FindIsobelGardner.com. This evening, only one email demanded her attention. She read it once, then sat perfectly still before leaning forward to reread it.

Dear Carla,

My name is Dylan Rae. We met for the first time when you were searching for your daughter in the Chalwerth Industrial Estate. We did meet again a second time but I imagine our first encounter is the one you remember most vividly.

I'd like to meet you again and discuss some information that may be of interest to you. I debated for a long time

*about sending this email and I'm following a gut
instinct by doing so. Please let me know a time and
place where we can meet. I look forward to seeing you
soon.*

  With warmest regards,
  Dylan Rea.

Effortlessly she slid back in time: the burned circles of wood,
the stale smell of urine and mould, the shadow that moved
from within the greater shadows and connected with her.
Now he wanted to connect with her again. She tried to
decipher the word 'information'. What could he possibly
mean? She moved restlessly from her office to the kitchen
and made coffee. Then, without drinking it, she ran back to
her office and clicked into the archival pages of her website.
Instantly, she was consumed by the past. The visual links
were almost impossible to watch. Their faces at the press
conference, their hands clasped, Robert's tears, her catwalk
smile, Leo trying to control the journalists, the fever and fear
and desperation. How had they endured? So long ago, over
fifteen years now. She clicked into *reply* and unhesitatingly
moved her fingers over the keyboard.

His eyes roved over the hotel foyer, seeking her out. She had
suggested the Gresham Hotel on O'Connell Street and had
arrived before him to secure a secluded table. He showed no
sign of recognition when he noticed her and continued
walking among the tables in search of her. He, on the other
hand, was instantly recognisable – a little older but with the
same spiked hair and hard-worn features.

  'Hello, Dylan,' she said.

  Unable to hide his surprise, he sat opposite her and grasped
both her hands. 'Carla! I wouldn't have recognised you.'

'I don't use that name any more,' she said. 'My appearance wasn't the only thing I changed. Call me Clare.'

He smiled and said, 'With or without an I?'

'Clare,' she said. 'Like the county.'

He nodded thoughtfully and signalled to the waiter. 'Would you like tea or coffee?'

'Tea is perfect.'

'When did you change your appearance?' he asked when the waiter had taken their order and departed.

'Years ago.' She self-consciously touched the back of her neck. 'Do I look very different?'

'On the surface, yes.' He nodded. 'You had a strong, iconic image. I expected you to look exactly the same.'

'That was the problem,' she said. 'It imprisoned me. What have you been doing with yourself?'

Did she care or was she simply delaying the moment? He spoke too fast, as if he too must go through the preliminaries before getting to the heart of the matter. He worked as a counsellor, dealing mainly with troubled young people. She could imagine them confiding in him. There was something reassuring about his eyes, intense and embracing. Her own eyes felt naked without their contact lenses which, on impulse, she had removed before she left her apartment.

The waiter returned with a tray and it was possible to draw breath while he laid the table. The clink of china was reassuringly familiar but Dylan's hand shook when he lifted his cup. No longer able to postpone the moment, she leaned towards him.

'Why did you want to see me?'

He placed the cup back in the saucer and linked his fingers together. Strong hands, knotted veins, leathery skin.

'I'm not sure any more. Seeing you like this . . . calling

you Clare . . . it's unnerving. I'd never forgive myself if I raised your hopes then destroyed them.'

Raised her hopes? Unable to mistake his meaning, she dug her fists into the chair and leaned towards him. Her surroundings had shifted, a dizzying tilt that wrenched her stomach and filled her mouth with a gush of hot saliva. She tried to swallow and felt an instant of panic before her throat muscles worked.

'I'm stronger than I look.' Her voice was barely audible. 'And my hopes have been raised and dashed so often I'm immune to disappointment. Tell me what you know and let me decide.'

In reply, he reached into his jacket pocket and removed his wallet. 'I want you to look carefully at this photograph.'

Two young people at a party, their faces close together, big cheesy grins. The young man was older than the girl but Carla barely registered his presence before her attention switched to the girl. She was wearing a red dress, low-cut, and with shoestring straps. Blonde hair fell to her shoulders and her brown eyes seemed to reach out and enfold Carla in an unquestioning gaze.

The noise from the foyer faded. Carla touched her stomach, an automatic gesture that used to register as no more than a tic. Now, suddenly, it was imbued with a terrifying meaning. She was on the edge of something and she did not know whether to stay or run.

'Who is she?' she whispered.

'Her name is Joy Dowling. Joey is her half-brother. I took the photo at a party in her house.'

'And you think . . . *What* makes you think she's Isobel?'

'I've no proof that she is your daughter.' He replaced his wallet, leaving the photograph with her. 'I've carried this image of you around in my head for years. But now . . . you look so different—'

'It's superficial, and not important—'

'But it *is* important.' He rushed his words towards her. 'Joy's hair was short until recently when she let it grow. Either way, the resemblance is remarkable. Your eyes. The shape of your head . . . your neck . . . she's so like you it's uncanny.'

She tried to remain calm. Impossible, under the circumstances, yet she needed to concentrate. If she took the next step forward and this turned out to be another false trail, she would be unable to survive. A woman at the next table bayed with laughter, the sound shrill and unpleasant. Carla moved her chair closer to Dylan.

'You must have more information or you wouldn't have contacted me.'

'Yes.' He nodded slowly. 'Joy Dowling was born at home. A neighbour assisted at her birth, or so it's generally believed.'

'And did she?'

'I suspect Phyllis Lyons rather encouraged that belief and I've never had any reason to doubt it until I spoke to her recently. After I probed a bit deeper into her story, I realised it was slightly different to the generally perceived version.'

She could imagine him drawing the truth from the woman, his quiet, probing questions.

'What did she say?' Carla wanted to reach across and shake him, force the story willy-nilly from his mouth, instead of having to endure this slow build-up. Her eyes remained riveted on the photograph. Dylan was wrong. Her resemblance to this young girl was illusory. It was Robert she saw, his mouth, the full lips she had kissed so often, his determined chin. Their daughter, she realised, bore a stronger resemblance to him than his two sons did.

'Phyllis admitted that Joy was already born when she arrived that night. Born and resting on her mother's stomach.

Susanne Dowling claimed she had been unable to make the hospital on time.'

'Why?'

'There were heavy floods in the area that night and for days afterwards. Phyllis had seen her earlier in the evening and she had seemed fine. No sign that her baby was due. Then she rang Phyllis at the height of the storm. That was the first night of Isobel's disappearance.'

Carla had expected to feel relief and joy, to rejoice that her long search was over. But she was aware only of pain. Her whole body ached but she had no idea where the pain emanated from. She welcomed the physical assault. Far preferable than dealing with this new possibility . . . probability . . . *actuality*.'

Vaguely, she was aware of Dylan's words rising and settling around her. He talked about the wind . . . no . . . windsurfing and an injured dog and how friendships had formed over the last few years.

'I know these people, Carla. I've been a guest in their house. There was never any indication that Joy was not their child. What I've just told you is based on remarks Joy made. She's no idea that what she was saying had any significance and I'm running purely on my instincts.' She had no idea who he was trying to convince, himself or her. 'I can't go to the police and tell them my suspicions. If I'm wrong I'll be destroyed.'

'And if you're right . . .'

'The people Joy believes are her family will be destroyed. But I can't ignore my suspicions. Joy is . . .' He hesitated, his expression suddenly noncommittal.

'Joy is your patient?' she said.

'She's had some difficulties adjusting to her mo . . . to Susanne's death. But I can't talk about her in that context, Carla.'

'*Death?*'

340

'Susanne Dowling died over a year ago from a massive haemorrhage.'

'I see.' But she did not see anything other than the photograph. Her feelings for the dead woman belonged to later. For now, all she wanted to do was devour the young girl's features, rest her eyes greedily on her long slender body and starry-eyed gaze that sparked off the young man who lounged so casually beside her. Her half-brother, Dylan said. They shared the same father, or so they believed.

'Who is this man who claims to be my daughter's father?'

'He's my friend.' Dylan leaned back in his chair and closed his eyes against this monstrous betrayal. 'His name is David. He was abroad at the time of Joy's birth. He didn't arrive home until two days later.'

'But he would have been with her during her pregnancy. He must have known she was faking.' She remembered Robert resting his head against her stomach, spooning against him at night, and Isobel's frantic pattering. What kind of marriage did not allow such intimacies?

'I don't know . . . I don't know. Jesus Christ, what am I doing?' He fisted his hands to his mouth and blew into them.

She understood his terror. He had set events in motion and nothing could stop the momentum. David Dowling was a geologist. Most of the contracts he undertook were abroad, which meant that Joy Dowling was without a father for long periods of time.

'Where will I find her?' she asked.

'In the county of Clare,' he said.

She no longer tried to hold back her tears, nor cared who saw her bend her head into his shoulder. When she recovered, she pressed the photograph to her lips and listened as he spoke about the stolen child who had once rested under her heart.

Chapter Fifty-Five

Joy

Kitten claws scratch her heart. That's the only way Joy can describe the sensation. Dylan would probably call it 'delayed grief'. He believes her decision to accompany her father to Arizona arrested the normal grief pattern she would have established if she had stayed at home. He's right, of course. Arizona was the Big Escape and Dylan can no longer help her. She's out of his league. Grief, it appears, is more difficult for him to handle than drugs and drink and violence and mood disorders. He suggested another counsellor who is skilled at dealing with bereavement. She keeps meaning to make an appointment but she does not want to talk to strangers about her mother. That outburst in Dylan's office was the last time Joy mentioned her name.

Her grandmother has offered her a summer job showing visitors around the studio. Joy has already done two trial runs under Miriam's supervision and, hopefully, has learned all the answers to any questions she will be asked. She starts work tomorrow.

'Better grab the last of your freedom hours,' her father warned before he went off to clear the grass in Dowling's Meadow. No more skulking with cans of cider in the long grass.

He uses a scythe to cut the meadow. When the hostel is built he will turn the meadow into a wildlife habitat. Soon he will bring heavy clearing machinery down the lane and the real work will begin.

The day is hot and the gang are sunbathing around Danny's swimming pool. That's where they gather every afternoon, but today Joy keeps changing her mind about joining them. Outside the air is still. Even the birds are too lazy to sing through the afternoon heat. She will cycle to the graveyard and head on from there to Danny's house. The flowers she placed on the grave last week will have wilted by now. She picks a bunch of stock and places them in the pannier of her bike. Splotch ambles over and licks her hand but does not follow her down the lane. Since his accident, he never ventures far beyond the house.

Her father has made short work of the grass. He is stripped to his waist and a fine layer of sweat gleams on his back. She leans over the gate and watches him at work. The smell of fresh-cut grass is so sweet Joy wants to breathe into it forever.

'Are you going to the cemetery?' He strolls over to her, noticing the bundle of stock.

'Yes.' Even now, sixteen months later, she can't believe her mother lies under the clay. *The worms crawl in . . . the worms crawl out . . .* She hates that song yet it keeps circling her mind . . . *They crawl in thin . . . and they crawl out stout . . .*

'You're too imaginative for your own good,' her mother used to tell Joy. 'Why can't you be happy in your own skin?'

'Where are you going afterwards?' her father asks. Why doesn't he just clap a ball and chain around her ankle?

'I'm meeting Lucinda.' It's not strictly a lie. Lucinda will be among the gang hanging out at Danny's pool. But Danny is out of bounds. Too many strikes against him as far as her

344

father is concerned. She still shudders with mortification remembering how he shouted over the phone at Victor Breen and ordered him to control his 'moronic waster of a son'.

'I'll come with you.' He lowers the scythe and wipes his forehead. 'Give me ten minutes to shower and we'll be on our way. I've been meaning to clear the overgrowth in the cemetery and get rid of that horsetail. It's spreading at a ferocious rate.'

'I'll go on ahead,' she says. 'I fancy a cycle.'

'See you there, then,' he shouts back at her.

Her father is a member of the Maoltrán Ramblers. Apart from hill walking, which they do every weekend, they keep the cemetery clear of weeds. When someone from Maoltrán dies they come together and dig the grave. Her father says it's an old tradition going way back. The Ramblers dug her mother's grave and formed a guard of honour when her coffin was carried into the church. Joy was vaguely aware of them standing on either side of her as she followed the coffin. What she remembers most was the tight clasp of her father's hand.

He's been doing some work on the overgrowth surrounding the cottage. She drops her bike and stands in the empty doorway. She remembers the time she found her mother uprooting the primroses. The loose clay is baked and crumbling under her feet. Another memory stirs. Her mother praying in that same place. The earth was dead then, brown stalks everywhere and mulching leaves. Tears dripped from her chin when she promised not to enter Joy's name in the Judgement Book.

Today there are bluebells at Joy's feet, a carpet of them nodding in the breeze, and the bees are droning above the clover. But there is no flash of blue among the leaves, no familiar voice warning her to stay away . . . stay far away from danger.

Chapter Fifty-Six

Carla

The road shimmered like a mirage as Carla passed through the limestone body of the Burren. From the brow of a hill, she glimpsed the Atlantic rollers crashing against the rocks. She reached Maoltrán in the late afternoon and parked outside the Catholic church. The church doors were open. She hesitated for an instant then entered and genuflected before an altar where two women were arranging flowers. Their murmuring voices reached her as she sat down on a pew and folded her hands on her lap. She had no inclination to pray, had not prayed since her tempestuous, desperate prayers had remained unanswered.

Her mind was in turmoil after her meeting with Dylan, darting feverishly from one scenario to the next. She had resisted her first inclination to go directly to the police, knowing, just as Dylan had known, that once she spoke out she would create an unstoppable momentum. She imagined the media moving towards her like a swarm of locusts, her daughter bleached to the bone in their passing. The protective urge she had experienced when she had stood over Isobel's cot and watched her tiny chest rising and falling came back to her with bitter-sweet force. On two occasions she rang

Robert's number but hung up before the call connected. She decided to confide in Leo and Frank, then changed her mind, knowing their advice and caution would weigh her down.

Joy Dowling – she must think of her by that name until such time as she and Robert could lawfully claim her – had lost the woman who had reared her. Soon she would lose the man she believed to be her father. Softly, softly, Carla warned herself as she tossed sleeplessly each night. She felt powerless to act in her own interests, yet the urge to go to Maoltrán and breathe the same air as her child drove her forward.

'I'm taking a break.' She had kept her tone casual when she told Frank she was renting a cottage for a month in Clare.

'What on earth for?' he had asked. 'We'll be going away to France for three weeks in September.'

'I know. But, right now, I want some time on my own.'

'Is it because I've asked you to marry me?' He glanced keenly at her. 'I'd no idea my proposal was going to have that effect on you.'

'This has nothing to do with your proposal. I feel stressed—'

'Then it has to do with me. I've destabilised you—'

'For goodness' sake, Frank, my life is not governed by your behaviour or your decisions,' she snapped. 'This has to do with me and my daughter. I'm thinking about writing my story.'

'You've always refused to even consider that possibility when I've suggested that to you.'

'I've changed my mind. She'll soon be sixteen. This could be another opportunity to bring her name to the fore.'

'And what about you? How will you handle the publicity?'

'I've a lot to consider, Frank. That's why I need some time alone.' The lie grew easily. She had provided him with a reason he could understand.

One of the women turned to stare curiously at Carla before resuming her flower arranging. She stabbed high tall lilies into an oasis. The scent reminded Carla of Edward Carter. She had read his death notice in the *Irish Times*. Two of the tabloids had re-run the scandal of their ill-fated attempts to find Isobel, and Janet had rung to inform Carla that her father's heart was broken once again.

A priest came from the vestry and spoke to the women. They laughed at something he said. Their laughter followed Carla from the church. A graveyard adjoined the grounds. She opened a low gate and walked along an avenue of yew trees. This was an old graveyard, filled with lichen-covered tombstones, the engravings barely visible. Further on she came to the more recent burial plots. These headstones, brash in their white marble or polished limestone, had clearly distinguishable names carved in black lettering. She walked up and down the narrow paths seeking only one name and finally found it on the border beside the old graves.

Susanne Dowling's family had gone for a simple block of limestone. Wilted flowers drooped from a vase and mini-ature rose bushes had been planted along the length of the grave. A perpetual flame fluttered inside a lantern. Two inscriptions were carved into the limestone but it was the second name that froze her to the spot. She forced herself to read the inscription.

In Loving Memory
Susanne Dowling
1957–2007
Beloved wife, mother and daughter
May she rest peacefully

How could such a woman rest peacefully? Carla longed for faith, the fundamental, fist-thumping creed that consigned those who sinned against others to everlasting flames. She wanted the smell of burning flesh in her nostrils, the hiss and spit of muscle and sinew, the crack of bone. She sank to her knees and covered her face. No hell or earthly retribution could give her back all she had lost. This woman was beyond her fury, beyond every worldly sorrow.

Footsteps approached. She glanced around and saw the black-clad priest approaching. She arose and turned to an old grave behind her, hoping he would keep on walking. As his footsteps drew nearer, she knelt down and pulled up a clump of weeds. The abrasive leaves cut into her hands but she kept pulling and flinging them to one side.

'Good afternoon.' He stopped at the opposite side of the grave and smiled across at her.

'Good afternoon, Father.' She allowed the weeds to drop from her hands and rose to her feet.

The priest nodded apologetically at the graves. 'Horsetail, it's such a pervasive weed. The rain this summer has helped it to grow out of control.' He walked around the perimeter and held out his hand. 'I'm Fr Davis, parish priest of Maoltrán.'

'Clare Frazier.' She rubbed her hands on her jeans and returned his handshake.

'Why does your name sound familiar?' he asked, stepping back to fully view her. 'You're not from around these parts, I presume?'

'No. I'm from Dublin. But I'm renting a cottage in Maoltrán for a month.'

'Really. How interesting. I hope the accommodation is to your satisfaction?'

'Absolutely.' She nodded, knowing his politeness was a cover for curiosity. 'I'm hoping to write a book.'

'Ah! A writer. No wonder your name is familiar. Let me see . . . let me see.' He frowned suddenly. 'Were you associated with that very sad book . . . something about screaming?'

'*Screaming in Silence*. Yes, Father. I was the ghostwriter.'

'Indeed . . . *indeed.*'

She waited for his anger but, instead, he looked troubled. 'A most disturbing book. I'm sad to say the church did not come out of it very well. These are difficult times to be a priest. But when God calls we have to answer that vocation.'

'I'm sorry the book upset you, Father.'

'It enraged me that such things were allowed to happen to the most innocent among us. This new book . . . will it be in a similar vein?'

'No, Father.' She moved the mound of weeds with her toe and noticed how it was beginning to root at the edges of Susanne Dowling's grave. 'I'm hoping to do some research.'

The priest stroked his chin and gazed thoughtfully at her. 'I'm something of a scribe myself. Oh, nothing very ambitious, some features in our local newspaper. What would you be hoping to research, if you don't mind me asking?'

'Oh . . .' At a loss for words she touched the old tombstone. 'It's local history. Tombs . . . ancient tombs.'

'Like our famous Poulnabrone dolmen?'

She nodded. What difference did it make if one more lie was woven into the web?

'I'm interested in the excavations that have been carried out at Poulnabrone.'

'Most interesting excavations,' he agreed. 'Children and adults were buried there at the end of the Neolithic era. Without a doubt, you've come to the right place. You'll find numerous examples of portal tombs right across the Burren. I've often thought about writing a history of the tombs myself. But time,' he sighed and spread his hands, 'time is the eternal winged enemy. If I can help in any way, please don't hesitate to contact me. My house is next door to the church.'

'Thank you, Father.'

'You're welcome.'

He bent, as she had done, and plucked at the weeds. The briars caught in his sleeve and he chuckled as he freed himself. 'Even in the midst of death there is life and very thorny it can be at times.'

'This woman was so young to die.' She turned back towards Susanne Dowling's grave.

'Indeed. Poor Susanne. So sudden. Amazing when such a vital person goes. You can't imagine life without them but it folds over the space they occupied and on we go . . . on we go.'

'You obviously knew her well.'

'Indeed I did. She was at the centre of our little community.'

'Her family must be heartbroken.'

'They are to be sure. Like yourself, she was a Dublin lass. She married a local lad. A bit wild in his day but she settled him down soon enough. However, I've dallied long enough.' Fr Davis prepared to leave. 'Don't forget to call. My door is always open.'

She watched him walk along the path and stop to talk briefly to a man carrying a scythe. The man nodded and lowered the scythe. He was dressed in khaki knee-length shorts, a floppy T-shirt, a sweatband tied around his forehead. Fleetingly, he reminded her of Robert, most tall, dark-haired men did, but he had a narrower build, and when he parted from the priest he walked with a loose, easy stride towards the grave. A girl ran and caught up with him. She carried white flowers in her arms and her hair was a golden banner, waving.

Chapter Fifty-Seven

Joy

Horsetail is a horrible plant, rough and hairy. It keeps spreading, no matter how often Joy uproots it. The flowers on her mother's grave are dead. She replaces the water and arranges the fresh stock. Every spring her mother planted it under the kitchen window. Miriam must have done so this year. The scent is heady at night, drenched with longing.

Her father drops to his knees beside her. 'You're crying,' he says and helps her to her feet, stands with his arm around her shoulders. He never tells her not to cry and she's been doing a lot of it since that day in Dylan's office. A woman kneeling at the next grave covers her mouth. The grave is a mess and she keeps pulling at the horsetail, pulling harder and harder. There is blood on her hands. Joy feels sick, remembering.

'It's impossible to get rid of it.' She did not mean to speak so loudly, to shout, actually, and the woman jerks her head to look up at her.

'It's horsetail,' Joy explains more quietly. 'It spreads everywhere.'

The woman touches her lips with her tongue and sighs. She sighs again, deep heaving breaths as if she can't get enough air into her lungs. She tries to rise but sinks back to the ground. Her hands flutter, as if she does not know what to do with them when she is not pulling weeds. She reminds Joy of a droopy swan, except for her cropped black hair, which somehow looks all wrong with her long thin face and cat-green eyes.

'Are you all right?' Joy's father asks. He bends forward to help her stand but she draws back and, this time, rises without difficulty. She stands still as a statue, staring at him.

'Your hands are bleeding,' Joy says.

The woman, noticing the blood, lifts her fingers and holds them like claws before her face. Then she lets them fall, as if all the energy has drained from her. A *dying* swan, Joy thinks, as the woman sways and sinks over her mother's grave, collapsing so suddenly that Joy's father is unable to reach her on time. The rose thorns snatch at her clothes when he lifts her from the grave. Her face and neck are covered with fine, red scratches. The crack and rustle of branches stirs a bird from the undergrowth and it flies upwards with a startled song. Joy's heart thumps and the flashback comes: the deadly stillness of her mother when she drew her last breath.

The woman's long legs hang over Joy's father's arms and her head lolls like the picture of the Michelangelo Pietà in Miriam's room. He lays her down on a grassy verge and uses water from the container to revive her.

'We need to bring her to hospital.' He sounds frightened and is about to lift her again when her eyelids flutter open.

'Please put me down.' Her voice is a hoarse command, her face ashen. Even the back of her neck is white. She stares at the sky then turns her head to one side and buries Joy in

354

her gaze. That is the only way Joy can explain it. Joy steps back, suddenly so nervous that the kitten claws start scratching at her chest again.

'You fainted.' Her father's shadow falls across the woman's body when he kneels beside her. 'We should bring you to hospital.'

'No, I don't want to go near a hospital. It's nothing . . . nothing. I'm fine, honestly.' She refuses to allow him to help her up. 'Don't touch me,' she snaps. 'I'm perfectly capable of managing by myself.'

Why is she so unfriendly when all they are trying to do is help? Her face is no longer white. It's red and angry and she looks as if she loathes them for interfering.

Joy gathers up the dead flowers. The stems are slimy, the smell unpleasant. She walks past the woman without speaking to her again and flings them onto the rubbish disposal dump.

'I'm meeting Lucinda,' she shouts across at her father. 'I'll see you later.'

Cold water gushes from the outdoor tap. She holds her hands underneath, runs it over her wrists. The woman walks towards her. Tight jeans emphasise the length of her legs and her red jacket, nipped at the waist, flares over her hips. Unwilling to speak to her again, Joy shakes droplets of water from her hands and heads towards the church gates.

'Thank you for your help.' The woman is breathless when she catches up with her. 'I don't know what came over me. The heat, I guess.'

'Are you okay now?' Joy asks.

'Yes, I am. Everything is perfectly fine. Can I drive you to your friend's house?'

'It's only down the road,' she lies. Danny's house is at least fifteen minutes' cycle away. 'I don't want a lift.'

The woman stops and nods, turns back towards the graves.

After the silence of the cemetery, the village sounds reassuringly loud. Music blares from the record shop, *Spinning Discs*, and her friend Jacinta waves from the window of Bella Fashions, where she is working for the summer holidays. Joy cycles past Breen's Estate Agency. She wonders who has taken her mother's place and if they will win awards and bonuses for being brilliant at selling apartments. Further out along the road, a car horn beeps. Lucinda's mother, with Lucinda in the passenger seat, pulls up beside Joy and stores her bike in the boot.

'You two behave yourselves,' she warns when she parks outside Danny's house. 'I don't want a repeat of that last experience.'

'Get a *life*,' Lucinda mutters from the side of her mouth but, remembering the grounding that followed their night in Dowling's Meadow, she makes sure her mother doesn't hear.

Danny's house is at the end of a sweeping driveway. It has two wings on either side, which Danny's mother named the North and South Wings. Joy lies on a sunbed beside the pool and thinks about the woman collapsing. If her mother had sunk to the floor with the same silent grace, instead of hitting the dressing table when she fell, Joy would never have known anything was wrong. Not that it mattered in the end. The most awful part is that a lot of the time she really doesn't miss her mother. Maybe that's why, when she does, she feels as if her insides have been scraped out. Now that she's at Danny's place, she wants to go home. The boys are watching Lucinda, who has changed into a string bikini. They stamp and whistle when she dives into the pool. They are oafs, oozing testosterone. Her father must have been like that once, chasing and catching Corrine O'Sullivan. If he hadn't caught her there would have been no Joey. She refuses to think about him. Only an E . . . stop . . . *stop!*

No one notices when she leaves the swimming pool and heads for home. She's tired and hot by the time she reaches Miriam's Glasshouse. She'll take a lift home with her grand-mother. Miriam has to catch up on her emails and will be with her shortly. Joy enters the Amber Café, which opened last summer at the back of the studio. The last visitors have left and Phyllis, who looks after the food, is closing the kitchen.

'You look hot,' she says when she sees Joy. 'Fancy a Seven Up?'

'Just water,' says Joy and relaxes in the café until her grand-mother is ready to leave for Rockrose.

Joy flings her bike into the boot of the car and settles into the passenger seat, glad to rest from the heat. No sign of Splotch as Miriam drives down the lane. Surprising that, considering he can usually hear a flea's wings beating. A silver Toyota Avensis with a Dublin registration is parked behind her father's jeep.

'Visitors,' says Miriam, parking behind the Avensis. 'I wonder if Tessa and Jim have arrived?'

'They haven't,' says Joy.

The front door is open. Sunlight spills into the hall, capturing dancing dust motes. The scythe, covered with grass and leaves, has been left outside.

Voices are audible from the kitchen. She hears her father's laughter. The woman sits in the sofa beside the Aga. Splotch, his tongue lolling like a discarded rag, lies on his back, his legs jiggling the air as the woman trails her fingers up and down his belly. He makes no attempt to move, even when he notices Joy.

'Splotch. *Here*, boy.' The pang of jealousy is sharp. Joy slaps her hands off her knees and he drags his paws across the floor towards her.

The woman also stands. Grass stains are visible on her white T-shirt.

'We meet again, Joy.' Her voice catches, the way it did in the graveyard, but she doesn't sound as if she's going to faint again. 'I'm Clare Frazier. Your father has very kindly invited me to dinner.'

Her father had prepared a casserole earlier and it has been simmering for hours in the Aga. He's set the table for four and uncorked a bottle of wine. 'It's the least I could do after all the hard work you did in the cemetery,' he says.

'I did very little,' she replies.

'You certainly know how to wield a scythe.' Her father is smiling, really smiling, like he doesn't have to pretend any more. 'We cleared a large amount of weeds from the graves.'

'About time someone took a scythe to that graveyard,' says Miriam. 'The Ramblers have been too busy rambling this summer to pay any attention to it. Is this your first time in Clare . . . Clare?' She laughs and carries the tureen to the table.

'I was here once as a child with my parents and my brother, Leo,' says the woman. 'We had a dog then too. His name was Miley. Splotch reminds me of him. The same collie breed but a different colour.'

Splotch, hearing his name, gambols over to her and leaps upwards, places his paws on her stomach. Fawning over a stranger. First her father, now her dog. And the woman doesn't seem to mind his dirty paws on her T-shirt.

'What a wonderful kitchen.' Her head turns slowly as she stares around the kitchen. 'It looks like the heart of the house.'

Her father seems pleased with the compliment. Joy's parents used to argue over the kitchen. Her mother wanted fitted presses and marble countertops. She would have loved a large American-sized chrome fridge and freezer, like Danny's mother has in her kitchen, but her father would say, 'You've always done what you wanted to the house but you're not changing a stick of furniture in the kitchen.'

He carved his initials on the inside of one of the wooden table legs when he was a boy. Joy did the same on her ninth birthday. He shows the woman the carvings and she hunkers down beside him. She traces her finger over Joy's initials and grips the edge of the table to keep her balance when she stands.

'You two obviously have a very close relationship.' Her eyes make Joy nervous. Even when she smiles, they remain hard and glassy.

'We're pardners in crime.' Her father puts on a fake cowboy accent and tugs Joy's hair. 'Isn't that right, ole buddy?'

'Sure thing, cowboy.' She pulls an imaginary shotgun from an imaginary holster and aims for his heart.

He clutches his chest and staggers into a chair. The woman sits next to him and opposite Joy. It's where her mother used to sit. Joy should be able to bring her to mind but she's conscious only of the woman staring then looking away every time Joy catches her out.

Miriam lifts the lid off the tureen. Steam and the scent of thyme gushes out.

Hopefully, there'll be enough food for four. Joy is ravenous and she does not want to share her dinner with a stranger.

Chapter Fifty-Eight

Carla

The garden in the cottage Carla had rented was filled with gnomes. They peered from behind the bushes, stood to attention on either side of the porch, and splashed merrily in an ornamental pond. Inside the cottage, enchantment still held sway with pictures of fairies on the walls, and pixies, elves and delicate fairy figurines arranged on every available surface.

Carla, returning from Rockrose and aware that her own world had shifted to another dimension, felt totally at home among these tiny, other-world creatures. Reluctant to go to bed, knowing sleep was impossible, she pulled an armchair to the window and sat gazing out at the gnomes. Darkness had settled over the countryside but in the garden the solar lights glowed and she would not have been surprised if the gnomes had begun to move, to dig and strut, and to empty their water vessels into the lily pond.

'Oh, what a tangled web we weave, when first we practise to deceive,' Janet used to chant at her children when they lied to her. If she realised how deeply Carla was mired in her own deception, she would chant it now, long and loudly, and remind her once again that she was breaking her father's heart. And not just her father's heart, Carla thought. A chain of hearts, soon to be wrenched apart.

She had lied to her lover and to a priest. In the echelons of sin, which one was graver? The lie had been cast in stone by the time Joy Dowling reached her and had hardened in the furnace of her anger as she faced the man who had stolen her child. She had no memory of collapsing. When she recovered consciousness, the clouds were heaving above her, forming strange, incredible shapes and she, caught in her own delirium, had turned to feast her eyes on a stranger who was her flesh and blood. Joy Dowling had looked askance at her. What had she seen? A demented woman, her face livid with hope and rage? Enough emotion, obviously, to send her cycling in the opposite direction.

David Dowling had started scything through the summer's weeds by the time she had returned to the grave-side. His ruddy arms had moved rhythmically in powerful, sweeping movements. Her hatred towards him was so intense she wondered if the hairs on the nape of his neck were quivering but he seemed oblivious of any tension between them.

He had stopped when he noticed her and lowered the scythe. 'How are you feeling now?'

'Fully recovered, thank you.'

'Fr Davis said you're doing some research on the Burren tombs.'

'Yes.'

'You're a writer?'

'Nonfiction. Ghostwriting, mostly.' She glanced down at the scythe. 'Is it very difficult to use?' she had asked.

'Not very.' He raised it again. 'I'll show you.'

She touched the blade with her fingers and shivered when she felt the keen edge. He had stood behind her and

362

guided her arm through the sweeping movement, laughing when she sliced the heads from a bank of nettles.

'I told you it was easy,' he had said, and she wondered what it would be like to sweep it towards him, cut him down where he stood. She was calm by then, calm as ice over a raging river. She helped him rake the clippings and carry them to the rubbish dump.

'Have you always lived in Maoltrán?' she asked.

'Apart from studying geology in Galway University, Maoltrán has always been my home,' he replied. 'But since I graduated I've mainly worked abroad.'

'Then you must have spent a lot of time away from home during Joy's childhood?'

'More than I wanted to.' He flung the last bundle of grass and weeds into the dump and wiped his forehead. 'This is thirsty work. I'm stopping off at Molloy's for a drink on the way home. Would you like to join me?'

'Thank you, I will.' She followed him along the narrow path towards the gate.

In the dimly-lit pub, they had sat on stools at the bar. She ordered a glass of cider. He drank beer, sighing with satisfaction after the first long sip. 'I needed that. The cemetery is not an easy place to visit.'

'I'm sorry about your wife. Joy must miss her dreadfully.'

'We all do,' he replied shortly and raised his glass again. Just before the silence became uncomfortable, he had said, 'So, how far have you advanced with your book?'

'I'm still at the early stages.'

'Have you seen the Poulnabrone dolmen?'

'Not since I was a child.'

'I know the location of all the Burren tombs. I mapped them when I was a boy. I know, I know . . .' He laughed and said, 'I had a sad childhood. If you like, I can show them to you.'

She had swayed forward on her stool and gazed at the bottles ranged on shelves behind the bar. 'That's very kind of you.'

'I'd enjoy revisiting some of my old haunts. What other books have you written?'

'Too many to remember,' she replied.

The bar door had opened and a group of hill walkers entered. They settled around a table, pulling chairs from the surrounding tables and raising the level of noise.

'Is this the only pub in Maoltrán?' She was keen to steer the conversation away from herself.

'There used to be more,' he replied. 'The country pub is a dying tradition. The smoking ban started the death knell. Now it's the drink-driving laws. But Molloy's has always been popular . . . too popular at times.' He frowned into his glass. 'Joy was drinking here one night.'

'But she's underage!'

Her reaction, instinctive and alarmed, startled him. He smiled wryly and said, 'I kicked up hell with the owner. He's lucky he didn't have his licence revoked.'

'Was Joy okay?'

He frowned and tapped the edge of a beer mat against the counter. 'She was . . . eventually. I try to be an understanding father but it's difficult at times. She's had some issues since her mother died.'

'They were obviously very close.'

'She was our only child.'

'A special child.'

'Very special. And you?' He glanced at her left hand then swivelled his gaze back towards the bar.

'Divorced. We also had one daughter.'

'Is she here with you? I'm sure Joy would love to meet her.'

'We lost her at birth. Do you mind if we don't discuss her?'

'I'm sorry. I didn't mean to pry.'

She had drained her glass and slipped down from the high stool. 'I'd better go. Thank you for the drink.'

'Why don't you come to dinner?' he said. 'Meet my mother. She's due home from her studio soon and she loves company.'

That was the moment to make a polite excuse and leave; set events in motion with a call to Detective Superintendent Murphy. But instead she had driven behind him, her car bumping over the uneven surface of a narrow lane which, he had told her, would soon be levelled and widened. She had passed the cottage he hoped to raze and turn into a hostel. The front door of Rockrose was unlocked. Shoes and boots were neatly aligned in the porch. She had followed him into a kitchen that smelled of herbs and simmering beef. It was cluttered with the bric-a-brac of living but nowhere in that warm, steamy space had Carla seen a photograph of Susanne Dowling. He had removed magazines and newspapers from a sofa and gestured at her to sit down. A dog followed them into the house and laid his head on her lap.

Shortly afterwards, Carla had heard a car and voices. Joy entered, followed by a striking, grey-haired woman in a navy business suit. Carla recognised her immediately. No wonder her son's face had tugged at her memory throughout the afternoon. As Miriam Dowling warmly grasped her hand, Carla remembered the craft fair in Dublin. She had stood face to face with her child's kidnapper, as blind as the stallion David had carefully wrapped, and which she had just as carefully carried all the way to Australia. Sweat broke out under her arms. She wondered if he caught the sour smell of her disbelief. She thought about the other horses, the colourful, jingling seahorses, now wrapped in tissue paper gathering dust, and allowed them to sway through her mind, to steady her nerves so that she could make conversation, answer questions, tell more lies. Was his mother oblivious to the truth or was she his confidante, his partner in a heinous crime? Miriam's eyes were serene, her face open and welcoming. Towards the end of the meal she had asked Carla if she had children.

'I had a daughter but I only knew her for two days before . . .' She stopped, aware of the sympathy in Miriam's eyes. David placed his hand over her clenched fist. His comforting touch almost unhinged her. Would her fury eventually become a conflagration and consume them both? She pulled her hand away before the desire to claw his face became uncontrollable.

'I'm so sorry, Clare,' said Miriam.

Carla sat silently for an instant. No one made any effort to rush in with heedless comments. Eventually, she spoke again. 'I bought one of your seahorse mobiles for her. I hung it over her cradle in the nursery we'd decorated for her.'

'Did you now.' Miriam's eyes moistened. 'Oh dear me . . . life can be so very tough at times.'

David nodded but made no attempt to touch her again. Joy glanced warily from her father to Carla, as if she suspected they were exchanging signals. Jealousy. She saw Carla as a threat, someone who could possibly replace the woman she had loved. She looked away when Carla caught her eye and stabbed her fork into a chunk of meat.

'Joy has a summer job, starting tomorrow,' Miriam said as the meal drew to a close. 'She'll be showing visitors around the studio. Why don't you drop in and see us? I've some meetings in the morning but I'd love to have lunch with you in the Amber Café. Phyllis is a wonderful cook. We're lucky to have her.'

'Phyllis?' Carla struggled to deal with this new piece of information.

'She's our nearest neighbour,' said Miriam. 'You probably noticed the canary yellow house before you turned into the lane.'

'Yes, I did.'

'Impossible to miss.' Miriam laughed. 'Phyllis had it painted after her mother died. Between you, me and the wall, she was celebrating the first fling of freedom she'd known in her life.' She smiled across the table at Joy. 'We've a special place for Phyllis in our hearts.'

Joy flung her eyes upwards in exasperation. 'Oh, for God's sake, Gran,' she muttered. 'I'm sick of listening to that story.'

'I'd like to hear it,' said Carla.

'Well, I wouldn't.' Joy sighed with exaggerated weariness and rested her elbows on the table, pressed her chin into her fists. 'It's no big deal.'

'Phyllis helped deliver Joy,' Miriam explained. 'Her mother was unable to make the hospital on time.' She glanced sternly across at Joy. 'Now, was that so difficult? Honestly, Joy, I don't know what's wrong with you lately. I've almost forgotten how beautiful you look when you smile.'

Joy grimaced, a mock smile that stretched her lips downwards, and said, 'Satisfied?'

Behind her posturing, she was clinging to the secure bindings of childhood while struggling, at the same time, to free herself from their clasp. And those bindings would soon be ripped from her. But how . . . and when?

David Dowling and his mother had made Carla welcome in their home. They fed her, poured wine into her glass, offered her second helpings, unaware that they had invited the enemy to sup.

Chapter Fifty-Nine

Joy

From the showroom window, Joy notices the silver car as soon as the driver enters the car park. Clare Frazier has lost no time accepting Miriam's invitation. Joy will probably have to show her around.

Last night her father had walked her to the gate after dinner and stood watching until her car rounded the bend in the lane.

'Why did you bring her here?' Joy had demanded when he came back inside. She had been so angry with him she wanted to smash glass. The urge quivered through her but it had no centre, no reason she could understand or control. Just an urge to smash glass. How crazy was that?

'I was simply being friendly.' Her father had been as cool as a cucumber as he began to clear the table. 'She seemed a bit lost, don't you think?'

'She knows the way back to Dublin,' Joy replied. 'The road signs are clear enough.'

'What's that puss on your face for?' he demanded.

'I don't puss. I pout.'

'So, what's up?'

'She scares me.'

'Who, Clare? Oh, for crying out loud!'

'Did you see her eyes?'

'Impossible not to. She has very striking eyes.'

'She was summing up *everything*. She wants to take Mammy's place.'

'No one will ever take your mother's place.' Miriam had turned from the dishwasher and smiled across at her.

'You have,' said Joy and wanted to bite down hard on her tongue. Smashing glass was safer than being rude to her grandmother but she couldn't stop. 'You're changing everything . . . like . . . like her bedroom and the living room. I hate those paintings you bought and those new armchairs are *really* tacky. Where have you put her photograph?'

'It's in the conservatory. I thought you'd like it to be in her favourite place.'

'Well, you thought wrong,' Joy shouted.

'Apologise to your grandmother this instant.' Her father had been furious with her.

'David, leave her alone. Joy and I can talk this out.' Miriam seldom gets angry. It's a negative emotion that interferes with her creativity. Hatred is another bad one. She burns scented candles and chants for ten minutes each morning so that her creative energy is channelled in the right direction. 'Mainly into my bank accounts,' she jokes but last night she had looked so hurt that Joy's anger disappeared as suddenly as it erupted. Yet she had been unable to apologise. She had plumped up the cushions on the sofa where Clare had sat after dinner. The faint lingering perfume reminded her of roses when they have been disturbed by a breeze.

Clare enters Reception and disappears from sight. A bus with Canadian tourists has just arrived. The visitors enter and fill the studio with voices. They're anxious to see the glass

370

blowers at work in the furnace room. Their accents remind her of Joey, although he sounds sort of Irish too. He always enjoyed showing off his skills as a glass blower to the tourists. Joy cannot believe how much she misses him. The longing to see him again shames her. Impossible to imagine Leanne or Lisa having the same tremblingly awful thoughts about their half-brother.

Clare Frazier can tag along with the Canadians. No way is Joy going to give her a private tour.

She smiles at Joy and says, 'That sounds perfect.'

Today she is dressed in sandals and a dress with triangles of material that sway when she moves. A light cardigan is slung over her shoulders, the sleeves tied under her neck. In the showroom she touches a seahorse mobile and sets it chiming. She walks to the window and stares into the car park. She must be thinking about her dead baby. Joy had no idea why she finds her so frightening. She's wearing the same perfume today. Joy can smell it, even though Clare is standing on the other side of the showroom. It's been in her nostrils since last night, which is such a crazy thought she can hardly concentrate when one of the tourists asks her about the legend of the blind stallion and Maura Rua.

Clare Frazier looks around as Joy holds the stallion towards the light. Then she turns to face the window again, but Joy knows she's listening to every word. She hears her own voice rising. Suddenly it's like being on stage, singing her heart out so that her mother will praise her afterwards, single her out, instead of saying, as she did after the opening night of *Annie*, 'It was a fine performance. Everyone gave it their best shot.'

When she finishes, Clare walks across the showroom and clasps both her hands. 'That was wonderful, Joy,' she says. 'I could have listened to you all day.'

'Time for lunch.' Her grandmother enters the showroom. 'Come with us, Joy. The next tour isn't for an hour.'

The Amber Café has wide windows overlooking the ocean. The tide is out and the rocks hunch like basking seals, wet and gleaming. Phyllis comes out from the kitchen to say hello. Her chef's hat is tilted to one side and there's a red stain on her white apron. Joy knows it's pasta sauce but she can't take her eyes from it.

'Delighted to meet you, Clare.' Phyllis shakes the woman's hand and asks where she's staying.

'The cottage with the gnomes,' Clare replies and everyone nods, smiles, even Joy.

'Lucy Baker's place,' says Phyllis. 'She's gone to the States for six months. How long are you staying, Clare?'

'A month.'

'And what's your book about?'

Phyllis is so nosy. Joy taps her foot against the floor. She's finished her lasagne and is anxious to email Joey on Miriam's computer.

'Do you mind, Gran?' she asks. 'I won't be long.'

Miriam nods and listens to the woman's reason for writing about tombs. It's some kind of guidebook on the Burren. She's come to the right place, Joy thinks, as she runs up the stairs. Her father could write that book blindfolded. The heat from the furnace room reaches out and grabs her. Joey used to strip off his T-shirt when he was working there. She remembers the intense concentration on his face as he rolled the blowpipe, knowing the exact instant to gather the glass and draw it from the furnace.

The low growl from the furnace room dies away as she closes the office door. Quickly she clicks into her email and sits staring at the screen. If she had a pencil she'd chew the tip.

Hi ½-Bro,

Greetings from the Burren where even the rocks suffer from boredom. Same old, same old here, except that I'm working in Gran's studio. I've just brought a group of Canadians on a tour and they were raving about your glass bowls. They loved the amber ones most.

How are things at your end? Italy sounds cool. I saw your glass designs on Facebook. Deadly.

Hot news from the home front. Dad has met someone. She is strangely beautiful and beautifully strange, at least that's what he claims. Personally, I found her a bit pale and weird. Turns out she's a ghostwriter so that's not surprising. He can deny it all he likes, but I believe he has the hots for her. Watch this space!!!

But on to more serious matters and the reason for this email. It's time I cleared the air between us. I'm sorry, Joey, for being such a stupid ass. I suspect it's something to do with the geographical distance between us. Leanne and Lisa had the opportunity to smell your dirty socks and spot your warts (metaphorically speaking, of course) but I, your other sister, half-sister, whatever, have only met you three times in my life. I'm also hormonally challenged at the moment and expect to develop acne fairly soon . . . I'm really sorry about that stupid, <u>stupid</u> email. Forgive me, forget it.

I took your advice and spoke to Dylan. He's brill and I'm now restored to my former sanity. I'm actually seeing Danny Breen. Don't tell Dad. Bit of bad blood going on there. Danny fancies me, although he has been known to cast a sly glance at Lucinda who's taken to wearing a string bikini. Not a good idea since she refuses to give up Big Macs.

Bye for now, bro.

Joy.

When she returns to the table, Phyllis is back in the kitchen and her father has arrived. She doesn't know anyone else who can look so uncomfortable in a suit. He had a meeting about the hostel with his bank manager in Ennis. He gives Joy a thumbs-up signal and leans back in his chair, tilts the front legs. He keeps stealing glances when he thinks Clare is not looking. When he sees Joy staring, his eyes flicker away. Guilty as sin. He's going home to change, then he'll bring Clare to see wedge tombs. It sounds as exciting as watching cows chewing the cud but Clare nods, like she's really interested.

They walk from the studio towards his jeep. Joy wonders what's on her father's mind. One thing she knows for sure, it's got nothing to do with tombs.

As soon as she finishes the next tour, she nips back into Miriam's office. Joey has replied.

Hi kid,
    Don't give it another thought. Forgive, forget, absolutely. Glad Dylan's working out. So Dad's hit it off with someone. Mmmmm. Italy is still amazing but Gran knows every bit as much as Alanzo. I miss you all and am thinking of heading back to the Glasshouse when I finish here. Be warned. I'll be keeping a close eye on Danny Breen. No monkey business now!
    Hang loose.
    Joey.

It's wrong to feel ticklish and warm when she thinks about him living with them again. But there's nothing she can do about feelings. Like her feelings for Clare Frazier. Joy doesn't trust her. It's to do with her eyes. Apart from the colour, they're like her own, bold and demanding. That's what her mother used to say.

374

'Stop staring at me with those bold eyes.' Joy can hear her voice inside her head. 'Those eyes . . . why are they always demanding something or other from me?'

She never explained what the 'something' or the 'other' was and now it's too late to ask.

Chapter Sixty

Carla

They stopped off at the rented cottage first. David followed her into the small living room and waited while she changed her dress. She pulled on a pair of jeans, then, as the heat of the afternoon had flushed her cheeks, she changed into shorts. She was hungry for information about her child. If that meant climbing over rocks with David Dowling, she would willingly do so. She walked briskly along the corridor towards the living room. Outside the door, she hesitated, unable to tolerate the thought of his gaze glancing off her bare legs. She turned and ran back to the bedroom, flung the shorts across the bed and dragged her jeans on again.

She stared into a full-length mirror and ran a comb through her hair. Her roots were beginning to show. She had hair dye with her. Tonight she would touch them up.

'Because I'm worth it.' She mouthed the words at her reflection then clasped her arms around her chest, allowed her terror to surface. Already she was sinking under the weight of all the information she had gleaned. These people were so open, so friendly. Especially Phyllis Lyons, who had managed in the short time Joy was absent to give a graphic description of the night she was born.

'How did you manage to cut the umbilical cord?' Carla had forced herself to ask the question, her skin prickling when Phyllis, without hesitation, answered, 'I used scissors and thread. You clamp both ends with the thread.'

David drove to Rockrose, where he also changed into jeans and a white T-shirt that emphasised his tanned arms. Halfway down the lane he stopped the jeep.

'Would you like to see the site of the hostel?' he asked.

'Why not.' She opened the passenger door and jumped down.

He led her through a gap in the hedgerow into a shadowy clearing. The cottage walls were still standing but the roof was missing, the stony window ledges covered in lichen. She sat beside him on a low boundary wall leading from the side of the ruin and studied the plans he had taken from the jeep. His earlier meeting with his bank manager had been successful. Work would begin shortly.

In the early evening they reached the Poulnabrone dolmen. She took notes and photographed the dramatic alignment of rocks. Translated from Irish, Poulnabrone meant 'the hole of the sorrows'. Ancient bones had been found there, a newborn baby among the remains. She thought about the bones in the Angels' plot. How desperately Robert had wanted them to belong to Isobel. A place of stone. Miranda May's prediction seemed so clear now.

'A friend of mine was buried in reeds.' Carla had no idea why the young prostitute should come so forcefully to mind. 'She lay there for four days before she was found. Her name was Anita.'

'I'm sorry.' He seemed taken aback by her sudden outburst. 'It sounds horrendous.'

'She was like a shadow passing over my life. But I was arrogant enough to believe I could save her from herself.'

'Did she need saving?'

'She was a teenage prostitute and a drug addict. What do you think?'

'I think you'd better tell me about her.' He helped her up onto a plateau of rock and sat beside her.

'She had a limp but she was born with two straight legs.' She was forced to take a deep breath before she could continue. 'Her father pushed her down the stairs when he was drunk. And he did worse . . . the *bastard*. Then she was killed because she owed money to a scumbag who, thankfully, is *rotting* in jail. Can you make sense of it? I sure as hell can't. I met her when I was going through a difficult time. I'm not sure whether she saved my life or my sanity . . . but I could do nothing for her . . . *nothing*.'

'You can't be the judge of that,' he replied. 'None of us knows what impact we have on the lives of others.'

'The proof was lying in the reeds. I didn't even know her second name until the guard who interviewed me mentioned it. I wonder . . .' she controlled a sudden urge to weep, 'what it was all about . . . her short life. Was it to save *me* from myself? Or to give some punter brief satisfaction in the back of a car? I don't know why I'm telling you about her . . . I really don't know what the hell I'm doing . . .' She tensed, thinking he might touch her hand, as he did yesterday when they were dining in his kitchen but he sat with one foot resting on the rock, his arms wrapped around his knee.

'I was in Arizona when my wife became ill,' he said. 'I tried to tell her I loved her. I don't know if she heard me.'

'I'm sure she did. Hearing is supposed to be the last sense that leaves us.'

Below them, a cow tore grass from the crevices of a narrow ravine. Faintly, she could hear the tug of its teeth against the grass but she was unsure if the sound was imagined. Anything was possible among rocks that had once honoured the dead.

'I hope so,' he replied. 'We didn't have an easy marriage.'

'But you loved her?'

'I told her I loved her. Two different things. If she did hear me, she probably knew I was lying.'

'How sad.'

'Yes, it's sad. After she died, all I could think about was the waste . . . the wasted years when both of us could have been happy with other partners. My parents were divorced. That's why . . . well . . . it's the reason I stayed in my marriage.'

'But why did you marry her?'

'Because I was in love with the idea of being loved,' he replied. 'Susanne was older than me, ten years between us. I thought she was the most sophisticated woman I'd ever met. I was flattered by her attention . . . beguiled . . .'

The sun highlighted the russet tones of his hair. His profile was as weathered and chiselled as the rocks surrounding them.

'How long since your divorce?' he asked.

'Eight years.'

'I'm sorry.'

'No need to be. We're good friends. It's all very civilized.'

'And since then . . . anyone?'

'Yes. He's interested in marrying me.'

'I hope you'll be happy.'

'Happiness is a demanding call. I'll settle for serenity.'

He bent down, touched the leaves of a dark-red plant that snuggled in a crevice. 'Orchids grow wild in the grikes,' he said. 'Species can be found here that normally could not exist side by side anywhere else. I belong here. Susanne did not. She tried but she never settled. In the end she wanted to leave, move to Spain. I fought her every inch of the way. So did Joy. And now it all seems so irrelevant.'

'Is Joy happy here?'

'She loves the Burren. From the time she was small, she's wanted to know everything about the place. She's an enquiring mind, not that you'd notice from the way she's been behaving. But that will iron itself out. When work starts on the hostel, she'll be too busy to get up to mischief. And she's been seeing a friend of mine, a local counsellor. He's helping her deal with her mother's death.'

The Dylan link. What inadvertent remark had Joy Dowling made that triggered off his suspicions and brought him back into Carla's life?

'Joy seems like a lovely young girl,' she said. 'Tell me about her.'

David talked until the sun loomed large and red behind the hills. She stared at the dolmen until it sank into purple shadows and in those shadows she saw her child skipping over the rocks, reciting, in Latin and in English, the names of peeking flowers, splashing in the shallows of retreating tides, sleeping soundly beside a polar bear that uttered profanities at the most unexpected moments.

When she interrupted him, unable to continue listening any more, he took her arm and helped her across the sundered slabs. She thanked him but refused his invitation to dine with him in Doolin. Too tired, she told him. Difficult to get used to a strange bed and she had not slept well last night. He made no attempt to change her mind. They spoke little as he drove her back to Miriam's Glasshouse to collect her car. She reached the gnomes shortly afterwards. She had no memory of falling asleep.

Chapter Sixty-One

Joy

It's been two weeks since Clare Frazier came to Maoltrán and her father seems unable to finish a sentence without including her name. Joy knows why he does it. She does the same with Joey's name. She never intends mentioning him but, somehow, his name slides out and her heart gives a little ping from excitement.

Clare has been twice to Rockrose to dinner. She went with them on a picnic to Inchiquin Lake and they surfed last Sunday in Lahinch for the entire afternoon. No sign of Dylan or Nikki, even though her father rang Dylan and told him they'd be there.

Joy sees her through the window of the Stork Club talking to Dee Ambrose. She must be pregnant. Why else would she be in Dee's shop? She's still slim so she must be in the early stages. Her father will be disappointed when she tells him.

Danny's car is parked on the other side of the road. She crosses over and meets him as he saunters from Daly's newsagents.

'Hi, Danny,' she says. 'How're things?'

'Same old . . . same old.' He tears the plastic off a pack of cigarettes and poses against the side of his car. 'I'm heading back to the pad. Want to come?'

Clare emerges from the Stork Club and glances over towards them.

'Who else is coming?' Joy asks.

'Lucinda and the usual outlaws. We can have a barbecue.'

'Sounds good.'

'Then hop in, babe,' he says in his fake American accent and opens the passenger door for her.

Clare stands on the edge of the opposite pavement, unsmiling, watching.

The inside of Danny's house is so different from Rockrose, Joy can't even make a comparison. It has lots of glass and skylights, and a lounge as big as a football pitch, or so it seems from where she's sitting. In the basement there's a home cinema with strobe lighting. No wonder it's where the gang like to hang out. Usually they hang out in Danny's den. She's never been in the lounge before. Glass sliding doors lead to the balcony. She steps outside and peers through a telescope. She can see the ocean, the sails of yachts fluttering like seabirds.

Danny hands her a cocktail. He calls it a Kamakazi Shooter, which makes it sound dangerous and exciting and like something her father would absolutely forbid her to drink.

'Where are the others?' She leans over the balcony but the driveway is empty. 'You said they were coming.'

'Relax,' he says and puts his arm around her. 'They'll be here soon.'

'Your parents will go mad if they see us drinking,' she says.

'They'd want a fucking strong telescope to do so.' Danny grins and tightens his grip. 'There're on an overnighter in Dublin. Come on inside.'

He puts on Snow Patrol, which is cool because he usually

prefers heavy metal bands like Wolfmother and Children of Bodom.

'A mojito,' he says and mixes a second cocktail. This one tastes even better. Still no sign of Lucinda and the gang. She knows, without looking at Danny's face, that they were never invited. He collapses onto the wide leather sofa and pulls her down beside him. Their isolation makes her nervous, especially when he tells her there are six bedrooms in this house, and he wants to do *it* to her in each one. After she finishes the mojito, he mixes two A-Bombs. They close their eyes and knock them back even faster.

'C'm'ere, babe, let's dance.' Danny slows the music until it seems as if she's floating in his arms. It's so bright outside, crazy to be drinking shots and dancing up close in the middle of the day. When he pulls down the blinds, the room is filled with a hazy, beige light. He presses his hands against the small of her back and moves them lower, caressing her and holding her so close it hurts. The thought of all those bedrooms would not be so frightening if only her head would stop spinning.

The first bedroom, he says, belongs to his parents and has a king-sized waterbed. She wonders what would happen if it burst. Would they drown or swim to safety? Weak with laughter, she trips and collapses to her knees. Danny demands to know what's so hilarious. She crawls towards her handbag when she hears her mobile ringing.

'Turn the fucking thing off,' Danny moans, and he tries to grab it from her hand. She holds it out of his reach and answers.

'Where are you?' demands her father.

'With Lucinda.'

'Don't lie to me. I've spoken to her. Are you with Danny Breen?'

'Yes. But there's a gang of us here. I thought Lucinda was here too—'

'I'm outside his house and I'm staring at a window with the blinds drawn. If you're not out of there by the time I count to ten, I'm kicking the door in.'

'*Dad*—'

'I've started counting. One . . . two . . .'

She clicks off the phone and flings it back into her handbag.

'Ah fuck, what now?' Danny moans when she staggers to her feet.

'My dad's outside,' she says. 'He's going to drive his jeep through the front door. See you 'round, Danny.'

'You're an effing minger,' he yells as she runs down the hall.

She hates her father and loves him in the same breath. He grabs her arm and pulls her outside the door, then marches down the hall to confront Danny. She hears their voices, her father shouting, and she cringes, her head spinning from the shots and the fresh air.

'Why don't you lock me in a tower?' she shrills when he storms back out and slams the front door behind him.

'I wish I could,' he yells just as loudly. 'I'd throw away the key until you're old enough to behave sensibly.'

'The way you behaved with Corrine O'Sullivan?' Her voice is so high it could split iron. 'Pity Gran didn't lock *you* in a tower.'

'That was different.' He's not yelling so loudly now. 'Corrine was older—'

'Only by *three* years. You're such a hypocrite.'

'Just because I messed up doesn't mean I'm prepared to stand by and let you do the same.'

'Let me have fun, you mean.'

'Fun? That creepy bastard has only one idea of fun. And don't think for one minute that he'd hang around to deal with the consequences.'

'Did you?'

'Too right I did. But Corrine had other ideas, which is why my son has been separated from me for most of our lives.'

'But if you'd married Corrine, you wouldn't have had me.'

'And think how much easier my life would have been,' he roars. 'You're going straight to your room. I'm grounding you until further notice.'

'Don't bother,' she yells back. 'I'm going to my room so that I never have to speak to you again for the rest of my life.'

Self-imposed isolation can only last so long and by the third evening Joy is ready to forgive her father.

When her grandmother opens the bedroom door and carries in her dinner on a tray, Joy tells her she will eat it in the kitchen.

'Don't think that's going to lift your grounding,' warns Miriam. 'You really pushed your father over the edge this time.'

'I know.' Joy's hangover was a hideous punishment for her stupidity. 'I'm reformed, utterly and forever.'

'I sincerely hope that includes ending your friendship with Danny Breen. Honestly, what were you thinking? If it hadn't been for Clare—'

Miriam stops and bites her lip, a dead giveaway.

'She *snitched*!' Joy is outraged. 'I wondered how Dad knew. She has a nerve *spying* on me. Who does she think she is with her—'

'Calm down, will you?' Miriam turns, still carrying the tray, and heads towards the door. 'You should be glad she was worried enough to ring your father.'

'Why should I be glad? It's none of her business what I do.'

'Maybe not. But she took Danny Breen's measure quickly enough, the little twerp. Can you imagine what your mother would say if she knew about your carry-on?'

'Gran.' Joy sits on the edge of the bed and stares at her feet. 'Why didn't you like Mum?'

'What makes you think I didn't like her?' Miriam places the tray on the dressing table and comes back to her.

'You can't hide your feelings.'

'I didn't dislike her, Joy. But Susanne was a very private person. It was difficult to get close to her.'

'Was it because she made Dad unhappy?'

'Two people make a marriage, Joy. And they were probably happy in their own way.'

The sound of a woman's voice drifts up the stairs from the kitchen.

'Is *she* here again?' Joy asks.

'She's having dinner with us tonight. Be nice to her, Joy. She's a sweet woman and she's no intention of stealing your father. She has someone special in her own life—'

'I know. Dad told me. I think she's pregnant. She was buying stuff in the Stork Club.'

'That would be wonderful for her.' Miriam smiles and gives Joy a hug. 'Come on, you. It's time to rejoin the human race.'

Clare smiles and rises when Joy enters the kitchen. She looks relaxed, as if she belongs in the house. Her skinny jeans emphasise her long legs. She certainly didn't buy *them* in the

388

Stork Club. Joy casts a sideways glance at her father, who knits his eyebrows in a 'behave yourself' warning.

The conversation around the table floats above her. Miriam is talking about *Annie* and how Joy played the starring role in the school musical.

'How wonderful.' Clare claps her hands and beams. 'You're a singer. I'd no idea. Personally, I can't hold a note in my head but my brother is a fabulous singer.'

She's always doing that, slipping in bits of information about her family. At the picnic by the lake she told Joy about her niece, who used to have an imaginary friend. Joy had told her about Polar and all the cursing he used to do. Clare had flung back her head and laughed so heartily that Joy had joined in. But when Joy told her about the Judgement Book, she had stood up abruptly and walked to the edge of the lake. She stood there for ages, staring across at the castle beyond the reeds.

Miriam rummages in the bottom of the dresser and draws out the album. 'I'll show you some shots of her in action.' She opens the album towards the end and shows the photographs of Joy singing 'Maybe'.

Joy's eyes sting when she notices the *Annie* write-ups and photographs from the *Clare Champion* and the *Maoltrán Mail*. Her mother had placed them in a plastic envelope and stuck it in the back of the album. She started the album when Joy was a baby and recorded every year of her life. It's enormous and Joy has not looked at it for ages.

Clare pushes her plate aside and places the album on the table, opens it on the first page. Joy wants to scream. All those dribbling baby photographs exposed. Oh Christ! She'd forgotten about the scans. The outline of her emerging self looks like the scribbles a small child would make.

The second scan doesn't look any clearer until her father says, 'I couldn't see anything either until the sonographer showed me.' He traces his finger over the scribbles and suddenly Joy can see her alien head and grub-like body, her skinny frog arms and legs. Despite her embarrassment, it's kind of cute. By the last scan, she's practically waving and saying 'Cheese!' to the camera.

Clare sucks a sound deep into her throat. 'Were you with Susanne when those scans were taken?' she asks.

'Just the second one,' he says. 'I was abroad for the other two.'

'I was with her when she had the first one taken,' says Miriam. 'It was a real walloper of an emotional moment when we saw it. The last one was a relief. She'd been worried because the placenta was low-lying but the scan reassured her everything was okay.' Miriam smiles across at Joy. 'All Susanne was short of doing was framing it and putting it on top of the television.'

'Pass the sickbag,' moans Joy. 'Fast.'

Clare looks equally squeamish. She presses her hand to her mouth and chews the side of her finger. Then she turns to the next page and looks at the photograph Phyllis took after Joy was born.

She's wrapped in a towel, lying against her mother's breast. Her mother's hair is plastered to her scalp and she looks exhausted. But it's her expression that brings a lump to Joy's throat; her shining smile of happiness and relief.

Clare wheezes, like she can't get enough air into her lungs. When Joy looks at her, afraid she will collapse again like she did in the cemetery, her lips are pressed so tightly together, they're almost invisible. She pushes the album away from her and leans against the table as she stands.

'I have to go now.' Her voice is shaking so much she has to wheeze again. 'Please don't see me out . . . Thanks again for the meal, Miriam . . . it was lovely . . . goodbye . . . goodbye.'

'What was all that about?' asks Miriam when the front door slams. It's like a draught ran through the kitchen and set the pots rattling but that's only the sound of Splotch whining. Her father sits staring at the door, as if he expects Clare to materialise through the wood at any moment.

A phone rings. Everyone looks at their own mobiles but the ringing comes from under the album. Her father picks up the mobile phone and runs to the front door but the car taillights are disappearing beyond the bend in the lane. The phone stops in the same instant.

'Frank.' He reads the name on the screen. Almost immediately it begins to ring again. 'No, she's not here,' he says when he answers it. 'She left it behind her.' He pauses then snaps, 'In a friend's house.' He listens again, his expression cross and impatient. 'Yes, I'll see her tomorrow. Yes, I'll tell her you phoned. Goodnight.'

Chapter Sixty-Two

Carla

She arose early and tossed her clothes into her suitcase. In a few hours' time she would be back in Dublin. Obsession was a dangerous madness and it had claimed her once again. To think she had considered contacting the police, had almost rung Robert and blurted out her farcical story. The photograph she had kissed so often it was smudged from her lips had told a lie. There was no resemblance between the girl and Robert. No bloodline flowing, no genes replicated. Carla had seen the evidence, three precious scans charting Joy Dowling's journey through the womb.

She would call in to Rockrose, pick up her phone and be on her way. A flying visit. With any luck Joy would not be there. Carla carried her suitcase to the car and locked the cottage, slipped the key under the nearest gnome. She reversed down the garden path, almost knocking over the gnomes nearest the edge. Outside the gate she indicated left and was drawing away from the pavement when she noticed the jeep approaching from behind. She switched off the ignition and lowered the window.

'Are you leaving us already?' David lifted his eyebrows quizzically when he saw her case in the back seat.

'Yes. I've enough research done to complete my book.'

'You left us so suddenly last night. Did something we do upset you?'

'You were very hospitable. I'm sorry if I appeared rude.' She fell silent, unable to think of a rational explanation for her sudden departure. She no longer needed to hate him but it was impossible to shake off the reason she had come to Maoltrán. 'I found it difficult looking at the album. Those scans . . . they reminded me of another time.'

'I understand.' His expression was sombre as he leaned in the window and handed her the mobile. 'Your fiancé was looking for you. He rang twice last night. He sounded suspicious when he heard my voice. I hope I reassured him.'

'Thank you. He's not my fiancé . . . not yet. I hope the hostel works out for you, David.'

He had done nothing to harm her. Nor had his wife or their daughter. They were innocent projections of her own obsession.

'Hopefully, it will.' He shook her hand. 'You'll have to come and see it when it's finished.'

'I'll certainly call in if I'm passing this way but—' She was still holding his hand.

'I'm not being polite, Clare,' he interrupted her quietly. 'I'd like you to pass this way again . . . and soon.' He too seemed equally incapable of releasing his grip.

'I'm sorry, David. I don't think that's a sensible idea,' she said.

'No, it probably isn't.' He was the first to draw away. 'Good luck with your life, Clare.'

'And you with yours, David.'

He gave her a half-salute and walked towards his jeep.

The shock of her discovery still trembled through her but with it had come another emotion, one she had not allowed

394

herself to appreciate until this instant. Relief. A tiny sprig that freed her from the responsibility of breaking up his family. It had the power to release her from an endless expectation, to allow her hopes to fade. Finally, she could be at peace with those tiny bones resting in the Angels' plot.

David Dowling stopped and came back to her car. He leaned in the open window. Before she could move, he clasped her face between his hands and kissed her.

'You've wrenched my heart, Clare,' he said. 'I wish I could tell you how I feel . . . this man who rang . . . you said he's not *yet* your fiancé. Am I to assume he soon will be?'

She nodded. 'Yes, David. I'm sorry.'

Her antennae would have been alert on any other occasion. She would have sensed his desire, been aware that there were undercurrents playing between them. But those undercurrents had been flowing in different directions. Now, freed from the fury and the longing that had driven her to Maoltrán, she could allow herself to see what had been obvious all along.

This time, when he walked away, he did not turn around.

She sat in her car until the sound of his jeep faded. No other sound distracted her except the thud of her heart. She drove without stopping until she reached the coast. The sand dragged against her footsteps. The waves cast spume in the air, sprayed her cheeks with salt. She cried then, hunched into a sand dune, until she no longer believed it was possible to shed another tear. But, somehow the tears kept flowing. She drove away, leaving nothing behind but the husk of longing.

On her return to Dublin she rang Frank and told him she had cut short her stay. He arrived shortly afterwards with wine and a takeaway. After they had eaten, she lay against

395

him, wanting him with an urgency she had never before experienced in his arms. He, responding, slid hard and smoothly into her. Her body pulsed with a needling ache that sweetly turned to pleasure as her mind reached out and reclaimed that moment in the car. The touch of lips so fleeting, so electrifying. Madness.

When Frank was sleeping, she pressed her head deep into the pillow and forced herself to count sheep. But there was no momentum to their jumping. They crashed and scrambled and flipped into impossible huddles. Suddenly, she recalled a letter from the past. Frank flung his arm, heavy with sleep, around her. She slipped out from under its weight and made her way to her office. In Maoltrán, she had been so obsessed with Joy that she had not allowed a flickering memory to surface. Too much effort needed to concentrate. But now it flickered again. She remembered the address. Surely it would be too much of a coincidence. In her filing cabinet she took out the mail she had received after Isobel's disappearance. Yellowed with age and ridden with unrealised hopes, she had not looked at these letters since the ending of the campaign. She separated those with a Clare postmark and, after a short search, found the one with his signature. She sat with it in her hands until she grew cold and shivery. She must have responded to him. What had she written? Did he still have it? Why should he? She had to let go. She searched for another letter. A place of stone . . . Miranda May. A fake name, as fake as the information she supplied. Carla placed his letters, along with Miranda's crazy ramblings, into the shredder. Before switching it on, she added the photograph of Joy Dowling, and watched them flitter into the past.

Chapter Sixty-Three

25 July 2008
Dear Dylan,

You were right about circumstantial evidence but wrong about Susanne Dowling. I saw the scans taken in St Anne's Clinic during her pregnancy. I understand you were trying to help and that, somehow, you believe you owe me a debt of gratitude. Nothing could be further from the truth. You have achieved much since the first time we met. I may have been a catalyst but what you have achieved is due to your own determination.

Since I returned home, I've had time to reflect. Now that I know Joy is not my daughter, I feel a sense of relief, especially after seeing her with her father and grandmother. They adore her and she adores them. They're a close-knit family and it would be impossible for me to sunder it.

In a peculiar way, I'm glad this happened. I've been sleepwalking through my life, unable to accept my own reality. Well, even Rip Van Winkle woke up eventually. Now it's time to rub the sand from my eyes. I want to move on with my life and accept that the search for my daughter is at an end. Soon I'll be married to a thoughtful and loving man. So please don't worry about me. My future is secure.

Joy Dowling is suffering deeply over the death of her mother. I recognise the symptoms of bereavement and hope you will be able to help her.

Yours sincerely,

Carla Kelly.

29 July 2008

Dear Carla,

I'm sorry. I know that's an inadequate apology but no words can convey my feelings of regret. I acted in what I believed were your best interests but, in doing so, I've subjected you to an incredibly traumatic experience. I hope you can forgive me.

If there is a sliver of a silver lining in this whole sorry business, it is the fact that you are moving on with your life. I wish you every happiness in your marriage.

I'm sorry . . .

Dylan.

5 January 2009

Dear Clare,

A very happy new year to you. The letting agent for the cottage you rented kindly passed on your address so that I could contact you. I'll be in Dublin on the 14th January, taking part in a glass designers' exhibition in the Three Lanterns Galley in Dublin with my grandson Joey. He's been working closely with me since he came back to us from Italy and will be displaying his latest piece, The Swan Maiden of Inchiquin Lake.

We had a lovely day with you by that lake and I thought it would be nice to see you again. If you're free,

why not drop by and have a glass of wine with us? David
tells me you're soon to be married, indeed, may already
be married by now. Obviously, my invitation also
includes your partner.

How is your book progressing? I'm sorry you had to
leave Maoltrán so suddenly. I was afraid we'd offended
you but, afterwards, David told us you were upset by the
album. I'm so sorry, my dear. You told us about the loss
of your baby and I can quite understand how those scans
would trigger your own memories. I'd no idea Susanne
had placed them in the album but Joy's pregnancy was an
anxious time for her.

We're all keeping well and busy. Work on the hostel
was delayed for a few months over some planning
objection but that's been sorted now and David is moving
things along as fast as possible. He hopes it will be up
and running by the summer and has already had lots of
enquiries. It should do very well, particularly as plans for
a hotel in Maoltrán have fallen through.

Joy is studying hard, although she's down with a dose
at the moment. Lots of snuffles and sneezes. It's that time
of the year again. Thankfully there's been no repeat of her
sillier behaviour earlier in the summer and Danny Breen
has been keeping well out of David's way.

My grandson is proving to be a talented glass designer.
I'm so proud of him. I hope you have an opportunity to
see what he has achieved.

Warmest regards
Miriam Dowling.

Chapter Sixty-Four

Joy

For over an hour Joy has been waiting to see Dr Williamson in a waiting room filled with sneezing, coughing, wheezing, spluttering patients. She's coughing louder than any of them. Her throat aches and her nose, according to her father who is sitting beside her, could steer ships away from rocks in a fog. When her name is finally called, her legs ache as she drags herself into the surgery.

She says 'ahh' and opens her mouth so that Dr Williamson can shine a torch down her throat. She shudders when she feels the stereoscope jabbing her back.

'Bronchitis,' declares Dr Williamson. 'It's bed, I'm afraid, Joy, and lots of tender loving care. How are you otherwise?'

'Fine.'

'You've been through a very tough time. It's okay not to feel fine. I'm sure you must miss your mother very much.' Dr Williamson sits back in her swivel chair and folds her arms. She's got an army of patients waiting outside but she doesn't appear to be in any hurry to call them into her surgery.

Joy nods, too miserable to pretend otherwise. 'Sometimes I wake up and think she's still alive. She should be, shouldn't she?'

'What do you mean?'

'She should have gone to you and got better. I begged her to do so when I saw the bleeding the first time.'

'The first time?'

'One morning. The blood was all over the bed. I can't stop thinking about it. Dylan says I'm suffering from un-resolved grief.'

'Dylan Rae?'

'Yeah. I went to see him after I came back from Arizona. Sometimes . . .' She begins to cough, that awful tickle in her throat acting up again. Dr Williamson gives her a glass of water and a throat lozenge. 'I get so furious with her at times. She must have known it was serious but she kept talking about the menopause and how it was perfectly normal . . . but it wasn't, was it?'

'She did come and see me, Joy. And she was attending her gynaecologist in Dublin.'

'What gynaecologist?'

'I don't know his name. Did she ever mention him to you?'

Joy shrugged. 'Not that I can remember. He didn't help her very much, did he?'

'Sadly not.' Dr Williamson frowns and writes a prescription for antibiotics and a tonic. 'Are you still seeing Dylan?' She hands the prescription sheet to Joy.

'No. He figured I needed a proper bereavement counsellor. He gave me a name, but what's the use in talking? Mum's still going to be dead, not matter how much I talk. And I'm still going to be furious with her. She wouldn't let me tell Dad . . . I shouldn't have listened to her, I know that now. Fat lot of good that is . . . me knowing.'

'That kind of anger is not good for you.' Dr Williamson stands up and walks to the surgery door with her. 'Take Dylan's advice and make an appointment with that counsellor. But in the meantime, go straight home to bed and stay there for the rest of the week. I'd like a quick word with your father. Will you ask him to come into the surgery for a moment?'

Her father doesn't speak until they arrive home. Joy falls into the sofa and huddles into the warmth of the kitchen. He makes tea and toast and places a tray beside her.

'I don't feel hungry,' she says.

'Try and eat something.'

'I can't . . . what did Dr Williamson say?'

'She wanted to know the name of Susanne's gynae-cologist in Dublin.'

'Who is he?'

'I never knew she had one . . . other than Professor Langley in St Anne's. She should have told me . . .' He presses his lips tightly together and sinks down beside her on the sofa.

'What else did she say?'

'She told me to talk to you about Susanne's death.'

'Did she tell you it's all my fault?'

'Of course not. Why on earth should she say such a thing?'

'Because it's the truth.' The tickle gathers at the back of her throat. She is going to cough again. Her eyes water from the effort of holding it back but it's impossible. Her breath splutters free as she bends over her knees, her chest heaving. Her father runs cold water and soaks a flannel, places it across her forehead. When she is able to speak she tells him about that morning and the expression on her mother's face when she turned and saw Joy standing at the door. That lost, hopeless expression that has been burning a hole in Joy's head ever since. If she starts crying she won't be able to stop. Never ever.

'All my fault,' she sobs. 'She said I mustn't tell you . . . it was women's stuff and you'd hate to know . . . it's all my fault . . . all my fault.'

'No, Joy. It isn't your fault. Have you been carrying those thoughts around in your head since she died? You silly, silly girl. Come here to me . . . come here . . .'

Then she is in his arms, crying against his rough tweed jacket. It doesn't matter if she can't stop because no matter what awful things happen he will always be there to look after her.

Chapter Sixty-Five

Statement of Dr Una Williamson.
Address: Wheat Acres, Maoltrán, Co. Clare.
Occupation: Medical Doctor.
Taken on Monday 14 January 2009 at Maoltrán Garda
Station by Garda Eoin Morris. I hereby declare that
this statement is true to the best of my knowledge and
belief and that I make it knowing that if it is tendered
in evidence I will be liable to prosecution if I state in
it anything that I know to be false or do not believe to
be true.

My name is Dr Una Williamson and I have been in
general practice in the town of Maoltrán for twenty
years. During that time, I saw Susanne Dowling
professionally on only two occasions. On one occasion
she discussed symptoms related to anxiety. On the
second occasion I had reason to be concerned about
dysfunctional uterine bleeding which began to occur
prior to the onset of her menopause. I found Susanne
Dowling to be evasive about her gynaecological records.
She was insistent that she had had regular smear tests
carried out by her gynaecologist, who was based in

Dublin. As she was originally from Dublin, I had no reason to doubt her word but I did find it strange that she never revealed his or her name. I knew her personally and she had been my bridge partner for a number of years. Shortly after her last appointment in my clinic she explained to me that our partnership was over as she was becoming increasingly involved in selling property in Spain. Again, my suspicions were not aroused. I was, however, shocked by her sudden death. If she had consulted her gynaecologist, which she claimed to have done, then her symptoms should have been immediately apparent. I contacted the Medical Council with my concerns but they failed to establish a link between her and any of the Dublin-based gynaecologists. I could only assume that she had lied to me for reasons that would always remain a mystery. I had occasion to speak to a counsellor, Mr Dylan Rae, who admitted that he had concerns about the identity of Susanne Dowling's daughter, Joy. He had reason to believe Susanne Dowling was not her natural mother. Although I found his suspicions almost impossible to believe, I decided to check the blood records of Susanne Dowling, her husband, Mr David Dowling, and Joy Dowling. My own suspicions were immediately aroused when I realised that both Susanne and David Dowling were rhesus positive while their daughter, Joy Dowling, was rhesus negative, thereby making it impossible for them to have conceived her. However, it was possible that David Dowling was not Joy's father. Susanne Dowling may have conceived her child by another man. But after a further conversation with Mr Dylan Rae, I reached the conclusion that Susanne Dowling did not give birth to the child she claimed was her daughter. I have read over this statement

and it is correct. I have been invited to make any
amendments or changes to it and do not wish to do so.

Signed: Una Williamson
Witness: Eoin Morris, Garda
Witness: Siobhan Comerford, Garda
Date: 14 January 2009

Chapter Sixty-Six

Carla

The speeches were over and the exhibition launched by the time Carla arrived at the Three Lanterns Gallery. She pushed her way through the crowd but was unable to see the Dowlings anywhere. In the centre of the gallery, the level of noise dropped to a murmur while Josh Baker interviewed one of the designers. Carla stopped abruptly when she saw him, then she merged back into the crowd. She heard the seahorses before they came into view, a kaleidoscope of flashing jewelled colours swaying gently above the laughter and conversation. Joey's design revolved slowly on a display stand. The plinth formed a glinting, rippling pool from which the swan maiden arose, translucent, ephemeral, her glossy hair drenched from the lake, pearls of moisture on her arms. She reached upwards, each delicate fold of her cloak and hood perfectly chiselled.

'What do you think of my son's work?' David Dowling had approached quietly and now stood beside her.

He was dressed once again in a suit, formally polite, except for his eyes, raking her.

'This is an exquisite piece of work,' she replied. 'You must be very proud of him.'

'It's receiving a lot of attention. We've very happy for him.' Their shoulders touched when he stepped closer to her. 'I'm glad you came, Clare.'

She nodded, laughed nervously. 'I had an hour to spare and thought it would be nice to say hello to Miriam.'

'She's around somewhere with Joy.' He waved his hand vaguely at the crowd. 'That creep Baker is interviewing Joey.'

'*The Week on the Street* is prime publicity.'

'I agree.' He shrugged, dismissively. 'But Baker's still a creep.'

'He's not one of my favourite presenters either,' she agreed. 'How is Joy?' Funny to mention her name and feel nothing except polite interest.

'Just out of bed. She's had bronchitis.'

'That's a tough one. Has she fully recovered?'

'Not quite. But nothing would keep her away. She has a severe case of hero worship of Joey. Is your fiancé, or should I say your husband, with you?'

'My fiancé. And no. He's launching a book tonight. It's quite a celebrity event.'

'Is that the book you told us about? Rocking your way from the bedroom to obscurity.'

'That's the one.' Carla laughed and leaned forward to look closer at the swan maiden. Why did legendary women emerge from their watery kingdoms, she wondered, only to retreat back again, heartbroken and betrayed?

An elderly woman with a young man in tow elbowed her way in front of them. Carla did not need an introduction; the young man's resemblance to David was immediately apparent. As the woman began speaking in a loud, authoritative voice about his design he looked sheepishly at David, who shrugged sympathetically and steered Carla away from the crowd.

'It's good to see you again,' he said when they reached a quiet corner of the gallery. 'I wanted to contact you and apologise for my clumsy behaviour—'

'It's okay, David—'

'No, it's not okay . . .' He stopped as the noise surrounding them increased. A government minister, surrounded by his officials, moved past and stopped a short distance from them. Josh Baker shook the minister's hand and they chatted casually to each other while the television crew set up the lighting and camera.

'Would you mind stepping out of the picture?' A young woman with titian hair and an angel tattooed on her neck gestured to Carla and David. 'We're about to interview the minister.'

Josh glanced indifferently in their direction then stepped into the space they had occupied. The minister assumed a dignified stance as he faced into the camera and his officials gathered supportively around him.

'Let's get out of here,' David said. 'Have a drink somewhere?'

Rain was falling when they left the gallery. He took her arm as they crossed the street and entered a small pub. When they were seated he lifted her left hand and held it lightly.

'Quite a sparkler.' He stared at her engagement ring. 'When are you getting married?'

'We haven't settled on a date yet.'

'I hope you'll be happy, Clare.'

My name is not Clare, she wanted to shout, and you are disturbing my heart. You are dangerous. I came to you in hatred yet when you kissed me it seemed as if I'd known the taste of you forever.

As if attuned to her thoughts, he said, 'I'd no right to kiss you. I'm not normally so impulsive but you were going away and I didn't know what to do.'

'We should forget that moment.'

'I can't.' He shook his head. 'All I knew was that I'd been waiting all my life for you to step into it. I couldn't get you out of my head. I was going to follow you to Dublin—'

'But you didn't.'

'No, I didn't. Joy told me she'd seen you in the Stork Club and well . . . there's only one reason why women shop there. I thought you were—'

'I'm not pregnant, David. Nor was I then. I was buying a present for my sister-in-law's new baby. But even if you had contacted me, it wouldn't have made any difference. Frank and I became engaged shortly after I returned from Clare.'

She had called into the Stork Club on an impulse. Raine's baby son gave Carla an excuse to browse among the rails of maternity and baby clothes. She had casually mentioned Susanne Dowling's name to the owner. Dee Ambrose was talkative and, after some prompting from Carla, she had started reminiscing about the amount of time Susanne had spent in her boutique when she was expecting Joy. As if Joy was aware she was being discussed, she had appeared in view then headed off with a young man, who, Carla had decided after summing up his flashy car, could only be Danny Breen. The sight of Joy going off with him had alerted such a strong maternal instinct in her that she had been unable to resist ringing David. The row that followed was now history, as was the maternal anxiety that had raged through her at the time.

David was still holding her hand. She should pull away and bring the conversation to a close, return to her apartment and gather its security like a protective cloak around her. When she made no effort to do so, his grip strengthened.

'Logic does not even enter into this,' he said. 'Nor does honour. I sensed something between us from the first time we met.'

'David, don't—'

'Let me say this . . . *please*,' he said. 'I need to tell you before it's too late.'

'It *is* too late.'

'Are you in love with him?'

'I think so.'

'You *think*?'

'I fell in love once,' she replied. 'Love at first sight. It didn't work.'

'So you believe it's possible, love at first sight?'

'Maybe. When you're young and foolish. I've been through too much to believe it can happen again.'

'But it has,' he said. 'And I can't imagine a future without you.'

'You know nothing about me—'

'What is there to know?'

'That I intend getting married to Frank. I wish it was different, David.'

'You're getting married to a man you think you love?'

'Yes.'

The lounge girl placed two drinks on the table. He drew his wallet from his pocket and handed her a twenty euro note. He lifted his glass then placed it back untouched on the table. 'If only I'd met you sooner . . . all those years wasted. Like you, I *thought* I was in love. But you don't *think* you're in love. You know you're in love because it hits you like an express train and you realise that nothing will ever be the same again.'

'I hope you meet someone, David. You deserve to have a happy life.'

'As you do, Clare.' His earlier urgency had been replaced by subdued politeness. He lifted his glass again and clinked it off hers. 'Here's to happiness.'

His mobile phone rang, startling them both. He checked the name and spoke to the person at the other end.

'Excuse me.' He turned apologetically to her. 'I have to take this outside. The connection is bad in here.' He stood up and walked towards the exit.

The lounge girl returned with his change. Carla accepted a ten euro note and some coins. His wallet had a seasoned look, well travelled leather. How many times in strange places had he taken it out and stared at the inserted photographs? She placed the note into the flap. The photograph of his daughter and son was similar to the one Dylan had taken. Seeing it again, she was reminded of the passion and fury that had driven her to Maoltrán. The second photograph, she figured, had to be his wife. The woman had short blonde hair and a heart-shaped face with wide-set blue eyes. The kitchen dresser was visible behind her and she was laughing, her hand raised in a startled gesture, as if warding off the photographer. Her other arm held a small bundle against her shoulder.

Pain shot through Carla's forehead, sharp as ice against her teeth.

She was still holding his wallet when he returned. 'Your wife?' she said, pointing to the photograph.

He nodded and accepted the wallet from her. 'I took that a long time ago,' he said. 'It was our happiest time.'

'I know her face,' said Carla. 'What was her maiden name?' She knew the answer but she needed to hear it from his lips.

'Sheehan. She was originally from Dublin.'

Carla picked up her handbag and clutched it under her arm. David Dowling had sensed something between them. It had been an earthquake shuddering deep within her and now it had cracked wide open.

'I have to go now.'

'But your drink.'

'I've something to do. It can't wait any longer. Goodbye.'

'I'll walk you to your car.' He shoved the wallet back into the inside pocket of his jacket and attempted to rise.

'No!' She would collapse if he moved any closer . . . or smash a glass and then . . . and then . . . she spun around and walked rapidly away from him. Outside the pub she ran towards the car park, expecting at any moment to feel his hand on her arm, holding her back, pleading with her to think . . . think . . . The street lights danced in dizzying circles as she drove from the city centre back to her apartment block. But her apartment was no longer a refuge. Its walls would be unable to contain her anger.

She parked by the canal and walked along the bank. A swan emerged and glided silently in a circle before disappearing again. No ghostly transformation would be played out among the reeds tonight. The swan maiden was trapped in glass, forged from the heat of a furnace. Solid mass until a crack or splinter shattered the illusion.

Edward Carter . . . Sue Sheehan . . . silent, the two of them, silent as the grave. This time Carla would not be deceived by fake scans and the gold circle binding Joy Dowling to her father. She would return to Maoltrán and reclaim her stolen child.

Chapter Sixty-Seven

Joy

The cars arrive just before Joy leaves for school. A white police car with yellow markings, followed by a grey Toyota Auris. At first, glancing out her bedroom window and noticing them, Joy assumes the policeman who emerges, Eoin Morris, her father's friend, is calling about the Ramblers. He's the secretary of the club and often drops in on his way home from work. But that's usually in the evening. Joy can't remember the name of the second guard who joins him . . . it's something Irish . . . Sinéad or Sorcha or Siobhan – yes, Siobhan *Comerford,* whose sister is in the same school year as Joy.

The doors of the grey car also open. A woman steps out from the driver's side. She's dressed in a navy suit and carries a briefcase, which she rests on the bonnet of her car. A man emerges from the passenger side and hurriedly buttons his jacket when the wind flaps it open. The woman removes documents from the briefcase while she talks to Eoin.

Joy's father comes into view from the side of the house and hurries across the grass towards them. His mood since they came home from the exhibition yesterday has been dire. Today he intends working on the cottages. His jeans are

417

tucked into his wellingtons and he's wearing the chunky fleece jacket Joy bought him for Christmas. His head jerks back when Eoin holds up his hand like he's stopping traffic and says something to him. The woman glances up and notices Joy at the window. The winter sun shines with a harsh, metallic glare. Her tinted glasses flash across the space separating them. Together with the man, she moves past the guards and heads towards the doorway.

Joy hears voices downstairs, Miriam's raised in protest. She opens her bedroom door as Miriam reaches the landing. Her grandmother's face is waxy, her hands trembling. Beyond her shoulder, Joy can see the man and woman standing in the hall.

'Joy, they want to talk to you.' Miriam sounds hoarse, her breath shallow.

'What do they want?'

'I don't know, darling. It's some dreadful misunderstanding but you'd better do as they say.' She takes Joy's hand and leads her to the top of the stairs.

'Are you Joy Dowling?' the woman asks when Joy reaches the hall.

'What's going on?' she asks. 'What's happening to my father?'

'Are you Joy Dowling?' The woman repeats the question in the same polite tone.

'Yes. Of course I am. What's wrong?'

'My name is Althea Egan,' the woman replies. 'I'm a social worker and this is my colleague, Hugh Colley. Please come with us, Joy. Everything will be explained to you shortly.'

'Explained? What will be explained? I've done nothing wrong . . . Gran, tell them to get out of our house.'

The woman keeps talking about Joy's welfare and how her safety is the most important thing to be considered.

Joy runs past her and out the front door towards her father. He's handcuffed to Eoin who, stiff and red-faced with embarrassment, is also talking about her welfare. He keeps going on about some Child Care Act and how Joy must be placed under the protection of the state.

'What are you talking about? *What* Child Care Act—' her father demands.

'The 1991 Child Care Act.' Eoin sounds as if he's reciting by rote but when her father tries to embrace her with his free arm, the policewoman barks an order that freezes him to the spot.

'Tell me what's wrong . . . what have you done?' she cries. 'I'm not going anywhere until I know what's happening. Please tell me.'

When her father reaches out to answer, his voice cracks. He hasn't shaved since yesterday and the rasping noise he makes when he rubs his hand against his chin reminds her of the night her mother died. That same nervous gesture, repeated again and again, as if he must touch something rough in order to focus. Nothing can be as awful as that time, she thinks. Miriam, reaching her, holds her hand so tightly that the ring she wears, the one with her birthstone – which she has promised to leave to Joy when she 'pops her clogs' – cuts into Joy's fingers.

Joy turns to Eoin. He used to crawl like a bear along the floor and let her ride on his back when she was small; now he stands still as a statue, no expression on his face, apart from his cheeks flaming, when he says, 'Joy, this is for your own good. Please go with the social workers. They'll take good care of you until all this is sorted out.'

'Fuck *off*!' Joy jerks away when the woman attempts to hold her arm. 'Don't you *dare* touch me.'

Her father speaks directly to Miriam. 'Contact my solicitor,

Maurice Doyle, immediately,' he says. 'There's been an appalling mistake and I want him to come to the Garda station immediately.'

'We have to go, David.' Eoin still sounds like a friend but Joy knows that their friendship is dead forever. 'Like you say, it's a cock-up but I'm just following orders.'

Joy moves back towards the house. 'But I don't have to go—'

'Go with them, please,' says her father. 'Miriam will stay with you.'

'No,' says the social worker. 'I'm sorry, sir. That's not allowed.'

Her father stumbles when Eoin moves forward, then falls into step beside him. The Garda car moves off. He is visible in the back seat, his face straining towards her until the car disappears between the hedgerows.

'We must leave now, Joy.' The man speaks for the first time. 'I'm sorry we've had to move so fast but your welfare is our responsibility now.'

If she hears one more word about her welfare she'll scream.

'I demand to know where you are taking my granddaughter.' Miriam sounds like herself again, calm and even more authoritative than the social worker. 'I'm warning you now. Heads will roll for this.'

'Visiting hours will be arranged as soon as possible,' says the woman. 'But, as of now, you are obstructing us in the discharge of our duty.'

It's too ludicrous for words but it is those commanding words that direct Joy into the car and away from Rockrose. The road stretches through Maoltrán and weaves through the Burren, past the broad Atlantic rollers and the kittiwakes swirling against the tide, onwards towards the signposts pointing to Dublin.

Joey is in Dublin. He stayed on after the exhibition to buy materials and do some more interviews. When her mobile rings she knows, without looking at the screen, that it's him.

'I've just been talking to Gran,' he says. 'What the hell's going on?'

'I don't know,' she sobs, and she arches her shoulder away from the woman. 'They just burst into my house and took me away . . . and Dad's been arrested.'

'I know. Can I speak to someone?'

'Yes.'

She holds her phone towards the woman. 'My brother wants to talk to you.'

Joy can hear the sound of Joey's voice but not what he's saying to the woman.

The social worker listens impassively and says, 'I'm not free to disclose that information.'

Joy can tell that Joey is becoming increasingly upset but the woman's expression doesn't change.

'Joy is under our care and will receive a full explanation as soon as we reach Dublin.' She nods at something Joey shouts then says, 'I'm sorry you think I sound arrogant but I'm not prepared to have this discussion with you over the phone. Of course Joy is free to ring you at any time. I'll pass you back to her now.' She smiles at Joy and hands over the phone.

How *dare* she smile? Joy wants to hit her, kick the seats, headbutt the man, leap from the speeding car. Her eyes are swimming in red.

'Ring me when you reach Dublin,' says Joey. 'It'll be sorted by then. I'll come straight away and take you home.'

The house, three storeys high, reminds her of Leamanagh Castle, except that it's not a ruin and, instead of fields, the smooth lawn is bordered by a high privet hedge. Joy enters a hallway with parquet flooring and steps leading upwards to a reception desk. The woman walks in front of her, the man takes up the rear. The handcuffs are imaginary, yet as tight as the ones that held her father captive.

'Try to understand, Joy,' the woman says when Joy is washing her hands after using the bathroom. 'Your safety is our only concern—'

'*Don't.*' She covers her ears. 'You take me from my home without any explanation and you want me to understand?' She has never known the strength of hatred until now. 'Where am I?'

'Everything will soon be explained to you.'

The woman *click click clicks* in her brisk high heels down a corridor and holds a door open. The room they enter is brightly lit with long oblong windows. An older woman rises from behind her desk and comes forward to greet Joy.

'These situations are very difficult,' she says and gestures Joy towards a chair beside the window. She must have nodded to the others because they melt from the room without a sound.

'My name is Patricia.' She draws another chair forward and sits opposite Joy. Her pink scalp shows through fine silver hair. She has old hands, wrinkled as dead leaves, and her eyes, staring at Joy from beneath her fringe, are compassionate, kindly, motherly. It is this concern that fills Joy with an unbelievable dread and the realisation that her world is about to be rent asunder.

Chapter Sixty-Eight

Carla
Three days later

In the arrivals hall at Dublin airport, Carla positioned herself beside a tall, young man with jutting cheekbones and dramatic curls. He carried a rose and a violin case, and leaned forward expectantly each time the sliding doors parted. A musician in love. She imaged a chaotic flat, the pizza wrappings binned, the clean sheets a sensible afterthought.

Robert's plane had landed twenty minutes earlier but there was still no sign of him. The sense of being under a microscope was sickeningly familiar. She peered through the cheap pair of glasses she had bought in Penneys – brown frames, nothing flash or glamorous to attract attention – and surveyed the latest surge of passengers. Her black jeans and tan jacket were unremarkable. At the last moment she had changed the woolly multi-coloured scarf that she usually wound around her neck for a plain, neutral one that blended into her jacket. No hat. Her black hair had grown slightly and the effect, although less severe, was also less dramatic. Apart from her height, nothing remained of the Carla Kelly who had once chased publicity with the same vigour as she now avoided it.

It was so simple in the end. Blood tests and a doctor with an enquiring mind had pre-empted Carla taking any action. Robert had rung her from Australia with the news, which Detective Superintendent Murphy had already broken to him. It was night time in Melbourne and he was weeping. She had imagined this moment so often and, now that it had arrived, they were separated by continents. Nothing to do but weep with him, her heart breaking all over again as she imagined their daughter's terror and distress.

The file on Isobel had been re-examined and the DNA tests – carried out on Carla and Robert when the tiny bones were discovered in the industrial estate – proved conclusive when they were matched to Joy Dowling. As the news spread among her family, they had arrived at her apartment and gathered around her. Carla was glad they did not bring champagne. To have popped corks and toasted the future would have been unendurable. No one seemed to know how to handle this revelation. A stranger would soon become part of their lives, carrying with her an entire childhood based on a falsehood.

'If only Gillian had lived to see this day,' whispered Raine when she embraced Carla.

'She always believed Joy . . . *Isobel* would be found,' Carla replied. 'You've no idea of the strength that faith gave me.'

David Dowling had been the target of their anger. Carla, listening, understood the instincts of a lynch mob. She wanted to be part of it and then, just as insanely, her rage gave way to such overwhelming confusion that she fled the crowded room.

Since then Robert had been in touch with her constantly. Orla Kennedy, who now carried the title Family Liaison Officer and was nearing retirement, was on hand to guide her through the following days. Fifteen years since she had held Carla's hands and batted off the media in the distraught atmosphere following Isobel's disappearance.

'This is the best retirement gift I could ever receive,' she said. 'I've never been able to forget you. You struggled so hard and for so long.'

'And then I disappeared.'

'I don't blame you.' Orla tut-tutted and shook her head. 'The media . . . a school of sharks. I was furious with some of the coverage.'

'They had so little to go on. No clues. Susanne Dowling was clever.'

'As well as devious,' replied Orla. 'And she'll never have to answer for her actions. Unlike her husband.'

'Unlike her husband,' Carla repeated.

David had been taken into custody, his initial period of detention extended by a further six hours. He had maintained his innocence throughout his questioning. On television she had watched him, shielded by friends, returning to his home.

'David Dowling will stand trial for abduction,' said Orla. 'He's been released on bail on condition that he presents himself at Maoltrán Garda Station every day.'

Joy was in the care of foster parents until she expressed a wish to meet her parents. So far, she was refusing point blank to consider communicating with them in any way.

'Give it time,' advised Orla. 'She's absolutely traumatised. With patience and good will, you'll meet your daughter soon.'

Carla, remembering Joy Dowling's impetuous personality, the adoration she had so openly displayed for the man she believed to be her father, wished she could feel so certain. Had Susanne Dowling, oblivious in her grave, created a gulf too wide for them to cross? Somehow, they had to build a different bridge. One that would bring them together, and that first step had to be taken by Carla. She would reveal her identity to her daughter before their first meeting. Give Joy time to adjust. A phone call was impossible. After numerous attempts to write a letter she gave up. Her excuses made her cringe. If only she had not gone to Maoltrán. If only she had walked away when she saw her daughter in the cemetery. If only she had ignored David Dowling who had filled her with such fury and, later, with a longing she had refused to name. It seemed inconceivable, those feelings that she believed had died within her, the jabbing excitement, the dizzying flights of fancy . . . and all the time he was a thief . . . *thief* . . . who had stolen her child . . . destroyed her future. She had gone to Maoltrán to break up the Dowling family. Now that the dream had become a reality, she was terrified by the consequences that would soon be unleashed.

Her mobile phone bleeped. *Luggage delayed. Will be with you asap.*

She grimaced wryly. They had planned for every eventuality except delayed luggage. Her nervousness grew as the delay stretched. The waiting crowd looked normal enough but she knew better than to trust appearances. Any self-respecting journalist would give his or her eye teeth to film the Anticipation parents reuniting.

On her other side, a stout businesswoman with a brisk jaw dangled a sign from one hand. Something about a language school. Carla's mind darted like a mayfly from one ripple to the next but she was incapable of absorbing more than fleeting impressions. The businesswoman wore silver high heels, confident stilettos to go with her ruthless chin. The musician had delicate fingers. How could it be otherwise? The young woman who rushed towards him was equally perfect: willowy limbs and dark, tempestuous eyes.

She too carried a violin case. Carla watched them lower their cases and collide, heard their joy as he lifted her high then folded her in his arms. It was too beautiful to last. This would be their golden season. Carla wished them luck then turned her attention back to the sliding doors.

The woman with the silver stilettos held her sign aloft and a group of Spanish students veered towards her. They spoke rapidly as they flowed past Carla, knowing their shrill conversation would soon be replaced by the stumbling blocks of the new language they had come to acquire. Josh Baker, still as eager as ever for the angle, the soundbite, the scent of suffering, moved from his vantage point behind one of the pillars. Carla, spotting him instantly, was not surprised. Of course he would have been tipped off, and now he was preparing to attach himself like a burr to her life once again. As he sank out of sight, she sauntered away from the waiting crowd and walked alongside the olive-skinned students. Josh never glanced in her direction. Nor did the camerawoman lounging beside him. Their indifference exhilarated her. Triumph when it came in quiet ways was all the sweeter for its containment.

Outside the arrivals hall she texted Robert. *Josh Baker waiting for you. Orla Kennedy will organise another exit. I'll meet you in my apartment.*

No candles on the kitchen table. No music playing softly on the stereo. Nothing to suggest intimacy as they sat opposite each other, just a dish of goulash and a shared bottle of wine. Occasionally, unable to control their emotions, they fell silent, then one or the other would pick up the story, go back over the details, as if repetition would make it easier to understand.

'How does Sharon feel about all this?' Carla asked.

'Threatened, jealous, angry – although she's tried not to

427

show it,' he replied. 'She's always believed I settled for second best . . . and I did, at the time.'

'And now?'

'I need her support, not her insecurities. She's my wife and nothing that's happened will change that. I think Isobel—'

'Joy. We must call her Joy.'

'Her name is *Isobel*. We've waited long enough to use her name.'

'She's lost so much, Robert. We can at least let her keep her name.'

'She lost what was never hers to lose.'

'But she doesn't believe that. She adores her father—'

'*I'm* her father.'

'Of course you are. But she needs to adjust to the shock of discovering who she is. We have to allow her that time.'

'What's the media situation?' he asked.

'It's been contained until now. But Maoltrán is a small community. They're now swarming over Rockrose.'

'Rockrose?'

'It's where she lives . . . lived.' She took a deep breath and blurted out the truth. 'I've been there.'

Robert grew increasingly agitated as she tried to explain, apologise, stumble past his constant interruptions.

'How could you go there without first consulting me?' he demanded when she finished speaking.

'What would you have told me to do?' she asked.

'Obviously, I would have told you to go straight to the police with your information.'

'And then what?'

'They would have followed proper procedure.'

'As they did when Dr Williamson gave her statement. And look what happened. Our daughter's in care now and refusing to meet either of us.'

'But what did you hope to achieve by going there?'

'I wanted to see that woman's grave . . . oh, I don't know . . . perhaps I wanted to dig her up, expose her for the liar and thief she was . . . I hadn't intended meeting Joy, not then, but she suddenly appeared and I was swept along—'

'Exactly. You were swept along, determined, as you always are, to do things your own way.'

'No—'

'Yes.' He banged his fist on the table. 'And now you've compromised your relationship with her. She thinks you're Clare Frazier.'

'I know . . . I know all that. But she will understand . . .'

'Understand *what*? I'm her father but you never thought about me when you decided to go off on this hare-brained mission.'

'You *buried* her, Robert. Remember?'

'Don't throw that at me. All the evidence—'

'All the evidence was circumstantial,' she replied. 'Just as circumstantial as the evidence Dylan Rae presented to me. I didn't want to get your hopes up and have them dashed again, especially when you were so far away.'

'I was *never* far away from you . . . or her. Every day . . . you've no idea . . .' His voice broke.

'But you *were* far away, Robert, in every sense of the word.'

An hour in each other's company and they were fighting. The urge to cry quivered effortlessly through her and was resisted. He too struggled to compose himself. As he drew her into his arms, his face, deeply lined with tiredness, was achingly familiar. They held each other without desire, friends now, unable to escape into the passion that had once bound them together. Like a flame that had raged too strongly, the love they had known was quenched that evening with a gentle puff.

Chapter Sixty-Nine

Joy

Hi Isobel,

My name is Jessica Kelly. I'm Carla Kelly's niece. I Googled your name and found your website. It's so cool. I just wanted to say Hi and to tell you how stunned and thrilled and excited and happy we are that you have been found.

When I was small, you were my imaginary friend. My parents never wanted to talk about you in case it would upset me but bit by bit I found out about my stolen cousin. I had a hidey-hole in my back garden that no one knew about. It's where I escaped from my brothers (your cousins) . . . oh my God!! . . . you don't want to know anything about them! I'd take down my tea-set and dolls and my xylophone. I invited my aunt in one day. She looked so sad until I told her about my secret friend. It helped her, knowing I didn't believe you were dead. I stopped having you as my imaginary friend when I was about eight but I never stopped hoping I'd meet you some day.

You must be feeling really frightened by all that has happened to you. My main reason for emailing you is to

431

*reassure you that my aunt and uncle are really nice
people. He used to love my aunt madly and I think he
still does but he has another wife and they have two
children so I guess it's not on. He's a cop. Funny, isn't it,
that he couldn't find the person he most wanted to find
in all the world?*

*Every year on your birthday, I visited the Angels' plot
in Glasnevin Cemetery with my family. But my aunt
never went there on that day because she had her own
belief. She went there other times and said it was to
honour the memory of a child with no name. She never
stopped believing she would find you and now she has.*

*I can't wait to meet you in person and welcome you
into our family. Don't tell my aunt I contacted you. She
wants to give you space . . . and so do I. You don't have to
respond to this email but it would be nice to hear from
you and maybe be each other's friends on Facebook.*

Love from your cousin,

Jessica.

Joy stands beneath the shower and switches it to cold. At
first she yelps, then grits her teeth as her body slowly adjusts
to the jets. This is a power shower, icy needles on the back
of her neck. She wants to be numb. That way she has control.
The sensation is almost unbearable, then *utterly* unbearable,
and she is forced from the shower to shiver in this strange
bathroom in this strange house in this strange city in this
strange situation, which is so ridiculous she needs to stand
back once again under the flailing jets.

Five days have passed since she was kidnapped. These
strangers, those impostors who have broken up her family
and caused an incredible miscarriage of justice, have decided
she will be in foster care until she is willing to meet her

so-called parents. To pretend to be Isobel Gardner. It's too ridiculous for words.

Most of the time she stays in her room and emails her friends. They are fascinated by her story. She's a celeb in Maoltrán. *Woo hoo* . . . send in the paparazzi. She bangs furiously on the keys and tells Lucinda to stop writing drivel about how she always wanted to belong to someone beautiful like a famous supermodel. Danny Breen also emails. He's in Trinity now and will call and see her soon. They can go for a drive in his Boxster. Anywhere she wants to go?

Rockrose, Joy emails back. *Bring me home.*

Patricia says it's out of the question. She had hoped Joy could stay nearer her home but both of her so-called parents are anxious to be near her. Joy doesn't care where she stays as long as this crazy situation is sorted out. Her father (no way will she call him Mr Dowling, as Patricia does) is allowed to see her once a week but always in the presence of Patricia.

The woman knocks on the door.

'Everything all right, Joy?' Her cheery question has an anxious undertone. Katie is her name and she must be used to disturbed young people wreaking havoc on her bathroom. Some of the tiles are cracked and there is a dent in the door, as if it has been kicked violently and often.

'Yes.' Joy can hardly speak. Her teeth chatter and the cold water wins. She switches off the shower and dries herself, drags her clothes back on. Katie and her husband Philip look after young people with what Katie calls 'issues'. Joy does not have issues. She is the victim of a grave miscarriage of justice. Those are her *father's* words. She clings to them, recites them to everyone who calls to see her. And many people have called, most of them in tears of shock and outrage over this appallingly grave miscarriage of

433

justice, which, claims Miriam, will result in heads rolling and lawsuits and compensation claims for millions.

Her grandfather and Tessa were her first visitors. Her grandfather looked stooped and walked with a cane. When he sat down, he placed his hands on the cane handle but he was still unable to stop them trembling. They wanted to look after her until her father is tried and proved innocent. But they are not allowed because, officially, until it is proved otherwise, she is not related to them. Her grandfather had snuffled so much that Joy handed him a box of tissues and ordered him to stop pretending he wasn't crying. He kept saying it was all his fault and going on about a baby boy until Tessa said he was upsetting everyone.

After they had left, she rang her grandmother (the idea that Miriam is not her grandmother is equally ludicrous) and asked her to bring the photo album when she visited the following day. Miriam told her it was in police custody but she would bring anything else Joy wanted. And that is precisely nothing. Joy does not want any of her possessions, except her laptop. Her grandmother has booked into a nearby guesthouse and won't leave Dublin until Joy is with her. Her 'creative drive' is kaput, she says. Joey can run the studio until their lives are back to normal again. But there is something about her voice that worries Joy. It's subdued, not furious and yelling the way it was when the social workers marched Joy into the car. Sometimes they don't talk much. They just sit, holding hands, like they're storing up memories to hold forever.

When Phyllis Lyons had visited it was okay to cry and be rocked in her arms, because Phyllis was the bearer of the truth, a witness to Joy's existence. The woman who drove her tractor through the flood and helped Joy's mother give birth. All that was true, Phyllis had agreed. It had been an awful flood right enough. One of the worst. And she had almost, but not quite, drawn Joy's head into the light. That part, she said, had already been done by Joy's mother. But, she added when Joy had begun to cry again, that only happened a second or so before her arrival because, not to put too fine a point on it, there was blood on the sheets and all over Joy. To be honest, admitted Phyllis, she was there so quickly it hardly made any difference, which was why she never *actually* corrected anyone who believed she was present throughout. She had spoken so breathlessly it had been difficult to follow what she was saying. Joy wondered if the guards had the same difficulty when they interrogated her in the Garda station. Phyllis burst into tears when she came to the bit about the interrogation. It was the first time she had ever been inside the station, except to get passports or driving licences signed.

Katie believes anger is good. Change is a journey and anger is the first obstacle to be overcome. It sounds like something Miriam would say. But there will be no anger journey, except for the journey back to Rockrose. Every day Joy expects it to happen. There's a view of the Dublin Mountains from her bedroom window. Most of the time they're covered in a blue haze and today she can see snow on the summits. Once this grave miscarriage of justice is sorted out, Joy will be gone from this house so fast there'll be roadrunner dust on her heels.

The media are crawling all over Maoltrán. Lucinda says the locals are giving interviews about Joy's family and how nice and ordinary they are, especially her mother, who was always the first to say yes when asked to volunteer for community work. But Joy does not read this information in the papers. Instead, she reads about home-schooling and the isolation of Rockrose, and how her mother once assaulted Joey. A sick journalist called Alyssa Faye writes about the psychological state of Joy's mind and makes her sound like a feral child. The tabloids are having a field day. *Weekend Flair* photoshops her face and transposes it on top of Carla Kelly's body. One of her catwalk shots. The clothes she wears are diaphanous and flowing, and she seems to be carried on a gale force wind that sweeps her long blonde hair from her face and moulds the clothes to her legs and breasts. She might as well be naked. Stark naked, and it looks so real that Joy feels as if the same wind is sweeping away another layer of her identity.

After crying so much that her throat feels like the inside of a glue pot, she hits the www.FindIsobelGardner.com site on her laptop. She has resisted the temptation since arriving in Dublin. It's like entering enemy territory but she can't take her eyes off the baby photograph. Isobel Gardner's eyes are closed and her tiny mouth pursed like a raspberry. The rest of her resembles a caterpillar inside a pink cocoon. Joy looks at Carla Kelly and Robert Gardner. Her heart does not dovetail in recognition of her long-lost parents. All she feels is sadness that their hopes, still alive after all those years, must be dashed, and dashed-quickly before she's drawn into their tragedy.

Joey emails every day, often twice. He came to see her as soon as she arrived in Dublin with the social workers. He held her so tight she thought she'd faint from lack of air. He'd been crying. She had never seen him cry, even that time her mother hit him. He had held Joy in the way she'd always imagined, like she was something tender and precious, instead of a sister who needed a bear hug. But she wanted that bear hug now. She wanted him cuffing the side of her head and teasing her and getting mad at her because she was acting off the wall and sending him stupid emails. Half of her is half of him, and he said, 'Yes . . . yes . . . of course that's true,' but his gaze kept sliding away, as if meeting her eyes would expose him to a terrible truth.

He's back in Maoltrán now, supporting her father. They are doing everything they can to end this grave miscarriage of justice. In the police station, her father's belt and shoelaces were removed. He was put in a cell and questioned by Gardaí from Dublin who had once searched for Isobel Gardner. They failed to do their job properly and so they concocted this ridiculous story to prove they have succeeded. To prove Joy Dowling is a stolen child. Not kidnapped for ransom, adopted or abandoned on the steps of a church. Stolen. Like a jewel necklace or gold bullion.

Joy burrows under the duvet until she feels warm again. She has phoned Dylan and asked him to visit her. But he hasn't come yet. She could do with him sorting out her head because sometimes, just sometimes, when she's really tired and weepy, she wonders what it would be like to meet them, Carla Kelly and Robert Gardner, just so they can see her and know it's all a sick mistake.

Miriam brought one other thing from Rockrose – Joy's father's hairbrush. Joy cut a strand from Joey's hair. She labelled it, as she labelled her own, and the hairs she drew from her father's brush. She has researched DNA on the internet. It's an exact science. Why should she trust the cops? They failed once to find Isobel Gardner. They will not admit to a second failure and have probably deliberately forged the DNA results. It's up to Joy to establish her own identity.

Before she switches off the light on another wretched day, she sends a final email.

> Hi Jessica,
> My name is Joy Dowling and I received your email. It was nice of you to contact me but I'm afraid you've made a terrible mistake. I'm not Isobel Gardner.
> Do you believe in heaven and hell? I don't, not any

more. Hell exists on earth and you enter it when you look out of your bedroom window one morning and see strangers walking into your house. Hell is having your own solicitor, social worker, foster parents, Family Liaison Officer, psychologist, everyone except your own family around you. Heaven will be the day I return to my proper home.

I'm sorry your aunt and uncle had their hopes raised and dashed again. I'm sorry your imaginary friend wasn't me. It sounds like you had fun in that hidey-hole.

I looked at your aunt's site. How did I ever get mixed up in her story? I guess it's because I look a bit like her and we have the same blood group. But so had my mother. She told me so herself, many times. They've obviously fucked up the forensic tests which is disgraceful and my family will be taking an action for compensation. Heads will roll. I don't plan to meet her or your uncle. It will only complicate this mess even further.

Goodbye,

Joy Dowling.

Chapter Seventy

Carla

Where is Carla Kelly? Anticipation Mum Under Cover. Model Mum Missing. Mother of Isobel Unavailable for Comment.

Carla watched the story unfold. The broadsheets and the redtops, all with the same prurient curiosity, demanding to see her tears of joy . . . joy . . . Joy . . .

Her defences held. Her apartment remained her fortress. She dreaded being swept along by the currents of the media, unable to think, to make decisions, to extricate herself from the morass of her own deception. She was protected by the internet but the FindIsobel mailbox was flooded with requests for interviews. She ignored them and Robert also remained under cover; a chameleon man, back in familiar territory.

Her family, after their initial gathering in her apartment, respected her desire for anonymity. Janet rang every day, complaining about the journalists lounging against her garden wall. They were breaking Carla's father's heart and Janet was forced to serve them soup and sandwiches, and have her photograph taken every time she put her nose outside her front door.

'How long will this go on?' she demanded. 'Isobel can't keep refusing to see you.'

Robert said much the same thing. Only four more days left before he returned to his family. He was apologetic, harried. Damian, his eldest son, was booked into hospital to have a tonsillectomy. Carla suspected Sharon had laid his responsibilities on the line. A son with engorged tonsils would have to take priority over a child he had buried many years previously. He spoke with Patricia every day but his daughter remained resolute in her refusal to meet him.

'And now she's going to give a press conference,' Carla complained when she called to Frank's house on the evening Patricia had relayed this latest information to her. 'She hasn't the slightest idea that she's walking into a snake pit.'

'I'm sure she's being well advised.' Frank placed a dish of vindaloo curry with rice and naan bread in the centre of the table. 'Sit. Relax. Eat,' he ordered. 'We never have time on our own any more.'

'This is delicious, Frank.' Carla gulped water and reached for a tissue. He had a heavy hand with spices and her eyes were already watering. 'I'm not so sure Joy will take advice. She's headstrong and stubborn—'

'As you discovered when you went to Clare.'

'Yes.'

He opened a bottle of red wine and poured it into two glasses. Initially his reaction when she had confessed her true reasons for being in Clare had been more muted than Robert's outburst. But she was aware that his annoyance simmered a little more strongly each time they discussed it.

'Going there was a bad idea,' she admitted. 'I'm so fright-ened it's going to drive an even deeper wedge between myself and Joy when she discovers the truth. And Robert will be going home next week. I'll be on my own again—'

'Hardly on your own,' he protested. 'You have me.'

'Of course I do.' She nodded and pushed her plate aside, leaned her elbows on the table. 'But I can't think about our wedding until I've sorted out my relationship with Joy.'

'Of course,' he replied wryly. 'First things first.'

'I wish . . . how I wish I'd let events take their natural course.' She knew she was talking too much about Joy. Talking compulsively, incessantly, unable to focus on anything other than the inevitable meeting. 'Six months, that's all I had to wait until the truth was uncovered but now . . . it's such a mess, Frank. What am I going to do?'

He broke off a chunk of naan bread, dipped it into his curry and continued eating, slowly chewing, digesting her question with the same deliberation.

'You were different when you returned from Clare,' he said. 'Softer, somehow. Like you'd finally let her go. And that was the reason you decided to marry me.' He ignored the wine and reached for a glass of water.

'It helped make up my mind, yes.'

'But you lied about your reasons for being there. You only told me the truth after you'd spoken to Robert.'

'He needed to be the first to know.'

'Are you still in love with him?'

'Of course not. I love you.'

'Somehow, I don't think so. Not the way I expected you to love me.'

'And what way is that, Frank?' she demanded.

'Everything's changed, Carla.' He ignored her question. 'What has happened to you and Robert changes the entire balance of our relationship.'

'Why should it?'

'You've been obsessed with finding your child since I've known you. Now you've succeeded. Isobel . . . Joy – whatever you want to call her – will always come first. And Robert will be back in your life again. You'll have decisions to make, events to attend, a daughter to share. Which begs the question. Where do I fit in?'

'Is this about *you* or me?' she asked.

'It's about our future,' he replied. 'You have your daughter back again. The reason you decided to marry me no longer applies.'

'Are you cancelling our wedding?'

'I'm not good with competition . . . and I can't compete against flesh and blood.'

'You're *jealous* of my daughter?'

'If you want to put it like that, yes. But I prefer to think I'm letting you off the hook. Sharing space with a teenage tearaway is probably not the best way to begin married life. Don't tell me the thought hasn't crossed your own mind.'

'I'm willing to take that risk.'

'I take enough risks in my business, Carla. But I don't extend them to my personal life. For that, I depend on certainties.' He stood up and began to clear the table. Leftover food disgusted him and had to be removed immediately.

She followed him to the kitchen and watched him scrape the remains of their meal into the bin. The clang of the fork against plates reverberated through her head.

'Nothing in life is certain, Frank. Even true love doesn't come with any guarantees.' She removed her engagement ring and placed it on the windowsill beside him. 'I'm sorry, Frank,' she said.

'I hope everything works out for you, Carla,' he replied. 'You deserve to be happy.'

She stared at the ring for the last time; a solitaire in a

simple setting that highlighted the purity of the diamond. Now that it no longer weighed heavily on her finger, she wanted to run light-footed from his kitchen. She should feel some emotion other than relief. They had been together for so long, lapping comfortably against each other's lives, priding themselves on the easy-going nature of their relationship. She had used him – just as she used her website and the persona of Clare Frazier – as her shield, and had envisaged their future drifting along at the same unruffled pace. A small price to pay for serenity, she had decided when she returned from Maoltrán and accepted his proposal.

But love, she thought, as she opened his front door and stepped into the night, was not easy-going, nor was it undemanding. It burned and bled and scoured the heart. The demands it made had haunted her for fifteen years and, now that an end was in sight, she was in turmoil. No wonder Frank had retreated from such unbridled emotion.

She smiled as she walked towards the canal and the moon, white and full with promise, skidded giddily above the rooftops.

Chapter Seventy-One

Joy

Dear Joy,

I know this will be a difficult letter to read but I hope you will finish it and understand that I seek only to protect you. I had decided not to contact you until you were ready to meet myself and Robert. However, I've heard that you are planning a press conference for tomorrow. I understand your reasons for doing so but I beg you to cancel it. The wrong publicity can do untold damage and only make things worse for you and your family. I speak from experience. If you ignore this letter, then please think carefully before you answer questions and remember that the truth, as you know it, can become someone else's torrid headline. <u>Please</u>, have good people surrounding you and listen to their advice.

My heart is breaking all over again when I think of the shock and confusion you have endured since you were removed from your home. I always believed that one day we would be reunited but I never understood, until now, how devastating that would be for you. Please do not feel threatened by me or by Robert. He, too, only wants what

is best for you. We will wait until you are ready to meet
us, no matter how long that takes.

Goodbye for now. My thoughts are always with you.
Carla Kelly.

Patricia did warn her in advance that the letter was from
The Other Side but Joy is still unprepared for the anger she
feels after reading it. She tears it in half and flings it into the
rubbish bin. How manipulative is that? Pretending to protect
her while at the same time trying to stifle her. The first thing
she did when her baby was stolen was to hold a press
conference.

She puts on her iPod and listens to Eminem until she falls
asleep. It's still dark when she awakens. Her head aches. She
wants to cry again but tomorrow is an important day. She needs
to look her best when she puts the record straight. The letter,
jutting from the litterbin, annoys her. She takes it out and
places the pieces together, a jigsaw with ragged edges that
will never join. She places it under her pillow and drifts
restlessly towards morning.

A green baize tablecloth, bottles of water, glasses that tinkle
with ice. Her solicitor wrote the statement he expects her to
read. She has studied it many times. It is filled with words
like 'allegedly' and 'purportedly' and 'adjustment period' and
'conciliation'. All it stops short of stating is that Joy is looking
forward to a happy-ever-after reconciliation. He has advised
her to read it slowly and clearly. Thanks to the school musical,
Joy knows how to breathe correctly and project her voice.
She has been warned about the media presence but the
crouching movements of the photographers and the blaze
of the television cameras is terrifying.

'Thank you all for coming.' Her voice, which sounded so

strong earlier when she was rehearsing, suddenly shakes. She ignores her solicitor's statement and opens her own one.

She had spent so much time writing it, then reading it aloud to herself, that she could recite it off by heart. She spreads it out on top of her solicitor's statement and presses her hands flat against the green baize tablecloth.

'My name is Joy Dowling. I'm fifteen years old and that is all I have in common with the Anticipation Baby, Isobel Gardner.'

She stiffens when her solicitor's hand rests commandingly on hers. He leans towards her and whispers that she must, as arranged, read what he has written. She ignores his warning and continues.

'A grave miscarriage of justice has been perpetrated against my father, David Dowling. Throughout my life he has treated me with kindness and love, as my mother did until her death. I was removed from my home without any warning on the 16th January 2009. Since then I have seen my father twice. We are not allowed to spend time alone. I believe this is an infringement of his civil rights. I demand to know why my father is being treated like a criminal when he has done nothing wrong. I'd like to extend my deepest sympathy to Carla Kelly and Robert Gardner for all the suffering they have endured. But I am not their child. I appeal to them to stay out of my life and allow me to return to my own home and family. Thank you for your time and attention.'

Cameras click and the lights flash like scattered firework sparks. The journalists, having remained silent while she spoke, rear upwards with questions.

'How can you explain the different blood groups?'

'Isn't DNA evidence irrefutable?'

'How will you feel if it's proved you are the Anticipation Baby?'

'When do you intend meeting Carla Kelly and Robert Gardner?'

'Had you any suspicions when you were a child that you were stolen?'

'Did you ever wonder why you were brought up in such an isolated place?'

'Why did Susanne Dowling home-school you for years?'

On and on the questions fly, their microphones jabbing at her like claws. Have they listened to a word she said? Her panic grows. A man stands in the front row and approaches her. He has wrinkles around his eyes, and a wide, narrow mouth that curves in a smile. A woman with a television camera closes in on Joy. He looks familiar but she can't think of his name. The journalists fall silent when he speaks.

'Joy, I'm Josh Baker from *The Week on the Street.*' His voice creeps over her like something furry and soft. 'On behalf of the assembled media, I want to thank you for speaking so frankly to us. Congratulations on your courage in holding this important press conference.'

She stretches backwards in her seat, suddenly scared, which is ridiculous because Josh smiles again.

'Joy, can you tell us about your first childhood memories?' he asks.

She remembers looking through the bars of her cot and seeing her father and mother smiling at her from their bed. The memory is so sharp she presses her hand to her chest, but it's not a true memory because her father's bed was always in the other room and he was gone so often . . . She remembers crying on the steps of his office . . . but that's not a good memory . . . And she thinks about the games they played . . . how she used to pull the duvet over her head and he would crawl underneath her bed and into the wardrobe, pretending he couldn't find her anywhere, and, how, when she jumped from under the duvet, she'd startle him so much he'd collapse on the bed, clutching his chest, yelling, 'I give in. You win again, Champ!'

So many memories pressing against her head. Josh is waiting and smiling and it's important to explain to the world that she did not have a weird, mixed-up childhood.

'My father used to tell me stories in bed. He'd bring me to the Burren and teach me the names of flowers and once he—'

'In your bed?' asks Josh.

She stops, unsure if she has heard him correctly.

'He told you stories in your bed?' Josh, no longer smiling, looks concerned.

'Yes. In . . . I mean . . . *on* my bed.' She shakes her head, willing him to smile again. 'We used to play games—'

She is aware that Patricia is pressing her knee, a hard squeeze from her dead-leaf hand, which is the signal for Joy to stop talking. But she can't because Josh looks so grave and the camera is an all-seeing eye that freezes her expression.

'Catching flies,' her mother would say if she could see her sitting here with her mouth open, gulping when she swallows. She is unable to look away from Josh Baker when he asks, 'Were there other men who played games with you at night?'

Her solicitor is on his feet, so angry that his hands bang off the table, and Joy is shrinking smaller and smaller, the way she felt when her father steered the boat through the towering walls of the Grand Canyon.

She stands at Patricia's command. Her feet wobble. Jelly on a plate . . . jelly on a plate . . . another childhood memory . . . and Patricia supports her, moves her away from the green baize table.

A face flickers at the edge of her eye, stands out for an instant from the crowd. The journalists are leaving the room, ordered out by a woman in a Garda uniform. She looks so formidable that they obey her instantly. All except Clare Frazier. She wears glasses now. They make her look stern and stand-offish but they cannot hide the tears on her cheeks.

Joy wants to go to her. The pull is so strong she stops and tries to walk back but Patricia, strong for an old woman, has such a tight grip on her arm that she's unable to break free. When she looks around again, Clare Frazier has disappeared.

Back in the foster home, when she is left alone at last, she does what she has wanted to do since that terrible morning. Katie, hearing her banging her head on the bedroom wall, holds her so still she can no longer harm herself.

Hi Joy,

Can you forgive me for being so stupid? I was so excited when I believed Isobel Gardner had been found that I emailed you without thinking it through. My mum says I'm always running off at the mouth and I guess that applies to email as well. You were right to be mad at me. I can't bear to think how I'd feel if the social services came into my house and took me away by force.

I watched your press conference. It was horrible. Josh Baker is a sicko and I hope he suffers from leprosy of the tongue. My father used to read me stories and lie on my bed too. It's disgusting the way that sicko twisted everything. But you were really cool.

If you don't believe you are Isobel Gardner, no one can force you to do so. Even if (and I know it won't happen) but even if your father is found guilty, you still can be who you believe you are.

If you want to email back that would be cool. But it doesn't matter if you don't. I'll understand.

Yours sincerely,

Jessica Kelly.

Chapter Seventy-Two

Carla

The media showed no mercy. Josh had set the honeytrap and her daughter had walked right into it. Carla watched that night's edition of *The Week on the Street*, read the papers the following morning. *No Joy for Anticipation Parents* was the kindest headline. *Was Anticipation Girl Victim of Paedophile Ring?* the most cruel. She was safe from prying eyes in her citadel, yet she was inside her daughter's skin, flashing back in time and spinning from the exposure.

She had hoped Joy would change her mind and meet them after the press conference. But the meeting she and Robert had attended this morning with Patrica had proved that their daughter was still determined to keep her distance.

'Joy has had to make huge adjustments and she's not yet ready for that final step,' Patricia had told them. 'It happens regularly enough when adoptive children prepare to meet their birth parents. They desperately want to make contact but the weight of their fear paralyses them. I know the situation is different with Joy—'

'Isobel,' Robert had snapped.

Patricia had nodded, apologetically. 'I must put Isobel's interests first. I'm sorry. Please be patient. The accident has further destabilised her. I'm so sorry your hopes have been dashed again.'

The meeting had been as frustrating as all the others and the social worker's apologies had only increased Robert's annoyance.

'As her parents we have rights. Don't you think we've suffered enough, *waited* long enough?' His expression had hardened. 'Does she think about us at all? Has she any consideration for the fact that we also have lives to lead. Can't you talk to her again, change her mind?'

'What would you like me to do, Mr Gardner?' Patricia had compassionate eyes but her steadfast gaze was capable of steel. 'Frogmarch her towards a meeting? That would hardly be the most auspicious way to begin a family relationship.'

With her reproof ringing in their ears, they had left her office.

Unable to stay still when she returned home, Carla tackled her apartment. She cleared out presses, swept mats, dusted the tops of picture frames, lifted armchair cushions to vacuum every crease and crevice underneath. She worked with a feverish intensity, as if by cleaning the hidden dust and grime of her surroundings she could bleach the confusion from her mind.

When her apartment was spotless, she soaked in a bath. Steam clouded the mirror and the bath bubbles slowly evaporated, every muscle in her body seeking relief. When the doorbell rang she sighed and decided to ignore it. Robert would not call to her apartment, nor would her family. Unable to ignore a second, more prolonged ring, she pulled on a bathrobe and checked the security camera.

David Dowling was standing outside the apartment entrance. She stepped back, as if he was physically confronting her. Robert had sought to prevent him or any members of his family making contact with him or Carla. But David was not breaking that injunction. He was calling on Clare Frazier, hoping, perhaps, that she could bring him comfort. His face had that askew appearance, as if the muscles aligning his features had collapsed. She recognised his loss of control, his all-consuming anguish.

'David.' Her voice was softer than she intended as she pressed the release button. 'Come on up.'

By the time he had taken the elevator to the sixth floor she was dressed in a skirt and top but was still in her bare feet. He hesitated at the front door, reluctant to enter.

'Joy saw you at the press conference,' he said. 'I wanted to thank you for not asking her any questions.'

'I'm not a journalist,' she replied and led him into the living room. 'I went there to offer her support.'

His hands, resting on his knees, clenched into fists. 'I wanted to kill Josh Baker with my bare hands. No knife or gun, just my bare hands. You've seen the headlines, the insinuations. I had to seek an injunction to stop them *alleging* I abused my child. As if I would harm a hair on her head. But the damage is done. She was taken from me and now my reputation's also gone.'

'I'd hoped to talk to her afterwards,' she said. 'But she was whisked away so fast.'

He slumped into an armchair and hunched forward. 'That sums it up.' His voice cracked. 'They just came one morning and lifted her.' He paused, still unable to grasp the enormity of what had occurred. 'It was over in a few minutes. My life . . . her life. Everything we'd shared . . . gone, just like that. You would think it couldn't happen, wouldn't you? The state can't come into your home and destroy you. But they can . . . and they have . . . I can only see her in the company of a social worker. It's one of the conditions of my bail.

This morning, before I could leave Maoltrán, I had to present myself to a guard I've known all my life. I don't know what to do, Clare. I'm lost . . .'

'But she never belonged to you. The DNA evidence is irrefutable.'

'Yes.' He shook his head from side to side. 'Irrefutable. Even Joy has to accept that now. Joey is with her, trying to convince her to meet her parents.' He continued speaking, more to himself than to her, the raw anger on his face giving way to bewilderment. 'Susanne never gave birth to Joy. How can that be? Who is going to believe I didn't know? I should have known . . .'

'David, listen. I need to tell you something.'

'How could she do this to me . . . to steal another woman's child?' He was incapable of hearing her. 'But the dead can't speak and I'm left to explain . . . what? Who will understand what I can't understand myself?'

His mobile phone rang. He answered it immediately and spoke tersely to the caller. 'How long since she left?' he asked. Already he was walking from her apartment. 'I'm on my way now.'

He clicked out of the call and said, 'That was Joey. Joy's missing. She's taken off with Danny Breen.'

Then he was gone. Carla heard the front door slam. The truth fell like a stone into the silence he left behind.

Chapter Seventy-Three

Joy

Dear Joy,

Your email has been brought to my attention. DNA testing is a very sophisticated tool for establishing identity and I wish I could give you a different answer.

Using tests on sixteen different areas on the DNA molecules submitted for Mr David Dowling and Mr Joey O'Sullivan, we have established a definitive profile on both. They are father and son.

Unfortunately, in the case of your own DNA molecule, the results were incompatible. No relationship could be established between you and Mr David Dowling or between you and Mr Joey O'Sullivan.

I am sorry to have to break this news to you as I have established from your correspondence that you had hoped for a different result. But I'm afraid you must take the result as definitive and capable of standing up in a court of law.

On a personal note, this sounds like a complex situation and I hope you have people around you who can help you come to terms with the changes taking place in your life.

With my best regards,

Jon Sutton
Managing Director
T.R.A.C.E. Laboratories Inc.

The seats in Danny's Boxster are heated. Joy wriggles deep into the passenger seat and opens a packet of Rolos, leans over and places one on his tongue. She remembers an old advertisement she used to watch on television. Something about loving someone enough to give them your last Rolo. Her mother used to chant it when she gave her a treat. *Do you love me enough to give me your last Polo, Rolo, jelly bean, jelly baby?*

'Where to?' Danny shouts and she shouts back, 'Follow the Yellow Brick Road all the way home.'

Danny doesn't want to go home. Home is misery. His father wants to sell the Boxster. Boom is over, he's told Danny. The Celtic Tiger has become a dead dodo and no one's buying or selling houses in Ireland, Spain or Timbuktu.

'He can go take a fucking jump to himself,' says Danny. 'No one's taking my car. Let him sell her fucking jewellery if he wants to lighten his load.'

His anger has been burning slowly ever since she got into the car but he can hardly expect her sympathy. Her, of all people.

'A car is *nothing*.' She has to yell above the music. 'I've to give back my father.'

For some reason he thinks this is hilarious and she laughs along with him until her sides ache. 'I've to give back my gran and my half-brother and my house and my friends and my identity,' she shouts. 'Beat that.'

He drives through the wide wrought-iron gates of Phoenix Park. The zoo is here. She used to visit it with her so-called grandfather and Tessa whenever her so-called mother brought her to Dublin for a visit.

458

'My granddad and step-grandmother,' she shouts. 'I've got to give them back as well. My mother doesn't count. Or does she?'

'Does she what?' Danny accelerates along a wide, straight road.

'Does she count as a give-back, seeing as how she's dead?'

'Guess not. I wish I got to shaft my family. My old man's turned the heat off in the swimming pool. Swear to Christ, it's like a fucking icebox.'

'Tough shit, Danny Boy.'

The car is powerful but small, only two seats. She wishes it was summer time so that Danny could open the roof and allow all the anger contained inside it to escape. Anger frightens her. She has tried to keep it under control since the press conference. Six stitches in her forehead. Her poor war-torn, scarred forehead. She had a fringe cut to hide them but they throb tightly when Danny turns the volume higher on the stereo.

Joy wants silence, not noise. She no longer wants to listen to voices talking reassuringly about grave miscarriages of justice and heads rolling. When silence settles she can hear her father's heart beating far too fast. She hears her grandmother's anxiety gnawing her chest. And Joey . . . what can she hear when she thinks about Joey? Chains breaking, sundering forever the links that once bound them together.

He sat for ages in her room today. Someone should have objected. He is not her brother and he was sitting with her on her bed. They could have done anything, kissed, even done *it* and that would have been all right. No incest involved. No even a molecule. He told her she would always be part of his family. No matter what DNA decreed, she was bound to them by love. On the night of the party, she wanted to kiss him. She remembers that crazy delirious longing to press her body close to his, closer than a brother and sister ever ought to be. It made sense at last, but all she wants is to turn back time. To be tortured and anxious because she was in love with her half-brother, and it felt half wrong, half right. Now, it's *all* right, and that's the most terrible truth.

'You must meet your real parents,' he said. 'You'll have to sooner or later. They're not to blame for what happened.'

'Do you believe our father knew?' She hated asking him that question but Joey, like her, believes the truth. Only one person knew and she will never have to confess her crime.

After Joey had left, she sent a text to Danny. *Need to escape these prison walls. Bring a rope ladder and rescue a damsel in distress.* She sat back to await his reply. Katie never noticed her leaving the house. Danny parked around the corner and they were gone in a flash.

He parks the Boxster under trees. No street lighting here, just the two of them alone together. They listen to Wolfmother. She wants him to play something gentle but all his CDs are heavy metal. She steps outside and walks between the trees. The wind has ice on its breath. Poor Danny and his icebox swimming pool. Poor Danny and his Boxster. What on earth is she doing here with him?

She leans against the trunk of a tree and stares through the bare branches. Soon they will bud. Her mother stole her when she was a bud, almost straight out of Carla Kelly's womb. The knowledge is a hard kernel rooting in her mind. Now that she has allowed it space, it can never be dislodged.

Danny puts his arms around her and pushes her back against the tree trunk. There are hundreds of trees. Maybe he wants to do *it* to her against every one. She giggles but he stifles the sound with his mouth.

Over Danny's shoulder she sees a sweep of headlights in the distance, a blue light revolving.

'Fucking cops,' says Danny, and hurries her back to his car.

'Where are we going?' she shouts.

'Who cares?' he yells. 'Watch this panther go.' The Boxster surges forward and slaps her against the seat, swerves her to one side when he turns corners.

'I want to go back, Danny,' she shouts above the music.

'Where to?' he shouts back. 'You don't belong anywhere.'

'You bastard!' She screams at him but he laughs and presses harder on the accelerator.

'Slow down, Danny.' She's frightened now. The car sweeps between the trees. Branches whip against the windows as Danny turns this way and that, seeking a gate that will lead him from the park. The headlights frame a deer as it leaps from the darkness and bounds into their path.

'*Fuck!*' Danny tries to straighten the wheel but the car skids sleekly towards an embankment. She hears a thump, as if someone has smacked the back of her head with a hammer, and she is suspended for an instant in midair. The car settles back on the road with a gentle bounce that turns into a grinding crunch. Danny, scared and howling, holds the steering wheel so tightly that the guard who opens the door has to prise his fingers loose.

'Are you determined to make an intolerable situation even more intolerable?' demands her father when he arrives in A&E. 'What will you do next? Hack out my heart?'

She can see by his face that he wants to embrace her and shake her at the same time. But he can do neither. Her leg is in a cast, hanging from a pulley and her head is still encased

461

in a block. Danny has a broken nose. Tough about the Boxster. Not much market value on scrap metal.

'I won't let you go,' she whispers so that none of the others, her so-called foster mother with her concerned expression, and her social worker, who is really her jailer, can hear. 'I can't accept the truth.'

'The truth?' He speaks more quietly. 'I wish I knew what the truth meant. We've all been living a lie for fifteen years but that doesn't make what we had any less real or meaningful. I will always love you as my daughter. No matter what happens, nothing can change that.'

'You could go to jail.' The thought terrifies her but facing it is easier than holding it back.

'I have a good defence team. The most important thing I need right now is for you to stay safe.'

'Do you want me to meet *them*?'

'You won't hurt my feelings if you do.'

He is lying, of course. She loves him more than ever. He's right about that never changing. Not on this side of the earth. But with her mother, Susanne Dowling, on the other side, so many things are clear now. Her possessiveness, smothering Joy. Her sudden rages when Joy refused to do things her way. Had she ever loved Joy? Was love possible when it was haunted by a deed too dreadful to confront?

Patricia has released a statement to the media, telling them that Joy's injuries are minor and asking for privacy. At last Joy is moved to a ward with four beds. With everyone swirling around her and the injections, it's difficult to remember who's coming and going. She awakens once and there is someone standing by her bed. She's like a ghost, pale face, trembling hands. She touches Joy's forehead. Her fingers are cool and soothing.

'Sleep tight, my darling child,' she whispers.

Joy floats on the sound, swaying in a rainbow boat and everything is wonderful. Then the pain comes again and when she opens her eyes she knows she was dreaming because no one is there – and how could Clare Frazier possibly have known where to find her?

Dear Joy,

I cried for ages when I got your mail. It's so cool that you've decided to keep in touch. But the crash! You could have been killed! My aunt is terribly upset. We all are. It's a relief to know you only have a broken leg. I know that's awful but you will get better. I broke my arm when I was ten and once I got the cast off it healed real fast.

You asked me to tell you about my family. There's five of us, two cats and a dog. The other animals are twins but I'm forced to call them brothers. My dad's a lawyer and my mum works in a health food shop. She believes brown rice and soya will save the world so I eat my Big Macs in a dark cave. My gran drinks gin and pretends not to, and worries all the time about my granddad's heart. It's weird, 'cause she's the one with the pacemaker. He's nice and gives us chocolates on the sly. More visits to the dark cave!!

Aunt Carla lives by herself in an apartment and ghostwrites books. We thought she was going to get married in June but that's over. Her fiancé was nice but he's one of those guys who only notices children if he falls over them. Uncle Robert lives in Oz but he's still here. I guess he'll go back soon. I wish they were still married. But they're not and Carla says that's just the way the dice falls.

Your taste in music is cool. I also adore Coldplay, Snow Patrol and Kings of Leon. My favourite girl band is Sugababes. The twins have a band. Imagine knives on a draining board – that's sweet music compared to the noise they make.

Gotta go now. Time for Quorn on the cob. Yuk.

Stay cool.

Jessica.

Chapter Seventy-Four

Carla

The restaurant Robert had chosen was intimately lit and fragrant with promise. Sheen's on the Green, where they had first met. Carla recognised the danger signals, his hand resting on hers for an instant longer than necessary, his eyes leading her back to other occasions, forcing her to remember . . . A dangerous business, straying into past territory.

'A nightcap?' he asked when he pulled up outside her apartment.

'Why not?' She was beyond caring, weary of it all: the waiting and anticipation, the hopes dashed.

She poured two brandies into glasses and sat down beside him. He lifted her hand and stroked her bare ring finger. 'He's a fool to let you go.'

'He didn't want to share me with my daughter.'

'An arrogant fool.'

'Will Sharon share you with her?'

'She has no other option. I hope to bring Isobel to Melbourne for a holiday in the summer. I'd love you to come as well.'

'Somehow, I think that would be stretching Sharon's tolerance to breaking point.'

'This whole business had been tougher than I thought,' admitted Robert, who had been able to extend the date for his departure by an extra week when his son's tonsillectomy was postponed. 'I'd stay on indefinitely only for Sharon and the boys. I want to be there when Damian comes to after his operation. But that means I'm walking out on you and Isobel. Why won't she accept the truth and agree to meet us? *Why?*'

'You heard what Patricia said. Our daughter is terrified. Once she meets us, she can't go back.'

'But *we* can go back . . . at least for one night.' Robert slid his arm around her shoulders.

'Stop it, Robert. It's not fair on Sharon or your sons.'

'It's crazy . . . but I still feel as if we're married.'

'Considering you've been married to Sharon for far longer than you were married to me, I'd say that's just your imagination working overtime.'

'I wish it was, Carla.' He stood up and poured another brandy. 'I'll take a taxi back to Raine's . . . unless . . .'

'No, Robert.'

He sank heavily back into the sofa. 'I hope to Christ that bastard is put away for life.'

'You think he'll be found guilty?'

'How can it be otherwise? The case is cut and dried.'

'But he was working on an oil rig when she was born—'

'Jesus, Carla, what is this?' Robert demanded. 'He *stole* our daughter. Give me one rational explanation why you think he's innocent of the crime that destroyed us . . . our relationship, the future we could have shared with our child . . . our children?'

'I've met him, Robert. I've seen how he is with Joy . . . Isobel. Susanne Dowling faked the latter stages of her pregnancy. The first scans are genuine, which means there was a baby until she miscarried. I'm convinced he genuinely believed Isobel was his daughter. But it doesn't matter what I think, Robert. A jury will decide his guilt or innocence.'

'Since when did you make this huge leap of faith?' He folded his arms, his face hardening. She imagined him cross-examining a suspect, his blank yet demanding stare. 'Have you any idea how defensive you become every time his name is mentioned? I'm beginning to wonder if you're in love with him.'

His words ran like an electric shock through her. 'That's ridiculous. Just because I believe he's innocent . . . how can you say such nonsense?'

'I once filled your eyes, Carla. No one else knows you the way I do. Tread carefully. You're walking a dangerous path.'

Chapter Seventy-Five

Joy

Hi Jessica,

    Thanks for your last mail. My leg is still in the brace. It's driving me nuts! But it's going to be removed next week and then the physio starts. Hospital is such a drag. If I could escape I would . . . but not in a Boxster. Do you know what that creep once called me? A minger! I'm glad his car was trashed, not the deer, but I could have done without the broken leg. All he got was a broken nose!! It looked like a pig's snout before the crash so the plastic surgery has to be an improvement . . . hope it isn't.

    I've so much time to think now. Carla Kelly and Robert Gardner keep coming into my mind. None of this was their fault. I look so like her, it's weird. But my baby photograph is hideous. I look like a trout. To think it was sent around the world and used in the FindIsobel campaign is <u>so</u> humiliating.

    I've been on a long journey and it's still only the beginning. Your emails have helped a lot to bring me to this decision. I now accept that my 'mother' stole me. But I will never believe my father suspected. If you knew the kind of marriage they had, well, you'd understand how he

never suspected. No matter what they do to him, I will
never accept that he's guilty. I hope you and all your
family will respect my belief.

I want to meet Carla first and then Robert and
afterwards the rest of you . . . not so sure about the
twins!! Oh my God . . . it's <u>so</u> scary.

Take care.

Joy/Isobel.

The FindIsobel site is addictive, especially the first awful press conference after her disappearance. That smile, anyone can see the agony behind it. This woman is her mother. Mother . . . mother. Joy presses her finger against the screen, her mother's face, her hair, the tears gathering in the corners of her luminous eyes. She wants to touch her. Just the tiniest touch to feel her skin. But there is glass between them and it is up to Joy to break it.

Dylan comes to visit her at last. He pulls up a chair and sits beside her bed. His fingers are linked, his knuckles clenched. When she tells him she has decided to meet her mother, the worry lines lift from his face and he tells her a story.

Joy imagines grey empty buildings, echoes, rats, cobwebs, rusting machinery, cops' voices, sirens, rubble, shadows. She imagines a woman walking between the shadows, tears like rain on her cheeks. She imagines Dylan with his pockmarked arms and lockjawed mouth and his breath wheezing out of him.

The dopehead and the angel. That's the way he makes it sound. Her mother laid her healing hands on him and he arose into the light and became . . . well . . . he became Dylan, someone she has always liked and trusted, and who is responsible for splitting up her family.

The key word that Joy had used? *Anticipation.* It had resonance, reverberations. It pulled him back to his past and she, sitting unaware in his clinic, had started the unravelling. She remembers the frantic drive in the ambulance, the claw-like grip on her hands . . . Anticipation baby . . . Anticipation baby . . . Joy moans and presses her fingers to her temples. She can't speak. What is there to say? Well done, Sherlock Holmes? She wants to lie in the silence. Then she will hear the crash of her friendship with Dylan shattering into a million pieces.

But his story is not yet over. He drove to Dublin and met Joy's mother. He alerted her, poured out his suspicions. But she was no longer the Carla Kelly he remembered. No longer the iconic image.

'Once I got over the shock of seeing her, the resemblance was even more pronounced,' he admits. 'You looked exactly like her when your own hair was short.'

She tries to imagine her mother with a boy's haircut. Impossible. Her hair blows in the wind. It streams along a catwalk. It hides her face when journalists shout, 'How do you feel . . . can you describe your emotions when you saw the empty cot?'

Dylan says her hair is black now. Black and short like a skullcap. Jessica's email . . . how did Joy not realise? A ghost . . . ghostwriter . . . she sees her mother's neck bending like a swan as she keels forward across the grave of the woman who had stolen her child.

Joy bends forward and touches the cast on her leg. The itch is a burn and she will scream if she can't ease it. She opens her mouth. Dylan draws back, suddenly silenced, and the other patients also look startled at her, as if they have been smacked by the sound rushing from her mouth. It brings the nurse running, and a doctor, too, but there's only one person she wants to see.

He drives to Dublin the instant she phones him. He doesn't bother about the guards or asking permission from Patricia and when he finally arrives he draws the screens around her bed so that she can cry against his chest and tell him about Clare Frazier who came like a ghost into their lives to steal back what was once stolen from her.

Chapter Seventy-Six

Carla

Carla crumpled the sheet of paper and flung it into the bin. Others followed. Finally, when words no longer made any sense, and excuses no longer had any meaning, she finished the letter to her daughter.

Dear Joy,
By the time this letter reaches you, Patricia will have told you the truth. I intend meeting her tomorrow morning and giving her permission to reveal my identity. My false identity, as you will know by now. I'm a writer, yet all my skills were useless when it came to finding the words that would make you understand the dilemma I faced.

I never meant you any harm. I simply had to be near you. What did I hope to do? Watch you from behind the drystone walls? Hide in the hedgerows? I still don't know what I would have done if you had not walked into the cemetery. Perhaps it was fate taking the decision from me but, once I saw you, I could not let you go.

Patricia will have the right words. She is compassionate.

She will comfort you. Please don't turn your face from me.
I've waited such a long time to hold you.
  I love you.
  Carla.

Carla addressed and stamped the envelope, knowing that if she did not post it now she would tear it up in the morning and try to write a more coherent, sensible, pleading one. As she was leaving her apartment, she noticed a bunch of freesias she had purchased earlier from the flower sellers on Grafton Street. She removed them from the vase and wrapped them in paper.

The cold night air gusted around her as she walked along the canal path. She fastened the top button on her coat, pulled her hat lower over her forehead. After posting the letter, she continued walking. Hopefully, she would be able to sleep through the night. She passed the lock gate where she had once hesitated for an instant between life and death. The ghost of Anita seemed to drift into view. But it was only a swan, an ungainly waddle of feathers until it reached the water and was transformed. The reeds grew high along the bank where her body had been dumped. She laid the flowers among the reeds and stood for a moment watching the flow of water. What had Anita thought of her? Had she seen her as a friend, a mother figure, or just an eccentric insomniac, killing time until dawn?

She reached the bench opposite her apartment where homeless men and women often sat at night, sharing a bottle. Tonight it was occupied by a solitary figure. He looked up as she approached and rose to his feet.

'It's you.' David Dowling stared at her in amazement. Perhaps he thought she was a sprite that had materialised from the watery reeds. A swan maiden, perhaps.

'What are you doing here?' she asked.

'I called to your apartment but you weren't there.'

'I'm sorry.'

'Which of you is sorry? Carla Kelly or Clare Frazier?' He shivered, his body braced against the wind and slumped back into the bench. 'Dylan called to see Joy today. She knows who you are.'

Too shocked to reply, she sat down beside him. He moved when their shoulders touched, creating space between them. She hunched into her coat, the sleeves forming a muff as she huddled her hands into them.

'Why did you lie to us?' he asked.

'How could I tell you the truth?'

He shook his head. 'Ever since Joy came to us, I've been living a lie. And now, I find out that you are also an accomplished liar.'

'I never intended lying . . . but things moved so fast . . . spun out of control. The night you were in my apartment, I was going to tell you then. But Joy was missing and you were gone . . .' Her voice trailed helplessly away.

'Why should I believe you?' he demanded. 'You came into our home and accepted our hospitality for only one reason. To destroy us. Well, you've achieved what you set out to do. You've taken her from me.'

She watched a waterhen rippling the still water. 'If she was your child, wouldn't you have done the same?'

'Yes.' He nodded. 'But I would have done it honestly.'

'How? *Fifteen years*, David. She'll never be my child. She'll always belong to you . . . no matter what happens now.'

He stood up and walked to the edge of the canal. For a terrifying instant, she thought he was going to jump in. She rushed forward, shocked by her need to protect him, but he stood rock steady, staring into the water.

'Come back to my apartment.' She took his arm and moved him away from the edge. 'We have to talk about this.'

'What more is there to say?' He drew his arm away and turned to leave.

'David, do you remember the words you once wrote to me . . . to Carla Kelly?'

'What do you mean?' He stared blankly at her.

'I memorised them,' she said. '"If faith can move mountains, then you have the power to create an earthquake. What lies beneath the surface is fragile and constantly shifting. Sooner or later, and I hope with all my heart it will be sooner, the cracks will appear and you will be reunited with Isobel."'

He was silent for an instant, his head bowed. 'If I didn't feel like weeping, I'd laugh at the irony of it all,' he said. 'I'll see you in court, Carla.'

She watched him walk away. The waterhen disappeared into the reeds, startled, perhaps, by a group of young women defying the wind in skimpy tops and bare midriffs. Their voices carried across the water, their laughter a shrill signal that their night was just beginning.

The following day Orla Kennedy phoned to inform her that David had broken his bail conditions. He had broken an injunction and visited Isobel Gardner without the knowledge of her social worker. For this reason, he would be remanded in custody until his trial.

Chapter Seventy-Seven

Joy

Her father writes to her every day. Snail mail. He orders her to be brave. He'll prove his innocence, never fear. Sometimes Joy believes him and then her mind swings the opposite way and she's convinced he'll be in jail forever. He won't have a chance in court. Not with Carla Kelly standing there looking forlorn and desperate. The judge will be putty in her hands. Joy hates her. Her hatred runs cold then hot. It shivers her skin until she feels as if tiny invisible insects are crawling under her flesh. Snitch, bitch, liar, spy, home-wrecker, heart-breaker, impostor . . . mother . . . *mother* . . .

Patricia tries to persuade her to forgive and forget. How can she? Her heart is ice and will remain ice until her father is released. She tore up Carla Kelly's letter. Too late . . . too late . . . too many lies. Impossible to forgive. Snitch, bitch, liar, spy . . .

Mary in the next bed agrees. She's had a hip replacement and is Joy's limping companion along the corridor.

'Forgiveness,' she says, 'is written in the book of repentance. When you are ready to forgive yourself, then your forgiveness will reach out to others.'

How can Joy forgive herself? She let her mother die

then led Dylan to the truth and now her father is in jail because she sent for him. It's as simple and as awful as that.

She dreams about her mother. Her thief mother. Joy knows she's dead yet she looks so alive as she stands in front of the cottage with the Judgement Book open before her. Angels fly around her head. Six angels with white robes and shimmering wings, shining baby faces. Joy wants to fly with them but the plaster of Paris holds her to the floor. Her mother is smiling as she looks up from the Judgement Book and gazes at the angels. She doesn't see Joy struggling to fly. The angels soar upwards and vanish but her mother is sinking into the earth. Joy wants to struggle free from her dream but then she realises that she is actually awake. Dreaming awake. She hears Mary snoring in the next bed. The jangle of the breakfast trolley along the corridor. The dark morning beginning to brighten outside the hospital windows. Her mother continues to sink lower and lower. She is still smiling but soon her face will disappear into the crumbling clay.

Joy rings the emergency bell beside her bed but by the time the nurse comes with the sick tray it's too late and she has thrown up over the bedclothes. The ward is empty of angels and ghosts.

'A bad dream,' says the nurse.

'It was real.' Joy huddles in a chair while her bedclothes are changed. 'I was wide awake the *whole* time.'

Another nurse checks her chart. 'Hallucinations,' she says. 'I'll talk to Dr Nolan about your pain medication.'

'Medical people!' Mary snorts when Joy is back in bed, sitting palely between the starched sheets. 'They know how to fix bones but they are clueless when it comes to interpreting the wonderful mysteries of the mind. Your mother was sending you a message.'

'She's *not* my mother.'

'No. She's a free spirit. That's why she's happy.'

'How do you know she's happy?'

But Mary hums as she gathers her black straggly hair in her hands and pins it in a beehive. She knows exactly where each sparkling clip goes and only reaches for the mirror when she is ready to make up her face.

'Not a good idea,' she says, as she always does when she sees her reflection. 'At my great age, a mirror is a dangerous friend first thing in the morning.'

Joy stretches her hands above her head and immediately lowers them again. Movement is pain, yet soon the physio-therapist will have her limping up and down the corridor, demanding impossible manoeuvres. The daily routine of the hospital makes it hard to think. She slides down in the bed and closes her eyes. Snatches of memory come and go.

'I'm writing your name in the Judgement Book.' How many times had she heard those words? And she heard them again in the ambulance when her mother's mouth slanted sideways as she held onto Joy, the words sliding free but garbled, so garbled . . . written in the blood . . . written in the book . . . which was it? Or was it both?

'The book?' says Joy. 'Or the blood?'

'Written in the book,' replies Mary. 'The blood is no longer flowing. It's found its source.'

Joy stares across at her. Mary's face is wrinkled now but soon she will be transformed. Her lips will glisten with bright red lipstick and her dangling earrings will sparkle. Somehow, her wrinkles will smooth out and disappear, or else people are so busy looking at everything else about her, including her black flashing eyes, that they won't notice she is actually quite old. Mary is not her professional name. She hasn't told anyone but Joy. As a psychic she has a certain image to maintain.

'It wouldn't do if word got out that Miranda May is hobbling up and down a hospital corridor like Hopalong Cassidy,' she whispers.

Joy has promised to keep her secret. The only problem is that everyone else in the hospital seems to know it too. The nurses keep asking her to read their palms and, yesterday, Dr Nolan had a tarot card reading done, but only after he drew the blinds around Mary's bed.

'Written in the book of repentance.' Mary clips on her crystal earrings. The transformation is about to begin. 'What did she tell you to do?'

'She never spoke.'

'Language is not always necessary for knowledge. You must read the signs she left behind.'

'Morning everyone. Rise and shine.' The patients resent the morning nurse. She brings the outside world with her, reminding them of swarming traffic and surging crowds and changing weather patterns.

'Good gracious me, what have we here?' She stops at the foot of Joy's bed and stares at her in amazement. '*Tears?* This will never do at all.'

'She'll be fine,' says Mary and, hearing the certainty in her voice, Joy feels strong again. Susanne, she whispers. Susanne . . . Susanne. The name hisses on her tongue, sibilant and unfamiliar. Using her name is the first snap of a thread that has bound Joy to a lie.

When breakfast is over and the doctors have done their rounds, Joy phones Patricia.

'I want to meet my mother,' she says. 'Will you ask her to visit me?'

'The shape of a family cannot be defined by blood alone,' says Mary while they wait for Patricia to arrive.

'But I belong to her and him,' says Joy.

'You belong to yourself, child.'

'It doesn't feel like that. I've lots of relations, all looking for me to be part of them.'

'Science has yet to measure the love our hearts can hold.'

'I've no space for *her*,' says Joy. 'She deceived me and she made my father fall in love with her. I *hate* her.'

Mary starts to hum again.

'*What*?' snaps Joy.

But Mary smiles and sinks deeper between the sheets.

Patricia arrives and helps Joy into her wheelchair. 'Carla's here,' she says. 'She's waiting for you in the dayroom. Good luck.' She briskly wheels Joy from the ward.

'I'll manage the chair myself,' says Joy when they stop outside the day room.

'You're sure?'

'Positive. This won't take long.'

After Patricia walks away, Joy sits perfectly still for a moment. She needs to compose herself but her anger continues to bubble out of control. Snitch, bitch, liar, spy . . . Her head aches from the power of those words. She pushes the door open and manoeuvres her way through. Carla Kelly is sitting in an armchair. A brightly striped coloured scarf is wound around her neck. Her glasses have disappeared and her hair looks longer than Joy remembers. She stands when she sees Joy. Two spots of colour appear on her cheeks. Her hands flutter, that same helpless flutter that Joy remembers from the cemetery. The sun was shining that day, the air still and breathless.

Her anger, that bubbling, sulphuric anger, suddenly evaporates. Joy has no idea where it's gone. She grapples after it, tries to claw it back, but it keeps slipping beyond her reach and in its place, unfolding in slow motion, is the memory of Danny's car skidding and turning over. The sensation of being suspended upside down. The knowledge that she was going to die and that it was too late . . . too late to know the strength of her mother's arms, holding her safe from harm.

Her mother shudders, as if she has peered inside Joy's mind. Her hands freeze and she is motionless apart from the slight tremble of her bottom lip. Waiting. Her eyes are bog brown and luminous. Not green and unsettling, as Joy remembers. They belong to her face . . . and to Joy. Her mouth opens slightly, as if she is about to whisper Joy's name. How many times over those long years did she call out her daughter's name . . . *Isobel* . . . *Isobel* . . .? How many nights did she lie awake, waiting for a new day to break so that she could rise and begin her search anew?

'Mammy . . .' Joy whispers and her mother's face breaks apart, like something has ripped through her chest and stopped her breathing. Joy doesn't know if the rip is her own heart aching, or her own hushed breath repeating, 'Mammy . . . Mammy . . .' but the sound brings her mother's face together again. Suddenly, there's no space between them. Her mother is on her knees, her arms holding Joy with a fierce tenderness, and they cling together, crooning words that make no sense, need no language, binding, rejoicing words that were once lost and are now found.

Afterwards, there is time to talk.

'I thought I hated you.' Joy stares at her hands, still scarred from the accident. 'I couldn't hate Carla Kelly for destroying my life but it was easy to hate Clare Frazier. But it was her . . . *Susanne*, she was the one I really wanted to hate. But I can't . . . I want to . . . I should . . .'

Her mother shakes her head. 'You have to give yourself time, Joy. So much has happened so quickly—'

'She wrote things down.' Joy needs to make her mother understand. 'She called it her Judgement Book.'

'You told me about it. Remember? By the lake. I was so angry I had to walk away from you.'

'I've been thinking a lot about it since this . . .' Joy gestures at the cast on her leg. 'I think it was *her* Judgement Book. Like a therapy, or something. In the ambulance on the way to the hospital, she kept talking about it. I believe she wanted me to find it. It makes sense. If she couldn't have me, then it wouldn't matter who knew the truth. It's written in the book . . . she kept repeating that . . . I thought she meant blood but that wouldn't make any sense.'

'Where did she keep the book?'

'There's lots. She used to keep them in the back of her wardrobe but the police searched our house for evidence. They found nothing. I think she buried them.'

'*Buried?*'

'In the cottage garden. It's where she went when we had rows. Like it was a grotto or something. She smacked me once for following her there. Sometimes I hid and watched her. She used to kneel and pray.'

'Oh, Joy . . . were you ever happy?' her mother asks.

'I believe I was.' She nods vigorously. 'But I was either clinging to her or pulling against her. Always trying to win her approval. At least now I understand why *that* was impossible. The best times were when Dad was home. I know he's not my dad . . . but I can't stop . . .'

'You don't ever have to stop, Joy.'

'Do you believe he's guilty?'

Her mother doesn't hesitate. When she says, 'He never knew,' Joy's body folds forward in relief.

'But he's in jail because of her,' she says.

'When he goes on trial he'll be able to tell his story. Then it's up to the jury to decide.'

'Will you tell that to the judge?'

'My word will carry weight but I'm only a witness, one of many. Everything your family has done over the years will be scrutinised and analysed. Then the jury will decide. So, you see, Joy, I'm only a very small cog in the whole process.'

'If you had proof . . . they'd have to listen.'

'What proof can I bring? All I have is a belief. That's not evidence.'

'The books might be.'

'But if you're right and she buried them, how could anyone possibly find them? I've seen that place. It's a wilderness.'

'Not in one space. There used to be flowers there, like they were planted, not growing wild. I've done research on the internet. If you find the journals and hand them over, the DPP will have to believe you.'

'You want *me* to find them?'

'Mary says . . .' Joy stops, embarrassed. Her mother will think she's a snowflake if she discovers she believes in psychics. But maybe her mother does too. Maybe they share lots of things in common. 'Mary says the truth is hidden in a place of stone.'

Her mother tilts her head back and stares at the ceiling. She appears to be deep in thought before she meets Joy's gaze. And nods.

Chapter Seventy-Eight

Carla

Carla did not stop driving until she reached Rockrose. Still exhausted from the events of the day, she was happy to allow Joey O'Sullivan to fuss over her and serve her a second helping of spaghetti bolognese. Tomorrow morning he was flying from Shannon to Dublin to see his family then flying on to London for a business meeting. He was reluctant to leave her alone in Rockrose; he was stressed from the sudden responsibility of running his grandmother's studio and still shocked by the events that had occurred. 'I won't be alone,' she said. 'I have Splotch for company.' She patted the dog's head and was rewarded by a slobbering lick.

'Joy told me why you're here,' he said when they were clearing the table after the meal.

'Do you believe in this so-called Judgement Book?'

'Anything was possible with that woman. But I never saw it or noticed her writing anything down. I think Joy's sent you on a wild goose chase. If there was any incriminating evidence Susanne would have destroyed it.'

'She died very suddenly. Whatever her intention was, she would not have had time to do anything before she collapsed.'

'Perhaps. But I'm not convinced.'

'You obviously didn't like her.'

He frowned and shook his head. 'There was something about Susanne. An aura, Joy would probably call it. It was invisible but at times I could feel a chill surrounding her. She was a cold woman, utterly possessive. I was Joy's half-brother but she still resented me having any part of her. I disliked her intensely. Now I hate her. My father may go to jail because of her. Who's going to believe he's innocent?'

'I do,' said Carla.

'I've never hated anyone before,' admitted Joey. 'But you must have carried that same hatred for all those years. How are you still standing upright?'

How indeed, Carla wondered after he had gone to bed. She walked through the rooms that had imprisoned her daughter. In the bedroom where Susanne Dowling had slept for her entire married life, nothing remained of her existence. Carla hesitated at the doorway and shuddered. They had made love in this room, conceived babies and lost them when fate decreed it was not their time to be born. The bed was new, as was the crisp bed linen. The drawers and dressing table were empty. Carla knelt and checked under the bed. Bobbles of dust made her sneeze but there was nothing to see, no hidden trapdoors or unwieldy boxes.

She entered David's room. A woolly jumper lay over the back of a chair and an anorak hung from a hook on the door. She caught a whiff of oil from it. The pockets were numerous and bulky, deep enough for pens and binoculars, measuring tools and goggles, and small razor-sharp chisels. She imagined him under desert suns, adrift on oil rigs, searching for the black tide beneath the surface.

He had stood too close to the edge of the canal. A step further and he would have entered the water. She would have dived in after him and pulled him to shore. She had the strength to do it, and then she would have kissed life back into his lips. Could she love such a man if she believed him guilty of stealing her child? No, a thousand times no.

Splotch followed her into Joy's bedroom. Posters on the wall, Coldplay, Snow Patrol, Kings of Leon, Sugababes. Similar posters hung on Jessica's wall. Her dressing table was cluttered with creams. Necklaces dangled from the fingers of a black, splayed hand. A teen magazine was open on her bed and the clothes Joy had dumped on her last night before being taken to Dublin were still crumpled in a laundry basket. Carla lay on the bed and held the pillow over her face. She had no tears left, nor any desire to cry. She fell asleep in her daughter's bed and did not awaken until morning.

The sun, rising above the hedgerows, streaked the clouds with blood-red energy. Frost hung in the air and froze her breath, tingled her fingers as she made her way towards the cottage. A digger stood abandoned beside it. Joey drove down the lane and stopped when he reached the cottage. His tousled hair, frank gaze and lanky stride reminded her of his father. He gazed over the dead foliage she had raked into neat cones.

'Good luck,' he said. 'I'll tell Joy you're hard at work.' He hesitated. 'I'm visiting my father. Is there anything you'd like me to say to him?'

She shook her head. 'We parted on bad terms,' she said. 'I don't think he wants to hear anything I have to say.'

The sky was gentler now, wispy clouds stippled pink and pewter. She removed her scarf and jacket, and continued working. Splotch snoozed under the plum tree.

At noon she drove to Molloy's for lunch. She ordered soup and a baguette, suddenly ravenously hungry. The baguette came with a generous filling that could be enjoyed comfortably only in private. She was unconcerned by the squishing salad dressing and tomatoes, mopping her lips after each bite, anxious to return to the place of stone. The psychic's words resonated with power and certainty.

Chapter Seventy-Nine

Joy

'How do you know you're in love?' Joy asks Mary.

'It shakes your heart to bits,' replies Mary, which, Joy thinks, is the first time Mary has given her an answer in plain English.

She is sleeping when Joey arrives. It's the afternoon and the patients have sunk into the hush that follows the rattling dinner trolleys. He calls her name so softly that when she sees him sitting beside her bed she is unsure if she is still dreaming.

He smiles and winks. 'Wake up, lazybones. I didn't come all this way to listen to you snoring.'

'I love you, Joey,' she says but she must be speaking to herself because his gaze doesn't flicker away from her, nor does his mouth go tight with disapproval.

He unwraps grapes and magazines and her favourite chocolate biscuits.

'How's Dad?' she asks. 'He's so cheerful in his letters it makes me want to scream.'

'Patient,' says Joey, no longer smiling. 'But convinced his legal team will mount a strong defence.'

'Did you tell him about the Judgement Book?'

He shook his head. 'No sense getting his hopes up.'

'You don't believe in it?'

'I've an open mind. Carla was working up a real lather when I left. How are you?'

'How do I look?'

'Ugly as ever.'

'Got lost, punk!'

'Cheeky as ever.'

'I love you, Joey.' This time she says it aloud.

His smile slides from his face. 'Don't, Joy,' he says but she flaps her hand at him, orders him to listen.

'It's just love,' she says. 'It's not weird or confused or messing with my head any more. I want us to be the way we always were. Just an E between us. Brother and sister. I don't want that to ever change. Do you understand?'

'Yes, I do.' He leans across the bed and rests his palm against her cheek. His eyes narrow and his gaze seems to pull her inwards, as if he too is remembering the night of the party when, for an instant, blood and kinship no longer mattered and forbidden kisses almost breached a dangerous taboo. 'No matter what happens in the future, you'll always be part of me.'

Families, Joy sighs. Who can define them? Are they made from flesh and blood? From circumstances or a whim? From a secret buried deep in a grave? And does it matter how they form as long as they are forged from love?

She hobbles with him to the elevator.

'See you, sis,' he says.

'Cheers, bro.'

She waits until the display signals that the elevator has reached the ground floor and he is striding from the hospital. Then, carefully, painfully, she swings her crutches and begins her long journey back to the ward.

490

Chapter Eighty

Carla

She scythed through the wild grasses, cutting deep and low into the stems until she could clearly see what she sought. It was the hint of gold that made her pause. The early blossoming cowslips and primroses were just beginning to open. She hunkered down, seeking a pattern among the stubbly growth, and noticed the small oblong bed of clay beneath the cottage window.

She found a pickaxe and spade in the garden shed and carried it back, swung the pickaxe over her shoulder and down into the earth. The budding flowers split, leaves and blossoms crushed to pulp before being covered by mounds of clay. The earth below was stony and unyielding. At times it seemed an impossible task to dig any deeper. No book was buried here, and if it was it would have disintegrated.

But she had known that all along. The evening shadows fell across the walls. Suddenly nervous, aware of the isolation, she rested, leaning against the handle of the spade. Something moved, startling her. A rat darted from the undergrowth inside the cottage. Head down, tiny paws scrabbling against the mounds of clay, it ran past her and disappeared into the ditch. Carla's feet slipped. Before she could regain her balance, she had collapsed into the excavated opening. Knee-deep in the earth, she tried to hoist herself upwards but the loosened earth moved under her hands. Clay and pebbles poured into her wellingtons. Something shifted beneath her feet, malleable, rootless. Once again, she reached forward, grasped the trunk of a plum tree and clambered out. Her skin crawled as the wind strengthened around this cottage with its suppressed secrets. She forced herself to look downwards at the shroud of plastic. She had found what she had sought. She brushed the clinging earth loose from her skin and walked away from the spot where Susanne Dowling had buried her unobtainable dream.

The last police car departed. When the headlights faded, Carla watched the darkness settle over the Burren. Back inside, she switched on the kettle and made tea. She had spoken to Joy on the phone and promised to be with her the following day. DNA tests would be carried out on the delicate substance that still clung to the blanket Susanne Dowling had wrapped around her child. Carla had no doubt they would provide a match with David's DNA. No wonder Joy had struggled so hard to win her affection, unaware that Susanne Dowling's emotions had withered as soon as she had turned that first sod of earth.

Carla entered the glass conservatory. Here, for the first time, she had a sense of the woman who had lived the life that should have belonged to her. The conservatory was an ugly appendage to the old house yet Susanne had made it her own. The willow sofa and armchairs, the metal-framed occasional table with the glass surface, the bric-a-brac and candles had been chosen by her. She had sat here in the evenings, watching the sun setting, writing in her Judgement Book, wailing against her glass wall.

The blind stallion stood on top of a small, stone rect-angular table, framed on either side by a potted yucca and a trailing ivy. The plants had died from lack of watering and the stallion was covered in dust. Carla studied the fierce expression, the drawn-back lips, the glimpse of teeth, the bevelled, angry eyes.

She walked to the back door where she had left the pickaxe. Clods of muck fell from its head as she slammed it against the wall. Splotch whined and scampered into the darkness, unnerved, perhaps, by the fury eminating from her. She carried the pickaxe back to the conservatory and swung it high. It was easy to slash the chintzy cushions, to shred the soft fabric. She smashed the occasional table and stepped back from the flying glass. She swung the pickaxe across the shelves of bric-a-brac and watched a photograph of Susanne Dowling shatter in its silver frame. Shards glinted between the wooden boards. Trembling so violently that she wondered if she would be able to continue standing upright, she crunched the glass to powder under her heel.

The stallion glinted under the light, flailing, always flailing to escape the reins of blindness. Carla brought the pickaxe down so violently she smashed open the surface of the pedestal table on which it rested. A deep wedge appeared. She lifted the pickaxe in a last violent swing. A lock snapped and the edge of a drawer was visible. It jammed, damaged and listing from her attack, but she managed to force it open. She carried the journals to the kitchen. The Aga burned brightly and she was able to draw strength from its heat as she turned the first page. Night turned to morning and she still sat in the same position, reading. She had been Susanne Dowling's conscience. The spectre breathing constantly against the back of her neck. All the strands coming together, weaving in and out of the same piece of tapestry. When she finished the last journal she began again at the beginning.

I buried my baby on the shortest night of the year. We were shielded by old walls when I laid her to rest in a shadowy wilderness of lilac and elderberry. She was my almost-child, my shattered dream. Sixteen weeks in my womb before she came away. Born on the longest day of the year, webbed fingers and toes, her veins delicate as skeins of silk. Sweet little monkey face.

Chapter Eighty-One

Joy

New faces, new places, embraces, awkward silences, sly glances, shy glances, handshakes, bear hugs, high fives, laughter, tears, curiosity, cousins, grandparents, aunts and uncles. Parents. Her real father is a tall man, stern-faced, his eyes red from weeping. He sits beside her bed and apologises for not having faith. He looks at her mother with such hunger that Joy wonders how a tiny baby such as she could have broken them apart. When he says goodbye, she promises to visit him and his wife in Australia and meet her half-brothers. Her mother drives him to the airport. Her gaze is calm and content when she returns to the hospital. There is no pull on her emotions. She has done what Joy has charged her to do and the decision rests with the law.

Her new relations come. Jessica wears leggings and Ugg boots and has pink streaks in her hair. Her brothers look like they have emerged from the underworld. Joy thinks they may stick pins in her to see if she's for real. Maybe some day she'll be able to tell them apart. Her Aunt Raine comes with her husband, Jeff, and their two children; two more cousins, a little girl and a baby boy.

Her grandmother weeps so alarmingly that Joy wonders if she should ring the emergency bell.

'Your grandfather's heart was broken so many times,' she confides to Joy in a low voice. Jessica must have heard because she snorts so violently into her hand that Joy is terrified to look in case she too breaks into hysterical giggles. Her grandfather smiles, as if he knows his granddaughters are having internal convulsions, and tells Joy she looks exactly like her mother when she was a teenager.

'And she giggled just as insanely,' sighs her grandmother, who obviously also doesn't miss much.

Miriam tries not to look scared when she sees Joy's new relations. Almost overnight, her hair has turned from grey to silver, or so it seems to Joy.

'I keep remembering moments,' she says. 'That's all memory leaves us, moments to cherish. But they never belonged to me. That's the hardest part, Joy. Knowing they belonged to someone else.'

She no longer wants to be called Joy. Nor Isobel. She is somewhere in between and she needs a strong name if she is ever to reach inside and discover her true identity.

'Ainé is your second name,' says Miriam. 'It means radiance . . . and happiness.'

Joy thinks . . . *maybe* . . . then finds the song from *Annie the Musical* running through her head.

'It's an ear worm,' says Jessica when she visits that evening. 'The only thing you can do to get rid of an ear worm is to sing the song the whole way through.'

And Joy does. Everyone in the ward claps, even the nurses pause to listen as she sings *Maybe*. Funny how she sang those words so many times and never realised she was living them.

Her mother is turning her guest bedroom into Joy's room. She brings swatches of material and paint charts for Joy to choose. The excitement ripples between them until visiting

496

time is over. Then Joy sinks back against the pillows, exhausted and confused.

Her father comes to see her. Just walks in, unannounced and free. When the Judgement Book was scrutinised by legal bigwigs and all those who claimed to have her welfare at heart, the DPP decided he had no charge to answer.

He hugs and kisses Joy, the two of them crying hard but quietly into each other's faces so as not to disturb the other patients. Blood doesn't matter. Nor facts. She thinks about Josh Baker and the questions he asked her. How he misshaped her words and made them drip with poison.

They're still sitting together, hands clasped, heads close together when her mother enters the ward. She blushes when she sees him, stops so suddenly that Mary, walking behind on her Zimmer frame, almost collides with her, and has to nudge her forward. Her mother sits on the opposite side of the bed. Joy feels like a tennis umpire, her head going this way and that, struggling to find something to say when silence falls.

'I've been speaking to your doctor, Joy,' her mother says before she leaves. 'You're going to be discharged on Friday. I think you should stay with me for a few weeks before returning to Rockrose. The media are still following the story. I can protect you from the publicity until they turn their attention elsewhere.'

'You want me to go back home?' Joy is unable to hide her astonishment. Her father seems equally stunned.

'You now have three homes where you are equally loved,' her mother replies. 'Be free to move between us. No one will ask you to make choices. I'll leave you alone now. You and David have a lot to talk about.'

Before her father can move, she's gone. 'How do you know if you're in love with someone?' Joy asks him.

'It's like an express train going through you for a short cut,' he replies. 'You know that nothing's ever going to be the same again . . . and all you want to do is run towards the future.'

'Was that how you felt about Carla when you met her in the cemetery?'

'Yes.' He smiles but it's a grim smile, without humour. 'Little did I know how right I was.'

'Do you still love her?'

'What does it matter? After the heartache she's been through, how could she possibly have any feelings for me other than anger?'

'But you didn't know—'

'That's beside the point. I lay beside the woman who stole her child.'

He looks older, more wary, the shock of betrayal etched deeply into his skin.

'Anger eventually burns itself out,' says Mary when Joy tells her afterwards. 'If a phoenix can rise from the ashes, so can love. Time and distance create their own healing path.'

Cameras flash when Joy is discharged from hospital. Journalists hurl questions.

'No comment. No comment,' shouts Leo and ushers her into his car. 'Sixteen years and nothing changes with the media,' he says, driving away. 'They still have your scent in their nostrils. But they lost your mother's scent a long time ago. You'll be safe with her.'

Five months have passed since then. Every Friday evening Joy takes the bus from Maoltrán and her mother picks her up in Busáras. It's where all the buses come to disgorge the passengers heading for the bright city lights and collect those escaping from them.

She should have lived in an old, end-of-terrace Georgian house. One weekend, her mother takes her to see it. The owners welcome them and allow Joy into the room that would have been her nursery. It has changed, of course, everything does, and it's now a breakfast room. But Joy sees the spot where her cradle rested and Miriam's seahorses lightly danced in anticipation.

On another occasion they drive to the industrial estate where her mother once walked in the dead of night. The factories are gone now. Bright apartments with satellite dishes stand in their place. Later, they visit the Angels' plot and there, among the flowers and candles and tiny whirring windmills, they laid flowers for that unnamed baby, just as her father did when the tiny particles that should have been his daughter were laid to rest beside his wife.

On Sunday evening Joy comes back to the rocks and the butterflies, back to the turloughs that rise and fall between the green grassy swards. She returns to Miriam, who holds her so close that at times it's difficult to breathe.

Back to her father, who rises at the crack of dawn each day and works until darkness falls. The cottage has gone and the hum of machinery, diggers and cement mixers turning the earth is so familiar she is hardly aware of it.

Back to Joey who will soon return to his own mother in Canada. The heart, thinks Joy, is a funny thing. Mary is right. It's porous and capable of many kinds of loving. Like Joey. The mixed-up crazy desire to kiss him, the longing to hear his voice that shivered her like a fever . . . all gone. It's warm and safe, the love she feels now. She has so much growing up to do, so much growing into her new skin, her new name. But everything changes . . . and if that happens, there will be nothing safe about her love for Joey O'Sullivan. It will shake her heart to its foundations, rattle it like an express train.

She lies on a flat rock and stares upwards. Birds glide above her, clouds sail, the sun dazzles. These sights will never change. The ice age came and scraped the earth from the Burren, leaving a moonscape in its wake, lifeless, barren. Yet purple orchids flutter at her elbows, the gentians are in full bloom, and the scent of wild thyme skims on the breeze.

Today is the longest day of the year, the shortest night. The road between Dublin and Clare shimmers, rises and falls. It runs in a straight line all the way to here.

Her father waits at the door. He knows the exact instant the car turns down the lane. When it stops outside Rockrose, Joy hangs back but he is striding forward, his gaze fearless, ardent, his arms already reaching out to wrap her mother close. Carla's hair is light and feathery now, and there is something fragile about her, as if she is slowly emerging into sunshine. But nothing ghostly, nothing secretive, nothing to stop her running forward until she is eye to eye with him, mouth to mouth. And when they kiss, it seems to Joy that they have been waiting all their lives to grasp and hold this moment forever.

Reading Group Questions,
Laura Elliot:

1. Consider the two women, Carla Kelly and Susanne Dowling. What values, concerns and priorities distinguish their characters? Do they share any similarities?

2. Why has Susanne focused on Carla Kelly? Does she only want her baby?

3. The role of motherhood is shown as having the greatest importance in *Stolen Child*. How does the fact that Carla only meets Joy when she is fifteen affect their relationship?

4. Examine Carla and Robert's relationship. Throughout the book we see it disintegrate. Can we understand why Robert felt he had to move to Australia? How much sympathy do we feel for his character in comparison to Carla?

5. In which ways is the theme of morality explored in the book?

6. How important is the media's influence upon the events in the book? How does the fact that Carla is a celebrity in Ireland affect the press's response to Isobel's kidnap? Why does Carla feel she has to cover up her abortion?

7. What is the significance of Susanne changing Isobel's name to Joy? How far does it illustrate her lack of concern for Carla's sorrow?

8. What is the major factor that causes the breakdown of Carla and Robert's marriage? How much is the media frenzy that centred around them to blame?

9. Throughout Carla has an unshakeable belief that she will be reunited with Isobel. Can we understand her obsession and why she is unable to move on?

10. Can we empathise with Susanne? Despite her reckless actions can we in some respects understand what led her to desperate measures?

11. Compare and contrast the different father figures within *Stolen Child*, Robert and David. In what way is fatherhood seen as less crucial than motherhood?

THE PRODIGAL SISTER
Laura Elliot

Can a black sheep ever return to the flock?

When 15-year-old Cathy Lambert runs away from her Dublin home, she is scared and pregnant. Settled in New Zealand with her new son Conor she believes the secret she carries will never be revealed . . .

Rebecca Lambert was eighteen when her parents died and she took responsibility for her younger sisters. Years later, she is haunted by fears she hoped she'd conquered.

Freed from family duties, mother of three Julie Chambers is determined to recapture the dreams of her youth.

Married to a possessive older man, Lauren Moran embarks on a frantic love affair that threatens to destabilise her fragile world.

Anxious to make peace with her three sisters, Cathy invites them to her wedding.

But as the women journey together through New Zealand towards their reunion, they are forced to confront the past as the secret shared histories of the Lambert sisters are revealed.

ISBN: 978-1-84756-147-3
Out now

What's next?

Tell us the name of an author you love

| Laura Elliot | Go ▶ |

and we'll find your next great book.

www.bookarmy.com